Praise for the work of Bentley Little

The Return

"Bentley Little is a master of horror on a par with Koontz and King.... *The Return* is so powerful that readers will keep the lights on day and night."   —*Midwest Book Review*

The Collection

"Memorable . . . bizarre . . . disturbing. . . . A fascinating glimpse into how Little's creativity has evolved over the years, this volume is a must-have for the author's fans."   —*Publishers Weekly*

"Thirty-two spine-tinglers. . . . Little's often macabre, always sharp tales are snippets of everyday life given a creepy twist."
—*Booklist*

The Association

"With this haunting tale, Little proves he hasn't lost his terrifying touch. The novel's graphic and fantastic finale . . . will stick with the readers for a long time. Little's deftly drawn characters inhabit a suspicious world laced with just enough sex, violence, and Big Brother rhetoric to make this an incredibly credible tale."
—*Publishers Weekly*

The Walking

"A wonderful, fast-paced, rock-'em, jolt-'em, shock-'em contemporary terror fiction with believable char̶a̶c̶t̶e̶r̶s̶ and an unusually clever plot. Highly entertai̶n̶i̶n̶g̶"   —*Dean Koontz*

"Bentley L̶i̶   f the year. If you like spooky

—*Stephen King*

continued . . .

"*The Walking* is a waking nightmare. A spellbinding tale of witchcraft and vengeance. Bentley Little conjures a dark landscape peopled by all-too-human characters on the brink of the abyss. Scary and intense."   —Michael Prescott, author of *Last Breath*

"The overwhelming sense of doom with which Bentley Little imbues his . . . novel is so palpable it seems to rise from the book like mist. Flowing seamlessly between time and place, the Bram Stoker Award-winning author's ability to transfix his audience . . . is superb . . . terrifying. [*The Walking*] has the potential to be a major sleeper."   —*Publishers Weekly* (starred review)

The Ignored

"This is Bentley Little's best book yet. Frightening, thought-provoking, and impossible to put down."   —Stephen King

"With his artfully plain prose and Quixote-like narrative, Little dissects the deep and disturbing fear of anonymity all Americans feel. . . . What Little has created is nothing less than a nightmarishly brilliant tour de force of modern life in America."
    —*Publishers Weekly* (starred review)

"*The Ignored* is a singular achievement by a writer who makes the leap from the ranks of the merely talented to true distinction with this book. This one may be a classic."   —*Dark Echo*

"Impressive. Chilling."   —*Science Fiction Chronicle*

"A spooky novel with an original premise."   —SF Site

"Little is so wonderful that he can make the act of ordering a Coke at McDonald's take on a sinister dimension. This philosophical soul-searcher is provocative."   —*Fangoria*

"*The Ignored* is not average at all."   —*Locus*

THE POLICY

Bentley Little

A SIGNET BOOK

SIGNET
Published by New American Library, a division of
Penguin Group (USA) Inc., 375 Hudson Street,
New York, New York 10014, U.S.A.
Penguin Books Ltd, 80 Strand,
London WC2R 0RL, England
Penguin Books Australia Ltd, 250 Camberwell Road,
Camberwell, Victoria 3124, Australia
Penguin Books Canada Ltd, 10 Alcorn Avenue,
Toronto, Ontario, Canada M4V 3B2
Penguin Books (N.Z.) Ltd, Cnr Rosedale and Airborne Roads,
Albany, Auckland 1310, New Zealand

Penguin Books Ltd, Registered Offices:
80 Strand, London WC2R 0RL, England

First published by Signet, an imprint of New American Library,
a division of Penguin Group (USA) Inc.

First Printing, September 2003
10 9 8 7 6 5 4 3 2 1

For Larry and Janice Weldon,
my uncle and aunt

One

1

He took off a day earlier than he'd planned, leaving in the middle of the night, halfway through Conan O'Brien, and two hours later Hunt Jackson found himself speeding past Palm Springs with the windows open, heading east. With the divorce finalized, there was nothing holding him back, nothing preventing him from doing whatever he wanted, going wherever he felt like going. He was no longer confined by the daily routines of married life, by the patterns and ruts into which he'd fallen, and he was filled with a delicious sense of freedom as he sped down the windswept highway. It was a moonless night, and the stars were out in force, great swaths of the Milky Way visible even through the darkened windshield of the Saab.

The Saab.

When had he turned into the kind of person who drives a Saab? He didn't know, but it was so far in the past that the question felt forced, something he thought he *should* ask rather than a query to which he genuinely desired an answer. Through the windshield, briefly, he saw a shooting star, far above and to the right. Though they'd been fixtures of the Tucson night sky when he was growing up, he realized that he hadn't seen a single meteor since moving to Southern California. He'd heard mentions of meteor showers on the news, comical weathermen occasionally announcing the phenomena and explaining why—because of air pollution or light pollution or the marine layer—the showers would not be visible in the Los Angeles and Orange County areas. He hadn't cared, hadn't even given it a thought, but now, out here on the open road, he realized that he missed seeing shooting stars, missed seeing the sky.

A semi flew past on the left, blasting its horn at him for some imagined slight. Feeling reckless, feeling brave, he flipped on his brights and leaned on his own horn, but the speeding truck was already far ahead and his attempted defiance fell flat, his high beams shining impotently on quickly retreating tires, his honk small and ignored.

He hit Blythe by three, and was past Phoenix and heading south toward Tucson well before the sun started lightening the sky above Casa Grande to the east. He stopped for breakfast at a trucker's coffee shop by the side of the highway, ordering an artery-clogging, meat-heavy meal that Eileen never would have let him eat, before continuing on.

Although the split was mutual—both of them had desperately wanted out of the screaming hell their relationship had become—he'd found himself thinking a lot about Eileen lately, his life with her and his life without her, and he'd tried to imagine the future, but he could not. He had decided that he didn't want to live in Southern California anymore, and it had been an easy decision to make. There was nothing tying him there. He'd been laid off at Boeing last month during the most recent round of cutbacks and hadn't yet caught on anywhere else. Eileen had gotten the house in the settlement, so he was temporarily living in an apartment complex on the border of Seal Beach and Westminster. He was freer now than he had ever been before and perhaps might ever be again.

But where did he want to live? San Francisco was a possibility. Hell, he could go anywhere he wanted. His options were

open. He could move to New Orleans or New York, Miami or
Seattle, Chicago or Honolulu.

But that wasn't what he wanted, was it? No. He wanted to
go back to Tucson. It was where he'd been born, where he'd
grown up and gone to school, where he'd met Eileen. Part of
it was comfort, retreat—and there was an element of failure
associated with that, the sense that he was crawling home with
his tail between his legs. At the same time, he would be starting anew, jettisoning the generic middle-class existence he had
created for himself and beginning again, perhaps taking his
life in the direction it should have been going all along.

And now here he was, at a truck stop in the desert, loading
up on fat and calories, staring out at a hand-painted sign that said
GET U.S. OUT OF THE U.N. But he felt good, he felt happy, and
twenty minutes later, he was on the road again, heading south,
past the lonely ruggedness of Picacho Peak, toward home.

Tucson had changed a lot in the decade he'd been gone, and
he drove around the periphery of the city, trying to get his
bearings, before diving into it. From the elevated freeway, he
saw that gated communities and generic shopping centers now
stretched around the side of the Catalinas well past Ina Road
to the north; new homes were creeping up the Tucson Mountains toward Gate's Pass to the west; an entirely new city
seemed to have sprung up south of the I-10 curve on the way
to the mission; and the Rincon district of Saguaro National
Park was no longer outside of town but on the eastern edge of
it. He turned back when he reached the Colossal Cave exit,
then got off on Speedway and headed toward the university.
Downtown, stores and restaurants had changed, entire buildings had been torn down and replaced, and a distinctly generic
appearance seemed to have been grafted onto the formerly
unique character of the city, part of the Californianization of
America that guaranteed a Burger King at every other stop-

light and a Mediterranean appearance to every new office building.

The old neighborhood was still there but shabbier than he remembered it, everything more run-down than he recalled. Their old house looked like hell. Whoever lived there now had poured concrete over the lawn in order to make room for a trio of 1960s muscle cars in various stages of renovation, and the side patio his dad had built, where his mom had had her hanging plants and potted flowers, was gone, torn out. His parents would be shocked if they could see the place now, and he was tempted to call them up and describe it to them, make them feel even more guilty for moving and selling, but he recognized the pettiness of the impulse and knew he would not act on it. They were happier back in Minnesota, and if he'd really cared so much about the old house, why hadn't he bought it from them when he had the chance?

He *didn't* care about it. He just wished his parents were here because he wanted a home to which he could return.

But they'd returned to *their* home, in Minnesota.

Everyone went back home eventually.

He spent the night at a Super 8 Motel, next door to a couple who fought loud and long about an outboard motor purchase before commencing an equally loud bout of lovemaking. In the morning, he bought a newspaper from the rack in front of the lobby and sat in the Waffle House next door, reading the classified ads over breakfast, looking for a house or apartment to rent.

Now that he was here, the romantic notion of pulling up stakes and resettling no longer seemed quite so romantic. He was suddenly aware of the practical minutiae that such a move required. He would have to put in a change-of-address form with the post office, make sure that none of his bills or important mail got lost in the transition, get a new phone number and inform all of his friends and family, cancel his *Los Angeles Times* subscription . . . the list went on and on.

Not to mention the fact that he would have to physically transport his furniture and belongings over here, probably via U-Haul.

Maybe it wasn't worth the effort.

No.

He needed to do this.

One plus was that rent was much cheaper in Arizona than it was in California. For the price of his little one-bedroom apartment over there, he could rent not merely a duplex but a full-fledged house—even if it wasn't in the city's best neighborhood. And that's exactly what he found after a short morning's search: a three-bedroom adobe on a sparsely populated street in the southeast part of town. The house was sandwiched between a run-down ranch-style home and what was little more than a plywood shack attached to a recently built and fairly nice two-car garage. The only other building on that side of the block was a Circle K on the corner. On the opposite side of the street was a cotton field—one of those corporate farms with no on-site house, barns, or storage shed.

He discovered the place by accident. He was traveling from one listing to another and stopped off at the Circle K for a cup of coffee, and when he glanced down the side street, he saw the posted FOR RENT sign. As shabby and out of the way as it was, something about the area appealed to him. It might not be the chic section of the city, but it was rural and real and reminded him of the way Tucson used to be when he was growing up. From the small desert-y yard he could see the Rincons to the east, the Catalinas to the north, and all around a gigantic expanse of sky. What more could he ask for? And when he read the stats of the house and the unbelievably reasonable price of the rent, he broke out his cell phone, called the number at the bottom of the sign, and waited in the driveway for the owner to arrive.

Forty-five minutes later, after a quick tour of the home and a security deposit withdrawn from an ATM at the Circle K, the place was his, contingent upon a credit check that he knew he would pass with flying colors.

It was more than he needed, really, but he liked the idea of being in a real house again. It gave him a solid, settled feeling, and even though he was only renting, he experienced a welcome sense of permanence that had not been his since before the separation. He drove back to the motel, spirits high. He'd have to return to California to pack up his stuff. He could find someone to help him load up a U-Haul with no problem—there were a couple of neighbors in his apartment complex with whom he was casually acquainted—but unloading here in Tucson would be difficult. He thought about the plywood shack and the shabby ranch house that bookended his new digs. He could probably ask someone there to help him, but he didn't want his first contact with his neighbors to be an imposition.

So he called up some of his old buddies—or rather, their parents. He could not seem to find any of his friends in the phone book, but their families were still listed and still at the same addresses, and he asked fathers and mothers for current phone numbers. It brought home to him how far out of his life he'd let them slip. It seemed to him that Jordan and his wife had sent Christmas cards within the past few years, letting him know that they'd moved, but he hadn't really cared and hadn't made an effort to keep track or keep in touch. He'd been living almost entirely in the present, letting his past erase itself, and he'd seldom even thought about his friends from childhood and early adulthood.

Now, it seemed, most of them were gone. Mike was a firefighter in New York, both Jordan and Eck had moved to Phoenix, and even Victor's own parents didn't know what had become of him. Joel was still around, though, and for that Hunt was grateful. Joel McCain had been Hunt's best friend in elementary school and junior high, and though they'd drifted apart in high school and after, there was still that connection, and Hunt called him up instantly, thankful for someone familiar in what was a suddenly strange and unfamiliar city.

Joel, oddly enough, was a teacher, a social science instructor at Mountain Valley Junior College. Oddly, because he had been at best an indifferent student—hostile was probably a more accurate description—and the last occupation Hunt expected to find him in was education. In junior high, Joel's goal had been to be a trucker. There was nothing better, he'd said, than cruising around the country, listening to tunes and getting paid for it. Hunt assumed his friend had changed his mind by the time he graduated from high school, but they'd been running in separate crowds by then, and he sure wouldn't have thought Joel would be interested in any occupation that required a college degree.

Joel laughed when Hunt expressed surprise at his choice. "I got used to that school schedule. Couldn't imagine a life where I didn't have summers off. Besides, a summer working with my old man in the hot sun would make anyone a model college student. What about you, though? What do you do? And are you just visiting, or have you come back for good?"

Hunt gave him the whole sob story—separation, divorce, layoff at Boeing, blah, blah, blah—and then explained how he'd decided—on the spur of the moment, while looking out his apartment window—to move back to Tucson.

"You get settled yet? Found a place to live?"

"Well," Hunt said, starting to feel a little embarrassed. "That's actually why I called. I found a place today. I'm going back to California to pack up my clothes and books and records, and what little furniture's left to me after the divorce. There's not enough to justify hiring movers, so I thought I'd do it myself and—"

"And you need someone to help."

"Yeah, I mean, there's not much. A bed. A sofa bed. A big TV. A dining room table. I can probably unpack the rest myself. It'll only take about a half hour or so—"

"Don't worry about it. I'm there. I was going to suggest we get together anyway."

"Thanks. I appreciate it."

"Say, what are you doing tonight?"

"Absolutely nothing."

"Why don't you come over, then? My wife and daughter'll be at a Brownie meeting. We'll be able to talk about old times without censoring ourselves."

"You have a daughter, huh?"

"Lilly. She's eight."

"Jesus, I remember when *we* were eight," Hunt said. And to him it did not seem that long ago. He could still recall vividly not only the things they did together but the way he felt—the all-or-nothing stakes that seemed to permeate every aspect of life, how neither of them ever gave a thought to a future that seemed open and endless.

"Yeah. Time flies, doesn't it?"

"Yes," Hunt said. "It does."

Joel gave him his address and directions to the house, and Hunt found a hotel notepad and pen, writing it down. The two of them said good-bye.

He had time to kill before seven, when he told Joel he'd come over, so he decided to drive around and hit some of his old haunts. He had the nagging urge to call Eileen and tell her he was moving, but he didn't know why. They hadn't gotten along at all the past year and a half, and the last thing she'd said to him, before the lawyers got involved and an institutionalized formality was imposed on their disintegrating relationship, was "Fuck you! I hope you die and rot in hell!" Still, it seemed strange that he didn't need to check in with her anymore, had no obligation to inform her of his whereabouts, was free to do whatever he wanted and go wherever he pleased. He wondered if there was some sort of divorce etiquette which dictated that he should give her a courtesy call and let her know what he was doing, just in case something came up.

But what could come up? They'd divided the assets, she wasn't getting alimony, and according to the law their obligations to each other were over.

He still wasn't used to being alone.

He spent the afternoon hitting used bookstores and record stores. A couple of his old favorites were gone, but there were still the two Bookman's shops, and he picked up a few Chick Corea albums and a copy of *The Killer Mountains*, a book on the Lost Dutchman gold mine that he'd read as a teenager but subsequently lost. In addition to the books and records in the living room of his apartment, he had at least five or six large additional boxes in the unused garage of the complex, and he realized that he was going to need more bookshelves for the new house. He checked out a Goodwill, a Salvation Army, and a St. Vincent dePaul thrift store but had no luck, and after a return to the motel and a quick swim in the pool, he ordered pizza, ate it while watching the news, then headed out.

Joel lived in a recently built subdivision only a few miles from Hunt's new house. The homes were big but the yards were almost nonexistent, and though the residences were stand-alone structures, they had the look of town houses. He assumed from the uniform appearance of the trees and bushes, from the perfectly matched mailboxes and identical color schemes, that some sort of homeowners' association held sway, and though these houses were obviously more expensive than his rental, he would not have lived here on a dare.

The generic neighborhood and the white SUV in Joel's driveway—indistinguishable from the vehicles parked in the driveways of adjacent homes—made Hunt wary at first, but Joel turned out to be the same wry, funny, cynical person he remembered, all grown up. The interior of the house belied the conventionality of the outside, as though the exterior were merely a deceptive cover; camouflage for the real home within. The furnishings were funky, eclectic. In the living room, what Joel described as a liquor cabinet he had "liberated" from the bar of an old ghost town past McGuane had been converted into a bookcase, and next to it a desert terrarium existed inside the oversized glass bulb of an antique gas pump. Across the room the skeleton of a saguaro cactus had been made into a standing lamp. In Joel's study, a rawhide couch sat next to an end table made out of a black boulder and a piece of glass. One entire wall was taken up with a neon sign rescued from a demolished hamburger stand that read: BURGERS, FRIES, SHAKES.

"This place is *cool*," Hunt said admiringly.

"Isn't it?"

"Remember our clubhouse? Roland stole that stop sign from the highway, and we had that old mirror we found in the garbage that we hung up next to that Mötley Crüe poster Mike's brother gave us? This"—he gestured around the room—"is what we were going for."

"You're right. We would've loved this. Especially the sign." Joel laughed. "I have the aesthetic taste of an eight-year-old."

"No, you've made it. And you didn't sell out. You are, after all is said and done—"

"The Man!" they shouted in unison.

Joel clapped a hand on Hunt's shoulder. "I'm glad you're back," he said. "I didn't know it, but I missed you."

"Me, too."

They walked back out to the living room.

"So," Hunt asked, "do you stay in contact with . . . anyone?"

Joel shook his head. "No. I get a Christmas card from Jordan each year, and I send him one back, but that's about the extent of it." He looked embarrassed. "I don't know why. I've never even thought about it before, and there's no excuse for it, but . . . it happened."

"Say no more, say no more," Hunt said, falling into his best Monty Python rhythm.

"Are you planning to reunite the old gang?"

"Not really. I called around and most of them are gone, scattered to the wind. Victor's parents don't even know where he is."

Joel frowned. "Victor?"

"Oh, that's right, he was a high school friend. High school and college. I don't think you ever met him."

Joel put on some music, brought out some beers, and they sat around for the next hour, laughingly talking about old times.

When Hunt looked at his watch, it was after eight. He made a move to get up.

"You don't have to leave, do you?" Joel asked.

"Well . . ."

"Come on, stay awhile."

"My motel's on the other side of town, and I wanted to get an early start. It's a long trip back to Seal Beach."

"I didn't realize you were going back tomorrow."

He thought for a second, settled back in his seat. "What the hell. I'm not."

"Good, good. Stacy and Lilly should be back soon. I want you to meet them."

Hunt saw framed photographs of the family on top of a stereo cabinet. "Is that them?"

"Yeah."

He got up to investigate and saw a picture of Joel and a pretty young girl standing in front of the Matterhorn at Disneyland, another picture of the girl with her smiling mother at the Grand Canyon, and a photo of all three posing by the giraffe pen at the zoo. Something about the woman looked familiar, and Hunt studied her face for a moment before an identity suggested itself to him.

He turned toward Joel, incredulous. "You married Stacy Williams?"

His friend grinned. "Yeah."

"Whoa."

"I tell myself that every day."

Stacy had been both smart and gorgeous, the valedictorian of their junior high and high school, head cheerleader, and— impossibly and simultaneously—editor of the school paper; one of those girls so far out of their league that she didn't even know they existed. And Joel *married* her?

Hunt asked the only logical question. "How did this happen?"

"We both went to U of A, and we met again in sociology class. Or, rather, she met me for the first time. Of course, I knew exactly who she was. That's why I sat down next to her. And when I casually let slip that I'd attended John Adams, too, it was like old home week. She was feeling alone and overwhelmed, and was grateful for someone familiar to talk to. Well, not exactly familiar, but someone who had the same background. We hit it off, and we even started studying together and had coffee after class a few times. I didn't think anything would come of it. I didn't think I had a chance because . . . well, because she was Stacy Williams.

"Then, at the last class, she gave me a Christmas card. Inside, she'd written a message thanking me for being someone she could talk to, for helping her through a hard semester, and at the bottom she'd put her phone number. I hadn't gotten her anything—it hadn't even crossed my mind—and on the spur of the moment I asked her out to dinner. Out of guilt. I thought of it as a Christmas present, not a date . . . but it was a date. And after that we started going out steadily, and"—he grinned—"after graduation I married her."

At that moment the front door opened, and Joel's wife and daughter bustled into the foyer, talking, laughing, noisily setting plastic bags atop the seat of the hall tree. Stacy looked, if possible, even more beautiful than she had in the photographs—more beautiful than she had in high school—and there was about her the no-nonsense practicality of a mother, which only added to her charm.

"You must be Hunt," she said, reaching around Lilly to shake his hand. "Nice to meet you. Joel said you'd called and were coming over. You went to John Adams too, huh?"

He nodded. "Yeah. And Bodie Junior High and Peppertree Elementary."

"Me, too!" Pushing her daughter in front of her, Stacy headed toward the stairs. "I'm sorry to rush like this, but the meeting ran late, and it's past Lilly's bedtime. School night," she explained. "Just let me put her to bed and I'll be right down. Say good night, Lilly."

"Good night," the girl said cheerfully.

"Good night," Hunt told her.

The two of them hurried up the steps.

Hunt shook his head. "Stacy Williams."

"Stacy McCain now."

"You are one lucky bastard, you know that?"

"Yes, I do. Hey, stay right there, will you? I'm going upstairs and say good night to Lilly. I'll be right back."

"Okay."

Joel started up the steps.

"Your wife doesn't happen to have any single friends, does she?"

Joel turned around, grinning. "She might," he said. "She just might."

2

After calling around, Hunt discovered that the cheapest way to transport his belongings back from California was not to rent a U-Haul or Ryder truck but to get one from a local agency called Eezee Rent, which undercut its lowest competitor by ten bucks and offered fifty free miles besides. He left his car in the driveway of his new home, had Joel take him to the rental place, and from there he took off, heading back to California on what he hoped would be a two-day trip.

He arrived shortly after dark and spent the evening packing. Most of the books and records he'd boxed before driving out to Arizona, but a lot of kitchen utensils and food and clothes and miscellaneous items still needed to be crated up, and it was after midnight before he finally crashed.

He awoke to the alarm at six in the morning, and finished boxing some last-minute items before going out for a quick breakfast of donuts and coffee. It was a Saturday, so most people were home, and as he'd hoped, the two of his neighbors with whom he was closest, Bill Curtis and David Vigil, saw him carrying boxes and offered to help him load the truck. He bought both men lunch as payment, and by midafternoon, the truck was packed and the apartment cleaned. After all that heavy lifting, he was too tired to make the nine-hour trip back to Tucson, so he drove down to Ocean Avenue and walked the Seal Beach pier one last time. Since the separation, he'd taken to strolling the pier, watching the fishermen, watching the waves, watching the seagulls, watching the babes. He found that it relaxed him. And as he walked against the offshore breeze toward Ruby's restaurant at the pier's end, he realized he was going to miss this.

He spent the night in a sleeping bag on the floor of his old apartment. In the morning, he left early, hitting the road before it was light. He made it back to Tucson just after one, and the first thing he noticed when he pulled the truck into the driveway was that his car had a cracked rear windshield.

"Son of a bitch," he said.

He got out of the cab and automatically glanced toward the plywood shack next door. There was no one about, only an angry skinny dog tethered by frayed rope to a metal stake. If he had to guess, the ball or rock or whatever broke his window probably came from there. He walked up to the back of the car to examine the glass. He'd expected to see dirt or rock chips, a pulverized area at the point of impact. But there was nothing—no indication that the crack was anything other than a natural occurrence.

"Goddamn it."

He called Joel, who helped him unload and arrange the furniture and took him back to the rental place. The next morning, he phoned his insurance company. The details of his policy were buried somewhere in one of the boxes still in the center of the living room, but he had a proof-of-insurance card in his wallet, and he took it out and dialed the number.

After one quick ring, a recording informed him that he had accessed the automated phone system of United Automobile Insurance.

United Automobile Insurance? He had Statewide Insurance.

Hunt frowned, hung up, and dialed again, but got the same recorded greeting. He stayed on the line this time and listened to a list of six options before the recording stated, "To speak with the next available representative, please press zero or stay on the line."

He pressed zero.

"Please wait," the bland recorded voice of a woman instructed him. "A customer service representative will be with you shortly. Please have your name, policy number, and vehicle make and model. Your call may be monitored to ensure better service to our customers."

Muzak came on, and he waited for one minute, two minutes, five, six, seven. He was about to hang up and dial again when the Muzak stopped and a man said, "United Automobile Insurance. How may I help you?"

"Hello. I, uh . . . I don't *have* United Automobile Insurance," Hunt said hesitantly. "I have Statewide Insurance. But when I called the number on my card, I got your company."

"We recently acquired SI. You should have already received a notice in the mail."

"I didn't."

"Well, we're now administering all former Statewide policies. Now how may I help you?"

"I have a cracked rear windshield on my—"

"Policy number?"

Hunt looked down at his card, read off the number.

There was a short pause. "You're Hunt Jackson? And the vehicle in question would be a Saab?"

"Yes."

"And you live at 114 Tenth Street, apartment B, Seal Beach?"

"Actually, no. I just moved to Tucson, Arizona. Yesterday, to be exact. I haven't had a chance to change my address yet."

"Where did the accident occur, sir?"

"I'm not sure I'd call it an accident."

"Well, where did the incident occur that resulted in the cracking of your rear windshield?"

"Tucson. In the driveway of my home." He realized that he didn't know the address. "Hold on a sec." He ran over to the kitchen counter, where he'd placed a copy of the rental agreement. He picked up the phone again. "That's 2112 Jackrabbit Lane."

"And how did it happen?"

"I don't know. I parked my car in the driveway and rented a truck to move my furniture from California. I was gone for two days, and when I returned the window was cracked."

"When did this occur?"

"Sometime in the past two days."

"I need a time."

"I don't know a time."

"I can accept an approximation."

Hunt was starting to become annoyed. "Look, can you just

tell me what my deductible is? If I can find someone to replace it for less than that—"

"I need the time of the incident."

"I told you. I was gone for two days, and when I came back the window was broken. It happened sometime in that two-day period."

"I have to put down something."

"It doesn't matter. You can put down whatever."

"Half past a monkey's ass, a quarter to his balls."

Hunt blinked. "What?"

"That's what I'm entering for the time."

"You can't—"

"These fields must be filled in, and since you're being uncooperative, I'm forced to use my own discretion and fill them in for myself. Now do you have an approximate time for me?"

"I told you—"

Hunt heard the clicking sound of keys being typed in the background. "Half past a monkey's ass, a quarter to his balls." This time the representative said the words in an exaggerated sing-songy Southern accent, stretching out the word "balls," to two syllables: *ba-wuls*.

"What the hell is going on here?" Hunt demanded. "I want to talk to your supervisor."

"Just a minute."

There was a click, and the line went dead.

What the—? The asshole had hung up on him! Hunt immediately dialed the number again. This time, after the prerecorded message and a five-minute wait, a female representative came on the line. She was courteous, efficient, and had no explanation for the bizarre previous call. Hunt gave the woman—Kara, she said, with a K—the pertinent information about his rear windshield, which she took down. She told him she did not need a precise time for the accident and that an adjuster would be out sometime this morning to assess the damage. She then took down his new address and phone number, asked him to send the company a photocopy of his Arizona registration once it had been transferred, and told him that a new policy reflecting his changed address would be issued and sent out within the next week.

"May I make a suggestion?" Kara said.

"Sure. What?"

"You should think about obtaining renter's insurance. According to the statistics in front of me, you're located in, not exactly a high crime area, but an area that is above average in the amount of reported vandalism."

"Aren't you a car insurance company?"

"We don't sell renter's insurance," she admitted. "But we are affiliated with All Homes Insurance, and they offer what is probably the most comprehensive coverage on the market. They don't redline, so you'll be assured of receiving a fair and reasonable price quote. I could transfer you if you'd like."

"Not right now."

"Well then, may I suggest that when you do buy renter's insurance, you sign up for the maximum limits. You're going to need it."

You're going to need it?

For some reason, that sounded like a threat.

"Is there anything else I can do for you?" Kara asked.

"What about that first guy who answered the phone? Are you going to tell your supervisor? He shouldn't be allowed to get away with behavior like that."

"What was his name again?"

"He didn't give his name."

"All phone representatives are required to state their names."

"Obviously that guy doesn't follow company procedures."

"Are you sure he was a real phone representative for United?"

"I called this same number and went through your automated system before I got to him. And he had access to my policy information. So, yeah, I would say so."

"Well, all I can say is, I'm sorry, and rest assured we will be investigating this incident."

"Thank you."

Hunt said good-bye and hung up.

Weird, he thought. *Weird.*

3

Hunt spent two weeks in a fruitless job search: reading classified ads, sending out résumés and haunting the unemployment office (or the Department of Economic Security, as it was euphemistically called). He filled out applications at every company and corporation, every hospital and school, every city, county, state, and federal office he could find. Most places were laying off, not hiring, and in this PC-based world, there did not seem to be much call for mainframe operators like himself. His severance pay was almost gone, and while the interstate paperwork had finally been sorted out and he was once again collecting unemployment, it was barely enough to pay for his rent. He needed a quick infusion of cash, but he could think of no solution other than to become a Kelly girl and get a temp job, or apply at a fast-food joint for a minimum-wage position flipping burgers.

As luck would have it, he was scanning the "Employment Opportunities" in the classifieds when Reed Abrams, personnel manager for the county, called to offer him a job. Only it wasn't the computer operations position for which he had applied, but tree-trimming work in the maintenance services department.

"When you filled out your initial application, you checked the 'Other' box as well," the manager explained. "Which means that you asked to be considered for any open positions.

So even though you're vastly overqualified, there's an opening on the landscape maintenance crew. It's an entry-level position with no prior experience necessary. While this might not seem like a job for someone with your background and qualifications, just let me point out that once you're working for the county, it's easier to effect a lateral transfer to another department or even a promotion once new positions become available. We're not looking for anyone in Computer Operations just now, but when we do, we'll look in-house before we advertise, and you'll be in prime position."

Hunt asked a few perfunctory questions, playing hard to get, but he'd already made the decision to take it. What choice did he have? It was either that or McDonald's.

Abrams told him to come in tomorrow, gave him a brief overview of what to expect, and Hunt hung up the phone. There was a moment of self-pity. *How the mighty have fallen,* he thought. But that was replaced almost instantly by a sense of renewed optimism. The pay was not significantly lower than what he would have earned as a computer operator at any number of private firms in Tucson, and county benefits were extremely generous. The insurance package easily matched the one he'd had at Boeing. Looked at objectively, this was really not a bad deal. Besides, this was why he had moved here. He was reinventing himself, starting over, and what could be more liberating than that?

"And," he explained to Joel later, "my job isn't my life, it's a way to earn money so I can live my life."

His friend grinned. "You keep telling yourself that."

"Asshole."

But he really did feel that way, and he realized that a sea change had occurred in his makeup since the divorce. No longer was he driven by a need to prove himself, by a desire to keep up with some imaginary yardstick of career milestones. He had been competing since childhood, striving for good grades, getting into a top college, making sure he got the job

he deserved, the promotions he deserved. He'd been successful but not necessarily happy, and he thought that this was his
opportunity to turn that around, to not worry about success and
allow himself to *be* happy.

Joel clapped a hand on his back. "Seriously," he said. "Congratulations."

"Thanks," Hunt told him. "I think things are finally looking
up."

The alarm woke him up at five-thirty, and Hunt tripped
over a chair as he clumsily made his way through the darkness
to the clock on the dresser. He shut off the alarm, then stood
there for a moment, holding on to the dresser's edge, trying to
will his sleep-fogged mind into some semblance of alertness.
In California, he used to wake up at five in order to beat the
rush-hour traffic, but during his time off he'd gotten out of the
habit of rising early, and this was like pulling teeth.

He showered, shaved, then stood in his underwear looking
through his closet. He was supposed to meet with the personnel manager at seven-thirty for an orientation, and then with
the manager of maintenance services at nine. The personnel
manager hadn't told him what to wear, and Hunt hadn't
thought to ask. A tie was obviously too formal, but he probably shouldn't wear his weekend clothes, either. Didn't tree
trimmers have their own uniforms? Orange jumpsuits or
something? Or were those prisoners? He wasn't sure.

He finally settled on new jeans and a nice dress shirt. A
compromise.

As it turned out, there *were* uniforms for tree trimmers, but
he'd made the right decision to wear what he did because he
spent most of the morning inside the offices of the county
building meeting with bureaucrats, watching a "Welcome to
County Government" video, filling out insurance forms and
tax forms and liability forms. Shortly after ten, he finally met
Steve Nash, the brusque maintenance services manager, who

took him out to the corp yard, exposed him to some of the tools with which he'd be working, and gave him a boxed tan uniform and cap before bringing him back and making him watch another video, this one on trees and trimming techniques. After a half-hour lunch, he was required to go to a nearby medical clinic and take a physical and a drug test. It was nearly three o'clock by the time he finished.

"Am I supposed to go back to the corp yard?" he asked. "I thought I was going to start working today."

"Tomorrow," the personnel manager told him. "Although your status is considered temporary until we receive the results of the drug test, and you will be on probation for six months, during which time you can be fired without cause."

"So what do I do now?"

"Go home, get a good night's sleep, report to Steve in the corp yard at eight."

Eight was late. The trucks and the trimming crews were already out and about, and the maintenance manager told him that while the office workers started at eight and got off at five, here they started at seven. Six in the summer months. "I won't dock you this time because it's that choda Abrams who screwed you up, but from here on in, you'd better be on time."

"I will," Hunt promised.

Steve stared at him suspiciously. With his mustache, stocky frame, and perpetual scowl, he looked like a meaner Dennis Franz. "Jackson," he said, squinting, "what the fuck are you doing here?"

Hunt was taken aback. "Excuse me?"

"College man like yourself. Why're you here? Writing a book?"

Hunt didn't know how to respond. "No," he said. "I just . . . needed a job."

"So this is just a temp job to you? You're going to move on in a month or so, when something else comes in, and leave us high and dry?"

"No," he lied.

"Just get out," Steve said disgustedly. "And don't be late again. You're on your probation period, you know."

He'd already been assigned to a three-man crew, with himself as the third man, so Hunt took the map Steve gave him and drove his car out to a park in the east end of the city. He found the county truck easily enough but locating the other tree trimmers was more difficult. He finally met up with them several hundred yards down a hiking trail that wound through a hilly area near a dry creek.

A burly white guy who looked like he could be a professional wrestler, Edward Stack stood atop a metal stepladder, sawing through the upper branches of a palo verde tree with a long-handled cutter. Smaller, skinnier and darker, Jorge Marquez was gathering up cut branches and loading them in an orange trailer attached to a small motorized cart. Hunt apologized profusely for being late, but neither of them seemed to care, and both men stopped working and casually introduced themselves. Hidden under a bush was a cooler filled with ice and Snapple, and Jorge grabbed three bottles of raspberry iced tea, taking one for himself and passing two around.

"I just had breakfast a half hour ago," Hunt said, declining.

"Well, we've been working for an hour already and it's hot as hell," Jorge said.

The two of them conducted their own unofficial interview while they drank, asking Hunt about his life, his background, how he happened to get this job. They didn't seem overly concerned about his utter lack of experience, which was good, and they seemed to like him, which was even better. After they finished asking questions and had satisfied themselves that he was all right, they showed him what to do. He'd watched the tree-trimming video and Steve had explained how the tools of the trade worked, but that superficial overview had been next to useless. Edward and Jorge gave him a hands-on demo and let him practice a bit before telling him to take over cleanup—picking up the cut branches and piling them in the trailer.

"You picked a good day to start," Jorge told him, walking over to the palo verde. "You get to see Big Laura."

"Who's Big Laura?"

Edward chuckled. "You'll see. What's the time, Whoreman?"

"Nearly nine-fifteen!" Jorge called.

"Big Laura's as regular as my fiber-eatin' grandma. She jogs on these trails every day. And on the days we're here . . . well, she likes to say hi." Edward pointed up the dirt pathway. "Face that direction. She'll be here any second."

Sure enough, he saw a glimpse of red through the trees and bushes, and a moment later, a young blond woman came jogging toward them. She was tall and she was hefty, but that wasn't why Edward and Jorge called her Big Laura. No, those two reasons bounced in front of her like jellied basketballs, pushing the limits of even the loose-fitting red sweats, and as she approached the three of them, she smiled and lifted her top, exposing the biggest breasts Hunt had ever seen.

Then she was gone, around the bend of the path, and Edward and Jorge were both laughing.

"There are a *few* perks to this job," Jorge said.

Hunt shook his head. "Wow. I guess so."

"Just wait until Thursday," Edward said.

"What's Thursday?"

"We'll be working on the east side, off the Rillito. There's a new housing development next door."

"Stripping Susan. That's a sight you won't soon forget."

"Stripping Susan?"

Jorge grinned. "Big Laura was just the opening act. Welcome to tree trimming."

TWO

No.

This couldn't be happening.

But though Sy Kipplinger had never experienced an earthquake before, he knew without a doubt that he was experiencing one now. The ground beneath his feet rolled and rocked, like a small boat in a rough sea whose hull was being pounded by hammerhead sharks. Time seemed to have stretched out, and the seconds seemed like minutes, his heightened, panicked senses acutely attuned to everything that was going on, seeing the swaying of the hanging plants in the kitchen, hearing the crack of the house's wood foundation beneath his feet, smelling the odor of the broken gas line from the hot water heater.

His breakfast flew into his lap, eggs and orange juice staining his pants.

Mary was screaming, and he was on automatic pilot as he stood, grabbed her, and tried to steer her out of the kitchen into the backyard. But plates and cups were falling about them from the open cupboards, a mixing bowl barely missing Mary's head, and then the refrigerator slid in front of the back door, blocking their way. The window above the sink shattered inward, pelting them with glass, and several shards cut his arms and face.

Sy had been through a lot in his seventy years, but nothing had prepared him for this, where the very ground beneath his feet was moving and shifting, no longer safe and stable, the earth actively trying to throw him off as though he were a flea on its back.

A chunk of ceiling collapsed in front of them as they hurried into the living room, and he nearly tripped over it, his grip on Mary's arm the only thing that kept him upright.

He had no idea how long the earthquake had been going on—less than a minute, probably—but it felt like an hour, and it showed no sign of slowing or stopping. If anything, the shaking intensified, all rolling motion gone and now just a wrenching series of successive jerks. The television tipped over, shattering on the hardwood floor; Mary's knickknack shelf hurled its contents onto the couch and coffee table and throw rug.

For a brief impossible second, he thought he saw a man silhouetted in the hallway off to the left, a husky man in a hat, but then they were staggering across the lurching floor toward the front door, avoiding falling furniture, and he forgot all about the figure.

They made it outside just as the eastern half of the house collapsed, his den and the bedrooms falling in on themselves as though a pin had been pulled and everything that had held the structure together suddenly dissolved. They hobbled, limped across the lawn, and at some point Sy realized that the shaking had stopped, that he was compensating for a pitch that was no longer there.

They reached the street and turned around, staring back at the pile of rubble that had been their home. Without warning, Mary began beating him, sobbing as her fists rained blows on his cut shoulders and chest. "I told you we should've bought earthquake insurance!" she shrieked. "I told you!"

He stared dumbly at the spot where his den had stood, wondering why none of the other houses in the neighborhood had fallen. "This is Tucson," he said. "We don't have earthquakes here."

Neighbors emerged from their homes, many in their bathrobes, some with cups of morning coffee in their hands, and all of them looked bewilderingly at the Kipplingers' ruined house. A few ran over to try to help.

"I told you!" Mary sobbed, hitting him.

"This is Tucson," he kept repeating. "We don't have earthquakes here."

Three

1

Stacy really did have a friend who was single, and though Hunt had been joking about it, Joel and his wife set up the two of them, inviting both over for dinner one Friday night. They were each forewarned, so it wasn't a complete surprise. Both were assured that it was not a blind date, that there was no pressure, but that in itself was pressure, and he found himself trying on outfits like a schoolgirl going to her first dance, consciously trying to look good but in a casual "I don't really care about my appearance" way.

Her name was Beth, and she worked with Stacy at Thompson Industries in the public relations department. For the first part of the evening, Beth stayed with Stacy in the kitchen, while Hunt and Joel remained in the living room, watching television and talking. Lilly shuttled back and forth between her parents. At dinner, all of them ate at the big dining room table, Hunt and Beth conveniently and not coincidentally seated next to each other. The two of them hit it off immediately, and though help was ready and available if necessary, no conversational rescues were required of the hosts, who were able to focus their attention on their daughter and her melodramatic account of her day.

Afterward, Stacy took Lilly up to bed while Joel retreated to the kitchen to load the dishwasher, discreetly leaving them alone. They sat next to each other on the couch, close but not too close, and eased into the subject of themselves by reminiscing about how they met the McCains. Beth described how she and Stacy had met on her first day of work at Thompson Industries, and Hunt explained that he and Joel had lived down the street from each other and been best friends in elementary school.

"Wow," she said. "You've known him that long?"

"Well, there was a gap. We sort of hung out with different crowds in high school, and after that we went our separate ways. I moved to California, got a job and got married, and I just looked him up again last month when I moved back after my divorce was final. Before that, I hadn't seen or heard from him in . . . I don't know, fifteen years."

Stacy returned from upstairs. "You two ought to go for a walk around the neighborhood," she said, passing through the living room on her way to the kitchen. "It's a nice night out."

"Subtle," Beth said. "Very subtle."

Stacy laughed.

But they decided to take her advice, and after informing their hosts that they'd be going out, they walked down the driveway and out onto the sidewalk, strolling past the closely built, nearly identical houses.

"So you're divorced," she said.

"Yeah. Does that bother you?"

"I don't know."

"What about you?"

"Never married. Never even lived with anyone," Beth admitted.

The surprise must have registered on his face.

"I haven't been a nun," she said. "I've had plenty of boyfriends, and I was with the last one for over five years."

"But you never lived with him."

"He stayed over sometimes, or I stayed at his place . . . but, no, we never lived together."

"So why did you break up?"

"You're awfully nosy, aren't you?"

"Sorry. I'm not . . . I haven't . . . I've been out of circulation for a while. And back when I was *in* circulation, we were all doing the confession thing. I'm not up on current . . ." He took a deep breath. "I don't know what the hell I'm doing. I'm just winging it. I'm sorry if I—"

But she was already laughing. "It's fine, it's fine. I wouldn't've said anything if I knew you would take it so seriously. It's just that . . . well, I'm not that great at self-examination, and you were making me—"

"Examine yourself?"

"Exactly."

"Sorry."

"Don't be. And for the record, the reason Tad and I broke up is because he dumped me. He met some bim at a bar, and the next morning he called me up and said it was over."

"*Tad?*"

"Your name's Hunt," she pointed out. "You don't have a lot of room to talk."

"Still."

She punched his shoulder, then took his arm. He felt the warm softness of her body next to his. This was going far better than he had hoped.

"Now that we're in such a nice confessional mood, why did you get divorced?"

He shrugged. "The usual reasons, I guess. We drove each other crazy. There was no one else, if that's what you're wondering. Neither of us were seeing other people . . . we just couldn't live together. Probably, we shouldn't've gotten married in the first place."

"Oh." She held him closer, held him tighter, and as they walked the talk drifted off to other, happier topics.

A half hour later, they returned, hand in hand. Joel and Stacy had finished the dishes and were seated on the living room couch, listening to an old Spyro Gyra CD. Beth excused herself and went to use the rest room. Hunt looked over at Joel and saw his friend grinning, wiggling his eyebrows in an exaggerated Groucho Marx manner.

He nodded, smiled back.

This just might work out.

2

It was not a whirlwind romance by any means. They had both been recently burned, and they took things slowly. It was a week before he even called her; a week after that before they went out on their first official date: the traditional dinner and a movie. He'd been afraid they'd have nothing new to talk about, that they'd used up their quota of original thoughts and interesting topics at the dinner party, that there would be long stretches of awkward silence punctuated by pathetically obvious attempts at conversation. But if anything, they were even more comfortable with each other than they had been at Joel's, and the talk flowed easily. They had a lot in common. Not so much that they'd be one of those pukey couples who never did anything apart, but enough that there was a foundation upon which to build a relationship. They ended up going to a coffee shop after the movie and talking until midnight. When he dropped her off at her house, she invited him to come in and spend the night.

After that, not a weekend went by that they weren't together. They did ordinary things like go to bookstores, go to malls, hike, and rent videos. They did touristy things like spend one Saturday at Tombstone and another at Old Tucson Studios. Edward and Jorge made fun of him for being so whipped that he spent a Sunday afternoon weeding Beth's garden—"I'm working on trees and bushes all week long," Jorge said. "Last thing I want to do is spend my weekends gardening."—but they both understood and they both liked Beth, and one uncharacteristically cool Saturday afternoon he and Beth; Joel, Stacy, and Lilly; and Edward and Jorge and their wives all went to the Sonora Desert Museum and then out to dinner at an Italian restaurant, where Lilly fell asleep on the floor and the rest of them closed the place.

Beth's house was newer than his and bigger, but it wasn't one of those Mediterranean lookalikes that seemed to be proliferating at an alarming rate on every side of the city, and it wasn't part of a gated community. It was a long, low pseudo-Santa Fe home on a lot large enough to have a vegetable garden on the side and a flower garden in back. She wasn't renting, she owned the place, and he found himself spending more and more nights there, to the point where Beth finally asked him if he wanted to move in. He could take care of half the monthly mortgage payment, she added quickly, worried that he might be offended by an offer of free rent. But while part of him definitely wanted to move in with her, he still wasn't ready to commit so fully so quickly, and he told her in mock macho tones that he was a man who needed his freedom. She laughed, but she understood the truth behind the joke, and she didn't press him.

So they dated and they had fun.

Eileen had not been much of a music fan. Even when they first started going out, she'd gone to concerts only out of obligation and only when he couldn't scare up some buddies to go with him. After they got married, they never attended a single live music performance together.

Beth was exactly the opposite. Over the years, Hunt had become lazy and set in his ways, more comfortable remaining at home and listening to CDs than venturing out. But Beth loved the nightlife, and through the Internet, the alterna-press and a host of mailing lists, she religiously kept up with the ever-changing schedules for both small clubs and large concert venues throughout the city. In their first three months together, he heard more live music than he had in the preceding decade.

One Saturday night, they were exiting a Santana concert when they saw a group of Chicano gang members with shaved heads and blue-ink neck tattoos standing in a circle outside the arena, pushing a geeky gangly guy wearing bright purple clothes back and forth between them. Hunt led Beth in the opposite direction as several policemen emerged from the arena, billy clubs drawn.

They saw the geeky guy again, four days later, outside a movie theater. It was an art house adjacent to the university, and they'd gone to see a French romantic comedy that was supposed to be one of the year's best films but bored them both to tears. There'd been no parking in the front lot so they'd parked behind the building, and while the rest of the audience headed back up the aisles, they left through a side exit in order to save time. The heavy door shut and locked behind them, and only then did they notice the commotion at the top of the stairs.

He had on the same purple clothes, but a different gang was attacking him this time—a foursome of bearded, overweight, denim-clad bikers who yelled rough obscenities as they punched him in the face and stomach, and then kicked him after he fell to the ground. He was probably a drug dealer, Hunt thought. But drug dealer or no, Beth was outraged by what they were doing. "Leave him alone!" she demanded, hurrying up the stairs. Hunt went after her, cringing, expecting to be beaten to a bloody pulp, but to his surprise the four bikers took off running, obviously afraid of being identified. The man they'd been beating was curled up, clutching his midsection, his face a grimace of pain. One or more ribs were probably broken, but that was not what frightened Hunt. It was the blood issuing from the man's ear—a shocking amount that was still seeping onto the dirty cement of the sidewalk and puddling in an irregular pool that looked like an upside-down map of the Americas.

"Oh my God." He fumbled for his cell phone. "I'm calling nine-one-one."

"No!" the man shouted through moans of pain. "No cops!"

"There's a hospital just down the block," Beth said. "Or maybe a couple of blocks away at the most. It'll be faster if we take him there."

"I don't think we should move him."

"No doctors!"

"Blood is gushing out of your fucking ear!" Hunt said. "You may have brain damage! You may die!"

That seemed to get though to him. Wincing, crying out, he rolled onto his side, then pushed himself to his knees, holding a hand over the bleeding ear. "Take me there, then. But no ambulance. No cops."

The doctors would ask what happened and would probably be required to inform the police, Hunt knew, but he'd let the man find that out himself. He handed Beth the car keys, and she ran through the parking lot behind the theater. He helped the man to his feet and supported him as they walked to the edge of the curb where Beth was pulling up. She had already taken a handful of napkins out of the glove compartment, and gave them to Hunt when he opened the rear driver's-side door. "Use these to stem the blood," she said. Hunt handed the man the napkins, which he promptly pressed against his ear. "Press hard," Beth said. "We'll be there in a minute."

The man lay down in the backseat, rolling instinctively on to his left side, and crying. Hunt slammed the door, ran around to the passenger side, hopped in front, and they took off.

Desert Regional Hospital was indeed close—less than a block away—and Beth sped up to the emergency entrance, parking in a spot usually reserved for ambulances. She dashed inside, and before Hunt could help the man get out of the car, two attendants wheeling a gurney emerged from between the sliding glass doors and expertly removed him from the backseat, placing him on the soft pad atop the cart.

Hunt followed them through the open entrance, but they were all stopped by a severe-looking woman leaning out of a windowed office who refused to buzz open the security door separating the waiting room from the medical facility. "I'll need insurance information before the patient can be admitted," the woman said. Beth stood next to the window, looking angry and exasperated.

"I don't *have* insurance," the injured man wailed.

"Then I'm sorry," the woman informed them, "you'll have to go to County General. We are no longer taking indigents."

"I can pay," he moaned. "Look in my pocket."

"We do not accept patients without insurance."

"You have to take him," Beth said. "This is unconscionable."

"I'm sorry."

"He was beaten severely and he's bleeding from his ear. There might be brain damage."

"Like I said, he'll have to go to County—"

"Fine," Hunt interjected. "Then stop arguing with us and get him there. The man's hurt."

"*You* have to take him," she explained. "We can't spare any ambulances, and it's not our responsibility. We're not responsible for the fact that you brought him to the wrong hospital."

"You don't have to be such a bitch about it!" Beth snapped. She turned toward the two attendants. "Can you help us get him back in the car or is that not your job either?"

The gurney was wheeled out back the way it came, and the embarrassed attendants placed the man in the backseat in as comfortable a position as they could arrange, leaving a pad from the gurney under his head.

Hunt got in the driver's seat this time, but he didn't know where they were going. "Do you know where the hospital is?" he asked.

Beth nodded. "It's about ten minutes away if we hit all green lights. Get going."

They took off. There was silence from the back, and Hunt readjusted the rearview mirror. The injured man's eyes were closed. He'd lost consciousness. Hunt was driving the speed limit, but he pressed down on the gas pedal and pushed it up another ten, half-hoping that a police car would try to pull them over and then end up giving them an escort to the hospital.

No such luck.

They hit a green light, sped through a yellow light, and were stopped by a red light. From that point on, they were trapped in traffic, forced to go five miles *below* the speed limit.

Their passenger woke up several blocks before the hospital. He cried out in pain as they passed a supermarket.

"Are you all right?" Beth asked.

"Of course not!" he shouted.

"We're almost there."

"Just drop me off," he ordered.

"You need to be seen by a doctor," Hunt said. "You might have internal injuries or—"

"I'm *going* to the hospital!" the man said through gritted teeth. "I *know* I need help!"

"Well, you didn't want to go at first."

"I'm in pain here! It hurts like a motherfucker!"

"We can't just drop you off and leave."

"I don't have insurance. This one might turn me away, too. If you just dump me and run, they'll have to take me. I'll pretend to pass out. They'll have no choice."

He was right, Hunt thought. He might be turned away again. Where would they take him then? Did Tucson have any more hospitals?

Hunt glanced over at Beth, who gave him a "What do you think?" look.

He pulled in to the hospital parking lot and drove up to the brightly lit EMERGENCY sign.

"Help me in. Leave. I'll take it from there."

There was no time to argue or chat. "Okay."

"Hunt—" Beth began.

"They'll have to treat him."

The two of them supported him on either side and helped him hobble into the ER waiting room. After every few steps, there was a sharp intake of breath. Once he cried out.

"What's your name?" Beth asked as they approached the front desk.

"Doesn't matter."

The nurse staffing the station glanced at them with concern. Already she was withdrawing a clipboard with some forms. "What's the matter?"

"I'll be fine," the man said. "Go. And thanks."

Hunt grabbed Beth's hand and pulled her away. "I was in a fight," he heard the man say behind them. "I think a couple of ribs might be broken, and my ear's bleeding and . . ."

Then they were out the door.

"This isn't right," Beth said.

"We've done all we can. More than most people would do. And we have no choice." He unlocked the car, got in. "We should have called an ambulance in the first place."

"But would they have taken him?"

He didn't know.

It was long after midnight and they were closer to his place than hers, so Beth came home with him. The assholes next door were having a party. Vehicles were parked up and down the block, and several pickups had recklessly pulled in to the cotton fields across the street. Redneck rap/rock blasted from an impossibly loud stereo. The party had obviously been going on for quite some time and showed no signs of slowing down. Some of it was spilling over onto his lot, but it was late, he was tired, and Hunt just wasn't in the mood to confront a horde of drunken white trash over property boundaries.

He and Beth ignored the revelers, went into the house, locked up, and went to bed. Too tired even for sex, they kissed chastely, then retired to opposite sides of the bed where they promptly fell asleep.

In his dream, Beth had been stabbed by the geeky guy in the purple clothes. Increasingly frantic, he drove her from hospital to hospital, from Tucson to Phoenix to Los Angeles.

But no one would take her in.

3

"Jesus," Joel said. "That's hard to believe."

Hunt nodded.

"What the hell happened to the health care system in this country? I mean, when we were kids and we were sick, we always went to the doctor. And when I broke my arm and when you had to have stitches, we went to the hospital emergency room with no problem. And our parents weren't exactly rich. It makes no sense to me that we have the best doctors and hospitals in the world, the researchers and companies who produce all of the breakthrough drugs, yet we can't even take care of beating victims and accident victims and people with simple treatable problems. Who was it that said a country should be judged by how it takes care of its least fortunate citizens? It's true, man, it's true."

"Yeah," Hunt said, but his mind was on Beth. How good was her insurance? he wondered. He hadn't asked, but he should have. Especially after that horrible dream.

"The whole damn medical process is being co-opted by insurance companies and run by accountants. Health care should not be a profit-making venture. It's a necessity, and it should be available to everyone."

The two of them were sitting in Joel's living room, listening to an old Meat Puppets album, which Hunt had chosen after sorting through a stack of vinyl records on the floor. Lilly ran through with a friend on her way to the backyard, and a second later, they heard Stacy's voice from the kitchen yelling at the girls to stop running in the house.

"There has to be some sort of consumer advocate I could complain to. Hell, maybe I'll write to our congressman and senators. They've got to be good for something."

Joel laughed.

"What's so funny?"

"You. Same old Hunt. Remember back in junior high? When Mrs. Halicki made you move your desk into the hallway and take your midterm outside because you were wearing that Ozzy T-shirt? And you started that petition to get her fired?"

Hunt chuckled. "Yeah. Only Mrs. Halicki found it and gave me a referral."

"You and all of us who signed it."

Lilly poked her head into the room. "Daddy! Do you and Uncle Hunt want to play basketball with us?"

Joel looked at Hunt, who smiled. "Sure."

"It's me and Uncle Hunt against Kate and Daddy!" Lilly announced as they walked out to the backyard.

"Hey! You don't want to team up with your old man?"

Lilly laughed. "Sorry, Daddy."

"That's it, then, girly. You're going down."

"What goes around comes around," the saying went, and while Hunt had never been exactly sure what was meant by that ubiquitous phrase, he thought it probably applied to the fact that his best friend from childhood was once again his best friend as an adult—after a nearly fifteen-year gap. His parents were happy to hear that he and Joel had met up again, and they reminded him of quite a few incidents involving the two of them that he had forgotten.

He was surprised at how easily he and Joel had reconnected. And he was grateful. It had made the transition much easier—so easy, in fact, that he suffered no pangs of regret and no lingering feelings of homesickness, not even for the beach.

He was happy he'd returned to Tucson, and as far as he was concerned, everything had turned out for the best—everything was going great.

It still amazed him that Joel had married Stacy. Moving to California with Eileen and cutting himself off from his roots, he'd been unable to observe the natural progression of postschool life for his old friends and acquaintances. His mind-set was still the same as it had been fifteen years ago, and something like a Joel-and-Stacy matchup seemed nothing short of miraculous. He felt like someone whose life had been put on hold while everyone else's had continued on. But he was making up for lost time, and it seemed as though he was on the phone to his parents two or three times a week with surprising news: Mr. Llewelyn had died two years ago! Hope Williams turned out to be a lesbian! Dr. Crenshaw went bankrupt!

His parents, his mom especially, loved to hear news from Tucson, but neither of them liked the fact that he was working as a tree trimmer. He'd known what their reaction would be and purposefully held off telling them for as long as he could before he finally came clean. He thought about saying that he'd taken this job only because there was nothing available in his field and he needed immediate funds, but while that was factually correct, it wasn't really the truth. The truth was that he had stopped applying for computer operator positions. *This* was his job. Maybe something would open up in the county's MIS department, but maybe not. Either way, he wasn't worrying about it. He'd take things as they came.

He and Lilly beat Joel and Kate in a game up to twenty. Afterward, Joel asked him to stay for dinner, but he begged off. He'd already eaten at the McCains' twice this week, and he didn't want to wear out his welcome. Besides, he was still tired from the night before. He just wanted to go home, call Beth, watch some mindless TV, and go to bed.

In his mailbox when he arrived home was a letter from

United Automobile Insurance. He tore open the envelope, frowning. What did *they* want? His bill wasn't due for another two months. He'd had no tickets or accidents recently. Was this about the rear windshield? He'd ended up not even using insurance for that. His deductible was two hundred dollars, and it had cost only a hundred and twenty-five to replace the cracked glass, so he paid for it out of his own pocket.

Hunt scanned the letter. He might not have used the insurance company for his rear windshield, but he had informed them, so they were required to act on the information provided, according to the letter. Although he was not at fault for the incident that resulted in his cracked window, the damage had occurred while in his care, while he was covered by his current policy, and the company had no choice but to adjust his policy accordingly.

He shook his head in disgust as he looked down at the last line of the letter.

His "good driver discount" had been revoked.

4

Beth and Stacy walked slowly through Foothills Mall, talking and window shopping. A few steps ahead of them, Lilly drank an Orange Julius as she glanced into Victoria's Secret. The girl shot a furtive look back, then turned bright red as she saw her mother watching her. Facing forward, she continued on to the Bath and Body Works next door.

Stacy motioned toward the lingerie store as they passed by. "Need anything?"

Beth laughed.

It had been a while since she'd been able to laugh about that subject, and her friend had obviously noticed the change. She didn't know whether to be proud or embarrassed, but either way she was glad that her love life had taken a turn for the better, that she had once again rejoined the living.

That she had met Hunt.

Hunt.

He was different from other men she'd gone out with since Tad—and different from Tad himself. Tad had been handsome, successful, and charming, but he was also petty, controlling, and irredeemably self-obsessed. Hunt was mellower and more even-tempered. Kinder, she supposed. Nicer. Although those were not necessarily the qualities she would have said she was looking for in a man. He was also, despite his apparent lack of ambition, much smarter than Tad, and that appealed to her greatly. Most important, though, Hunt made her happy. She liked being with him, looked forward to seeing him, and it was that indefinable intangible that cemented her feelings and made her believe that they could make it over the long haul.

If it were up to her, they would have moved in together immediately, but she understood his reluctance to proceed too quickly. He was gun-shy after his divorce. Despite her own emotional history, she felt no such hesitation. She'd always been willing to take chances, and she'd always been one to make quick decisions.

And she'd decided that first night at Stacy and Joel's that Hunt was a keeper.

A trendy-looking woman who could have been a fashion model strode out of Victoria's Secret and nearly ran into her. The woman was talking into her cell phone, and she barely acknowledged them as she breezed past and continued on her way. "No, Tristan," she said. "After swimming lessons you have karate, and then tomorrow is your craft class . . ."

"Did you see that?" Beth asked incredulously.

"Did you *hear* that?" Stacy replied.

"Yeah. I feel sorry for her son."

"Children today are so overscheduled. They all have gymnastics and dance class and piano lessons and karate practice and soccer practice. We've tried to keep that to a minimum with Lil, but even so, she's in Brownies and signed up for band. It's hard to avoid it. Things aren't like they were when we were kids. Girls these days don't have time to just hang out at the mall or sit in each others' rooms and gossip and try on different nail polish."

"That's kind of sad, isn't it? There's enough of that when you become an adult. Children at least should be able to have some unstructured time. Let kids be kids."

Stacy nodded. "And time flies by so fast. It seems like just yesterday Lilly was in diapers. Now she's only a few years away from being a teenager."

"You've done a great job with her, though. She's a fantastic girl."

"Yeah. She is." Stacy glanced slyly over at Beth. "Have you ever thought about having children?"

"Stace!"

She held up her hands defensively. "In a general way, I mean. Not anything specific, not necessarily with Hunt. I was just wondering if you ever see yourself as a mother somewhere down the line."

"Since my clock's ticking."

"I didn't say that."

"No, *I* did. And yes, of course I've thought about it. In a general, nonspecific way." She paused, smiled. "And recently in a not so general way."

"Aha!" Stacy grinned.

"He could be the one."

"*Valley Girl*."

"What in the world are you talking about?"

"At the end of *Valley Girl* when Nicolas Cage is walking out of the prom with the girl, the band on stage, Josie Cotton, I think, starts singing this song: 'He could be the one, he could be the one.'" She must have seen the blank expression on Beth's face. "Sorry. Before your time, I guess."

"I'm not *that* much younger than you."

"Take your compliments where you can get them."

"Mommy!" Lilly called.

As the two of them walked up, the girl was peering through the front window of a pet store at a trio of orange kittens who were rolling across a carpeted shelf, playing.

"Can we get a cat?"

"You have to ask your father," Stacy said. "You know that."

"That means no."

"I told you before, if you can prove to him that you're responsible enough to care for a pet, he'll let you have one."

"But I can't prove that I can take care of a pet unless I *have* a pet! It's a catch twenty-two."

Stacy laughed. "Catch twenty-two? Where did you hear that?"

"I listen," Lilly said. "I pay attention."

"Little pitchers," Beth warned, smiling.

"What about Hunt?" Stacy asked. "Do you think he likes cats?"

"He will," Beth promised. "He will."

"Courtney!"

Beth put her packages down on the kitchen table and looked around for the cat. Usually, he greeted her the second she walked through the door. But the rattle of keys in the lock and her own entry noises had not drawn out the animal this time, so she called out again: "Courtney!"

There was a meow from the living room, and she followed the sound. "Courtney?" she said. He was sitting in front of the entrance to the hall, stock-still, staring fixedly toward her bedroom at the far end. Beth felt an involuntary shiver of fear, an emotion she refused to acknowledge. "What are you doing?" she asked, picking up the cat. Courtney's muscles were stiff, tense. She held him in front of her face, looked into his green eyes, and he relaxed, meowing happily at her.

"Let's go get a snack." She carried him back into the kitchen. She didn't know why he had been so tense, didn't know what he thought was down the hall, but it creeped her out, and she didn't want to go down there just now.

She wished Hunt were there.

That was another reason she wanted him to move in with her, though it was not something she had consciously articulated even to herself. She'd been having weird feelings about the house lately, little moments here and there where she was spooked or uneasy. It was probably the result of living alone for too long, something she was doing to herself, but it was still disconcerting, and she'd feel a lot better if Hunt were with her.

Beth grabbed the Friskies box from the cupboard and poured some into Courtney's bowl. The cat immediately started chomping.

"Let's see what we bought today," she said, wanting to hear a voice in the house, any voice, even if it was hers. She dug through the first sack. "New tennies. And new socks. Finally." She opened the second bag. "Jeans! Now I'll be able to button my pants again."

From somewhere in the back of the house—her bedroom, it sounded like—came a tapping, a low but insistent knocking, as of wood upon wood, that seemed far too loud in the silence.

Courtney growled, his back arched, and moved away from his bowl.

It was nothing, Beth told herself. But as she ran through a list of possibilities in her mind—water pipes, kids outside, settling house, wind, rats—none of them seemed plausible.

What did seem plausible?

Ghosts.

She wasn't going to go there, she didn't want to think about that. But she *was* thinking about it. And though it was midday, though the drapes were all open, the interior of the house seemed dark, forbidding. Through the kitchen window, she could see the world outside: her car, the Valdezes' yard next door, an airplane in the sky. Normal everyday sights that suddenly seemed a million miles away.

Beth opened the kitchen utensils drawer, drew out a long carving knife. Gripping it tightly, she walked out of the kitchen, through the living room, and with only a slight pause, into the hallway. The tapping had stopped for a moment, like a cricket alerted to the presence of an intruder, but it resumed almost immediately, and she could tell now where the noise came from: the guest room.

She moved forward slowly, trying not to make any noise. The guest room door was closed, though she always left it open, and Beth stood in front of it, listening to the low knocking inside. She didn't know what to expect, but the image that came to her mind was a scene from a children's book, a scary story about a house haunted by the ghost of an old cobbler. She imagined going into the room to find a wizened figure in the far corner, a white-haired wraith with a grinning death's-head face, sitting in an ancient chair next to a small table, obsessively working on a pair of spectral shoes.

The tapping grew softer . . . slowed . . . stopped. Then returned full force, a loud knocking that made her think of huge green knuckles rapping on a door, demanding entrance.

Instinct was telling her to run, get out of the house, get help, but she held her ground, forced herself to remain in place.

Steeling herself, she opened the door and walked inside.

There was nothing there.

Four

1

The day was bad from the get-go.

It was a Monday, to begin with—always the worst day of the week. And when Hunt arrived at the maintenance yard for the assignment meeting with Steve, he learned that there'd been a complaint lodged against them by an elderly woman who said that chips expelled from their woodchipper had damaged the hood of her parked Cadillac—not a good development when one member of the Board of Supervisors was already making noises about contracting out maintenance services.

Steve, typically, was furious. "Do you know how this makes me look?" he yelled at them. "Every time you jackoffs screw up, it's a black mark on my record. And I don't want to take the heat for your incompetence. Ever hear the phrase 'Shape up or ship out'?"

"Ever think that maybe the old biddy's lying?" Edward countered. "Maybe she wants a free paint job and wants it on the county's dime?"

Steve met his eyes, stared him down. "You really think that's the case? You think that lady researched the type of equipment we use, decided that the chipper's the most likely candidate for car damage, and now she's claiming it caused scratches to her paint job because she wants to grift the county out of a couple hundred bucks? Huh?"

"No," Edward admitted.

"No."

"Hey," Jorge offered. "Accidents happen."

"Well, they'd better not happen on my watch, and they'd better not happen on your shift. Got me?"

They said they did.

As if that weren't bad enough, when he, Edward, and Jorge reached the stand of sycamores where they were to work for the next three days, they discovered that someone—teenagers or U of A frat boys most likely—had overturned a Porta Potti and dragged it around the dirt support road before messily smashing it against one of the trees.

But that was not the worst of it.

No, the worst was when he arrived home that evening to find the front door wide open and his house trashed.

He stepped carefully inside. The stereo was gone, he noticed instantly, though whoever had taken it had left the speakers. Likewise, his TV, VCR, and DVD player were missing. He didn't know if the thieves had taken any of his books, videotapes, CDs, records, or DVDs, but they had certainly made a mess of them, knocking over bookcases, clearing shelves, throwing everything onto the floor. In the kitchen, the contents of the cupboards and refrigerator were strewn over the linoleum, the breakfast table smashed. He was dialing 911 on his cell phone even as he walked gingerly through the debris and into the hallway. He'd been using the second bedroom for storage and there wasn't much in it: a few boxes, his luggage, wood-and-block shelving filled with extra records. That room appeared to be untouched. But the master bedroom was a shambles. The drawers of his dresser had been pulled out, their contents dumped on the floor. The mirror over the dresser had been smashed, and the mattress of his bed had been sliced open, the stuffing welling out from parallel incisions like blood from open wounds.

"I want to report a break-in," he told the police dispatcher who answered his call. He described the scene, said the perpetrators no longer seemed to be in the house, then gave his name and address. Someone would be right over, the dispatcher promised, don't touch anything, there might be fingerprints or other evidence.

Before he even finished the call, he heard the sound of a siren from somewhere to the north, and a few minutes later, two police cars pulled in to the driveway. He made his way back through the wreckage, and once outside, found himself staring with suspicion at the white-trash shack next door. He was tempted to tell the police that as far as he was concerned, those losers should be considered the prime suspects. But he knew he was being irrational, and after giving the arriving officers the information they asked for, he stepped aside and let them do their work.

He did call Joel and Beth from the front yard, and while a machine answered at Joel's, Beth was already home from work and immediately drove over.

"Oh my God," she said when she arrived and saw the extent of the damage. The forensics team was still dusting for prints and searching through the debris for evidence. "Who do you think did this?"

"I have no idea," he admitted. The presence of police cars had piqued the interest of his neighbors, and though none of them had been brave enough to come up to him and ask what was going on, a growing line of people stood on both sides of his property, squinting at the house and talking amongst themselves. They looked as clueless as he felt, and against his will, he had to admit that his neighbors had probably not been the ones to break into his place.

But who, then? And why?

Immediately after calling Beth, he had phoned his landlord

to explain what had happened, and the man arrived now in a cloud of dust and a clatter of gravel. Leaping out of his pickup truck as though the seat were burning his ass, Sid Sayers ignored Hunt and Beth and the gathered crowd, striding up the porch and directly into the house, "Who's in charge here?" he demanded. "Who's in charge of this case?"

He emerged several seconds later with Lieutenant Badham, the one who had interviewed Hunt about the damage. The lieutenant led him firmly onto the porch so the forensics investigators could continue their examination of the rooms, but he remained to answer all of Sayers's questions.

Afterward, the landlord came over to where he and Beth stood in the driveway, and the three of them stared silently at the house for a moment.

"You have any enemies?" Sayers asked suspiciously.

Hunt shook his head. "Not to my knowledge, no."

"What about those piece a crap no-count neighbors? Have any run-ins with them?"

"No."

"I don't know what, then."

The police finished soon after, allowing everyone back in. Sayers got a Polaroid camera from his pickup and took his own photos of the home's interior. He had insurance, but other than broken windows the building didn't appear to have sustained any structural damage. The real damage was to Hunt's belongings. He had rental insurance, though, and the landlord suggested that he contact his insurance company and have them send out an adjuster ASAP. Hunt just hoped that he had enough to take care of all this. Only last night a representative from All Homes had called him to suggest that he increase his coverage, and he'd hung up on the man, saying that he wasn't interested.

He didn't know his policy number, didn't even know where his policy was in all this mess, but he knew the name of the insurance company, so he called Information to get the phone number, and dialed it.

He explained what had happened, gave his name and social security number, and the phone rep looked up his policy. After verifying that he was who he said he was by providing his date of birth and mother's maiden name, he was told that he had coverage for the loss of up to ten thousand dollars' worth of personal property.

Ten thousand. That might not cover all of it but it was close enough for government work. Maybe he wouldn't need that extra insurance after all.

The phone rep took down some additional information, then explained the claims process and said that a living allowance of sixty dollars a day, up to a thousand dollars total over the life of the policy, would be provided so that Hunt could stay in a motel while restoration work was performed.

"An adjuster will be out to look at the rental unit tomorrow morning, and once he determines the extent of the damage and files a report, we'll arrange to have everything cleaned up. Your home should be looking as good as new by the end of the week."

"The adjuster'll be coming tomorrow morning?"

"Yes, sir."

"I'm not sure I can get off work tomorrow. Wednesday would be better."

"There's no need for you to take off work."

"I have to be there."

"It's not necessary. Leave a key under the mat, and the adjuster will let himself in. He does this every day. We'll call you back with the estimate or fax you a copy of the report if you wish. Just leave a number where you can be reached. A cell phone number if you have it, or a work number."

"But when you're cleaning up—"

"Don't worry. The company we use is really good. They'll salvage whatever's salvageable, call you on anything questionable or personal, and replace the rest. If there are important papers, documents, or items of sentimental value that you wish to retain, I suggest you retrieve them now and take them with you. Otherwise, simply leave a note taped or tacked to the inside of the front door with a list of things you do *not* want replaced, and it will be taken care of."

Hunt borrowed a pen and scrap of paper from Beth and, writing against the living room wall, jotted down his claim number and the name of the representative with whom he'd been talking.

"So what's the news?" Beth asked after he'd hung up.

He told her.

"They're going to do it while you're at work?" She frowned. "You *have* to be there to supervise."

"That's what I said. I don't want some stranger going through all my stuff. But the insurance company said this is a routine procedure for them, they do it all the time, and they don't need me there."

"Still . . ."

"Well, I'm going to try to get off early tomorrow and stop by, but I'm not sure I can really take any time off. Technically, I'm still on my probation period."

"Jorge and Edward'll cover for you."

"Yeah, but Steve can be a real pain in the ass, and he could make it tough for me if he wanted. Besides, I'll gather up the important stuff right now. The rest . . ." He gestured around. "It's just furniture. It's replaceable."

"What are you going to do tonight? You can't sleep here."

"I get a living allowance to stay someplace while they do the work. It's part of my policy."

"You're staying with me."

He'd been about to say that he would spend the next few days at a Motel 6 or something. "You don't have to—" he began.

"I want to."

He had to admit, that sounded nice. The prospect of living out of a motel did not appeal to him at all, particularly since they were working all the way down by Green Valley this week, and with Jorge's Saturn in the shop for repairs, the two of them were carpooling. The thought that he could spend his evenings with Beth, eating home-cooked meals and sleeping next to her on her comfortable king-sized bed seemed very attractive indeed. Especially after dealing with this mess.

Outside, the sun was already sinking in the west, stretching long shadows in the opposite direction and giving everything a skewed expressionistic perspective.

Sayers emerged from the hallway, shaking off a Polaroid picture. "Bastards took a dump in the toilet," he said, grimacing. "I hope those cops got some DNA off it."

Beth looked disgusted. "They didn't flush it?"

"That's his job," he said, pointing at Hunt.

"God."

The landlord walked outside, letting the screen door slam. "Let me know what happens," he said. "I expect to be kept informed. This *is* my house, you know."

"Friendly guy," Beth said dryly.

"Yeah."

"So what's the plan? Are you just going to lock up and . . . go?"

"I have to look for some things first, make sure they weren't stolen or destroyed. Insurance policies, receipts and guarantees, addresses, photos. Stuff like that."

"But afterward, you're coming home with me."

He looked at her, nodded. "Yeah," he said. "I am."

2

"I think there's someone out there," Nina whispered.

Fuckers. Steve was out of bed, Smith & Wesson in hand,

running down the hall toward the addition before Nina could even get the next sentence out. It was those cholos. He was sure of it. Fucking wetbacks were pissed off that he was doing all the labor himself, that he hadn't hired any of them or their illegal alien buddies to work on the addition, and they were hell-bent on making him pay. Last Saturday morning when he'd gone out to put up Sheetrock, he'd found an empty tequila bottle in the middle of the plywood floor and a puddle of piss in the corner. Bastards had had a party in his new addition while he and Nina had been asleep.

That's what he got for staying here in the shitty part of town, for not moving when the brown wave crested over the neighborhood.

But he'd vowed it wouldn't happen again, and if there was someone on his property right now, he'd shoot first and ask questions later. Worse came to worst, he'd claim he saw a gun, that he'd shot in self-defense. He doubted it would even come to that, though. That's what was great about the old Wild West states. They believed in property rights, and if someone was on your property and needed shooting, then you could go ahead and do what had to be done and everyone would understand.

He reached the door at the end of the hall. The only thing he worried about was if it *wasn't* some anonymous illegal alien, but someone from work. Or, worse yet, someone he'd fired or who'd quit in anger. God knew there were enough of those. Maintenance services was a sludge catch for the dregs of humanity, and a lot of men had passed through there and hated his guts. It would be a hell of a lot harder to prove it wasn't intentional if he shot someone he knew.

He paused, listened. Nina was right. There *was* someone in the addition. Just on the other side of the door, by the sound of it. Where the bar was going to be. He heard the knock of boot heel on wood, heard what sounded like a sniffle.

He looked at the door, not certain that this was the right approach. Because the door opened onto the addition and the addition was little more than a partially roofed frame, open to the outside world, there were three locks on the door: the regular knob lock, a dead bolt, and a chain. By the time he got all three open, with the attendant clattering and clanking, the trespasser would be alerted and gone. It might be better to go out the back door and sneak around the side of the house to confront him.

He crept away from the door, back down the hall, careful not to make any noise. Nina was peeking her head out of the bedroom, and he angrily waved her back in. "Stay there!" he hissed as he hurried quietly past the bedroom.

The back door was closer, he decided, and offered the cover of shadow. He carefully slid open the dead bolt, turned the knob, then hastened through the darkness at the rear of the house, gun at the ready. Too much time had passed since he'd awakened—he'd had time to think, and he no longer planned to just shoot the intruder in cold blood. That would bring a world of problems on his head that he didn't want to deal with right now. He'd scare the shit out of the bastard, threaten to shoot him, but then he'd hold him for the cops and let them take care of the problem.

He'd prosecute to the full extent of the law, though. He didn't care if this was just a prank or an accident. It was a crime, and he was going to see that the criminal was punished.

He reached the end of the house proper and peered around the corner at the indented outline of the addition. In the far corner, faintly illuminated by moonlight, he saw a burly man in a hat—one of those old detectives' hats from the 1940s, what he'd always thought of as a Humphrey Bogart hat. The man appeared to be fooling with the knob of the door that led into the hallway.

Anger coursed through him, and Steve ran across the backyard grass toward the power box, gun extended. *Freeze!* he'd yell. *Hold it right there!* With any luck, the guy would piss himself or brown his shorts when he saw the old S&W pointed at him.

He reached the switch, flipped on the lights.

There was no one there.

The addition was empty.

3

It was great living with Beth. Hunt had been so poisoned by those last few years with Eileen that he'd been expecting explosive anger over small transgressions, irrational arguments followed by grim silent treatments. But the truth was that they got along beautifully. Of course, he and Eileen had been happy together for a long time before things went bad, so that wasn't really a good barometer, but just the fact that he could be with Beth every day and still enjoy her company—still look *forward* to the time they spent together—gave him confidence. He'd been afraid to take this relationship to the next level not because he didn't want to, but because he thought that might ruin it, and the discovery that what they had together was stronger and less fragile than he'd supposed gave him hope.

The biggest surprise was Beth's cooking. She'd cooked for him before, of course, but because they lived apart, those were special events—dinners meant to impress. But she whipped up fantastic little gourmet meals every night, and he did not get the sense that it was entirely for his benefit. This was just the way she lived. He had known that cooking was one of her hobbies, known that she was a devotee of the Food Network, but he hadn't realized that it was more of a passion than a casual interest.

He liked that.

Eileen had been big on eating out a lot. And frozen food. And tacos.

Hunt had never considered himself to be a traditional "Hey honey I'm home what's for dinner?" kind of guy, and he felt embarrassed and a little guilty to be thrust into such a role, but

Beth was no subservient suburban hausfrau, she just genuinely enjoyed cooking for him, and that made him more grateful than ever that the two of them had met.

On Friday morning, he was on break when a representative from the insurance company called him on his cell and said that his house was ready. He told Edward and Jorge, but delayed calling Beth until lunchtime. The truth was that he didn't want to go back. He'd been at Beth's for only four nights, but they'd grown much closer during that time, and he felt so comfortable there that it was like home to him now. Returning to his rental house seemed like taking a step backward. Despite the fact that he'd paid rent through the rest of the month, he had no desire to continue living there. So when Beth asked him not to leave, he gratefully agreed to officially move in with her. Behind him, Edward and Jorge, eavesdropping on the conversation, cheered.

He and Beth laughed.

Still, all his stuff was back there at the rental house, so after work they drove over to survey the renovation. The locks had been changed, but, as promised, new keys were hidden under a rock to the right side of the front porch. He picked up the keys, unlocked the door, and walked inside.

"Jesus," Hunt breathed.

The walls of the house had been painted black. In place of the framed classic movie posters with which he'd decorated the living room hung grotesque paintings of mutilated women in inappropriately gaudy frames. The books on his shelves had not merely been picked up off the floor and put back, they'd been replaced with far more gruesome fare: an illustrated history of Nazi medical atrocities, texts on mortuary science, the collected works of the Marquis de Sade, a series of graphically titled fetish novels with titles like *I Lick Your Blood* and *Foot Fucking Daddy*. Ditto for the videos and DVDs, which were all sadistic hardcore porn. In place of his vinyl albums—a collection of rock, jazz, blues, folk, and country that he'd been amassing since childhood—were boxes and boxes filled with multiple copies of the same record: Debbie Boone's *You Light Up My Life*.

"What . . . is . . . this?" Beth said.

He shook his head, stunned. "I don't know."

"Someone fucked up royally."

"Yeah." He walked numbly into the kitchen. An ax was embedded in a freestanding bloodred butcher block that replaced the table in the breakfast nook, and an old-fashioned hand pump had been substituted for the faucet in the sink. In the center of the new black linoleum was a throw rug that appeared to be made from the pelt of a gorilla. The ape's mouth was wide open, fangs bared.

"I thought they were just supposed to replace the broken furniture and damaged items. Not toss out all of your stuff and substitute it with . . . this."

"Me, too."

"And if they were going to replace something of yours, they should have exchanged it with something identical or asked you what you wanted. They're not supposed to make unilateral decisions."

"No, they're not," Hunt said. He walked into the bedroom, anger building within him. Although his pillows and mattress had been ripped open by whoever had vandalized the house, the bed itself had not been damaged. Still, it had been replaced—with a penis-shaped water bed. In place of his dresser was a red glitter-covered bureau topped by what looked like a gynecologist's plastic model of female genitalia.

Beth was incredulous. "This has to be illegal. You didn't sign any papers giving them approval to do any of this, did you?"

"Of course not. I was only here that one time, Tuesday, and everything seemed perfectly normal then. I didn't tell them they could do this, they didn't tell me they *were* going to do this."

Beth opened the closet door, revealing a solid row of black goth clothing

He gritted his teeth. "We need to go back to your place—"

"*Our* place."

"*Our* place, so I can read through the fine print of my policy. You're right, this can't be legal. They didn't just replace damaged items. They completely remodeled this place, stole my personal stuff, and forced me to accept this . . . weird shit."

"Bring a camera when we come back here," Beth suggested. "You need pictures, in case you have to take them to court. We have to document everything."

"Let's get out of here."

"Don't you want to check out the garage and the back-yard?" she asked.

"The sun's going down," he said.

He was only half-joking.

It was nearly six by the time they got back to Beth's, and even if the insurance company *wasn't* based on the East Coast—a *big* if—it still probably closed at five. He'd have to call in the morning.

No—today was Friday—he'd have to call Monday.

"Goddamn it," he said angrily.

He found a copy of his rental insurance policy in the box of papers he'd taken from the house, and he spent the next hour reading through the fine print. He half-expected to find a clause that said he had to file any complaint within twenty-four hours or else it would not be considered valid, but thankfully there was no such restriction. Still, just to be on the safe side, he called the insurance company's main office in Delaware, and after winding his way through their convoluted electronic phone system, finally found a place where he could leave a message. Speaking slowly and distinctly, he stated his name, policy number, and claim number, then described what had happened.

After he hung up, Hunt looked over at Beth. "What kind of homeowners' insurance do you have?"

"Don't worry. They're great. I had to call them when my roof leaked two years ago, and the year before that when a branch of the tree in the backyard fell during a storm and broke the bedroom window, and they fixed everything with no problem. I can't complain."

"You're lucky."

"Yeah, well, I pay through the nose for it." She paused. "In fact, that's why I didn't tell them when I had the master bathroom remodeled last year and that sunken tub put in. Any home improvements and the rates jump tremendously. I made the mistake of coming clean when I had my closet enlarged, and it was like I'd added a whole other wing to the house. I couldn't believe how much my premiums were raised. So this time I didn't say anything."

"If they catch you, that's called fraud."

"It's not fraud."

"And your policy'll be null and void. They won't pay off if something happens."

"No," she said.

"Ask them."

"I'll think about it."

He phoned the insurance company Monday morning right after breakfast—six o' clock Arizona time, nine o'clock Eastern time.

The man who answered the phone was brisk and officious. "May I have your claim number, sir?"

"Five two one, five six four U."

"U?"

"Yes, as in 'unhappy.'"

"Mr. Jackson?"

"Yes."

"What seems to be the problem, Mr. Jackson?"

"What's the problem? What's the *problem*?" He had been rehearsing this diatribe in his head for the past two days, and he let the man have it, both barrels blazing, as he described the black walls, the freakish substituted furniture, the pornographic books and videos and DVDs. "I don't know who did this or why, what kind of sick company you hired to do this work, but they screwed it up royally, and your company utterly failed to rein them in or provide any oversight. There is no way in hell this would have happened if you guys had been on the ball. I expect that house to be fixed up the way it was originally, and I want all of my belongings either repaired and returned to me or replaced with *exact* replicas. Do you understand?"

The man remained unruffled. "May I ask when the restoration work was completed?"

"Friday morning, I assume. I got a call around ten-thirty telling me the house was ready."

"You *assume*?"

"Well, I don't—" Hunt paused, suddenly suspicious. "Wait a minute."

"I need to enter a precise time," the man continued. "And since you don't know . . ." There was the sound of typing, and in a sing-songy Southern accent he chanted, "Half past a monkey's ass, a quarter to his *ba-wuls*."

"Who is this?" Hunt demanded. "I—"

He was interrupted by a short manic burst of laughter.

Then the connection was severed. There was only a dial tone.

He stared at the receiver in his hand. He felt the same anger he had last time, but now there was an uneasiness there as well. His mind made the connections that would logically enable this to occur—his car insurance company, UAI, and the company carrying his rental insurance, All Homes Insurance, were under the umbrella of the same parent corporation and used the same bank of employees to answer the phones; the man had transferred from one company to another and had somehow remembered his name—but each scenario he came up with seemed to be a stretch, and Hunt found that he could not believe any of them.

What did he believe?

He didn't know, wasn't sure, and that was part of what made him uneasy.

Taking a deep breath, Hunt dialed again, and, as before, a thoroughly professional woman answered, this one immediately identifying herself as "Alice." He gave her his name and claim number, and proceeded to describe once more the vandalism to his rental house and belongings, and the bizarre items that had been used to replace his own. He was less angry the second time around, having spent most of his rage on the first telling, but he was still plenty annoyed, and the phone rep was clearly aware of his dissatisfaction. Unfortunately, she also toed the party line, and rather than assure him that a prompt investigation was forthcoming, she read through the information on her computer and stated that the insurance company had done everything properly.

"That's what I'm telling you," he said, exasperated. "You didn't."

"I appreciate your position, Mr. Jackson, but I'm afraid that All Homes did everything it was contractually obligated to do. Our responsibilities are very specifically defined under the terms of your contract."

"Then why is there a dick-shaped water bed in my bedroom? Why are there three hundred copies of *You Light Up My Life* boxed up in my living room? Why are videotaped suicides now part of my movie library?"

"If you'll look at your policy," Alice said, "you'll see that all conditions are met. All Homes is required only to replace the damaged items with objects of *equal value*, not to replace them with *identical* items."

"I have the policy right in front of me, I've been reading it all weekend, and that is most definitely *not* what it says."

"Have you read the exception clause?"

"The exception clause?" He was thrown off balance. "What exception clause?"

"It's in the fine print at the back of your policy. Appendix D, subparagraph one-A. And it states very clearly that for all renter's insurance policies of ten thousand dollars and under, every effort will be made to replace the damaged items, but in the event that replacement items cannot be found or it is unfeasible to obtain them, items of equal value are to be substituted, with All Homes determining the equal value amount. Now, if you had purchased additional coverage, as one of our representatives recently suggested to you, then all of your belongings would have been replaced."

Hunt grew suspicious. "How do you know I was pressured into upping my coverage?"

Alice sighed tiredly. "What I can do, Mr. Jackson, is send you a Disputed Claim form. You can explain what the problem is, spell out your side of the story, then one of our arbitrators will take a second look at the case and make any necessary adjustments. We have a very high customer satisfaction rating, and the last thing we want is for any of our loyal customers to be—"

"Send the form," Hunt said.

She verified his mailing address, started to give him a happy-talk good-bye, and he hung up on her. "Assholes."

Beth had been listening in to his side of the conversation. "You didn't tell them about the repainted walls. They changed a lot of things that are part of the house itself, not just your stuff."

"Let the owner figure it out," he said. "I don't live there anymore. I live with you."

"Yes." She smiled, kissed him lightly on the lips. "Yes, you do."

Five

Everything happened at once and Brian Kutz couldn't think, couldn't sort out what was critical and what wasn't, what needed to be done immediately and what could wait. He acted on instinct, responding to each split-second change.

The fire alarm didn't go off.

That was his sole conscious thought, and his brain repeated it endlessly like a tape loop as he jumped out of bed and ran naked through the smoke to where he knew the bedroom door to be. Only it wasn't there. He hit a wall—and far sooner than he should have, as though their bed had been moved during the night while they slept—and when he staggered back, there was warmth and wetness flowing down his eye, over his cheek. He'd hit his head hard enough to break the skin. But the smoke was thick and the room was hot—

The fire alarm didn't go off.

—and rather than stop to assess his injuries or gather himself together, he pressed on, moving left, hands against the wall, until his fingers reached the door frame. His eyes were teary, stinging from blood and sweat and smoke, and far off—from the front of the house, he thought—he heard something crash: TV or microwave, computer or stereo.

The fire alarm didn't go off.

In the hallway, too-hot flames licked his left hand, the one not touching the wall, and his skin burned, blackened, peeled, exposing new underskin to the searing heat, his entire arm erupting in agony, as though it had been rent with a sharp scalpel. He wanted to hear screams from the twins' bedroom— wanted to know they were still alive—but there was nothing, only the crackle of the flames and more crashing from the front of the house, and then there was an earthquake shift in the floor, a roar from the roof. He sprinted forward through the blinding choking smoke, heedless of the danger, needing to grab his girls and get them out before the whole place collapsed in on them.

He found a doorway that should have been theirs, but the air was too thick with smoke to tell for sure, and when he started to turn in, his face was met by a blistering blast that made his eyes feel as though they were going to melt and sent him staggering back against the hall wall.

"Deb!" he cried. "Michelle!"

"Daddy! Mommy!"

"Mommy! Daddy!"

The voices sounded faint against the roar of the fire and the crashing/groaning/cracking of the dying house, but they were ahead of him, toward the front of the home, and he tearfully stumbled forward through the smoky darkness, grateful that they'd had the presence of mind to try to escape. "Get out!" he yelled at them, but his throat was dry and his voice not as loud as he'd intended. He tried to yell it again but dissolved into a fit of coughing.

They were in the front of the house anyway, in the family room or living room or kitchen, and the worst part of the fire seemed to be back here, toward the rear.

He only hoped Nanci was following him or had sped past him or had broken the bedroom window and climbed out. He was starting to think more logically now, his brain had shaken off the haze of sleep and the chaos of panic, and he was able to understand what was happening and where he was and what he was supposed to do. He wished he wasn't naked, wished he had at least put on underwear, wished he had been wearing slippers or shoes, but none of that was really important, and he moved forward as quickly as he could, still keeping his good hand on the wall and not running *too* fast in case some burning piece of furniture lay in his way.

He was still coughing, each postcough inhalation bringing with it new smoke and soot, and when he finally made it out of the hallway and through the living room, stumbling onto the front porch, he vomited. It splashed on his feet, spattered on the welcome mat, and for a brief second he thought he was going to choke to death—he couldn't seem to take a breath—but then he was moving away from the house, staggering toward the crowd of gathered neighbors, where old Mrs. Childiss was holding the desperately sobbing twins, and he felt the welcome coolness of fresh air—smoke-free air. He was sobbing himself as he reached the girls and grabbed them, hugged them.

"Daddy!" Michelle cried.

"Daddy!" Deb.

But where was Nanci? He stood, panicked, terrified to the core of his being. He called out his wife's name, turning around, looking for some sign of her, knowing he shouldn't frighten the girls this way but too frightened himself to care. "Nanci! Nanci!! Nanci!!!"

"Watch them," he told Mrs. Childiss, giving the twins back to her. Screaming his wife's name, he dashed around the side of the flaming house, through the backyard, then around the opposite side, looking for some sign that she'd escaped, cursing himself for not being quick and alert enough to rescue her when he had the chance.

The motion-detector light above the kitchen door had been off, but it switched on at the sight of him.

And he saw the insurance agent.

Brian stopped in his tracks.

The man was standing next to the broken kitchen window, through which were billowing plumes of smoke that had been dissipating into the night but were now starting to saturate the air. He was wearing what appeared to be a trench coat and a fedora. Although those accoutrements made him look like a film noir detective, they did not seem out of place, and for the first time, Brian realized that the insurance agent did not seem quite of this era.

He never had.

"Tsk, tsk," the agent was saying, and Brian thought absurdly that he had never heard anyone actually *say* "Tsk, tsk." It was one of those phrases you read in books but never heard in real life, and indeed it sounded artificial and mocking in the agent's mouth.

Nanci's burned body lay twitching on the ground at his feet.

Brian felt as though he'd been punched in the gut. "No," he managed to get out.

"Yes."

"This isn't be—"

"I'm afraid it is."

"I was going to send it off tomorrow!" he shrieked. "I already wrote the check! It's by my wallet!"

"That's too bad," the agent said. "That's a shame."

Brian threw himself on the ground next to his wife. She was burned almost beyond recognition, and this close he could see the blood beneath the charred flesh, the twitching movement of muscles that were now visible. No sound came from between what was left of her incinerated lips, and somehow that was the most horrible thing of all. She was dying, in agony, but she could not scream. Her throat was sealed shut. He wanted to hold her, wanted to comfort her, but knew that he could not. He sobbed, screamed. "No!"

The insurance agent tipped his hat and walked into the front yard, toward the darkness between the arriving fire engines. "It's been a pleasure doing business with you."

Six

1

Time passed.

Hunt had a chance to move up in the county hierarchy, to work in an MIS office rather than on the street, but to everyone's surprise but his own, he turned it down. Oddly enough, he found that he liked maintenance services. Besides, between Beth's salary and his own, they were making more than enough to get by. There was no reason for him to change.

It was almost as though he'd led two separate lives, he thought. His predivorce life and his postdivorce life. Before, he'd had a big suburban house in Southern California and a relatively high-paying tech job with a multinational corporation, and now he lived in his girlfriend's home and performed manual labor for Pima County.

But it was nice. It was good. He had never been one of those Thoreau-ian back-to-nature guys, one of those simplifying simpletons craving some nonexistent rural utopia. Yet he found it refreshing and invigorating to work outside on trees and bushes, to be back in the clean air of the desert after all of those years in metropolitan Los Angeles, where a clear day was one on which the outline of local mountains could be seen through the smog.

Besides, he actually liked his coworkers.

That was something he'd noticed almost immediately after

Boeing had laid him off: he didn't care if he ever saw any of his coworkers again. There was no one at work he'd hated, and for the most part he'd gotten along with everyone, but he hadn't formed any real friendships; there was no one with whom he was genuinely close. It was not something that had really registered before. He'd gone to work each day and he'd always had someone with whom he could spend break, with whom he could eat lunch, and not until he left did he realize his colleagues were acquaintances rather than friends.

Edward and Jorge *were* his friends, though. They hung out together, did things on weekends, went to each other's homes. And what surprised him most—he and Joel both—was that the familiar stereotypes did not apply. Edward was a fan of classical music. Not just a casual fan but a real aficionado. And not just mainstream classical music, but cutting-edge stuff—Monk, Lentz, Reich, Andriessen—a whole bunch of composers Hunt had never heard of and didn't understand. Jorge read more books than anyone he'd ever known—not just the usual assortment of bestsellers, but obscure literary South American authors who were not yet published in the United States. Ironic as it was, these two tree trimmers were more genuinely intellectual than Hunt or Joel or any of their urban professional peers—not that it was something to which they would ever admit.

It was a weird world. He'd grown up in a somewhat rarefied environment, the son of a librarian and a junior college instructor, and despite his well-meaning efforts to cultivate a small-D democratic worldview, in his heart of hearts he'd always bought into the notion of class, ascribing certain tastes and characteristics to manual laborers and the uneducated masses that he and his peers did not possess. It had taken this job to disabuse him of such nonsense and make him realize that prejudices and preconceived ideas really were as harmful and inaccurate as they were cracked up to be.

Tree trimming also continued to surprise him. The county

was so big and the vegetation so diverse that they were constantly working in what was to him new territory. Oh, they had a schedule of sorts—specific in-city sites that required regular maintenance—but that schedule was rotated between all of the crews, and at least a couple of times a month, they were out in far-flung locales, down seldom-traveled roads.

The strangest place he saw had to be The Jail. At least Edward and Jorge called it a jail. The truth was that neither of them really knew what it was. It was located southeast of the city near the remains of an old ghost town, at the bottom of what had once been an old reservoir but was now a bone-dry basin overgrown with desert vegetation and ringed by densely packed mesquite trees. The past year's drought had made the area a fire hazard, and they were there to prune back the trees; another crew would be coming along later in the week to clear out the worst of the dried brush.

First, though, Edward and Jorge led him down a steeply sloping gravel path into the basin, where tall thorny thistles grew waist-high around an odd stone structure slightly bigger than an outhouse. It had no windows, and the door, a rusted rectangle of criss-crossing iron bars, was frozen in a half-open position. Inside, the walls were mossy, and the floor was wet and slimy with algae, as though it were atop a spring and the water was bubbling up, refusing to be capped.

"We can't figure out why The Jail's here," Jorge admitted. "I mean, it's obviously old, probably as old as that ghost town, but at that time it would've been underwater."

Edward tried to move the door. "I think they imprisoned people in it when the water was low and left them there to be drowned when the water level rose. Like witches and stuff."

Jorge nodded. "Could be. Could be."

It was early in the morning but already hot, and they trekked back up the trail to the trucks. But The Jail remained in Hunt's mind the rest of the day, and for some reason he didn't tell Beth about it.

Aside from that, he and Beth were closer than ever, their relationship progressing, moving smoothly forward like that of lovers in a Lifetime movie. They *were* in love, though neither of them had yet said the words, and while he wasn't sure why they hadn't, he intended to rectify that soon. After Eileen, he hadn't been able to see himself getting involved in another serious relationship, but now he thought that he wouldn't mind spending the rest of his life with Beth.

Outside a club where they went to watch Jimmie Dale Gilmore perform one Friday night, they saw their old buddy, the geeky guy with the purple suit. He was alive and well and in the parking lot, no doubt plying his old trade. Although he saw them, he did not appear to recognize them. Just as well, Hunt thought. The guy was not exactly the type of person with whom they wanted to cultivate even an acquaintanceship.

He found himself wondering whether the hospital at which they'd dropped off the man had treated him or whether he'd been turned out on the street like some Dickensian pauper due to his lack of insurance. He was here now, so Hunt assumed that the injuries had been taken care of, but in the back of his mind was the thought that if he shouted out a greeting, the man would not look over—because he was deaf in the ear that the hospital had refused to treat.

Hunt was still fighting with *his* insurance company over the replacement of his property back at the rental house. As far as the company was concerned, he had been fairly compensated, his furniture and belongings had been exchanged for items of equal value, and on their books the case was closed. But he refused to accept that verdict, and he had appealed to the state insurance commission in an effort to correct this injustice. The wheels of bureaucracy turned slowly, however, and he didn't know when there'd be a ruling—or if it would be in his favor. He was already planning to send his state senator and assemblyman, as well as his U.S. senator and congressman, detailed guidelines that he thought should become law in order to keep such abuses from happening to someone else in the future. His proposed regulations were sensible, logical, and reasonable, and he couldn't think of any reason that anyone other than insurance companies would oppose them.

Theoretically, that meant that his voice should be heard and action should be taken.

But the insurance companies had professional lobbyists and deep pockets.

And, deep down, he didn't really think anything was going to change.

2

"Jorge!"

He didn't hear his wife yelling until he shut off the lawn mower, but he could tell from the frantic pitch of her voice that she had been calling him for some time.

"*Jorge!*"

If it was so important, why hadn't she come out to get him?

Maybe she *couldn't* come out.

That sent him running. He dashed into the house without wiping his feet, tracking mud and grass on the carpet as he called her name. "Ynez? Ynez!" She wasn't in the living room or family room, he could see that immediately, but he heard her voice from the kitchen, along with a strange sound he couldn't place, and he hurried in there.

It was like a scene out of a movie—a comedy, although there was nothing comedic about it. She was standing in front of the dishwasher, trying desperately to stop a steady spray of water that was shooting outward in all directions from the sides of the closed door. Not only was the floor wet and the counter wet and the front of the refrigerator wet, but Ynez was soaked as well, her hair dripping as though she'd just emerged from the shower, her top clinging to her skin like a wet T-shirt.

"Help me!" she yelled. "Shut off the water! Do *something*!"

A mist of cold water sprayed his face and a stream hit his crotch as he moved next to her and desperately started pressing the control buttons on the dishwasher.

"I already tried that!" she yelled at him. "Go outside and shut the water off!"

"Wait. I have an idea." He dropped to his knees, threw open the cupboard doors under the adjacent sink and looked around in there. As he'd hoped, there were two sets of valves, one for the sink and one for the dishwasher, and he began frenetically turning both the red knob and the blue one, and the spraying water slowed, lessened, then stopped. He stood. "What happened?"

Ynez tried to wipe the dripping water from her forehead, but her hands were as wet as her face and it did no good, so she tore off a length of paper towel and used it to dry her skin. "I don't know," she said. "I didn't even turn it on. I was just unloading it from this morning, and I got down to the last bowl and then all of a sudden the thing exploded. I shut the door and tried to press the buttons, but nothing worked and then I called you." She patted her neck with the paper towel. "What took you so long, anyway?"

"I was mowing the lawn. I didn't hear you."

She looked at the dishwasher. "I guess we'll have to call someone in to fix it."

"I'll take a look at it first, see if I can figure it out."

"Yeah, right."

He grinned at her. "You look pretty sexy, all wet like that."

"Not now."

"Why not? We used to. You could get on your hands and knees. I'll take you from behind, milk you like a cow."

"Let's just get the dishwasher fixed."

There was a loud gurgle from beneath the sink and a sickening glug from somewhere down the drain, and then all of a sudden water was flowing out from the dishwasher—not shooting out like before, but seeping under the bottom of the door onto the floor in a constant wave.

"That's impossible," Jorge said. "I shut off the valve."

"I told you we should've bought that extended warranty," Ynez said. "I told you." From the laundry room at the far end of the kitchen came a clanking crashing sound and an accompanying noise of jetting water. They rushed over to see the washing machine spewing suds, its front-loading door flapping improbably open.

Jorge looked at his wife. "You're right," he said. "We should have."

3

In October, he and Beth hosted a Halloween party. Hunt wasn't much of a party guy, but once again, she drew him out of his shell and made him participate, even dressed him up like a cowboy, and to his surprise he actually had a good time.

The guest list was made up primarily of Beth's friends, people from work, but Joel, Edward, and Jorge were there, Joel dressed as Michael Myers, Edward as a hillbilly, and Jorge as some effeminate person no one could figure out but whom he explained was the most popular member of a currently hot boy-band. "My niece suggested it," he said lamely.

Hunt mingled and met everyone, but ended up with his friends out on the patio. Joel had taken off his Michael Myers mask, and the two of them reminisced about boyhood Halloweens where they'd scared the crap out of younger kids and harassed some of the more crotchety elderly neighbors.

"*We* used to do the old 'dogshit in a burning bag' routine," Edward said. "There was this one asshole who would throw rocks at us every time we drove by his house. He'd be out there watering, and if we cruised down the sidewalk, he'd pick up a stone and heave it at us. He was afraid one of our bike tires would touch a microscopic corner of his lawn, so he tried to force us to drive on the other side of the street. We got him back, though. And we didn't wait until Halloween. We used to put the flaming dogshit-in-a-bag on his porch at least once a month and the stupid fuck fell for it every time."

Jorge grinned. "Speaking of stupid fucks, did you hear about Steve and his vandal?"

"What now?" Hunt asked. The maintenance services manager was in the process of remodeling his home, adding on a "rumpus room"—a term Hunt hadn't heard since childhood, and one that brought about significant snickers from his fellow maintenance men. The project was supposed to have been finished long before Hunt was even hired, but Steve was such a perfectionist that there was still no end in sight.

"Some guy came in, took a dump on the floor, and beat the shit out of the walls, knocking holes in Steve's great plasterwork. It was at least several hundred dollars' worth of damage, but the insurance company says it's not covered. He has to pay for the whole thing out of his own pocket."

"Yeee doaggies!" Edward said, doing his best Jed Clampett.

"Damn insurance companies." Joel shook his head.

Edward chuckled. "You wouldn't say that if you knew Steve. This guy deserves it."

Hunt and Jorge laughed.

"Still, it's the principle of the thing. You pay money to these bastards all your life, and then when you need them, they refuse to give you the service you've already paid for. Am I right, Hunt?"

He held up his hands in surrender. "You won't get any argument from me. Hell, I'm still trying to unload those Debbie Boone records."

They all laughed.

Beth walked up. She was dressed as Pocahontas and looked so sexy that Hunt thought if there hadn't been other people around, he would have taken her then and there. She must have been able to read his thoughts, because the smile she gave him promised that later he would be able to do exactly that. "How's everyone enjoying the party?"

There was a chorus of approval.

Beth beamed. "Well, thank you all for coming. We appreciate it." She took Hunt's hand, squeezed. "I'd stay here with you if I could, but someone has to be sociable, tend to our more high-maintenance guests and make sure this party doesn't jump the shark." She fixed Hunt with a look of mock reproach.

He laughed and gave her a quick kiss.

"Can you wait a minute?" asked Ynez.

"Certainly," Beth said. "I'm sorry. I didn't mean to be rude. I just—"

"No, it's not that."

Behind them, the sliding glass door opened. Stacy, who knew the same people as Beth did and who'd been inside the house chatting with some of her Thompson Industries coworkers, walked over and pulled Joel's mask down over his face again. "It's a Halloween party," she said. "Maintain your persona." She was dressed as a beauty queen. "She's Vanessa Williams," Joel had explained when they first arrived. "I have the lesbo pictures in my wallet."

Ynez took a deep breath. "Okay," she said. "Now that we're all here, I have an announcement to make." She looked at Jorge, put a hand on his arm.

He nodded, smiled.

"We're going to have a baby!"

Jorge? A baby? Hunt didn't know about the others, but he was shocked by the news. Jorge had always seemed the least likely of any of them to have children. Joel and Stacy had Lilly, but none of the rest of them had kids, and Jorge was always defiantly unparental in his attitude toward the nieces and nephews he occasionally watched. Hunt found himself wondering if this baby was planned or an accident.

Still, he was happy for his friend, and he gathered around with the others, offering congratulations.

Jorge was beaming. "Thanks, man. Thanks."

Edward clapped a big bear hand over his friend's shoulder. "Let's just hope the little guy takes after Ynez's family, hmm?"

"I don't like the guest room," Beth said out of the blue.

They were eating an early dinner at the kitchen table, and Hunt looked up from his plate of turkey étouffée. "What?"

"Courtney doesn't like it either."

The cat rubbed against her leg, purring as though it understood.

"What are you talking about?" Hunt asked.

"Do you believe in haunted houses?" She didn't wait for him to answer. "I never did. I always assumed that there was no such thing, that they were fictional, and that anyone who believed in them was probably just projecting their own neuroses on an inanimate object or had a screw loose somewhere. But . . ." She trailed off.

"But what?"

"The guest room. I hear things there," she said. "Not all the time, and not even on a regular basis . . . but sometimes."

Hunt was silent.

"You'll probably think I'm crazy—and maybe I am, maybe *I'm* the one who's projecting—but I think it's haunted."

"Since when?"

"I don't know. Recently." She looked down at the table. "Since I met you."

"It's my fault?"

"I'm not saying that, no. But that's when I started hearing noises. Or noticing them."

"I've heard things, too," he admitted.

"You have?"

He nodded.

"Why didn't you say anything?"

"I thought maybe it was my imagination."

"It wasn't. There *are* noises there."

"I still think maybe it's my imagination."

"Both of us? Independently? I don't think so." She pushed her chair away from the table. "Come on. Let's check it out."

Hunt looked down at his food. "Now?"

"Why not?"

"We're eating."

"It'll only take a second."

"Well, why don't we wait until we hear a noise or something? I mean, it comes and goes, right? It's not there all the time."

"Let's find out."

Hunt sighed, wiped his hands on his napkin, stood. "Okay."

They walked out of the kitchen, through the living room, into the darkened hall. Hunt was in the lead. He stopped for a second in the hallway, opened the guest room door, peered in, and damn if it wasn't spooky. He didn't know if they'd psyched themselves up for this or if their response was legitimate, but they both felt it: a stiffening of neck hairs, a subtle chill, an involuntary focus on the twin bed against the wall.

Hunt wanted to slam the door shut again. He didn't like the fact that he kept looking at the bed, didn't like the fact that *Beth* kept looking at the bed. There was nothing unusual about the frame or headboard or mattress, nothing out of the ordinary, but somehow its very plainness lent it a kind of inverse aura, made it seem more prominent and important than it should have amidst the Southwest décor of the room.

They stood there for a moment, listening, neither of them making an effort to enter the room.

"I don't hear anything," Hunt said.

"Me either."

And he understood that she was afraid, that she didn't want

to go into the guest room, that she wanted to leave right now and go back to the kitchen and get as far away from the guest room—

and the bed

—as possible.

"Do you want to move?" he asked.

She sighed, and the mood was broken. "No. Besides, we wouldn't be able to afford anything this nice. Not now."

"Well, what should we do? Hire an exorcist?"

"No, nothing, I guess. I've lived with it this long, and it hasn't harmed anything. Still . . ."

They both peered into the small room, and Hunt's gaze was once again drawn to the nondescript bed.

He quickly closed the door, and, not speaking, the two of them walked back into the kitchen to finish their dinner.

4

Steve looked out his office window at the corp yard. He hated Monday mornings most of all. He used to enjoy them. This was the time when he handed out assignments, when all of his troops were assembled and he got to lord it over them, show them who was boss. But now he hated seeing all those lowlifes gathered in one place. The losers of the world worked for the county: white trash and drunken Indians, angry spades and dumb wetbacks. There was even one worthless gook. And the bitch of it was, he couldn't fire any of them. There was a long drawn-out appeals process for any employee who was terminated, and at the end of the process, for fear of lawsuits, the county always caved and reinstated the employee with back pay.

In the yard, Edward Stack said something loudly but unintelligibly that was greeted with howls of laughter by the gathered workers. Stack, as usual, lifted his hands to acknowledge the praise in that annoying way he had.

At the administrative level, there was talk of contracting out tree trimming, and Steve was all for it. Hell, if they could outsource the entire workforce of maintenance services, that would be great. He'd get to deal with vendors instead of employees, just tell business owners when their men were doing a crappy job and let them deal with the shitwork of telling the grunts. He'd sit here and shuffle papers and be taken to fancy lunches by contractors desperately wanting to get on the gravy train.

The phone on his desk rang, and he picked it up, swiveling his dirty chair away from the window. "Corp yard. Steve Nash speaking."

"Mr. Nash!" Steve recognized the voice. It was that insurance agent, the one who'd called last night. *Sunday* night. The one who'd shown up on his doorstep *Saturday* morning with a briefcase full of brochures and a line of smooth salesman patter. The one who'd been pressuring him to purchase additional homeowner's insurance for damn near a week now. He didn't know how the man had gotten his work number, but he didn't appreciate being harassed during business hours, and he said bluntly, "I'm not interested," and hung up the phone.

It rang again, instantly.

"Mr. Nash," the agent said in a voice at once soothing and chiding.

"Look, I told you. I'm not interested in buying any more insurance. Now stop calling me."

"You're playing with fire here, Mr. Nash. Literally. None of the new construction is covered under your existing homeowner's policy. You need expanded coverage—"

"When it's *done* I'll get it covered. I'm not shelling out good money for a frame and plywood and Sheetrock."

"And wiring and plumbing . . ."

"I told you. No. Besides, I've read my policy and the addition *is* covered. In fact, I've already filed a claim with my insurance company over water damage. So I'm not looking for anything else."

"Your existing policy provides only partial limited coverage."

"It's good enough for me."

"But you've invested much more in your rumpus room than the amount it would take to fully insure it," the agent said smoothly. "Not to mention all of the labor and man hours."

"I'm not buying anything else. Not now."

"It would behoove you to purchase some hazard insurance as well, should some sort of *accident* befall you as you work on, say, the roof?"

"Good-bye," Steve said firmly. "And don't call back again." He hung up the phone. Swiveling in his chair, he frowned as he looked out the window. A few of the crews had already left, but the majority of men were milling around the open garage door where the coffeepot was located. Two of the men in the crowd he didn't recognize, however—men who didn't belong, who shouldn't be there.

Burly men in Humphrey Bogart hats.

His blood ran cold as he recalled the night when he'd seen that figure in the addition. He'd almost convinced himself that it hadn't happened, that it had been a figment of his imagination, but he and Nina had both heard noises and *something* had caused them, and before he'd flipped on the lights he'd seen a man in the corner who looked exactly like—

Where did they go?

Frowning, Steve stood, practically pressing his face against the window. The men were gone. Both of them. One moment they'd been in the middle of that group of workers by the door of the garage, then he blinked and they'd disappeared. He shifted to the right, looking sideways through the glass, then turned the opposite way, but saw no sign of either of the men.

That was impossible. They could not have just vanished

into thin air. Yet they were nowhere in the corp yard. Maybe they were in the garage. Yeah. That was it. They'd gone into the garage and that's why he couldn't see them.

But he didn't want to go over and check; didn't want to ask any of the other men to find out for sure.

Steve turned away from the window, sat back down in his chair. The phone on his desk rang—the insurance agent again—and he picked up the handset and dropped it back into its cradle without answering. He thought of the tequila bottles and piss puddles and piles of human shit that he'd found in his unfinished rumpus room.

Maybe he *should* buy additional insurance.

No. He straightened in his seat. There was no need. He already had insurance. All the insurance he needed.

He kept it in the nightstand next to his bed.

And he had plenty of ammo for it, too.

5

Joel had always heard that the majority of traffic accidents occurred in parking lots, but he'd never seen any evidence that that was the case. Most of the accidents he'd seen in his life took place in or around intersections.

Insurance company propaganda, he'd assumed.

His first accident since he was a teenager, however, occurred in the school parking lot. He was leaving late as usual—a group of students in his Wednesday afternoon Principles of American Government class *always* stayed after to discuss current events with him—and he decided to take a shortcut through the student lot instead of driving back through the faculty lot exit and then around the east side of the campus.

The car backed right into him.

He was traveling up one of the east–west rows, keeping a

wary eye out for suddenly lit brake lights, well aware of the fact that many first-year students, boys in particular, acted like they were in thirteenth grade rather than college and peeled out of the parking lot in a juvenile attempt to impress their peers, when a clunky old Dodge abruptly pulled out of its spot on his right and hit his front passenger door. It wasn't a hard hit, more of a gentle tap, but the car was a metal behemoth from Detroit's golden age, and he knew without even looking that his Toyota had probably sustained damage.

He stopped where he was and immediately got out of the vehicle. The other driver did, too. She was Vietnamese, and when he walked back to inspect the damage she was shaking like a leaf. He could see visible perspiration above her upper lip, like a shiny mustache. As he'd feared, there was a noticeable dent on the lower half of his passenger door. Her bumper and trunk were okay, but the Dodge's right rear taillight had been smashed.

"I need insurance," she said in jittery heavily accented English.

"You don't have insurance?" *Great*, he thought.

"No. I need . . ." She took a deep breath. ". . . *Your* insurance." With shaking hands, she passed him a pen and a piece of paper.

"Oh." He wrote down his name, address, phone number, make and model of car, license plate number, driver's license number, and insurance policy number. She looked down at the information, then tried to hand the paper back to him. "No. State Farm."

"What?"

"State Farm Insurance."

"I don't have State Farm," he explained. He pointed at the name on the paper, speaking slowly. "I have UAI. United Automobile Insurance."

"No! State Farm!"

Clearly, she didn't understand that there were other valid

insurance companies besides State Farm. He tried to think of a way to get across to her that UAI was legit even though it didn't advertise on TV the way her carrier did.

"I call police."

Joel looked at his watch, sighing. "Fine."

They retreated to their respective cell phones, she calling the police, he phoning his wife to tell her that he'd been in an accident and was going to be late. Stacy panicked at the word "accident," but he immediately assured her that he had suffered no injuries and that even the car had only a few minor dents. He told her that she and Lilly should go ahead and eat dinner since he didn't know how long this was going to take or when he was going to be home.

"Police coming," the girl told him after he'd clicked off the phone.

He nodded in acknowledgment, then took down her information. Her name was My Nguyen, and she lived not far from campus on a street he recognized as being in one of Tucson's poorer areas.

There was nothing more for them to say, so they each waited next to their own vehicle for the cops to arrive. A minor traffic jam was soon caused by the placement of his Toyota as the six o'clock students began to arrive, but he was an instructor and a voice of authority, and he redirected the drivers, making those in the rear back up to the main aisle so that those in the front could escape. How ironic was this? Just last night he'd hung up on an insurance agent who'd called out of the blue and wanted him to increase his auto insurance coverage, stating that the insurance company had analyzed his policy and his needs and had determined that a higher liability limit and expanded coverage was necessary. Joel had hung up on him.

Now he sure hoped that analysis was wrong.

It was a full half hour before the police arrived—not campus security but a patrol car from the Tucson PD—and he waited for what seemed an interminable length of time for the girl to give her side of the story, before succinctly describing to the officer the accident as he recalled it. Joel handed over his driver's license and insurance card, and waited for the policeman to give him a copy of the report. He assumed that would be the end of it and that he and My would both go their separate ways and let the insurance companies fight it out, but to his surprise, the officer went back to his patrol car and began radioing for two tow trucks.

"Wait a minute!" Joel interrupted.

The policeman held up a hand for silence.

"My Toyota's fine! It's just a dent. I certainly don't need a tow truck."

The policeman finished relaying his radio message, then looked up in annoyance. "Mr. McCain," he said, "Mrs. Nguyen *requested* that I call a tow truck for her, and I did. I am required by *law* to request towing service for any driver with a UAI policy. If you'll read the back of your card . . ." He handed Joel his insurance card.

Joel turned the card over and read the fine print. Underneath the 1-800 number for claims and complaints, there was indeed a stipulation that if any police officer was called to make a report, that officer was required to notify a towing service and have the vehicle towed to the nearest participating dealer's service department or body shop.

It made no sense, though. Why make the policeman call for a tow truck rather than the client? And why not specify the level of damage required before requesting a tow—why leave it open?

The officer returned the girl's insurance card to her as well, and gave both of them a copy of the report he'd taken. "Drive safely," he said, before closing the door to his patrol car.

Joel was tempted to take off and drive home, get some estimates and fix the dented door at his convenience, but he knew that such an action would probably lead to his insurance company not paying for his repairs or not defending him

against the student's insurance claims, and possibly even dropping him.

So he moved his car out of the aisle into a parking space
and waited for the tow truck.

They both waited.

His came first, thankfully, a long flat truck with the name
Bricklin Brother's Towing stenciled on its doors. A beefy florid
man who could have been forty, could have been sixty,
emerged, squinting against the setting sun. "Joel McCain?" he
said.

"Yeah."

"That Corolla there?"

"Yeah."

"Pull it out here and we'll get rolling."

Joel backed his vehicle into the aisle once again, and the
tow-truck driver unspooled a length of cable, connected two
hooked lengths of chain to the undercarriage of the Toyota, put
the car in neutral, and used a motorized winch to pull it up the
slanting bed of the tow truck. Another motor righted the bed,
he placed the Toyota in park, blocked the wheels, and said,
"Let's go."

Joel got into the high passenger seat. "I'm not sure where
to take it—"

"Dealer," the man said simply. "Your insurance company
already called."

That was weird, Joel thought. He hadn't even notified his
insurance company. But maybe the cop had. Or maybe Stacy
had.

No, Stacy hadn't. And he doubted if the cop had, either. He
wasn't sure how his insurance company had learned about the
accident so quickly, and he found that a little unnerving.

They drove for the first few miles in silence. Finally, the
tow-truck driver picked up a coffee can from the seat next to
him and spit into it. Joel smelled chewing tobacco. "You work
at the college?"

Joel nodded.

"You a professor there?"

He tried to smile pleasantly. He already knew where this was headed. "Yeah."

"Must be a pretty good-paying gig, huh?"

"Not bad."

"Mmm."

There was a pause.

"How much you pull down a year, average?"

"Not as much as most people think."

"Really?"

"Yeah."

"I always wondered something. How is it that professors and teachers get three months off each year? I don't blame *you*, you understand. But you know how much vacation I get each year? Two weeks. Sometimes we're so busy I can't even take that. So even on a good year, I gotta work a minimum fifty weeks. Minimum. From where I'm sittin' you got yourself one hell of a good deal. Know what I'm sayin'?"

"Yeah," Joel said again. It was a conversation he'd had more times than he cared to remember, an anti-intellectual insinuation that his job wasn't real work because it wasn't manual labor. An angry elitist part of him wanted to say, *I get more time off than you do because the job of teaching our future leaders, scientists, artists, and engineers the knowledge they need to know in order to succeed in their respective fields is a hell of a lot harder and more important than driving a truck back and forth*, but instead he let it slide and stared out of the dusty windshield at the passing buildings.

Another pause.

"So you don't really make that much money, huh?"

"No."

"But teachers get paid for workin' twelve months a year and you only gotta work nine, right? Only reason I ask is because I'm a taxpayer, you know what I'm sayin'? Those salaries're comin' out of my pocket."

Joel was tempted to point out that he was a taxpayer, too, and that a portion of his taxes went to paying his own salary, which meant that he was making even less, but instead he simply corrected the driver's misinformation. "We work nine months and get paid for nine months. That means we have three months of no salary. That's why a lot of instructors get part-time jobs delivering soft drinks or working as mechanics or what have you."

That ought to get the bastard.

Sure enough, the tow truck driver looked impressed. "Really? I didn't know that. Hmm." He spit again into his coffee can. "So what do you do during your vacation? Where do you work?"

The truth was that he did nothing. He played with Lilly, read a little, went hiking, hung out.

But he couldn't tell the driver that. He'd already gone this far, so he said, "I'm trying to start my own business."

"Really? What kind?"

"Computers."

The driver nodded sagely. "Lot of money in computers."

Luckily, they'd reached the Toyota dealer, so no further conversation was required. Joel climbed out of the cab once the tow truck had stopped and watched while the driver lowered the truck bed and unhooked all of the chains from his car. He signed the appropriate form, thanked the driver, then walked over to the office where Toyota's service manager, a skinny mustached man with a stitched name tag that read "Bud," was waiting for him. His insurance company had called ahead, and all he had to do was show the service manager the damage to the vehicle and then sign a form authorizing the work.

"Even got your loaner ready," Bud said. He led Joel out of

the office and around the corner of the service area to a small parking lot.

Joel stared.

There was only one vehicle parked amidst the marked empty spaces. It looked like a clown car or one of those strange little micro autos he'd seen in European movies from the 1960s. Vaguely Volkswagen-shaped, it was almost small enough for him to sit on, and he didn't see that there was any way possible for him to fit *inside* it.

"What the hell is this?" he asked.

"I'm sorry," Bud said. "That's what your insurance company specifies."

"What?"

The service manager shrugged. "I don't make the rules. Most insurance companies have a cap on loaner prices—and we have specific rental rates for all of our vehicles—but UAI requires that we provide their customers with this particular car."

"Why?"

"I have no idea."

Joel walked across the small lot, put his hand on top of the tiny car. Bending down, he peered through the driver's door window. "How am I supposed to drive this?"

"I don't know," Bud said. "But people do."

Ten minutes later, Joel was crammed into the miniscule front seat, hunched over the steering wheel, driving up Swan Road, the object of ridicule for every vehicle around him, as, at irregular intervals, the tiny car's exhaust pipe blatted comically.

"My insurance problems started with the car, too;" Hunt said. "Then they expanded from there."

Once upon a time, Joel would have put his friend's opinions down to an acute case of paranoia, but he'd seen and heard far too much lately to dismiss any conspiracy theories out of hand. "You have UAI too, right?"

Hunt nodded. "I was going to change, and I called three other companies, but they all considered my cracked window an 'accident.' One wouldn't even take me. With the other two, my rates would've jumped sky high. Although UAI revoked my good driver discount, they were still cheaper than everyone else . . . so I stayed."

"Maybe you shouldn't have."

"Maybe not. Sometimes it's worth paying extra just for peace of mind."

Joel took a pull off his beer. "Did I ever tell you that my grandfather was killed by Howard Hughes?"

Hunt blinked. "What?"

"Yeah. In a traffic accident in Hollywood, long before I was born. He was there on a business trip—he was a buyer for a furniture manufacturer in Phoenix and was there to look at material—and he was driving back from the textile factory to his hotel when this lunatic sped through a red light and plowed right into him. It was Howard Hughes. Hughes took him to the hospital in his own car, paid for the best doctors, but my grandfather died the next day. Howard Hughes even paid for the funeral, although he didn't go."

"What happened? Was he arrested? Was there a trial? Did your family get a fortune?"

"No. Nothing happened. That was it. People were stupider in those days."

"Jesus, I never heard that story before."

"Yeah, well it just goes to show that my family and car problems have a long history together."

The phone rang, and a moment later Stacy poked her head around the corner. "It's the dealer," she said. "It's about the car."

Joel gave Hunt a significant look as he stood and walked into the kitchen. He took the phone from Stacy. "Hello?"

It was Bud. "I'm afraid I've got some bad news," the service manager said. "We submitted our estimate, but your insurance company won't authorize the full amount. In fact, they will not authorize any repairs to this vehicle. They *will* give you the Kelly Blue Book value if you junk it and buy another car, but that's it. That's all they're offering."

"Jesus Christ. I can't believe this."

"It's pretty standard practice for most insurance companies when cars and trucks are beyond hope, held together with spit and baling wire. But UAI's the only company I know of that goes this far."

"Maybe I'll just pay for it myself. How much is it?"

"Well, the thing is, we also found some other problems. Drive train problems. I don't think they were caused by the accident, but you still need a new tranny and a head gasket. Including body work, the whole thing'll run you about four thousand five hundred, give or take. So as I see it, you have three options. One, you pay out of pocket, although frankly, I don't think that car's worth it. Two, you live with the problems until she dies completely. Which will probably be pretty soon. Three, and this is the one I recommend, you scrap it and get yourself a new car. Or a new used car. For the amount you'd pay to repair this one, plus what the insurance company'll give you, you can get a decent preowned Celica or Corolla."

Joel was gripping the phone so hard his fingers hurt. The anger he felt went far beyond the mere annoyance he usually experienced when dealing with intransigent corporate lackeys or governmental bureaucrats. This was personal, a white-hot hatred that made him want to lash out. If he'd had the president of UAI in front of him at that moment, he would've strangled the bastard.

Still, his voice when it came out was quiet and controlled, professional. One adult discussing business with another. "Let me think about it and I'll call you back."

He didn't wait for a reply but hung up the phone—slammed it down, really—and Stacy looked over at him. "What is it?"

Hunt, by this time, was standing in the kitchen doorway.

"The insurance company won't pay to get the Toyota fixed. They said it's too expensive and the car's not worth it. So they've offered to give me the blue book value so I can put it toward a new car."

"That's bullshit," Stacy said. From the backyard, they heard Lilly and her friend Kate giggle. Stacy lowered her voice. "You should be able to get estimates from different places, then let them pick the cheapest and get the damn car fixed."

"*Should* is the operative word here. Our policy requires us to use the dealer, and now the dealer's estimate has been rejected. They're not paying a dime to fix that car."

"That's crap!"

More giggles from outside.

"This isn't the end of it by a long shot. I'm calling UAI and going all the way up the chain if I have to. I want some answers, goddamn it. And I'm reporting them. I'm going to the insurance commission, the Better Business Bureau—"

"This sounds familiar," Hunt said.

Joel looked at him. "Well, there must be some way to get these sons of bitches and make them pay."

"No," Hunt said, "I'm beginning to think there isn't."

Seven

The insurance agent stood before the register counter wearing a high-buttoned vest with a gold-chain pocket watch that made him look like the conductor on a Victorian train. Dolores Bessett pretended to add up the day's receipts, not wanting to look at the agent, not wanting him to think that she was even listening.

She was afraid of him.

It was true, though she was not sure why. In the ten years since she'd opened up her own business—if you could *call* this hole-in-the-wall bookstore a business—she had to deal with problem people on a daily basis: homeless panhandlers, obnoxious vendors, pedophiles who cut out pictures of children from old photography books, wackos who whacked off in her bathroom. But she'd never been afraid or intimidated by any of them.

Until the agent.

There was no reason for it, really. Despite his marginally offbeat garb, the man looked like what he was—an insurance salesman. He had that soft, doughy, pale face typical of middle-aged men in service professions, and there was a blandness to his voice and demeanor that connoted an uninteresting existence, a prosaic life. Still, each time he came in, he frightened her, and she wished a last-minute customer would walk through the door . . . or a high school kid wanting a job . . . or the UPS man or . . . *somebody*.

But she remained alone in the store with him, and she pretended to be busy with bookkeeping minutiae as he tried to pressure her into buying more insurance.

"What you need is commercial insurance," he was saying. "Small business insurance. That includes liability, property, worker's comp, personal, medical, life, disability, the whole shebang. You probably have every red cent tied up in this store, and one misplaced match, one teenage vandalism spree, and you'd be filing for bankruptcy and looking for a job at Wal-Mart. All of that can be avoided . . ."

She folded up her register tape and placed it in the lockbox at her feet before flipping the sign in the window from OPEN to CLOSED. Looking up at the agent for the first time since he'd started his spiel, she tried to affect a detached businesslike manner. "We're closed now. I'm afraid we'll have to leave."

He smiled at her. " 'We'll?' "

Heat flushed her face. Her voice hadn't sounded nervous, but strong and self-assured, but the lapse had given her away. She had never before tried to take charge in her dealings with the insurance agent, had always behaved submissively and followed his lead, and now her one attempt to stand up for herself had backfired. "You'll," she corrected herself in an attempt to regain lost ground. "*You'll* have to leave."

His smile grew wider, and maybe it wasn't quite so bland, wasn't quite so agreeable. "*You'll* have to purchase small business insurance."

"Look," she said, trying to appeal to reason. "I have no other employees. So I don't need workman's comp and . . . all the other things you mentioned. I have plenty of insurance for myself. *You* sold it to me."

"Yes. And after analyzing your needs, I have determined that you require small business insurance."

Her heart was pounding, but she walked around the front counter, past him, and opened the front door, jiggling the keys in her hand. "I simply can't afford it right now."

"You can't afford *not* get it."

"I can't afford it," she repeated more firmly. "And the store is now closed. Good day."

He nodded in a way that might have been deferential, might have been patronizing. "Very well," he said. "But don't say I didn't warn you." He smiled at her, nodded, and stepped onto the sidewalk.

Dolores quickly locked the door behind him. Her palms were sweating, her hands shaking, and she had to take a series of deep breaths just to get enough air into her lungs, as though she'd been holding her breath for the past several minutes. On the counter, she noticed, he'd left a pamphlet advertising commercial insurance for small business owners, and she crumpled it up and threw it away.

She took out the register tape and this time *really* counted the receipts—not that there were many to add—and checked the number against the cash on hand before putting everything in the lockbox, turning off the lights, and exiting through the rear of the store. She put the lockbox and her purse in the car, double-checked both the front and back doors to make sure everything was secure, then headed for home.

Not until she pulled into the driveway of her apartment complex did Dolores realize she had forgotten the box of Fawcett Gold Medal paperbacks she'd bought off a longtime customer that morning for an unconscionably low price. She was hungry and tired and wanted nothing more than to heat up a Healthy Choice lasagna, sit in front of the TV, and watch a rerun of *Friends*. But if she didn't get the books tonight, she wouldn't be able to put them up on eBay until tomorrow evening and she needed an infusion of cash as quickly as possible.

The Internet was a godsend when it came to unloading collectible books. Things that would have sat in her store for months, maybe years, before finding a buyer, were now selling in a matter of weeks, sometimes days.

The sun was dropping fast, the Rincons in the east already lost in the gloom of night, the Tucson Mountains little more than a black shape against the orange sky of dusk, and it was nearly dark by the time she reached the store. She pulled up in front, parking next to the sidewalk, not wanting to drive through the alley and park in the small back lot at night.

She got out of the car, locked it. Only then did she notice movement inside the bookstore.

She stopped where she was and stood unmoving on the curb, looking in the window, her heart rate accelerating so fast she could feel the pulse of blood in her ears. Inside, in full view of anyone walking or driving by, a gang of young toughs were ostentatiously tearing out the pages of books, throwing paperbacks at each other across the room, pulling whole shelves of books onto the floor. Only they weren't all young. Standing near the back wall, by the bathroom, was a hefty stoop-shouldered man in a broad-brimmed hat. She couldn't see his face from this far away—he was little more than a silhouette to her—but she knew somehow that he was older than the rest of the attackers, and that he was the instigator of this melee.

She wanted to rush back, grab the baseball bat she kept under the counter and just start whaling on those punks, ordering them to get the hell out of her store.

And she probably would have.

But the man in the hat scared her.

He scared her in the same way the insurance salesman did, in some instinctive gut-level manner, and she found herself withdrawing, moving off the curb, onto the street, staying in the shadows as she made her way carefully back into the car.

The punks were now toppling the bookcases themselves, and one knocked over the two behind it, like dominoes.

I guess I should've bought business insurance, she thought.

In the back of the store, the man in the hat remained unmoving.

Dolores started the car and pulled onto the street without turning on her headlights, not wanting to be seen. She did not flip on her lights until she reached the end of the block.

She turned right and sped toward the police station.

Eight

1

Hunt asked Beth to marry him in January.

They'd been dating for nearly eight months, living together for the past four. He talked it over with Joel first, told Edward and Jorge before he asked her, and while that didn't sit right with him, he felt he needed some perspective, some outside opinions to make sure he wasn't moving too fast or in the wrong direction.

No, they all assured him, Beth was great, the two of them were a perfect couple, marriage was the next logical step.

Beth not only said yes, but she wanted to do it as quickly as possible. "I hate long, drawn-out engagements," she said. "Once a couple makes the decision, they ought to just go for it."

And that's what they did.

Neither of them was enamored of the idea of a big church wedding, particularly since neither of them went to church, but they also did not want the dry formality of a civil ceremony at city hall. So they opted for nondenominational nuptials conducted by a friend of Joel's from the college philosophy department who was also an ordained minister from one of those legally recognized but spiritually suspect mail-order New Age churches. They planned to have both the wedding and the reception in a cabana at one of Tucson's prettiest parks, a park that would conveniently be closed for the day to the general public for tree trimming and repairs.

Beth's father had passed away, but her mother flew out a week early from her home in Las Vegas to help Beth pick out a dress and flowers and get ready. She slept in the guest room, and if she heard any unusual noises or saw anything out of the ordinary in there, she didn't mention it. When she awoke each morning, she appeared refreshed and relaxed, so Hunt assumed that all was well.

His own parents came out from Minnesota, dragging along a caravan of distant half-remembered relatives: aunts and cousins, and his father's uncle, whom he had never met. There was deep snow on the ground in Park Rapids, his mother reported, and he could tell by the way she said it that she wished they'd never left Tucson. But his dad seemed rejuvenated by the move, happier and more alive than he'd been since . . . well, since as far back as Hunt could remember.

Joel was his best man. Since they weren't having a regular wedding, there wasn't a whole lot for Joel to do other than give a toast at the reception, but he still seemed touched by Hunt's invitation. In lieu of the traditional bachelor party, the two of them returned to William Bodie Junior High for an extended game of Horse, just as they used to do when they were thirteen. The gym was locked up, but the outside courts were free and empty, and the two of them practiced shooting baskets before settling down to the game. The school seemed smaller than Hunt remembered, but oddly enough the baskets seemed taller—and the metal backboards were just as annoying as ever.

Joel did a reverse layup, then tossed the ball to Hunt. "Remember when we stole that beer from my dad's refrigerator in the garage and we shared it and came over here to play and halfway through Pig you were puking all over your shoes?"

Hunt laughed. "Yeah," he said. "I remember."

"And Mr. Hunter was grading papers and saw it from his

classroom and came out to investigate? And I told him that Bill Groff made you eat a bug and that's why you were heaving?"

Hunt laughed harder. "And Groff got detention for a week?"

"Those were the days, my friend."

"We thought they'd never end." He perfectly copied Joel's layup, then attempted a hook shot from midcourt that bounced off the rim of the backboard and sailed into the chain-link fence.

He had missed Joel all those years, although he hadn't realized it until he'd returned. Hell, he missed all of his old buddies. Life had a way of pulling people apart, of winding away in different directions, of breaking up childhood friendships and substituting them with less intimate, more superficial relationships. As the narrator in *Stand by Me* said, he never had better friends than the ones he'd had as a boy, although Beth maintained that the same was not true for girls.

Hunt looked over at his friend, trying to see in this sedate and settled college instructor the rabidly anti-intellectual, anti-authoritarian rabble-rouser of his youth. That boy might have been in there somewhere, but he'd grown up and his edges had been softened and he'd become exactly the type of person he'd once scorned.

It happened to all of them, Hunt supposed. He himself had changed a lot since junior high. He was less arrogant, less cocksure, more willing to bend and compromise, less judgmental, more sympathetic.

Yet, somehow, they were friends again. They were both totally different people than they had been as children, they'd both grown into adults far different than either they or the people around them would have ever supposed, but they were once again in sync, their lives having come full circle.

Joel made an easy jump shot. "So, you told your ex yet?"

"Eileen?" Hunt shook his head. "To tell you the truth, I'm not even sure where to reach her." He perfectly imitated Joel's jump shot, then put his hands on his knees and crouched down for a moment to rest. "I thought about it, though. It seems weird not to have to . . ."

"Check in?"

"Exactly. I mean, I wasn't *happily* married, but I was still married, you know? It feels like I'm lying or something to pretend that it never happened, that she doesn't exist."

Joel crouched down next to him. "You don't still have, you know, *feelings* for her, do you?"

"Oh God, no. At least not any positive ones. And Beth . . . Beth's great, she's perfect. I just wish that this was my first time, you know? That I wasn't bringing all this baggage with me."

"Does Beth care?"

"No. At least she says she doesn't."

"Then why should you? Forget about it, man. You're getting married for real this time. That was just a practice run."

"You're right. You're right."

"I know I am."

Joel won the game, and afterward, they went over to Pancho Muldoon's, a bar by the U of A that had been one of Hunt's college hangouts. It was still a college hangout, though, and they were a decade past the target demographic, and after one beer they both felt so hopelessly out of place that they left and headed home.

"Adulthood," Joel said. "Ain't it a bitch."

The big day was chaotic. There seemed to be a hundred people at Beth's house—*their* house—all of them getting ready at once: he and Beth, her mom, his parents, assorted relatives from both families, friends.

He was going over minister payment and tip etiquette with Joel in the kitchen when Beth's mother popped in for a quick glass of water. "I was watching the news last night, and they said it might rain today," she declared. "You should have gotten wedding insurance, just in case. That way, you're not out a bundle if everything gets ruined by rain."

Insurance.

Hunt met Joel's gaze and saw there the same uneasiness he felt at the sound of that word.

"Don't worry," Hunt said. "Everything'll be okay. Everything'll be fine."

And it was. The ceremony itself was short and sweet, and though clouds did indeed roll in around noon, they served only to keep the temperature down; the threatened rains never came. Afterward, at the reception, Edward got drunk and nearly got into a fistfight with the philosophy professor, and Jorge and Joel had to hold him back. "I'll rip your arms off, you dickless scrim!" he shouted. One of Beth's old club-hopping friends puked into the duck pond.

His parents seemed slightly taken aback by these events, and in a delayed-adolescent-rebellion way, Hunt was proud of that. This was his wedding, these were his friends, and he was an adult. He could choose to hang with whomever he pleased.

But he might have been reading more into that than was there, for later he saw his dad deep in conversation with Jorge and caught his mother laughing uproariously at a ribald joke told by one of Beth and Stacy's work friends.

Both of his parents seemed to love Beth, and for that he was grateful. He wanted her to like them and wanted them to like her. He'd been a little nervous about it because they'd been genuinely fond of Eileen, but he needn't have worried. Apparently, they saw the same qualities in Beth that he did, and it was a load off his mind to know that they were all going to be one big happy family.

They spent their wedding night at Westward Look, a luxury resort at the foot of the Catalinas with an awesome view of the city at night. There were thunderstorms to the south, toward Tubac, and from the window of their suite they could see jagged flashes of bluish white lightning beyond the array of multicolored lights that was downtown Tucson.

"It's beautiful," Beth said, snuggling next to him as they stood before the window.

It was. The lightning gave brief delineation to dark night-time thunderheads, illuminating a billowing majesty that he would not have suspected was there, and the juxtaposition of the wildly random weather with the stationary artifice of the city's electric lights seemed somehow magical.

They stood like that for quite a while, until the lightning storm died down, and then moved back to the bed, where they removed each other's clothes and made slow passionate love. Originally, they'd had a much more elaborate scenario in mind. In an effort to make their wedding night special, to differentiate it from an ordinary evening, they'd planned to engage in a series of exotic offbeat sex acts that neither of them had tried, but they found that that wasn't necessary. The night was special on its own; it didn't need any forced distinction. The regular way was fine.

They fell asleep in each other's arms.

The next morning, they set off on their honeymoon. Hunt had wanted to go to Montana or Wyoming or maybe even Canada, spend time alone together in the wild, but Beth wanted to go to California, hit all the tourist spots, and he had readily acceded to her wishes. He missed California, and he liked the idea of taking her around, showing her the sights.

They went to Hollywood, Disneyland, Griffith Park, the Huntington Library, but what she really wanted to do was spend time at the beach. The weather was warm and sunny, more the summery splendor of August than the gloom of June, and he took her to Seal Beach, where they walked his favorite pier and then ate at a Mexican restaurant on Main Street. But she wanted to swim, and the water at Seal Beach was usually filthy and contaminated. So they drove down the coast to Crystal Cove. A lot of other people obviously had the same idea, because it was impossible to find a parking spot. Hunt drove around the lot twice, slowly, before finally seeing two teenage girls walk across the asphalt to a topless VW bug. He stopped, waited, but the girls took their time. When they finally backed out, a red Mustang swerved around him and took the space.

Hunt leaned on his horn, rolling down his window. "You stupid son of a bitch!" he yelled.

Beth put a hand on his arm. "It's not worth getting all worked up about. Look, there's another spot opening."

Sure enough, the brake lights of a Nissan pickup two spaces ahead had come on. This time Hunt took no chances. He pulled almost directly behind the vehicle, blocking off any possible end runs. His plan was to creep slowly in reverse as the truck backed up, keeping as little space as possible between them—a technique he'd perfected in college when competition for campus parking spots had been at a premium.

The pickup started to pull out, and Hunt put the car into reverse, but an old Chevy van was right on his tail, blocking him in. The truck continued backing up. Hunt pressed his horn, but both the truck and van drivers either ignored it or did not hear it. He had no room to move.

The pickup hit him.

Instantly, the driver was running out to survey the damage. "I'm sorry!" he said "Oh my God, I'm so sorry! I didn't see you there! Are you all right?"

Hunt and Beth got out of the car. "We're fine," Hunt said. He gestured behind him. "That moron was blocking me in. I couldn't get out of the way."

The Chevy van had backed up and was waiting for a red Jeep to pull out of another parking spot several spaces back.

"My truck's okay. How's your car?"

Hunt and Beth both examined the Saab's front end but could see no dents or damage. The other driver looked, too. "I don't see anything," he said hopefully.

"No," Hunt admitted. "I don't either. Looks like we all got off lucky this time."

"Maybe we should exchange insurance information just in case."

Insurance.

Hunt shivered involuntarily despite the warm day. "No," he said. "It's all right."

"You might find something later—"

"Don't worry," Hunt assured him.

"Are you sure?"

Half past a monkey's ass, a quarter to his ba-wuls.

"I'm sure."

"Maybe we should," Beth suggested.

"It's fine," he said. "It's fine."

2

Jorge met Ynez at the obstetrician's at lunch. She was sitting uncomfortably in one of the leather waiting-room chairs, thumbing through a women's magazine whose cover featured the female host of a television talk show standing next to a bouquet of flowers. "Sorry I'm late," he said.

She smiled, squeezed his hand.

The door next to the receptionist's window opened, and a nurse holding a clipboard kept it from closing. "Mrs. Marquez?"

Both Jorge and Ynez stood, following the nurse down a short corridor to a utilitarian exam room, where the nurse weighed Ynez and took her blood pressure and temperature. She'd gained five pounds from two weeks ago, and everything was normal. "Dr. Bergman will be with you in a minute," the nurse said, closing the door behind her.

Ynez remained on the cushioned examination bed, while Jorge nervously walked the perimeter of the small room, looking at the jar of cotton balls, the antibacterial soaps lined up at the back of the sink, the full-color poster of a woman's reproductive system. "We could change doctors if you want," he said. "There are a lot of other doctors in our group."

"I *like* having a woman doctor," she told him.

"I'm just saying."

After a polite knock on the door, Dr. Bergman entered. What worried Jorge wasn't that she was a woman. It was the fact that she was so damn *young*. She looked like she'd just graduated from medical school, and though she might have graduated at the top of her class, in his book that was no substitute for experience. This was their first child, and he would have felt a lot more comfortable if Ynez's obstetrician were an old white-haired gent with a bushy mustache.

Still, he admired Dr. Bergman's professional, no-nonsense attitude, and he had to admit that she seemed to know what she was doing. Besides, Ynez trusted her. That had to count for something.

The doctor pulled up Ynez's blouse and began to palpate her distended abdomen.

"Everything okay?" he asked worriedly.

"Everything's fine," she assured them. She finished pressing on Ynez's abdomen. "Ready to hear the heartbeat?"

Ynez smiled happily. "Yes."

This was the part of the visit she enjoyed most, but to Jorge it was nerve-racking. There was the miracle of life and all that, and technology and modern medicine were truly awesome— but he could not help worrying that there would be something wrong; that the doctor would hear an irregular heartbeat, evidence of a congenital heart defect, an indication that their baby would be born with severe and crippling medical problems.

Dr. Bergman squirted a jellylike substance onto Ynez's stomach—the stuff even *looked* cold—and then picked up the portable gadget that to Jorge still looked like a modified ohmmeter. Harsh static issued from the device's small speaker. She moved it slowly over Ynez's belly, and gradually a pattern emerged from within the white noise.

"There it is," the doctor said, smiling.

Even after all these times, it still didn't sound like a heartbeat to Jorge. It was too fast, for one thing. Kind of a whooshing, swishing sound that, at the same time, held a hint of the mechanical. Dr. Bergman had been through this often enough with them to anticipate his next question, and before he could ask it she said, "Your baby's heart sounds fine. It's very strong."

Jorge exhaled gratefully. Another hurdle cleared.

They listened for a few moments longer, then the doctor turned off the machine, put it away, wiped the goop off Ynez's stomach and began making notes on her chart. She flipped through a couple pages, then looked up. "I assume they called you with the results of the amnio, right?"

"Yes," Ynez said.

That had been another nightmare. It had been bad enough to see that gigantic needle sinking into his wife's abdomen, then to watch the ultrasound monitor and see the needle pause in its descent while the fetus moved so it wouldn't stab the tiny head, but the waiting had been far worse. First, they waited twenty-four hours to make sure that none of the possible side effects of amniocentesis—like miscarriage—occurred. Then they whiled away the next few days waiting to find out if their child would be born retarded or severely deformed. Receiving the phone call from the lab three days later was like a reprieve from the governor.

"And I assume they told you that everything's fine."

"Yes."

She paused and looked from Jorge to Ynez, smiling. "So . . . do you want to know?"

Jorge turned toward Ynez. That was the question. They'd discussed it many times, and they'd always decided that they did not want to know the sex of the baby, they wanted to be surprised. But the woman standing before them knew already. So did the technicians at the lab and probably a couple of nurses. And now that they were faced with the decision of whether or not to receive the knowledge or pretend it didn't exist, Jorge was not so sure they should stick to their guns, despite all of their self-satisfied philosophizing. He looked questioningly at Ynez.

She smiled, nodded, reached for his hand. "Tell us," she said to the doctor. "We want to know."

"Congratulations," Dr. Bergman said. "You're going to have a son."

3

The light in the guest room was on.

It had not been on ten minutes ago, when Hunt left for work. Beth was sure of that. But it was on now, and the sight of that yellowish light seeping from beneath the closed door in the predawn darkness of the hallway made her blood run cold. "Courtney!" she called.

The cat's responding meow came from far away—the kitchen or the laundry room.

She had to go to work, too. It was her first day back after the honeymoon, and she couldn't afford to be late. She should leave and come back later with Hunt, preferably when it was all over.

When it was all over.

Yes. Whatever was happening in there, it was still going on.

She reached for the light switch and flipped it, but there was no response. The hallway remained dark.

Except for the bar of light at the bottom of the guest room door.

She hesitated for a moment, unsure of what to do. There was a noise coming from the room. Not knocking this time, but an eerie sort of low whistle, like the sound of a forgotten teakettle almost out of water. The whistle was barely audible, almost lost beneath her own frightened exhalations of breath and Courtney's far-off meowing.

Dawn was only a few minutes away. If she waited, light would come into the house through the east-facing windows, dispelling the darkness. But she couldn't wait. Work traffic would be getting heavier by the minute and she needed to leave if she was going to make it to Thompson in time. Taking a deep fortifying breath, she walked quickly down the hall. She grabbed the knob to the guest room door, turned it, and pushed.

And the door wouldn't open.

She leaned into it, pressing against the wood with her shoulder, constantly aware of the light spilling from under the door onto her shoes, but it would not budge.

The noise within the room seemed slightly louder, and now it sounded less like a teakettle and more like the distracted tuneless whistling of a man waiting not so patiently for someone.

A chill passed through her.

And the door swung open.

She screamed. In the brief second before the guest room light shut off, Beth saw in the dresser mirror the shape of a man standing beside her, a hulking figure with stooped shoulders and a broad-brimmed hat.

And then she was running as fast as she could through the living room, through the kitchen, and out of the house.

"How you feeling down there?"

"What?"

"If your dick's not rubbed raw and damn near falling off, you're not a man."

Hunt laughed and threw a stick at Edward. It flew end over

end toward the big man's face before he stepped aside and it clattered harmlessly on the gravel.

"You were on your honeymoon, dude."

"Yeah?"

"So that thing should be red and chapped."

"What's the point? You want to pull down my pants and take a peek at my pecker? What exactly are you shooting for here?"

"Details!" Jorge announced from his perch in the tree. "We want details!"

"Well, you're not getting any."

"My guess is *you're* not getting any," Edward said. He laughed his deep wrestler's laugh, and the three of them paused while two moms pushing babies in sports strollers jogged by.

"Seriously," Edward said, "how was the trip?"

"A week off, squiring my new wife around my old haunts? How do you think it was?"

"It sucked?"

Hunt laughed. "It was *great*. There were a few minor inconveniences, just enough to make the trip memorable—"

"You need inconveniences to make your honeymoon memorable?" Edward shook his head. "Like I said: not a man."

"You know what I'm talking about. We got food poisoning at Olvera Street—"

"Diarrhea's always sexy on a honeymoon," Jorge offered, climbing down.

Hunt ignored him. "Then I got into a little fender bender at the beach."

Edward shook his head in sympathy. "What'd your insurance company say this time?"

"Nothing. I didn't tell them. There was no damage to either car, so we just left it as is."

"Probably a wise decision. You hear about Steve's homeowner's insurance?"

"No. What?"

"Canceled!" Jorge called out.

Hunt looked at Edward, who nodded. "It's true. I guess he filed what they considered a frivolous claim, and they dropped him."

Jorge laughed. "There he is with his half-built house and no insurance. It couldn't happen to a nicer guy."

"You know, Steve may be a dickwad," Hunt said, "but this insurance stuff is scary."

"I know where you're coming from . . . but it's *Steve*."

"I understand. But I don't think you *do* know where I'm coming from. I've been thinking about this a lot lately, and do you realize how much we depend on insurance? We need it for our cars, for our houses, for our health, for our lives. People stay at jobs they hate just for the insurance, especially if they have kids. It affects *everything*. I think more dreams are derailed because of the practical necessity of having insurance than anything else." He faced Edward. "How many more people would be writing music if they didn't have to make those car insurance payments, if they didn't need homeowner's insurance?" He looked up at Jorge. "How many more people would be writing the novels that are locked in their heads if they didn't need to work a job that guaranteed them health insurance for their kids?"

There was silence as the two of them digested this.

"People don't need more art," Edward said gruffly. "They need their trees trimmed. Let's get back to work."

"Yeah," Jorge said. "Besides . . . it's *Steve*."

Hunt got home before Beth and immediately went into the guest room to investigate.

She had called him on his cell early that morning to tell him what had happened, had called him again at lunch to go into more detail, and while it had sounded somewhat ridiculous when he was out there in the real world, away from the house, it didn't seem quite so unbelievable now that he was here.

She hadn't touched anything, she said, but the first thing he noticed when he walked into the room was that the covers of the guest bed were pulled down. That bedspread had remained unmoved and unchanged ever since Beth's mother left, and the sight of it crumpled at the foot of the mattress along with the flat sheet underneath raised goose bumps on his arms. Nothing else in the room appeared to be disturbed. The switch was down and the light was off. There were no noises.

From outside, he heard Beth's Saturn pull into the driveway, the slamming of her car door, then the opening of the kitchen door. "I'm in here!" he called when he was sure that she was within shouting distance.

Her footsteps sounded hesitant on the floor, but a moment later Beth was standing beside him, looking at the unmade bed. "I'm assuming you didn't do that," she said.

"Nope."

She glanced around the room, searching for something else out of order but apparently not finding anything. "I really did see something in the mirror," she said, and he could hear the fear in her voice. "A big man, standing right beside me. Only no one was there."

"Did you feel threatened by him? Did you have the sense that he meant you harm?" Hunt could not believe he was talking this way. There was no getting around it, though. Not after what had happened. The room was haunted. It was as simple as that.

Beth shook her head. "I didn't feel anything specific, if that's what you mean. I didn't have the feeling that his purpose was to harm me. But I've never been more terrified in my life, I can tell you that." She pointed to her arms. "Look," she said. "Goose bumps. They've been there all day."

Hunt pulled up the flat sheet, pulled up the bedspread, half-expecting that at any second they would be ripped out of his hands and go fluttering across the room. But nothing happened. He remade the bed and the bed stayed made. Inwardly, he breathed a sigh of relief. "People live with ghosts, don't they? Give them cute names like 'Georgie' or 'Louie' and tell everyone that they're friendly and don't mean any harm? Maybe that's what we should do."

"A haunted house," Beth said, echoing his thoughts. "We live in a haunted house."

"Yeah." He looked at her. "What do you want to do? Sell it and move somewhere else?"

"No," she said. She paused to think about it. "At least . . . not yet."

Nine

1

Steve had been riding their asses all week, and Hunt was grateful when Friday finally rolled around. On the way home, he stopped for gas at a Circle K. Across the street was a Waffle House, and as he pumped the gas he looked over at the restaurant, wondering what kind of people ate waffles at this time of day. Night-shift workers, he supposed. Truck drivers and train men. His attention shifted to the homeless man selling newspapers from the concrete island dividing the northbound and southbound sides of the street, and then to the bus stop in front of the Circle K. He frowned. Two women were waiting for a bus, and one of them seemed very familiar. He didn't recognize the clothes or the hair, but there was something about the set of her shoulders, the positioning of her head . . .

The woman turned to the left, giving him a profile.

It was Eileen.

He had not seen her since the divorce, had not even considered that she might move back to Tucson, too. Yet here she was, in one of the downscale areas of the city, using public transportation.

She looked old and unhappy, and that depressed him. He would have been depressed as well had she been looking fabulous, with a new husband and a young baby in tow, but somehow this was worse. He hadn't thought he had any tender

feelings left—not after the bitterness of the breakup—but obviously he did. Once intimate always intimate, he supposed,
and he could not help thinking back to when they'd first
started dating, their senior year in high school. They'd been
voted "Couple Most Likely to Last the Longest" in the year-
book and had literally spent every spare moment in each
other's company. She'd been beautiful and smart, he'd been
popular and high-achieving, and they'd both been young, with
their entire futures ahead of them.

Now she was middle-aged and all alone, and he could not
help wondering if her life would be different today had they
stayed together. Or had they never met. It was impossible to
say how much of an influence one person had on another, and
perhaps everything would have turned out this way no matter
what. But he had his doubts. He saw in his mind that bright
young girl, filled with promise, and there was an ache in his
heart so painful he felt almost like crying.

The bus arrived just as his tank filled and the pump nozzle
cut off. Hunt watched her stand, climb listlessly up the bus
steps, disappear into the vehicle, and he remained unmoving as
the bus pulled into traffic, heading east. It was only when the
bus was finally lost from sight that he hung up the hose,
screwed on his gas cap and got back into the car.

He went home to Beth.

And held her close.

They awoke to the sound of thunder and the *drip-drip-drip*
of water somewhere in the bedroom.

The roof was leaking! Hunt sat up in bed, opening his eyes
wide to clear them and looking toward the digital alarm clock
on the dresser, trying to make out the time. Two-thirty? Three-
thirty? Next to him, Beth was turning on the lamp atop her
nightstand. He got up to flip on the light switch—

—and nearly slipped in the water that had puddled on the
hardwood floor. "Jesus Christ!" he yelled, grabbing the bed-

post to steady himself. He tiptoed through water that seemed surprisingly deep—this must have been going on for some time—and was about to turn on the ceiling light when Beth told him to stop. He turned and looked where she was pointing. Even in the dim light from her lamp, he saw that rain was soaking through the ceiling in two places, one above the high-back chair in the corner, the other next to Hunt's side of the bed.

"That means the attic's wet," she said. "I don't know if that affects the wires, but I don't want you to short out the light or electrocute yourself or anything."

He didn't know enough about electricity to know if that was a possibility, but he didn't want to find out firsthand, so he backed away from the light switch.

Beth was already out of bed and pulling the chair out from under the leak. "Check the living room," she ordered. "Make sure it's not leaking in there."

He did. It was. He switched on one of the floor lamps. Again, there were two spreading spots on the ceiling, both dripping at a constant rate onto the coffee table and the couch. She came up behind him. "We need to get this fixed!" she shouted over a peal of thunder. "It's going to ruin all the furniture!"

"We will."

"Now!"

"Well, we *can't* call someone right now!" he snapped at her. "It's the middle of the night! We have to wait for morning."

She was already pushing past him. "I know that, asshole. But we need to move things around, put pots under the leaks. We can't just go back to sleep and let everything get washed away."

"You said we need to *fix* it right now."

She pushed the coffee table away from the leak. "Sorry I didn't speak as precisely as I should have. I guess I was more concerned about my furniture being ruined than finding exactly the right words."

They glared at each other for a brief second, then both hurried to opposite ends of the couch and dragged/lifted it out of harm's way. Together, they headed into the kitchen to look for containers to catch the water. It was their first fight as a married couple, and Hunt could tell by the expression on Beth's face that she felt as bad about it as he did. Before she bent down to dig through the pots-and-pans cupboard, he gave her a quick hug. "Sorry," he said.

"Me, too."

She found a stew pot and an aluminum turkey pan, and from under the sink he grabbed the plastic bucket she used when mopping the floor. That still left one leak with nothing to catch the water, so Hunt ran back into their bedroom, put the bucket where the chair had been, then got the wastepaper basket from the bathroom and set it on the floor next to his side of the bed.

They met back in the living room. Neither the kitchen nor the master bathroom had leaks, and no water was seeping through the hallway roof. Likewise, the laundry room, study and small bathroom were dry. That left only . . .

Beth said it aloud. "What about the guest room?"

"We'd better check," he said, though it was the last thing he felt like doing. Outside the storm still raged, and the hallway suddenly seemed darker than it had a moment before. Thunder and lightning could make *any* house seem haunted, and they certainly accentuated the spookiness of the guest room.

The door was open—

hadn't it been left closed?

—and he could see even from this angle that the bed was unmade again. The bedspread and sheets were crumpled at the foot of the mattress, and there was something unpleasant about the shape they formed, something about the wrinkles and overlaps and the peaked center of the disordered linen that reminded him of a figure he could not quite place but knew he did not like. Beth's hand closed around his, and he could feel fear in the tightness of her muscles.

Lightning flashed, and he stopped, waited, realizing that he was afraid to see that dresser mirror illuminated by lightning. He did not even want to look in the mirror's direction until an electric light in the room was turned on.

The lightning stopped, the thunder followed, and between episodes, he dashed in turn on the desk lamp. His first instinct was to simply flip the wall switch—going into a dark guest room was *not* something he wanted to do—but for all he knew rainwater was puddled in the attic directly above the overhead light, seeping down its wires, so he stumbled through the unlit room to the writing desk.

There was another flash of lightning, a bolt so jagged and strong that its outline burned through the curtains. He was already looking toward the dresser, and in the split-second before the bulb came on, he saw in the mirror exactly what Beth had described: a hulking man with stooped shoulders and a broad-brimmed hat. She saw it too, and she screamed next to him, a piercing cry that made him jump and practically knock the lamp off the desk.

Then the room was awash in electric light, the mirror reflected back only the furnishings of the room and themselves, and whatever had been there was gone. Beth's scream cut off abruptly, and she looked frantically behind her to verify that they were alone, that the figure they'd seen in the mirror was nowhere around. She turned to him, eyes wide. "You saw it, didn't you? In the mirror?"

He nodded, not trusting himself to speak.

"A man in a hat."

"Yeah."

Thunder cracked hard, this time unaccompanied by lightning. Rain splattered loudly against the window. Emboldened by Hunt's presence and the light from the lamp, Beth walked over to the dresser and looked closely at the mirror. He took the opportunity to go over to the bed and throw the covers back over the mattress, messing up that disturbing shape.

Both of them walked slowly around the room in opposite directions. There was no leak, and for that they were grateful, but . . .

But there was still . . . *something*.

A noise, Hunt thought. Kind of a whistle.

"Listen," he said. "Is that what you said you heard? That whistling sound?"

"I don't—" An expression of horrified recognition came over her face: "Yes! Only it was louder last time."

Lightning flashed, thunder clapping instantly on its heels.

And the whistling was gone.

They waited but it didn't return, and they searched through the room for another five minutes, checking the closet, opening the dresser drawers, looking in the desk, peeking under the bed. They didn't want to find anything, were *afraid* to find anything, but somehow the rational mechanics of a methodical search served to demystify the room, weakening its power over them at least on an emotional level.

Beth quickly made the bed, they shut off the lamp and closed the door, then went to mop up the floors and check on the pots and pans and buckets to make sure they weren't being filled up too fast. Either the rain had slowed or the leaks were not as bad as they'd originally seemed, because the drips were slow and infrequent, and it was clear that unless things worsened appreciably between now and dawn, the existing containers would be more than able to handle the problem.

"Maybe we should stay awake," Beth said. "Watch a movie or something. Make sure that no other leaks spring up."

"It's three o'clock! We'll be dead in the morning with only three hours of sleep."

"What if the couch gets ruined?"

"What are you going to do? Stare at the ceiling all night

long? That'll put you to sleep quicker than anything else. Besides, I think the worst of the storm's over."

He was right. The rain appeared to have tapered off, and the last peal of thunder had seemed farther away.

"I don't know." Beth yawned.

"See?" Hunt said. "Let's go back to bed."

But he could sleep only fitfully, tossing and turning, waking up every twenty minutes or so, and in the one dream he remembered upon awaking, a large stoop-shouldered man in a hat that shadowed his face looked at his watch and said in a sing-songy Southern accent, "It's half past a monkey's ass, a quarter to his ba-wuls."

2

Ordinarily, Steve slept through everything. Nina was a light sleeper, but she'd long ago learned that it was better to just lie awake by herself than to wake him up. He'd taught her that much.

Something had changed, though. Either the stress was getting to him or this storm was a hell of a lot louder than most, because he jerked awake to the sound of hard thunder, heart pounding in his chest. Rain splattered furiously in haillike strikes against the window, creating a muffled roar on the roof.

The addition!

He sat bolt upright in bed. As always, Nina was wide awake next to him. "Why didn't you wake me up?" he demanded.

"I—" she began, but he didn't wait for her simpering answer. Swearing, he threw off the covers, slipped on his pants, shirt, and slippers, and sped down the hall. He'd tarped the new room when he'd finished work this evening the way he always did, but he hadn't heard the weather forecast tonight and had made no effort to tie the tarps down or weatherize the addition against a possible storm. The tarps could have all blown away by now, and the wind and rain could be battering his new plaster job on the west wall. He'd left exposed wires out there, too. The water could cause plenty of damage.

Not to mention the lightning.

There was a sustained flash, an almost simultaneous crack of thunder.

He was such an asshole, such a stupid stubborn asshole. If something happened, it was his own fault. That insurance salesman had come by again today at lunch, offering home-owner's coverage, and Steve had turned him down flat. It was a dumb move, and he'd known it even at the time, was aware he was slitting his own throat even as he did it. He had no insurance to speak of, only a simple policy from a fly-by-night company he'd gotten out of the yellow pages after those bastards at All Homes had dropped him. And the policy the salesman offered seemed legit, seemed good. But the man's dogged persistence seemed annoying rather than admirable, and Steve had almost physically thrown him off county property, telling him to leave him the fuck alone.

Now he wished he *had* purchased that insurance. The addition was supposed to be covered by his new policy—at least partially—but there were so many exception clauses that if the addition did sustain some damage, he didn't know if the company would pay out at all.

He reached the end of the hall, quickly unlocked and opened the door, and for a brief second saw three of those big behatted men: one standing in the center of the addition, one on the lawn next to the sycamore tree, and one in the tree it-self, standing on the trunk at the fork of the branches.

Then the thunder hit with the sound of a rocket explosion, and the tree split in half. The improbability of the men and their positions was lost in the panicked realization that a large section of the tree was falling on the frame of his rumpus room and about to crush it. He ran forward blindly, stupidly, think-ing he could save his roof, wall and frame by somehow di-

verting the falling sycamore, but at the last minute a stronger
survival instinct made him swerve away from the toppling tree
and take refuge back in the house.

Lightning had not touched the tree, he realized. The section
of the tree had broken off while the thunder sounded.

Thunder couldn't splinter a tree, he thought. *Only lightning
could do that.*

Then that idea, too, was lost, as the heavy branches
smashed through the lone section of completed roof, bringing
water and leaves and plywood and two-by-fours down on the
rumpus room. A buttressing wall collapsed, taking wiring with
it, and sparks flew for a few brief seconds as his electrical
work was demolished before his eyes. A broken spiky branch
landed at the exact spot where he'd been headed before turning around.

Steve held the doorjamb for support. Gone. Weeks—no,
months—of work demolished in seconds.

Lightning flashed again, and he remembered to look for the
men in hats.

But they were not there—if they ever had been.

They were gone.

3

Hunt called their homeowner's insurance company first thing
in the morning, but there was already a telephone queue, and
he had to wait forty minutes until a real person came on the
line, listening to endless Whitney Houston, Mariah Carey, and
Celine Dion songs in the interim, putting up with annoyingly
regular "Your call is important to us, thanks for waiting" messages.

Finally, a customer service representative broke in during
the middle of a Kenny G solo with "This is Carole. May I have
your policy number?"

He gave it, and, after a pause, she said, "How may I help you?"

Hunt described the leaking roof and said that they needed someone to come out immediately and fix it before the next rainstorm hit.

"There are several homeowners in your area with nearly identical situations who have called in this morning to file claims," Carole said. "And I'm sure there are a lot of others who are with other insurance carriers and need similar assistance. So it may be a while before we're able to send someone out to assess the damage. There are only a limited number of qualified professionals we work with in your area."

"I understand," Hunt told her, trying to ingratiate himself with the woman and resenting the fact that he had to do so. He added, as if an afterthought, "You don't by any chance prioritize these things according to need, do you? Or severity? Because our roof seems to be in pretty bad shape. This isn't just a minor leak here. We have multiple leaks throughout the house. I'm just afraid the roof might be so compromised that it's dangerous."

"I'll note that, sir, and I promise we'll have someone out there as soon as possible."

No one came or called that day, or the next. On the third day, Wednesday, they were working in Flowing Wells, taking care of a tree that had fallen over a sidewalk during the storm, when he got a call that someone would be out to inspect the roof within an hour.

"We're almost done here," Edward told him when he explained the situation. "Go ahead. I'll cover for you." He grinned. "And when I happen to be MIA on the first day of deer hunting season, you'll do the same."

Hunt laughed. "Deal."

The man who came out to inspect the roof was sullen and surly. Hunt's original plan was to bond with the man, schmooze him, and maybe get bumped up a little higher on the to-do list, but the two of them just didn't connect. He was a tree trimmer, this guy was a roofer, they were both men who worked outside with their hands, but when push came to shove, he was a slumming computer operator, a white-collar worker pretending to be a blue-collar man, and the difference between them was glaring and obvious.

His name was Gary Donnell, the name of the company was Donnell Roofing, and Hunt had the feeling that he was the owner and sole employee. Dutifully, he followed the roofer around, pretending he knew what the man was doing when he scrutinized the now-dry spots on the ceiling, peered into the attic crawl space with a flashlight, or examined the top of the flat Santa Fe–style roof. Donnell did not speak much, and when Hunt tried to engage the man in conversation, he received only annoyed monosyllabic answers.

Finally, the inspection was done. "You need a whole new roof," Donnell said, writing out an estimate. "That's what I'm going to recommend, but I don't know if your insurance company's going to go for it. So they'll get back to you, and you get back to me."

"About how long do you think it'll be before everything's fixed?"

The roofer shrugged disinterestedly. "I don't know."

"What's your guess?"

"Don't have one." Donnell tore off a copy of the estimate and handed it to him. "Here. I'll fax a copy to your insurance company."

He'd been told that someone from his insurance company would contact him, but when a day passed and he still hadn't heard back, he called. He spent his entire lunch break on the phone, only to discover that no decision had yet been made. Yes, the roofer had faxed over the estimate, and, yes, the case had been assigned to a representative, but there were just too many claims to process. They would get back to him as soon as possible.

He called again the next day.

Then it was the weekend, and while he tried to call again on Saturday, a prerecorded voice informed him that the offices were closed. If it was an emergency, he could leave a message after the beep and someone would get back to him.

He left a message.

No one got back to him.

Someone finally did call on Monday to inform him that the request for a new roof had been turned down. The insurance company was willing to pay to have the leaks patched, but that was it.

"It's going to leak again the next time it rains," he told the woman. "The roof is shot. It would be a lot smarter and more cost effective if you redid the whole thing now instead of waiting for this to happen again."

"I'm sorry, sir. We pay for legitimate repairs to sustained damage. We do not pay for repairs to damage that has not yet occurred."

"It's called preventative maintenance."

"As I said, we take care of damage that actually occurs. It is up to you to maintain your own residence. We do not do that for you." Before he could argue further, she said, "We will contact the roofing company, let them know you are approved, and they will be out to repair the damage to your home as soon as possible. Thank you for choosing AHI." The line went dead.

Hunt was livid, and he was tempted to call back again, talk to the woman's supervisor and file a complaint, but under the circumstances he figured he'd better wait until all of the repairs were done and all of the bills were paid. Just in case.

Luckily, there was no rain for the next two weeks, because that's how long it took for Gary Donnell to return. As Hunt had suspected, Donnell Roofing was a one-man operation, and it took the roofer two days to finish what should have taken him only a few hours. When he was through, he left a big mess outside: nails on the lawn, scraps of tar paper on Beth's garden, black splatters on the back stoop and the front walkway.

Joel, Stacy, and Lilly came over for dinner that evening, and before the sun went down, he took Joel up on the roof to survey the job. It looked amateurish even by Hunt's low standards. A sloppy border of pitch ringed a square of tar paper that had been affixed over each leaking section of roof. Joel bent down and examined the first patch skeptically. "You actually think this is going to hold?"

"I hope so."

"After the first two rains, this is going to be leaking again. That's my prediction."

"Thanks."

"Did you or the roofer even test it? Spray some water up here with the hose or something?"

"To be honest," Hunt said, "I was afraid to. I know this is a supremely crappy job, but it's all I've got, and I don't want to put any unnecessary wear and tear on it. I want it to last as long as possible."

"Rots a ruck."

"Scooby-Doo!" Hunt exclaimed, pointing at him in the exaggerated manner they'd used as children.

"Close, but no cigar. Astro."

"I knew it was a dog."

"Let's get off this roof, go inside, and drink."

"Sounds like a plan."

After dinner, while the women and Lilly were in the kitchen talking or washing dishes or getting dessert ready or doing whatever it was they did, Hunt and Joel sat on the back patio looking up at the stars, trying to see the space station, which, according to the news, was supposed to be visible in the southern sky right about now. The talk turned, as it often seemed to these days, to insurance companies.

Joel reached down and picked up a triangular piece of tar paper from the concrete floor of the patio, flinging it across the backyard. "Did you hear, a couple years back, that either Wal-Mart or The Store was taking out insurance policies on its employees? So if an employee died, the company would get a death benefit?"

"You're lying."

"God's honest truth."

"That's like slave labor."

Joel nodded. "Tennessee Ernie Ford time."

The idea of it sent a chill down Hunt's back. The thought that someone could take out a life insurance policy on you without your knowledge was at once offensive and horrifying. Not only was it morally heinous, it was a gross violation of privacy. What was next? People taking out insurance policies on unsuspecting derelicts? Corporations betting that career criminals would bite the dust and pay off handsomely?

"Like I said, it was couple of years ago, and Wal-Mart or The Store or whoever it was took a lot of flak for it. But the insurance company that issued the policies got off unscathed. I guess the rationale was that they were an unknowing participant. But do you know what I read recently? That one insurance company, it might even have been the same one, was purposely issuing life insurance policies to violent career criminals, covering them for accidental death. These were guys who were uninsurable to anyone else, but this company allowed them to buy insurance so their wives or whatever could get some cash when they died. The catch was, though, that survivors got only half the benefits. The other half went to the insurance company. So they not only got the premiums but if they were forced to pay off, they got to keep half of it. I think the Justice Department shut them down, but I can't remember the exact details."

Insurance companies soliciting murderers? Hunt thought of legitimate claims like his own denied in order to finance elaborate schemes and scams designed to maximize profits and was filled with a righteous anger.

Joel must have been thinking along the same lines. "What we should do," he said, "is get together our own monkey-wrench gang and go after the insurance companies, damage *their* cars, put holes in *their* roofs, make *them* file insurance claims for *their* buildings and equipment. You, me, Jorge . . ."

"Dessert's ready!" Beth called from the dining room window. "Come back inside!"

Hunt and Joel roused themselves from their chairs and made their way into the kitchen, where they took cups of coffee and plates of pie and carried them out to the living room. The wives soon joined them, but Lilly remained in the kitchen, eating her pie in the breakfast nook and watching *Iron Chef* on Beth's kitchen television.

Hunt turned on the TV in the living room and switched the channel to a satellite radio station that played smooth jazz.

Beth motioned toward the kitchen. "Lilly's great," she said. "She's such a good kid."

Hunt nodded in agreement. "Yeah."

"So, do you two want kids?" Stacy asked. She looked from him to Beth and back again, and Hunt realized that he didn't know the answer to that question. He'd thought about it, of course, but not enough to have an opinion, and he and Beth had never discussed the subject with each other. He supposed that they might want a child in time, but certainly not for a while, not before they had a chance to spend some time together.

Beth performed a smooth save. "We're not thinking about that yet. Maybe eventually but not right away."

She gave his leg a small squeeze, and he was glad to discover that they were on the same wavelength.

Just the opposite of him and Eileen. Even when the two of them had gotten along, they had seldom if ever thought along the same lines.

Against his will, he'd been thinking a lot about his ex-wife lately. He supposed it was because he'd seen her at that bus stop. He still didn't know why she was back in Tucson, and at odd times he found himself wondering what she was doing, where she was going, whom she was with. It was a disinterested interest—he didn't really care, and he had no desire to see her ever again—but he kept it from Beth nonetheless, and for that he felt a little guilty.

He realized that although he'd known Beth for over a year now, though they'd been living together for nearly that long and were married, they were only in the infancy of their relationship. There were so many things about each other that they didn't know.

Like whether or not they planned to have children.

From across the coffee table, Joel grinned. "Wise decision," he said. "Have your fun first, *then* have children. Because afterward, your sex life will be . . . well, let's just say charitably that it will never be the same."

Stacy elbowed his side.

"Ow!"

"Serves you right."

"I heard that!" Lilly called from the kitchen, "Don't corrupt the youth!"

They all laughed.

The McCains left shortly after nine, waking up Lilly, who had fallen asleep on the couch, and half-carrying her out to the car. Hunt closed and locked the door behind them, then he and Beth went into the kitchen to do the dishes.

Beth was putting the leftover pie back into the refrigerator and Hunt was rinsing off plates, putting them into the dishwasher, when Courtney dashed into the kitchen and jumped onto the counter, back arched. A second later, there was a sharp sound from the guest room. A kind of quick snap, as of a whip cracking. He heard it, she heard it, but neither of them said a word and neither of them looked at each other. Instead, they both pretended it hadn't happened.

If they ever did have a child, Hunt thought, and they still

lived in this house, the guest room would have to be his or her bedroom.

He pushed the idea out of his mind.

There was another loud crack, and then the room was silent.

Hunt opened the dishwasher and started putting away the plates and glasses that Beth rinsed out in the sink. He looked out the kitchen window as he accepted a salad bowl from her, but all he could see was his own reflection against an inky blackness. His reflection looked transparent, like a ghost, and he glanced away. He didn't like it.

"I had fun tonight," Beth said, and gave him a kiss on the cheek.

"I had fun, too."

Eileen had never kissed him spontaneously after they'd gotten married, he remembered. She had when they were dating, but all that had stopped after they left college.

Things were different now, though. And he was much happier.

He was happier, but was he *happy*? Hunt asked himself.

Yes, he answered. All things considered, he was.

4

Jorge sat on the couch, sorting through the mail and drinking one of Ynez's fruit-and-vegetable concoctions. Orange mango carrot this time.

He never should have gotten her that juicer for Christmas.

On the coffee table before him was a Carlos Fuentes novel that he hadn't read before and that he'd been trying to get through for the past week. Ordinarily, he would have finished a Fuentes book in a few days, spending every spare minute drinking in that wonderful language, basking in the invigorating politics, but lately he'd been having a hard time concentrating on anything deeper than the daily newspaper. He'd been tired and mentally sluggish, and instead of reading he'd found himself sitting in front of the TV, flipping channels and watching hours of various *Law & Order* reruns.

The stress of impending fatherhood, he assumed.

He separated the envelopes into two piles: one for him and one for Ynez. Hers were primarily ads for bed-and-bath stores, upscale catalogs of items they could never afford, and solicitations from various environmental groups, who appeared to be decimating entire forests in order to raise enough money to save trees. His were mostly bills. There was one from the gas company, one from the cable company, one from the electric company, one from Visa, one from Sears, one from—

—Dr. Bergman's office?

Frowning, Jorge opened the envelope. He read over the bill, then jumped off the couch and strode angrily into the kitchen, waving the piece of paper in front of him. "I don't believe this!" he said.

Ynez, cleaning the components of her juicer in the sink, looked up. "You don't believe what?"

"This says we owe five hundred and eighty-eight dollars for your amniocentesis!"

"What?" She stopped washing the strainer, wiped her hands on a dishrag and took the bill from his hands, looking it over. "That's supposed to be covered!"

"I know."

"We can't afford five hundred and eighty-eight dollars."

"Don't worry," he promised. "I'll get this straightened out."

But twenty minutes later, as he sat on hold, his arm becoming numb from lack of movement, the ear to which the phone was pressed growing hot and red, Jorge thought of Hunt's endless quixotic tilts at the insurance company windmill, his doomed efforts to find satisfaction for the wrongs perpetrated upon him, and he was overcome by the sinking feeling that they would end up paying out of pocket for Ynez's procedure.

Sure enough, after a long and heated discussion with the

flunky manning the phones, and then an equally long and equally heated discussion with his supervisor, Jorge was forced to concede defeat. Apparently, their medical policy had an exception clause in which the insurance company paid for amniocentesis only if the expectant mother was over forty years of age. Ynez was thirty-eight.

"The doctor said my wife was in the high-risk group because of her age," he tried to explain. "Amniocentesis is recommended for *all* women over thirty-five."

"Recommended but not required," the supervisor stated. "Read your policy. The wording is very specific and very clear."

"I don't believe this."

"We will continue to pay for all checkups and routine office visits. Minus your deductible, of course. It is only voluntary and elective procedures that are not covered by your policy."

"It was not voluntary," Jorge insisted. "The doctor required it. You can ask her. I can get a signed statement from her."

"I'm sorry."

"What about the birth? Will I be footing the bill for that, too?"

"No, Mr. Marquez. Delivery is covered in full."

There was no winning, and he didn't know where else to turn. After hanging up, he called Hunt, but Hunt and Beth must have gone somewhere because after six rings the machine answered. He didn't feel like talking to a tape recorder at this point, so he dropped the handset in its cradle, intending to call back later.

"So what does that mean?" Ynez asked. "We have to pay it?"

"It looks that way."

"But that's almost six hundred dollars. We can't afford that much."

Jorge shook his head, disgusted, disappointed, discouraged. "I don't think we have any choice."

Ten

1

Hunt had just come home and gone to the bathroom when the doorbell rang.

"I'll get it!" Beth called from the kitchen. But he was already out of the bathroom and in the living room, and they both reached the front door at the same time. The bell rang again, and Hunt opened it.

He stood in the doorway—a man in a hat, silhouetted against the setting sun.

For a brief second, Hunt considered slamming the door, locking it, and retreating to someplace safe deep in the house. It was an instinctive reaction, brought about by that silhouetted form, a primal archetypal figure he'd seen before but did not recognize.

Then the man stepped forward, and he was just a man. Nothing special, nothing frightening. Hunt's impulse disappeared as quickly as it had arrived, and he looked at the visitor, a fellow of average build, ordinary height, and pleasant countenance. He was wearing an old-time hat, the kind they used to wear in detective movies—what were they called? Homburgs? Fedoras?—which seemed odd but not particularly threatening, and he was carrying a thin leather briefcase that he held underneath his arm. "Yes?" Hunt said.

"Hello," the man said. "I'm your new insurance agent. I'm here about your new insurance."

"New insurance . . . ?" Hunt frowned, glanced around at Beth, who shook her head uncomprehendingly. "We don't have any new insurance."

"You will when you hear what I have to say. May I come in?"

Now Hunt did start to close the door. "I'm sorry," he said. "We're not interested."

"You will be. May I come in?"

"This isn't a good time. We're about ready to eat—"

"Only take a minute."

The guy was pushy. It was a requirement for the job, Hunt supposed, but there also seemed to be . . . something . . . else in it. An urgency. A need.

"You're not happy with your current auto policy, are you? Your health policy or homeowner's? Life and dental? Let me in and we'll talk about it."

"Look—" Hunt began.

"Come in," Beth said.

He looked at her in surprise. He'd been about to brush off the salesman in no uncertain terms—guys like him did not understand hints and subtle clues—and her decision to not only hear him out but invite him into the house came out of the blue. She met his gaze, and from the expression on her face it seemed that she was just as surprised by what she'd done as he was.

Hunt was forced to step aside as the man walked past him and, just for a second, there was a rush of cold air against his face. *Vampires* had to be invited into a victim's home, Hunt thought, and though he wasn't sure what made him think of that, the comparison seemed appropriate.

Once inside the house, the insurance agent was all business. He strode directly to the living room couch, sat down, took off his hat, and opened his briefcase on the coffee table, withdrawing a manila folder with "Hunt and Beth Jackson" stenciled across the top. Hunt didn't know how the agent had gotten their names, but just the fact that he *had* made Hunt angry. It was not only presumptuous but seemed like an invasion of privacy, and the idea that their capitulation was a foregone conclusion made him dead-set against buying any insurance from the man.

The agent took a pen out of his pocket, clicked it. "Now, there's just the two of you, right? No children in the immediate future? Say, the coming year?" He eyed them inquisitively.

"Uh . . . no," Beth said.

"Excellent, excellent." He began writing furiously on a piece of scratch paper, then filling in blank lines on a densely printed form. Over his bent head, Hunt met Beth's gaze and the two of them exchanged a look of bewilderment.

"Now, you were both born in Tucson and neither of you have any preexisting conditions . . ." He was talking to himself, not asking questions or looking for confirmation, and again Hunt wondered where and how he had gotten this information. "She: homeowner's, two claims . . . he: renter's, one claim . . ." The agent scrawled notes on the scratch paper and filled in the form. "Last boyfriend Tad . . . former wife Eileen . . ."

"Hey!" Hunt said.

The man held up a hand. "Almost done."

"As far as I'm concerned, you're done right now. I'm not interested in buying any insurance from you."

"Mr. Jackson, Mr. Jackson. We can beat any offer by any competing company and can save you up to fifty percent on your existing homeowner's insurance alone. I think it will be worth your while to hear me out."

"We're not interested," he told the agent.

"*I* am," Beth said, and this time she looked neither surprised nor bewildered but sure and certain of herself. She faced Hunt. "It won't hurt to listen."

"Exactly so," the agent agreed.

Hunt tried to appeal to Beth's common sense. "This is a door-to-door salesman. We don't know anything about him *or* his company."

The agent looked at Hunt with an expression of utmost gravity. "Let me assure you, Mr. Jackson, that we have been providing insurance to satisfied customers for far longer than all of our well-known competitors and have a sterling reputation for quality, fairness, reliability, and accountability. As I said, we have a very high customer satisfaction rating and an equally high AAIO rating. We take what we do very seriously, and we are very good at it." A note of the messianic had crept into the agent's voice. "Insurance is . . ." He breathed deeply, smiled. "A higher calling."

Hunt tried to shoot Beth an "I told you so" look, but she refused to meet his eyes.

"It's true! Insurance is at the root of *everything*. What do you think marriage is? Insurance against loneliness, insurance that love will last. Religion? Insurance against the afterlife, insurance of the soul's survival. The truth is that the universe is chaotic, life and everything in it impermanent, and the only way we can go on, the only way we can live our lives and go to our jobs and do the thousands of pointless tasks that keep this world functioning is if we have some assurance that if we do so everything will remain as is. We need a stable guaranteed order placed on this disordered and transitory existence." He gestured expansively. "And that is the purpose of insurance."

Neither Hunt nor Beth knew what to say after that, and the agent did not allow them time for a response.

"I have a quote for you. Currently, you are paying eight hundred a year for your homeowner's insurance. Broken down, that's sixty-six sixty-six per month. We're prepared to offer better coverage with a lower deductible for only fifty dollars a month. And I can guarantee you that if your roof had started leaking under our watch, the entire roof would have been replaced immediately, with no charge to you other than the hundred-dollar deductible."

How did he know how much they paid for insurance? Hunt wondered. *How did he know about the roof?*

But Beth was already nodding approvingly. "Do you have any information about the policy? A brochure or anything? We'd like to read about it."

"By all means." The agent withdrew a pamphlet from his briefcase, handed it to them. "Here's a description of the coverage. Look it over, take all the time you need. If you have any questions, I'd be happy to answer them." He leaned back on the couch and read over the form on which he'd been writing to allow them time to read the pamphlet.

Heads together, they scanned the slickly printed brochure.

"This looks good," Beth said.

Reluctantly, he nodded.

The agent sat forward enthusiastically. "And that's not all . . ."

For the next twenty minutes, he spelled out the details of the homeowner's policy and explained the ways in which it differed from their current insurance. After he was done, Hunt had to admit that it did sound like far better coverage than what they had right now.

Beth glanced over at him, eyebrows raised. "What do you think?"

"If you two would like a moment to yourselves . . ." the agent said. "To discuss this . . ."

Hunt already knew Beth's opinion. And against his better judgment, he found himself in agreement. "That won't be necessary," he said.

Beth smiled. "We'll take it."

"Excellent. Now, if I could just have you sign these forms and date them, we should be all set." He pushed a pen and series of papers toward both of them. Small red arrows affixed to each page indicated where they were supposed to initial and sign.

Not reading the fine print on contracts had gotten him into trouble before, so Hunt took the time to read through each page. There was a *lot* of fine print. It all seemed to be pretty standard, though. He wasn't a lawyer, but to his surprise there didn't appear to be any hidden minefields or trickily worded time bombs that would substantially affect their coverage.

Beth was more used to reading contracts than he was, and she went over her copy at the same time, but she was unable to find any concealed drawbacks either. She glanced over at him. "Looks okay to me," she said and started signing the top page.

What were they doing? Hunt had a moment of irrational panic as she put pen to paper, suddenly filled with the certainty that they should not be going through with this. Then Beth finished initialing and signing, handing the pen to him, and the moment passed. There was no reason for him to overreact. All they were doing was switching insurance companies, something that people did every day, something that they probably should have done after that debacle with the leaking roof.

How had he known?

Hunt initialed the pages indicated by the arrows and signed his own name on the line next to hers.

"Thank you." The agent collected the forms, placed them in the folder, then looked up. "Now, about automobile insurance . . ."

They spent the next half hour going over the differences in price, coverage, and benefits between their current UAI policy and the new policy being offered. Hunt didn't need much convincing. After what he and Joel had experienced—

Half past a monkey's ass, a quarter to his ba-wuls.

—he was ready and willing to dump UAI for someone else. Still, something about this still made him feel a little uneasy, and he had to keep telling himself that he could dump this company, too, if things didn't work out.

They signed the application.

"Okay. What about medical and dental? We have a comprehensive medical/dental/life insurance plan that would fit both your lifestyle and budget, and would provide you with the security you need in these days of economic uncertainty and rising medical costs."

Hunt's stomach was growling. They'd been sitting here for well over an hour, and it was long past his usual dinnertime. The drapes were still open, and outside dusk had become night. He stood. "I'm getting tired, and my brain doesn't want to think about insurance anymore. I think that's enough for one day."

Beth nodded. "It's getting late."

The agent closed his briefcase and nodded professionally. "Very well. Here's my card. Should you have any questions or concerns, feel free to give me a ring. I'm an insurance agent, so I'm on call twenty-four hours a day, seven days a week. Leave me a message, and I'll get back to you within the hour. Guaranteed. When you want to talk medical/dental/life, we'll arrange a meeting, and I'll set you up with the most comprehensive coverage available at any price."

"We get insurance through our work," Hunt said.

"Yes. Thank you, though," Beth told him.

He put his hat on and stood. "Your policies should arrive within the next two weeks. They'll arrive through the mail, but if you wish, I can come by and go over them personally with you."

"We'll see," Hunt said.

"It's no trouble at all, I'd be happy to do it. Just let me know." He paused, turned. "Are you sure you wouldn't like to purchase maybe a small supplemental policy to complement the coverage you receive through your employer? It can end up saving you a ton of money."

"No thanks."

"You might want to think about it—"

"No," Hunt repeated.

"Okay."

They accompanied him to the door, where he shook both of their hands. His touch was surprisingly warm and dry. Hunt had been expecting clammy, but it felt more like touching a leather glove that had been left out in the sun.

In the doorway, he turned once more. He stared at Beth, assessing something. "I really suggest that you purchase some supplemental dental insurance," he told Beth. "You never can tell when problems will arise that require extensive and expensive dental work. A lot of procedures that are absolutely necessary are considered cosmetic by many companies these days and are not covered."

"We're fine," she assured him.

"All right then. It's been a pleasure doing business with you." He tipped his detective's hat. "I'll be in touch."

Hunt closed the door and instinctively locked it. He suddenly realized that the agent had not given them his name. That was odd. Insurance sales was a cutthroat business, and agents were prone to plastering their names on pot holders and refrigerator magnets and any mundane household item that would hold print in order to emblazon themselves on their customers' consciousness. All he had been given was a card, and when he looked at it, there were only two words and a phone number: QUALITY INSURANCE 520-555-7734. He was not even sure if Quality Insurance was the name of the agent's business. It might be simply a description of the type insurance he was promising to provide—quality insurance as opposed to mediocre insurance.

Strange, Hunt thought. *Very strange indeed.*

2

Joel lay down on the couch, eating Cheez-Its and watching a game on television. A commercial came on for car insurance, and he picked up the remote, flipped the channel.

You couldn't avoid it. Those insurance companies were everywhere.

The front door opened, and Stacy and Beth walked in, each carrying a fully loaded Nordstrom's bag. He sat up. "Back already?"

Stacy frowned. "Where are Lilly and Kate? I thought you were supposed to be watching them."

"I am."

"Unless they're on television, I don't see how that's possible."

He chuckled. "They're upstairs in Lilly's room. And they don't want me spying on them. They're discussing important things."

Stacy put down her bag, hung her purse on the hall tree. "I thought you were supposed to get them out of the house and play with them outside."

"I tried. I offered to play some B-ball, but they turned me down. They didn't seem to be in a playing mood. Kate was upset about something and Lilly was being her shoulder to cry on, so I left them alone."

"They've been up there the entire time?"

"Well . . . yeah."

"Make yourself at home," Stacy told Beth. "I'm going up to see."

She took the stairs two at a time, and Beth put her bag down on the floor, sitting on the couch opposite Joel. "Sorry Hunt couldn't make it. But they had a chance for that overtime, and Jorge needs the money . . ."

"No biggie. Besides, baby-sitting isn't all it's cracked up to be."

She motioned toward the television and the Cheez-Its box. "Yeah," she said dryly. "Looks tough."

He laughed.

Stacy came down the stairs and into the family room. "They're fine. Listening to CDs."

Joel grinned. "Kicked you out, too, huh?"

"Yes, if you must know."

"And you thought I was a lax parent."

Stacy and Beth retired to the kitchen, and Joel turned his attention back to the game. Or tried to. But his mind wandered, and he found himself thinking about My Nguyen, the Vietnamese student who'd hit him in the parking lot. He'd seen her today on campus for the first time since the accident. He'd smiled and waved, wanting to show that there were no hard feelings, but she'd been deep in conversation with an oddly dressed man near the physical plant, and when she'd glimpsed him, she'd quickly turned around as if to hide from him. The man, a brawny, stoop-shouldered fellow wearing a hat, remained where he was, but the shadow of a tree fell across him and Joel could not make out his features.

Something about that bothered him.

It bothered him even more now, and he wished that he had walked over to Ms. Nguyen and spoken to her. Not because he particularly wanted to talk to her or had anything to say—but because he wanted to know who that man was.

Another commercial came on, and he went into the kitchen to get something to drink. Stacy and Beth were sitting across from each other at the breakfast table.

"My gum hurts," Beth said. "When I chew."

"Where?" Stacy leaned forward.

"Here." Beth opened wide, pointed to her upper left gum.

"It looks pretty red," Stacy admitted. "You ought to get it checked out."

"Yeah," Joel offered, opening the refrigerator. "I stopped going to the dentist for several years—until I met Stacy and she badgered me into it—and when I finally had a checkup, I had six cavities, three at the gum line, and it hurt like hell to get them fixed."

"I hear that," Beth said. "I don't even remember the last time I went to the dentist."

"Take care of your teeth and they'll take care of you," Stacy told them.

Joel found a Sam Adams and closed the refrigerator. Talk of dentists had reminded him of dental insurance, which reminded him of a strange pamphlet he'd received the other day in his box that touted the benefits of employment insurance, guaranteeing that the purchaser of such insurance would be immune to demotions, firings, and layoffs. It was a ridiculous joke, but he had to admit that the pamphlet was very well produced. That was one thing about home computers, they'd democratized publishing technology. He'd looked into the adjoining boxes of other department members, but his appeared to be the only one who'd received the brochure. One of his students, he'd assumed.

It was funny, and he thought of mentioning it to Stacy and Beth, but they were already onto another topic—the annoying obtrusiveness of department store salespeople—and he walked back into the family room. By the time he settled back into the loveseat and checked the score of the game, he had forgotten all about it.

3

"What's this?" Hunt asked as Edward handed him a printed flyer.

"Employees' association meeting. They're going to be talking about contracting out jobs in maintenance services. Our jobs, to be precise."

"I thought that was all over. I thought we won."

"Oh no. When the supervisors have an opportunity to hire private companies to do the jobs of public employees and throw a little business their friends' and relatives' way, they're not about to give up so easily."

Hunt read the flyer. The meeting was scheduled this afternoon at five, immediately after they clocked out. "Kind of short notice, isn't it?"

"It's an emergency. The subject came up at the board meeting last night, and word in the corp yard is that Steve gave us up, told them that the county could save money and there'd be no loss of services if they outsourced tree trimming."

"That son of a bitch!"

"Shit," Jorge mumbled.

"Yeah. So like I said, it's an emergency."

"I'll be there," Hunt promised, and after work, he carpooled with Edward to the Cholla Community Center, where the meeting was to be held. Jorge, as always these days, headed straight home, alone.

"Tell me what happens tomorrow," he said.

The association president and the union's part-time legal counsel were standing in front of the large room when they arrived. Other employees were filtering in, sitting in the folding chairs, office workers as well as field workers. There was a palpable sense of anxiety among the gathered men and women, and the individual conversations that collectively made up the buzz in the room were all concerned with budget cuts and job security. Rumors were flying about individual positions that would be cut, but the only discussions of wholesale layoffs or outsourcing seemed to revolve around maintenance services.

Finally, at five-twenty, the president called the meeting to order. There was no beating around the bush, no concessions to the niceties of procedure. He stated flat out that the rumors were true, that because of reduced revenues and incorrect projections there was going to be a $3.4 million budget shortfall this fiscal year and that the county intended to balance the budget on the backs of the employees.

"There are currently two proposals on the table," he said. "One involves a reduction in benefits. They're talking about cutting back on insurance coverage: either increasing co-payments and eliminating life, dental, vision, and cancer insurance; or limiting coverage to just the employee and not the employee's family."

There was a murmur of disapproval.

"The other is more specific. Contracting out a division of maintenance services—namely tree trimming."

Hunt was disheartened that this announcement was not greeted with a similarly unified reaction. Instead, the tree trimmers all voiced their dissatisfaction, but the majority of employees remained silent, apparently thankful that they would be spared and their jobs were not in jeopardy.

"We're here to see if we can come up with an alternate plan to present to them. One thing they're not going to go for are revenue enhancements or increased fees. That's not going to fly this year. So we have to find places to cut."

"Management!" someone in the back called out, and everyone laughed.

The next hour was spent brainstorming. The president wrote shouted suggestions on the board, and then the lawyer explained why each of them was not feasible. The more those two spoke, the more it became clear to Hunt that they were steering this discussion where *they* wanted it to go, that they had most likely made a decision already and they were going through the motions to pretend that it was a democratic solution agreed upon by the majority. He didn't like where this was headed, and one look at Edward's scowling face told him that his friend was thinking exactly the same thing.

At the end of the hour, it was obvious that the lawyer and the president thought the most sensible course of action was to let the Board of Supervisors outsource tree trimming. And they had not had to work too hard to convince the other employees of that.

One old-timer, not a tree trimmer but a warehouse supervisor, spoke up. "Let me get this straight. You're in *favor* of letting them cut jobs?"

The president held up his hands. "Now, we don't want *any* cuts. That's our position and we're sticking to it. But somewhere down the line, if we have to sacrifice a finger to save the hand . . . well, that's one of those hard choices we're going to have to give serious consideration."

"Bullshit!" Edward roared, and everyone turned to look at him.

The lawyer smiled thinly. "I'm sorry, Mr. . . . ?"

"I'm not giving you my name because you don't really care what it is! Let's just say I'm that finger you're thinking of sacrificing!"

The president cleared his throat. "That sort of talk is *way* premature—"

"I don't think it is, you spineless jellyfish! Your job is to represent our interests. You hire this rent-a-lawyer with the money from our dues to make sure that we're protected, and instead you're bending and spreading them for management!"

A buzz of agreement ran through the crowd.

"Now, hold on a minute, here!"

"No, you hold on. I've been trimming trees for the county for the past twelve years, and if I do say so myself, I do a damn good job. So do the other men on my crew. So do the other crews. We know these parks, we know these trees, and we know damn well that no one's going to do it better or cheaper than we do. This is all just politics. The supervisors want to look like they're doing something, want the public to think they're on the ball, so they're going to contract us out. They're going to use taxpayers' money to support a private business. And they'll probably hire a tree-trimming company owned by their cousins or brothers-in-law or something. It may seem cheaper at first, but a year from now, when no one's looking the company'll raise their prices, and they'll be paying more than they do now with us."

"We're still negotiating with the county," the president said. "And we don't want any jobs cut. That's our goal."

"If I'm laid off, I want a refund of all union dues I've paid over the past twelve years, because if you don't fight for my job, that means you collected that money under false pretenses. That means I paid for services I didn't get."

The other tree trimmers were nodding, voicing their support. "Damn right!" one of them shouted.

Hunt stood. He was not a rabble-rouser, was not a firebrand like Edward, but he too was angry. It disgusted him that the union that was supposed to fight for them was so passive, so unwilling to stand up for its members. They were a bunch of scared little sheep, and he had no respect for them whatsoever.

He addressed the association president. "I think the problem is that we don't have outside negotiators. We have him"— he pointed to the lawyer—"but he's only a consultant and you only use him to answer your legal questions. So we end up with employees sitting across the table from their bosses, and of course they're not going to bargain hard, because they're afraid of reprisals. Because *they're* concerned about offending management, *we're* left out to dry. Edward's right. This association is not doing its job."

"Our job," the president said, "is to do what's best for *all* employees, not to cut our nose off to spite our face."

Edward frowned. "Enough with the amputation imagery, you gutless weenie—"

There were peals of laughter throughout the crowd, and the president turned red.

Chris Hewett, another tree trimmer, pointed an angry finger at the president. "You're supposed to *fight* for all employees, not give up at the first sign of trouble."

"What do you suggest we do?" the president asked. "Go on strike?"

Hewett nodded. "If necessary."

"I'm not going on strike and jeopardizing my job for tree trimmers," a computer programmer said. "I can't afford it. I'm sorry, but that's the way it is."

Hunt looked over at the man and was glad he had not transferred over to MIS. He might lose his job, but he felt proud to be aligned with Edward and Chris and the rest of the tree trimmers. These were good men, honest men, and he had no doubt that if the shoe were on the other foot, most of them would be willing to put their jobs on the line in order to help out their fellow employees.

"Your job's not even needed!" Jack Hardy, Hewitt's crewmate, shouted out. "They'd save a lot more money if they contracted out you guys instead of us!"

The room erupted in chaos, other maintenance services employees, fearful of a trend, siding with Hewitt and Hardy against the technocrats in MIS.

Edward put a hand on his shoulder, motioned toward the exit. "It's the Do Long Bridge. There's no one in charge here."

"We'll see what we can do!" the lawyer promised from the front of the room. "Everyone's job is important!"

"Come on," Edward said disgustedly. "Let's go find a bar and get drunk."

Eleven

1

Beth had just finished picking the last of her ripe tomatoes when the alarm clock sounded in the kitchen.

She carried the tomatoes inside and shut off the alarm. She tended to lose herself in her garden, so to tether herself to the real world, she'd taken to setting the clock when she needed to be somewhere or do something at a specific time.

Today she had to go to the dentist.

While she knew that she should have been going all along, getting regular checkups and cleanings, she'd let it slide for so long that, eventually she'd been afraid to go, afraid she'd have cavities or need a root canal or be subjected to some sort of *Marathon Man*-ish procedure. But the pain in her gums had gotten so bad that if she chewed anything on the left side of her mouth it hurt like hell, and Hunt had finally convinced her to get it checked out.

She had no regular dentist, so she'd called the customer service number listed on her insurance card and got the name and number of a participating dentist. That had been nearly three weeks ago. She'd tried to get an earlier appointment, had impressed upon the receptionist the extent and severity of her pain, had argued that this was an emergency and needed immediate attention, but the woman had doggedly insisted that the schedule was completely booked and she could not possibly fit Beth in until the end of the month at the earliest.

Beth washed off her tomatoes, placed them on the counter to dry, then went to get dressed and brush her teeth. She'd been obsessively brushing her teeth ever since she'd made the appointment—three times a day at the minimum, sometimes up to six—as though a last-minute flurry of good dental hygiene would negate the years of inattention and reverse the problem affecting her mouth.

She brushed, flossed, gargled with Listerine, then went into the bedroom and sorted through her purse to make sure she had her insurance card and enough money for the co-payment.

The dentist's office was not located in a medical center or suite of offices but rather in a converted adobe house. What had once been a residential street had been widened into a commercial boulevard, and many of the former homes had become businesses. There was an interior decorator, a tax accountant, even a café. The outside of the dentist's office still retained the look of a family residence, but the interior had been completely remodeled and did not bear even the slightest resemblance to a home. There was a surprisingly large waiting room dominated by a huge aquarium populated with primary-colored saltwater fish, and behind an open sliding glass window a receptionist spoke on the phone to what sounded like a very insistent patient demanding an appointment at an unavailable time. There was no one else in the waiting room, but from behind the closed door next to the receptionist's window, Beth heard the unmistakable high-pitched whine of a drill cutting through tooth.

She signed in at the window, then headed over to one of the yellow vinyl couches against the wall. On the table next to her was a stack of *Maxim*, *Details*, and *FHM* magazines. Not the usual dentist's office fare, but she picked one up and glanced through an article on fetish websites.

"Mrs. Jackson?"

She still wasn't used to having Hunt's last name, and though she heard the receptionist's voice, she didn't immediately realize that she was being called.

"Mrs. Jackson?" the receptionist said again, a little louder.

Beth quickly put down the magazine and stood up, embarrassed. A dental assistant was holding open the door and had in her hand a file folder. "Right this way," she said, smiling.

Beth followed the young woman past the receptionist's desk, down a short corridor to a small exam room, where she awkwardly contorted herself into the dental chair and then allowed a wax-paper bib to be clipped around her neck with a metal chain. The assistant—Dora, according to her name tag—swung a metal tray holding several wicked-looking instruments into place above Beth's chest. "The doctor will be with you shortly," she said before stepping out of the room.

Beth waited, remembering all too clearly why she'd been avoiding dentists for the past decade. Her mouth was already filling with too much saliva, and she imagined what it was going to feel like when the dentist began working on her teeth and the saliva puddled up in the back of her throat, threatening to choke her as she waited for some suction.

God, she hated dentists.

There was a jaunty knock on the wood of the open door, and Dr. Blackburn breezed in, smelling of Old Spice and Listerine. He could easily have been a television game-show host from the 1960s. He had the plastic, perfect-smile, every-hair-in-place look of a Bob Eubanks or a Wink Martindale. When he came closer, though, and sat down on the round stool next to her, she saw there was a cowlick on the left side of his parted hair that refused to remain down. It was not an Alfalfa, but it was obvious and completely out of place. There was something disturbing about that, and as he talked to her, asked her questions about her dental history, she could not help focusing on that one wild section of hair. It bothered her. It seemed so at odds with the rest of the dentist's appearance, so out of character, that it seemed *wrong*, and though she didn't know why, it made her feel uneasy.

Another assistant came into the exam room—not Dora—and there was something not right about her, either. She was wearing the prim white uniform of a dental hygienist, but her eyes had far too much mascara, her lips were too red, and there was an incongruously sharp-nosed, white-trash cast to her features. She looked like a character in a porno movie, the nasty nurse who would take her clothes off for a patient and then get drilled on top of a rising dentist's chair.

Dr. Blackburn spoke quietly to his assistant for a second, then flipped on the swivel-armed light above the chair and turned back to Beth. "Open wide," he said. She did so, and he poked and prodded the teeth on her upper left side with a metal pick until he found a spot that made her flinch.

"Does that hurt?" he asked.

"Uh-huh," she grunted.

He adjusted the light, exchanged his pick for another equally sharp tool and then propped her mouth open with a rubber wedge. The suction hose was turned on, hung over her lip, and he began to systematically examine the rest of her mouth. Once more he muttered something unintelligible to his assistant, then he started wiggling each of her teeth with his fingers. On several, it felt as though he slid a band or clamp over them. He used the sharp pointy tool to painfully trace her gum line.

Something was wrong.

"What are you doing?" she tried to say, but her mouth was still propped open, the suction hose was vacuuming out her saliva, and it came out more like, *"Uh ah oo oo eh?"*

"We're going to have to replace your teeth," the dentist said.

What?

A bolt of panic shot through her. She tried to protest, tried to tell him that there was no way she'd agree to anything so extreme or radical, but again the words sounded like gibberish. The dentist seemed perfectly able to understand her, however, and he pressed her down with one restraining arm when she tried to sit up. "I'm sorry. Tooth decay is so far advanced and you have so many cavities and such enamel loss, not to mention your rotting roots, receding gums, and gingivitis, that I'm afraid such a drastic course of action is necessary. Besides, my hands are tied. It's these new regulations and insurance company requirements. Even if such a procedure *were* feasible in your instance, I'm not allowed to cap; it's considered cosmetic and your insurance won't pay for that. I'm also required to treat distressed mouths aggressively. It's part of their preventative maintenance program. If I find evidence of widespread tooth decay, I have to do everything I can to immediately resolve the problem." The assistant—Rene, Beth could now see her name tag said—handed the dentist a steel hypodermic, and he maneuvered it into her mouth, the needle pressing painfully against the inside of her cheek. "Don't worry. This won't hurt a bit."

Preventative maintenance.

The phrase leaped out at her. That's what Hunt had insisted the homeowner's insurance company do for the house when he wanted them to pay for replacing the whole roof, and as the relaxing drug spread through, her body, loosening her muscles, loosening her mind, the thought occurred to her that this was payback, the insurance companies were getting together in order to punish them for complaining and demanding their rights. Collusion. Wasn't that illegal? Already her thought processes were breaking down, and her brain began leapfrogging from one paranoid scenario to another: the insurance companies were after them . . . and the AMA . . . and the credit card companies . . . and the car manufacturers . . . and the ADA . . . and the government . . .

Before she went completely under, she could have sworn she heard the dentist singing a strange little ditty. "Pussy for breakfast, pussy for lunch, pussy for dinner and a midnight snack."

"I love the taste of balls in the morning," the dental assistant said from somewhere far away.

When she came to, she was in the waiting room, propped up in one of the couches. Her entire skull throbbed. She opened her eyes and stared dumbly for several minutes at the fish tank. Air bubbles from the filter, she noticed, percolated upward from between a set of upper and lower teeth that sat flat on the blue gravel, moving up and down as though laughing.

All of a sudden the receptionist was next to her and helping her stand up. "Come on, Mrs. Jackson. It's time to go now."

She was dopey and she knew she was dopey, and a part of her thought that it was unprofessional and possibly illegal for the dentist to be sending her out like this, but she didn't have the will or the wherewithal to argue, and she allowed herself to be led out docilely. The receptionist did not even accompany her out to the car. She positioned Beth on the front porch of the office, then went back inside, closing the door behind her.

Feeling unsteady, her head suffused with a dull pulsing pain, she walked down the porch steps and then around the side of the building to the tiny parking lot. Her mouth was dry, and she kept running her tongue over her lips and teeth, but the teeth felt strange. Too cold, for one thing. And they had a faint taste that was almost familiar.

Concentrating hard, trying to focus on each menial task before her so that the drugs in her system didn't entirely overwhelm her ability to function, she took the key ring out of her purse and carefully unlocked the driver's side door. She got into the car, sat in the seat, pulled down the visor, and opened her mouth to look at herself in the mirror.

All of her teeth were shining, sparkling silver.

*　　　*　　　*

Beth was on the bed and crying when Hunt got home. She'd called him from the car, blurting out the entire story between sobs, and he asked her to stay where she was; he'd leave work early and meet her there. But she hadn't wanted to wait by the dentist's office—she'd been *afraid* to remain anywhere near it—and she told Hunt she was going home.

Once again he had Edward and Jorge cover for him, and he sped from the west to the east side of Tucson as fast as the midday traffic would allow.

He was stunned when he saw her mouth. She'd described it to him over the phone, and he'd believed her, but he hadn't been able to imagine how freakish and horrible it looked, hadn't been able to anticipate the way it changed the appearance of her entire face. Her nose now seemed off center, her cheeks chubby. She looked ugly, and if he did not know her as well as he did, he was not sure he'd be able to recognize her. To top it all off, her lips were swollen grotesquely, and she kept dabbing her mouth with an ice-filled washcloth to stem the bleeding.

All of this must have shown on his face, because the second she caught his expression, she was sobbing anew. He rushed forward and sat down beside her, cradling her in his arms. "Don't worry," he said. "We'll get this fixed. I don't know what possessed that lunatic or how he thought he'd get away with something like this."

"I didn't even consent."

"Of course not."

"I mean to the procedure at all. I wouldn't let someone yank my teeth out without getting a second opinion. But I didn't even have a chance to tell him. They were drugging me and putting me under, and when I woke up, I was like this."

"How's the pain?" he asked gently.

She closed her eyes for a moment, took a deep breath. "Unbearable. And the anesthetic hasn't even worn off yet. Once it does . . ." She left the sentence unfinished.

"They can't get away with this." Hunt felt like smashing his fist against the wall in frustration. He had never felt so powerless or so overwhelmed. This made no sense. Absolutely none at all. There was no reason for anyone to do something like this to Beth. She had no enemies, and no one could profit from knocking all her teeth out and replacing them with silver posts.

Was the dentist insane?

It seemed a distinct possibility.

"We're going back there," Hunt said. He went to the closet and got out his camera and camcorder. "I'm recording the whole fucking thing, and we'll see those bastards in court. I don't care if they fix your teeth and then get on their knees and kiss our asses till their tongues are brown. This should not have happened in the first place and, goddamn it, they're going to pay."

Beth managed a small swollen-lipped smile.

"Let's go."

The address and directions to the dentist's were still in Beth's car. The vinyl of the driver's seat was spattered with drops of blood that had leaked from her mouth on the drive home, and Hunt wiped them up with napkins from the glove compartment before taking off. "You shouldn't have driven in your state," he said as he backed out of the driveway. "You could've gotten in an accident."

Beth took the washcloth away from her mouth. "It would've been *their* fault," she told him.

"True enough. But you would've been the one hurt. Or killed."

"I wasn't staying there. I couldn't stay there."

He nodded, understanding.

The dentist's office was gone when they returned.

That was impossible. It had only been a few hours, and there was no way that all of the furniture and equipment could have been moved out of the building in that short a time. But there were no shades on the windows, and they could see through the dusty glass that the rooms were empty, the walls bare, the floors uncarpeted. The house was just a house, a vacant structure waiting to be converted into some small business like the other dwellings on the block.

They both got out of the car and walked up the concrete path to the front porch. "This was it, I swear it!" Beth insisted.

"I believe you."

"But how could this happen? An hour ago, two hours at the most, there was a waiting room with rugs and couches, and a five-hundred-pound aquarium. There was a receptionist's desk and several exam rooms filled with dentist's chairs and sinks and lights and cabinets."

It *couldn't* happen. They both knew that, and later Hunt supposed that that was the moment when he started to realize he was up against more than just an out-of-control corporation, that something far less concrete was at work here, something closer to supernatural than natural. But that thought wasn't conscious, not yet, and in response to her question, he said, "I don't know."

The house next door was an accountant's office, and though it appeared to be closed and a sign on the door said "By Appointment Only," Hunt rang the bell and knocked, hoping to find someone who could give him a little background on the dentist, tell him how long the dental office had been there or what had happened to it. But no one was at the accountant's, and the travel agency on the opposite side was closed, too. Across the boulevard, a smoothie shop was open, but the employees inside knew nothing about the dentist's office and hadn't seen anything unusual at that location today.

There was nothing to do but leave. Beth's head was really throbbing now, and the anesthetic was wearing off enough that she was starting to feel spasms of agony from individual points in her gums where old teeth had been pulled out and the silver posts had been jammed in. She kept a bottle of Tylenol in her purse, but she'd already taken two doses and the acetamino-

phen did not seem to be working, so before heading home,
they stopped by the offices of Beth's regular GP, Dr. Panjee. It
was getting late and she didn't have an appointment, and the
way things were going, neither of them would have been surprised had the doctor and his staff told her to go to the emergency room of the hospital. But she looked pathetic and needy
enough to rouse their sympathy, and the office manager was
able to fit her in before a late patient arrived.

Dr. Panjee was appalled by what had happened, but after a
careful examination, he had to admit that technically the dentist had done a good job. He applied a topical clotting agent to
her gums to stem the bleeding, and gave Beth a prescription
for some heavy-duty medication that he said would numb the
pain and not interfere too much with ordinary day-to-day living. He told them to have the prescription filled tomorrow, and
gave her several samples of another painkiller for the evening.
That was quite a bit stronger and would knock her out for most
of the night.

"Thank God," Beth said.

"You're going to be okay," Dr. Panjee reassured her.

"Yeah. Except for my silver teeth."

By the time they got home, it was not yet five, and after
making sure Beth was comfortably ensconced in the couch in
front of the television, Hunt took her insurance card and immediately headed for the phone. Their DentaPlus Plan was
part of the larger HealthPlus, a company with headquarters on
the West Coast. That meant they were still open, and he dialed
the customer service number on the back of the card.

"I hate dealing with those insurance company people," he
told her.

"Who doesn't?" She paused. "Give 'em hell."

"Oh, I will. I will."

After an uncharacteristically short wait, he was rescued
from the endless loop of the automated phone system by a

flesh-and-blood customer service rep. "Hello, DentaPlus. How may I help you?"

"Hello," Hunt said curtly. "To whom am I speaking?"

"My name's Tim," replied the young man at the other end of the line.

"Listen, Tim. My name's Hunt Jackson. My wife Beth called this number three weeks ago to find the name of a dentist in our area that is part of our HMO and would take her insurance—"

"Could I have the group number and member number off her insurance card?"

"No," Hunt snapped. "I'll give you that information afterward. First, you're going to sit there and listen while I tell you what happened."

"Sir—"

"Listen! She went to this dentist, Dr. Blackburn, and I know it sounds crazy but he yanked out all her teeth and replaced them with silver dentures or caps or whatever they're called. Fake teeth. Now her mouth's all swollen and bloody and she has these silver teeth that she didn't even agree to. Basically, she was drugged and mutilated. Now the dentist's disappeared. I want some information on this guy, and I want some satisfaction. You recommended him, so obviously he's part of your HMO, and I want him taken out of there. I want him prosecuted and disbarred—or whatever they do to dentists."

There'd been no response on the other end of the line, no acknowledgment of understanding or even a courtesy "Uh-huh." Only silence. Hunt didn't like that. He wasn't sure if Tim was still there, but he kept talking anyway.

"I also expect you *not* to pay him for this travesty of a procedure that was done to my wife and to find someone to fix it. I don't care what you have to do or how you have to do it, but she'd better have normal-looking teeth again instead of the metal mouth that monster gave her."

"These are serious accusations. I'll need your wife's name, and the group number and member number off her card."

"Her name is Beth Jackson. J-A-C-K-S-O-N. The group number is 44135. Her member number is A476B3588."

"Can you tell me the time of the visit?" Hunt heard the man's voice slide upward into a twangy Southern accent and suddenly felt cold. "That's okay," he said. "I know." Hunt heard the tapping of computer keys. "Half past a monkey's ass, a quarter to his *ba-wuls*."

Hunt hung up quickly, filled with a wild rush of unexplainable fear. Everything that had happened suddenly seemed a lot less random, a lot more interconnected.

"What is it?" Beth asked. "What happened?"

His heart was still pounding, but he immediately called back. He expected to get a normal customer service rep after going through the automated phone system, a person on the line to whom he could logically and comfortingly make his complaint. But the same man answered on the first ring, and before Hunt could even get a word out, he was shouting. "I told you not to call me here! Stop harassing me!"

"I'm—" Hunt began, flustered.

The man laughed. "Moron," he said. "Half-wit."

"Get me your supervisor," Hunt ordered.

"No."

"What?"

"I know what you look like when you're taking a shit," the man said nastily. "There's a photo in the file of you wiping your ass!"

Anger, white-hot and pure, blew away any leftover shred of fear. "I want to speak to your supervisor right now!" Hunt demanded. "I'm not going to put up with—"

"I'm sorry. We're closed." There was a click and a dial tone.

Hunt tried to call back, but three times in a row, the line was busy. Finally, it rang, but a recording stated: "Our office is closed. Hours are eight A.M. to five P.M. Pacific time. Please call again."

He hung up the phone and stared for a moment out the living room window at the house across the street. A photo of him wiping his ass. It was such a bizarre thing to bring up, a strange thing even to think. He knew the man was just trying to get to him, just trying to rattle his cage, and he didn't believe it, but . . .

On an impulse, he reached for the white pages next to the telephone. He turned to the Hs and flipped through the tissue-thin pages until he found what he was looking for.

Beth's medication was already starting to take effect. "What's going on?" she asked groggily.

"They're closed."

"So what are we going to do now?"

"We're going to the HealthPlus offices here in Tucson. We'll confront them in person."

"Now?"

"Tomorrow," he said.

She leaned back in the couch and closed her eyes. "Good," she said. "I'm too tired today."

The HealthPlus offices were not in a downtown high-rise as he'd expected but in a single-story pink stucco building located between an art gallery and a resort on Ina Road. They pulled up next to a green curb in front of the building where stenciled letters read: 20 MINUTE PARKING.

"It better not take us any longer than that," Hunt said. "And if it does and we get a ticket, they're paying for it. We wouldn't even *be* here if it wasn't for their incompetence."

Beth took his hand and tried to smile. "I like that attitude. Go get 'em, tiger."

The sprawling structure had several entrances, and they followed a sign with an arrow to a wing marked ADMINISTRATION. Hunt demanded to see whoever was in charge—CEO, president, district manager, whatever they had—but the secretary at the front desk pawned them off on a man named Ted Peary who was identified to them as the HealthPlus "Customer Liaison." Hunt made short work of him, and they moved up the ladder to Bill Chocek, head of the Customer Services division, before being transferred to Vice President Kenley Cansdale's office.

Luckily, Beth's lips were still swollen, the gums above her silver teeth raw and red, and it made everyone very uncomfortable to face her while discussing her problem. They all kept passing the buck upward until finally the two of them were in a boardroom, meeting with a group of upper-echelon managers headed by HealthPlus's Southwest Regional Director, Ryan Fielding. Hunt and Beth stood at the foot of a very long cherrywood table and explained for the fifth time what had happened, emphasizing that the psycho dentist had been recommended by someone at the insurance company and was a member of the DentaPlus network.

"Now, I know you're in a position to make decisions," Hunt said, "and I want that dentist found and punished."

"And I want my teeth fixed," Beth told them.

"Well, it's not our policy to second-guess the opinions of our highly qualified doctors and dentists," Fielding explained. Around him, the other men nodded.

Beth slammed a fist down on the table. "What?"

"We trust the experts in regard to specific procedures and treatments. We do not make medical or dental decisions. Those we leave up to the doctors and dentists."

"Look at my teeth!" she cried.

"It is not our fault that you're dissatisfied with the results of your dental work."

" 'Dissatisfied with the results'?" Hunt shook his head incredulously. "Are you blind?"

"I'm a freak!" Beth screamed at them.

Mr. Fielding nodded sincerely. "I understand. And we'll do

everything in our power to rectify the unfortunate outcome of this misunderstanding. But I must reinforce the fact that we have done nothing wrong. I'm not implying that you're litigious people or that you have any hidden agenda, but our agreeing to pay for a new procedure, in essence paying for the same procedure twice, in no way implies that we are in any way liable or responsible for mistakes that may or may not have been made by your original dentist."

Hunt took her hand. "Then you *will* pay for her teeth to be fixed?"

"Of course."

"What about Dr. Blackburn?"

"There will be an investigation, and if it is determined that he acted unethically or illegally, as you suggest, then he will be dealt with in the appropriate manner."

"'Dealt with.' That's kind of vague."

"He will face disciplinary action from a peer review board. If the offense is grievous enough, he will lose his license, and, if warranted, criminal charges may be filed against him. I trust that you will find that satisfactory?"

Of course it wasn't, but what did they expect? The past could not be undone, and the best they could hope for was that the problem be remedied.

There was no graceful way for them to exit. If they said thank you, it implied that they had been granted a favor, that they were in the board's debt. If they showed no gratitude but simply acquiesced to Fielding's proposal, they were effectively cutting off the possibility of any future legal action. If they turned the director down, the insurance company would not pay to fix Beth's teeth. It was damned if they did, damned if they didn't.

"Fine," Hunt said tersely, and still holding Beth's hand, the two of them walked out of the boardroom, back through the corridors and out of the building to where their car waited in its twenty-minute space with a parking ticket fluttering on its windshield.

2

The man who stood in the doorway of Joel's office was of average height and build, with the forgettable features of a career bureaucrat, but the fact that he suddenly just *appeared* out of nowhere caused Joel to start. He regained his composure almost immediately, however, and looked at the stranger with what he hoped was an expression of authority. "Hello. May I help you?"

"May I help *you*?" the man said, and walked uninvited into the office. "I was wondering if you had a chance to look over the information I provided regarding employment insurance."

Was this a joke? It had to be, but the man was not one of his students, indeed did not look like a student at all, and there was about him an air of experienced professionalism that led Joel to take him seriously. "I thought that was a prank by one of my students," he said.

The man looked offended. "You thought our employment insurance was a prank?" He shook his head in annoyed disbelief. "If you had bothered to read the provided information, you would have learned that this new and innovative coverage was created in order to provide career security in this highly unstable work environment, a security that every American was once able to count upon but that has become increasingly scarce in our current economy."

Joel still found it hard to believe that this was real, but the man's earnest demeanor seemed to indicate that it was. "I have tenure," he said, going along. "I wouldn't have any use for such insurance."

"Perhaps you have other insurance needs that I would be able to help you with."

"I'm sorry," Joel said.

"Come on. I *know* you're not happy with your automobile insurance. You're with UAI, correct?"

Joel grew suspicious. "How do you know that?"

"A good insurance agent gets to know the needs of his clients," the man said. "That's the only way to effectively provide the type of tailored coverage that suits your individual needs. Now, if I may be so bold as to make a suggestion—"

Behind the insurance salesman, a shaven-headed kid in dark baggy clothes had walked up and was milling around the corridor outside of the office. Luis Monteros. A sullen gang-banger who sat in the back of his Tuesday/Thursday class and was headed straight for the probation list, Luis was ordinarily the last person Joel would want to see on his office hour. But right now he was a savior, and Joel motioned him in, grateful to have an excuse to kick out the insurance agent.

"I'm sorry," he said, "but I have a student conference right now. Why don't you just leave your card, and I'll get back to you."

The expression on the man's face was cold and hard, and for a brief, wild second Joel was actually afraid of him. The agent seemed filled with an irrational hostility toward Joel and more than capable of doing something about it. Then the moment passed, and with the plastic smile of the practiced salesman, the man took out a card and handed it over.

QUALITY INSURANCE, the card read.

A phone number was listed, but that was it, and Joel was about to ask the man his name, when Luis pushed his way into the office. The agent slipped back out into the corridor. It suddenly seemed important that Joel find out who the agent was. "Who should I ask for if I call?" he shouted.

The agent smiled, waved.

And was gone.

3

Beth refused to look at herself in the mirror as she fixed her hair. She brushed it intuitively, by rote, doing everything she could to avoid looking at her mouth.

It was possible to forget for brief periods of time that she had metal teeth, particularly when she was around Hunt or her friends. But such respites were short-lived. Any deviation from the routine of her daily life, even so small a detour as a simple trip to the store, turned out to be a horrific disaster. She felt like Quasimodo, a monster among men, an object of gossip and ridicule, and she was acutely conscious of the stares— and the avoidance.

The swelling in her lips had gone down and the pain in her gums had settled into a low-level discomfort, but according to Dr. Mirza, her new oral surgeon, it would be at least another month or two before she had healed sufficiently for him to extract the silver teeth and replace them with more realistic-looking enamel facsimiles.

As it turned out, they were having to pay a good deal out-of-pocket for the upcoming operation. The insurance company was willing to cover only the cost of a procedure equal to or less than the original. As if anticipating that this would occur, Dr. Blackburn had charged a ridiculously low amount for the first removal and replacement, and Dr. Mirza's estimate could not come close to that price. She and Hunt were still fighting DentaPlus on this, but they both knew that the result was a foregone conclusion, and they'd resigned themselves to making up the difference. Once all appeals had been exhausted, she suggested that they sue, and Hunt thought that was a good idea, too. At the very least, a lawsuit might encourage the company to settle and pay up what they owed rather than risk the bad publicity.

She finished combing her hair and quickly put on some lipstick. She *had* to look at her mouth for that, and while she chose a color that would de-emphasize her lips and applied it carefully, she still did so as fast as possible. Grabbing her purse, she walked out of the bedroom, shouted out a quick good-bye to Courtney, then locked up the house and walked out to her car, preparing to leave for work.

It was early in the morning, most people were inside their homes getting ready for work or already gone and on their way, but next door Ed Brett was hosing off his Lexus while his youngest boy sat on the curb, throwing gravel into the street.

Beth was on pretty good terms with most of her neighbors. The family on the right had been there since the subdivision had been developed, and they had welcomed her to the neighborhood by throwing a party shortly after she moved in so that she could meet some of the people on the street. They weren't friends, but they were friendly, and she fed their dog when they were away on vacation. They watered her plants and watched out for her place when she was gone. The two old Molokan sisters across the street often stopped by to chat while she was pulling weeds or trimming her plants in the front yard, and at least every other weekend, she went over to their house for tea. The young man in the house next to them, a mechanic who spent most of his spare time working on a motorcycle in his garage, was always nice to her, although they'd never socialized.

But she had never liked the neighbors on her left, the Bretts. They'd moved in about a year ago, buying the house from Tom and Jan Kraal, who'd been her closest friends on the block and who had moved to Tarzana, California, when Tom's company had transferred him. She'd tried at first to make friends with them. Everyone on the street had. But Sally Brett was a harried housewife who seldom left the confines of her home, and her husband Ed was a rude and belligerent boor who soon alienated most of the people on the block. Their two sons were spoiled brats with a powerful sense of entitlement.

Beth noticed with annoyance that the boy was throwing

gravel right at the spot where she'd be backing up, but she didn't say anything. She unlocked and opened her car door.

"Hey!" the kid yelled at her. "What's wrong with your teeth?" He laughed and his father laughed, too.

Beth was suddenly filled with anger. She slammed the car door shut and walked over to where the boy sat on the curb. "That's not very polite," she said to him.

Ed Brett threw down his hose and strode over. "You can't talk to my boy like that!"

"He was being rude."

"He was just being honest. That's what kids do."

She should have left it alone, but she couldn't help herself. "Someone has to teach him some manners," she said. "He's certainly not learning them at home."

"What *is* wrong with your teeth?" Ed Brett squinted in mock puzzlement.

Beth closed her mouth and turned away, striding quickly back to her car, trying to keep back the hot tears that were stinging her eyes, trying to ignore the laughter of Ed Brett and his bratty son.

When she told Hunt that evening, he was furious. He wanted to go straight over there and make the man apologize. But antagonizing their neighbors wasn't going to make things any easier, and she convinced him to drop it and just let things slide.

"I'm oversensitive," she said. "I shouldn't let things like that get to me. It's just . . . these . . . teeth."

"I'd love you if they were green or brown or red, white, and blue."

"I know," she said, and gave him a quick kiss. "That's why I keep you around."

Twelve

1

Saturday, they awoke late, grateful for the chance at extra sleep. Hunt was up first, and he reached between Beth's legs, rubbed her, but she grumpily pushed his hand away. "Later," she mumbled. So he reached for the remote, turned on the television, and changed it to a channel that showed cartoons. *SpongeBob SquarePants* was on Nickelodeon, and he watched it for a while before heading out to the kitchen to feed Courtney and pop a bagel in the toaster for breakfast. Beth got up while he was reading the newspaper. She poured herself a glass of juice and, since her teeth still hurt, cooked some soft Cream of Wheat.

After breakfast, they planned to go to Home Depot and get a new rake and a couple of hanging plants for the back patio. Hunt showered and shaved, then quickly combed his hair and slipped into a pair of old jeans and a T-shirt. Beth put on her own weekend yardwork uniform. They opened the door—

—and the insurance agent was standing on the porch.

"I'm glad I found you home," he said, smiling broadly. "Your insurance policies have arrived. This is a big day indeed. May I come in?" He didn't wait for an answer but pushed past them into the living room.

They followed him. He seemed taller, Hunt thought. Something else was different about him, too, although it was not anything he could put his finger on.

The agent stepped between the couch and the coffee table, placing his briefcase on the tabletop. He looked at Beth, frowning in an exaggerated manner. "What in the world happened to your mouth, Mrs. Jackson? No offense, but it's a disaster area in there."

She covered her mouth with her hand, embarrassed, a hot flush blooming on her cheeks.

"Now, wait a minute," Hunt sad angrily.

"That problem would not have occurred had you availed yourself of our supplemental dental insurance, as I suggested, and it could be fixed tomorrow should you sign up for one of our many excellent dental plans. We work with only the best dentists and oral surgeons. In fact, we audition *them*. Ordinarily, it's the doctors and dentists who decide whether or not they will accept insurance coverage from a specific carrier. But in our case, *we* decide whether or not we will allow our customers to be seen by a given practitioner. That's why we have access to the best and the brightest in all of the medical and dental disciplines." He smiled engagingly. "We'll get to that, though. Don't worry. First, let's look over your brand-new, freshly issued policies, shall we?" He was already opening his briefcase and taking out two slickly printed booklets, laying them out lovingly on the coffee table. "I'd like to go over this with you, if I may. You might have a few questions regarding your coverage that I would be more than happy to answer." He motioned toward the couch. "Sit, sit."

Compliantly, they sat down. The agent handed them each a copy of the first booklet, perfect bound and with an olive green cover. "This is a copy of your new homeowner's policy. I'd like you to turn to page one and make sure that your names are spelled correctly, then we'll go on to page two and begin looking at the terms and conditions of the policy and how they will affect you."

Curious, Hunt opened the booklet and looked at the top of the page for the name of the issuing company.

The Insurance Group.

The Insurance Group? That was it? He riffled through the pages, scanning the documents for another name or a more detailed description but found none. He'd thought that knowing the name of the insurance company for which the agent worked would make him feel better, would put a corporate face on their new policies and allow him to feel more secure, but the name was so generic as to be suspicious.

"You work for The Insurance Group?" Hunt asked.

"Yes, indeed I do." The agent grinned. "And a finer organization I could not ask to be affiliated with. Now, let's turn to page two, paragraph one . . ."

It took nearly fifteen minutes for him to describe the information on that page. Hunt's eyes glazed over after the first fifty seconds, but the agent was rapturously delineating the variety of benefits they would receive under different scenarios, speaking so quickly and forcefully that neither he nor Beth could get a word in edgewise. Hunt flipped to the end of the booklet. There were thirty-five more pages to go. Not to mention the other policy booklet lying on the table.

He put his foot down. "We're a little busy here today," he said. "Why don't you just leave the policies with us, we'll look them over and if we have any questions, we'll call."

The agent seemed disappointed. He was clearly enjoying giving them his in-depth description of every minute detail. But he recovered quickly and collected the policies, handing the booklets to them. "I understand," he said. "Sometimes, with something like this, you'd just like to experience it for yourself in the privacy of your own home. Perfectly understandable.

"Now, let's see what we can do about solving your other problems."

As before, he took out a single-spaced form and a piece of

scratch paper. He muttered unintelligibly to himself, wrote furiously, then looked up at them, beaming. "Okay. We can provide both of you with a comprehensive dental/medical package—Denta-Med, we call it—for what I think will be a fraction of the cost charged by our closest competitor."

"That sounds great, but even if we wanted to switch, we couldn't," Hunt said. "I get my health and dental through work. She does, too. And both of our open enrollment periods aren't until fall. We're stuck with our plans until—"

"Wait a minute!" the agent said, shocked. "You two haven't even consolidated your policies? The moment you got married, the spouse with the most desirable package should have added on the other person as a dependant, and the other person should have taken those benefits deductions and switched them over to a deferred comp plan." He sorted through his briefcase, took out a sheaf of papers and several pens. "Now let me go over this with you."

"I'm sorry," Hunt said. "We're not interested."

Beth put a hand on his arm. "It won't hurt to listen."

"But we get our insurance through our work—"

"And you still can," the agent interrupted. "That's what I want to show you. For pennies more a month you can have the satisfaction and piece of mind that comes with knowing you are insured by the best, that you have the most comprehensive insurance available. And you don't have to wait for open enrollment. How it works is this: we take over your existing policies, collecting the premiums paid by both you and your employer. We then send you a modest bill each month for the difference, and—voilà!—you're enrolled in the best program available at any price. Deregulation has allowed us to offer a wider variety of services than ever before and to utilize creative approaches to recruitment. It's a boon for the consumer, and men and women like yourselves who were previously locked into plans that might have turned out to be unsatisfactory when put to the test can now partake of the foremost insurance coverage in the county as documented by the AAIO twenty-five years running."

"Look," Hunt said firmly. "We're not looking for new in-surance. You can stop with the hard sell."

"You're not the one with silver teeth," Beth pointed out. She nodded toward the agent. "Go on."

He withdrew from his briefcase two small booklets and handed one to each of them. "This is the package of which I was speaking. If you'll turn to page one . . ."

It took nearly an hour for him to enumerate the benefits of the Denta-Med insurance, and after he was done, Hunt had to admit that it did sound like far better coverage than what either the county or Thompson Industries provided. Plus, if what the agent said was true, they would actually be saving money by consolidating their policies. Although they'd have to pay part of the premiums themselves, Beth would see substantially more money on her monthly paycheck because she would be on Hunt's plan and an employees' contribution to her insur-ance benefits would no longer be taken out.

"I like it," she said.

Hunt sighed. "Yeah. It sounds good."

"Excellent. I just happen to have the application right here. So if I could just get you to sign and initial it, we'll get the ball rolling."

Pen in hand, Hunt paused. "What if we change our minds? What if we want to opt out?"

"Ah," the agent said. "Well, in that case, I'm afraid you would have to wait until your usual open enrollment period as determined by your employers."

"So we're rolling the dice here."

"Not at all, not at all. Our customer satisfaction—"

"And your AAIO rating. I know, I know." Hunt met Beth's eyes, saw the determination there and, breathing deeply, signed the form. What did he care? He was hardly ever sick anyway. He probably wouldn't even use the insurance before the open enrollment period. Beth would be the guinea pig, and she's the one who wanted it.

They signed and dated four pages apiece, then traded and signed the others.

The agent took the forms from them, put them in his brief-case and closed it, placing the briefcase next to the couch. "Thank you very much. Here's my card, and, like I said, if there's anything I can do for you or if you have any questions, feel free to give me a call."

It was the same card he had given them before. QUALITY INSURANCE. Phone number. No name.

"If we do call," Hunt said, "whom do we ask for?"

"Why me, of course."

"No, I mean what's your name?"

He smiled. "Don't worry. I'll always be the one to answer the phone." He stood, shook both of their hands—

not quite so leathery

—and started toward the front door.

"Aren't you forgetting something?" Beth pointed to his briefcase.

He shook his head, smiling ruefully. "Sometimes I think I'd forget my head if it wasn't screwed on. Last week I forgot an application for term life and had to go all the way back to my office to get it."

"Absentmindedness is always a good quality in an insur-ance agent," Hunt said. "Inspires confidence."

The agent fixed him with a look so venomous, so com-pletely at odds with the friendly, enthusiastically helpful persona he'd been cultivating, that Hunt was taken aback. Beth, too, seemed startled. But the look was gone as quickly as it had come, replaced by the familiar cheerful expression they'd come to expect, and Hunt thought of a human mask being pulled over a monster's face.

For an instant, he thought, they'd seen behind the mask.

"I hope you enjoy your new policies," the agent told them,

picking up his briefcase. "Look them over, read them at your leisure, let me know if there's anything else I can do for you."

He turned just as he was about to step out the door. "Did I mention that we now offer employment insurance?"

Neither of them responded.

"It's not like unemployment insurance, it doesn't guarantee an income if you are temporarily out of work. Rather, it ensures that you will *not* be out of work, that your job will remain stable and secure, that you will not, let's say, lose your job to budget cuts or privatization." He smiled at Hunt. "Or resent your job because of extraneous factors at work." The smile turned toward Beth. "With this coverage, you will be guaranteed happy tenure in the job you love. And who can ask for anything more?"

Before either of them could respond, he was walking out the door. "I'll let you two talk it over. I have some other clients I'm supposed to meet with, but I'll be back this afternoon."

"No," Hunt insisted.

"We'll talk about it and we'll call you if we decide to take it," Beth promised.

He waved them away. "No problem at all, I'll be glad to do it. You're on my route back anyway. I'll stop by sometime after one."

"We might not be home," Beth cautioned him.

"That's okay. I'll wait."

"We're busy," Hunt said firmly. "Today is not a good day."

He finally seemed to take the hint. "Some other time, then." He waved and walked up the cement path to the street.

A pickup went by at that moment, so Hunt could not be sure, but he thought he heard the agent whistling.

2

"Employment insurance," Jorge said. "You ever hear of such a thing?"

They were in a remote part of a remote park where they very seldom worked, clearing a dead palo verde and four mesquite trees that had been uprooted during a flash flood several weeks ago. Jorge was using a shovel to dig an intransigent branch out of the solidified mud. Edward and Hunt were repositioning the logs that lined the hiking trail so they'd be able to bring in some heavier equipment.

"What kind of scam have you gotten yourself into?" Edward asked. "Next you're going to be telling us you're going to lose weight by taking pills you bought from an infomercial."

"I know," Jorge said. "Now I'm thinking we should've bought that supplemental health policy from someone else. Anyone who offers something like employment insurance can't be on the level."

"You can always cancel."

Hunt was being awfully quiet, and they both looked over at him, "Hey, bro," Jorge said. "It's not like you to be so silent. You've got to have an opinion on this."

"I was offered employment insurance, too."

"No shit?" Jorge was surprised . . . but at the same time not. Hunt's unusual behavior resonated with him, and he realized that his friend's uneasiness mirrored his own. "Who's your insurance agent?"

Hunt shook his head. "I don't know. I mean, I don't know his name. The company's called The Insurance Group."

"Did he just . . . show up? Walk in off the street and invite himself in your house and just stay there until you bought something?" Jorge was feeling chilled for some reason, discomfited.

"He didn't invite himself," Hunt said, more quietly. "We

invited him in." There seemed something ominous about the way he said it.

"Some guy off the street? What's wrong with you guys?" Edward asked "Jesus H. That's Consumerism 101. Never buy anything from a door-to-door salesman."

"We *didn't* buy employment insurance," Hunt told him.

"But you bought other insurance from him. Mark my words, nothing good can come from patronizing solicitors."

"As opposed to buying things off the Internet?" Jorge countered.

The big man shrugged. "Do what you like, it's your money. But don't come crying to me when it comes up and bites you on the ass."

Neither of them answered. Jorge didn't know about Hunt, but for his own part, he was more than half-convinced that Edward was absolutely right.

"He was here," was the first thing Ynez said when Jorge arrived home. She was upset, but he couldn't tell if she was angry or frightened or both. "He came at lunchtime."

"Who?" Jorge asked.

"That insurance agent."

This was getting weird. "What did he want?"

"He said we needed to buy *more* insurance, that if there are complications, we won't have enough to cover the delivery and all the related expenses."

"So what did you tell him?"

"I told him I'd talk to you about it. He gave me this pamphlet." She handed Jorge a slickly printed brochure.

It was the photo on the cover that caught his eye rather than the bold exclamatory words.

A newborn infant with an oozing gaping hole in its chest and batlike wings where the arms should be.

"This Could Happen to You!" the text proclaimed.

He looked up, sickened. Ynez started to cry. "I didn't know

what to do. He sat there and made me read it, and he wouldn't leave. He said I might have some questions, and he wanted to be there to answer them." She threw her arms around Jorge and held onto his neck, sobbing into his shoulder.

Jorge was filled with a white-hot rage. He opened the pamphlet and inside saw a photograph of a shrunken purple infant with an oddly bulbous head.

Ynez pulled away, wiping her eyes. "I think we should get it," she said.

"Hell with that. I'm canceling our supplemental insurance."

She grasped his arm. "No! You can't!"

"We'll get it from someone else. But I'm not giving in to these scare tactics. Like Edward said today, why would we buy *anything* from this guy? We don't know the first thing about him."

"I'll pay for it out of my own money, then!"

"Don't you see what's happening? You're doing exactly what he wants you to do." Jorge waved the pamphlet. "You're giving in to this."

"Everything will be covered," she beseeched him. "No matter what happens, we'll be able to get the best care." She held him, looked into his eyes. "It's our *son*. We have to think of what's best for him, not us."

She was right, but he was not sure that buying insurance from that creepy nameless agent *was* what was best for their child. Still, he understood her concern, and he told her that they'd keep the insurance until he was able to find alternative coverage.

"Just don't listen to that insurance agent," Jorge said. "If he comes back, don't let him talk you into anything, don't let him try to sell you any new insurance."

"Don't worry," she said, and he heard the fear in her voice. "If he comes back, I'm not even going to open the door."

3

"Hello!"

It took Hunt a moment to recognize the voice on the phone, and when he did, he was immediately put on edge.

The insurance agent.

"How are you today, Mr. Jackson? I'm just calling to give you a heads-up about a new type of coverage we're offering for a very limited time to our best and most loyal customers. Technically, it's a rider attached to our deluxe personal injury policy, which means that in order to qualify you will have to *purchase* a personal injury policy, but I guarantee that it will be worth your while."

Hunt sighed. "I'll bite. What is it?"

"Legal insurance."

"So . . . you'll pay for lawyers if I get sued or something?"

The agent laughed. "Legal fees are already covered under the appropriate policy, such as auto or home. No, this insures that you will not be falsely accused of a criminal act and will not be arrested if—"

"What the hell is this?"

"I'm trying to explain that, Mr. Jackson."

"Let's stop right here," Hunt said. "I don't know what kind of insurance company would offer something so ridiculous—"

"The Insurance Group is a consortium of well-established and highly respectable carriers."

"—but I can tell you that neither of us would waste a single penny on such crap."

"What is it?" Beth asked, poking her head out of the kitchen.

He put a hand over the mouthpiece of the phone. "Insurance agent," he said disgustedly.

"I really think you should discuss this with your wife," the agent said.

"Sorry. Not interested."

"I could come by and—"

"No," Hunt told him. "And please don't call again."

There was a long pause. "Very well. As I said, I would advise you to partake of this generous, limited-time offer, but the ultimate decision is, of course, up to you."

"Yes it is."

"May I just say, though, that you ignore your insurance needs at your own risk. Let me assure you that when tragedy strikes, when lives are disrupted due to natural or man-made catastrophes, it is not policemen or firemen who help put those lives back together. It is insurance men."

"Thanks for the civics lesson," Hunt said, and before the agent could say another word, he hung up the phone.

"What did he want?" Beth asked, wiping her hands on a dish towel.

"He wanted to sell us legal insurance, which would guarantee that we wouldn't be arrested and falsely imprisoned for crimes we did not commit."

"You're joking."

"Indeed I'm not."

She stared at him, at a loss for words, and he knew exactly how she felt. There was something unreal about all of this. No, not *un*real. *Sur*real. It was as if they'd suddenly been thrust into a *Twilight Zone* world where the rules of normalcy did not apply.

"Is this a real company?" Beth asked.

"I've been wondering the same thing. And I'm thinking maybe it's time we contacted the Better Business Bureau and made a few inquiries about The Insurance Group."

Thirteen

1

The next few days were busy and stressful for both Hunt and Beth, and on Wednesday night they decided to go to bed early and catch up on some much needed sleep. Hunt dozed off first. Beth remained awake awhile longer, reading a collection of horror stories by Barry Welch, but they were both sound asleep before ten o'clock.

They were awakened by policemen pounding on their front door.

The policemen didn't ring the doorbell, just knocked, and thinking about it later, Hunt found that odd. If the intent was to intimidate them, however, the tactic worked. That constant barrage of fists on wood and the shouted cries of "Open up! Police!" served to frighten them as they hurriedly put on robes and pants and went to answer the door.

"What if they're not really cops?" Beth whispered as they came close. "I saw that on the news once. Home invasion robbers pretended to be cops to get into the house. Then they raped and killed the family."

Hunt put his eye to the peephole. "They look like cops."

"Open up now or we'll have to break down the door!"

He started unhooking the latch.

"What are you doing?"

"They're going to knock down the door and get in anyway. If they *are* cops, we'll be better off if we're cooperative."

"And if they're not?"

He unlocked the door, and the second it opened, they were on him, two uniformed officers slamming him against the wall, yanking his arms behind his back and slapping handcuffs on his wrists. A punch to the side left him gasping for air, and a fist to the groin accompanied what was supposed to be a pat down. Beth was screaming, backing away, but he could not tell if it was fear or an effort to alert the neighbors that accounted for the edge of desperation in her cry. It sounded to him like she was saying something, not just screaming incoherently, but the pain in his balls and his side made it hard for him to concentrate.

He was whirled around to face forward, and he saw the two cops, one young and brash with a wide dumb face, the other older and tired but still crafty, like a weary Lee Van Cleef. Both looked like they wanted to beat the living hell out of him.

He sucked in breath. "What am I being charged with?"

The young cop pushed his dumb face right against Hunt's. "You are under arrest for child molestation, unlawful sexual congress, contributing to the delinquency of a minor and any other charges the DA sees fit to throw your way, you disgusting piece of shit."

"Hank," the older officer warned.

"I know, I know."

"We don't want to void this one."

"Whatever it is, I didn't do it," Hunt said. "There's been a mistake. You've got the wrong guy!"

"Don't say anything!" Beth ordered. "Wait until we get a lawyer!" She turned on the younger officer. "And I heard that 'piece of shit' remark, you piece of shit. And so help me God, when this all gets sorted out, you're going to pay through the fucking nose for it. We'll sue you, your department, the city,

and you'll end up scrubbing toilets in the park with your min-
imal wages garnished, you incompetent fucking asshole."

"Classy wife you got there," the cop told Hunt.

If he'd been tougher, if he'd been cooler, he would've responded, "She's got *your* number, dickwad." But he was
scared and confused, the handcuffs hurt like hell, and he didn't
want to antagonize these idiots even more. Obviously, this was
all part of some huge screwup, and the faster he was taken to
the police station, where he could explain the situation to
someone in charge, the quicker it would all be sorted out.

"What's your name?" Beth demanded. "What's your badge
number? Who's your commanding officer? I want all of that
information before you leave here."

"Your husband's a child molester and you're mad at us?
What kind of woman are you?"

"He's not a child molester, you assholes have made a *huge*
mistake, and I'll tell you the kind of woman I am: I'm the kind
that will not rest until unqualified thugs like you are thrown off
the police force."

Hank was obviously all set to argue, ready to go toe-to-toe
with her, but the older cop put a restraining hand on his shoulder. "Come on, we've gotta take him in."

"And why did you come in the middle of the night, huh?
Needed to cause a scene, have a show? Why didn't you arrest
him this afternoon? You couldn't've just found out about this
trumped-up charge just now. Why'd you wait until now to act
on it?"

Her fearlessness, her righteous anger, bolstered Hunt's own
confidence, blew away some of the cowed deference that had
started to settle over him. He was wearing nothing but jeans
and an unbelted bathrobe, and he held up his chin, met the eyes
of the older cop. "I want a shirt," he said "I'm not going to the
police station dressed like this."

"Oh yes you are," Hank said.

The older cop nodded. "We have plenty of orange jumpsuits that'll fit you." He turned Hunt around, pushed him toward the door. "Come on, get going."

"I'm coming," Beth promised. "I'll follow you in the car."

He wanted her to accompany him more than anything. He wanted a witness to this Kafkaesque nightmare just in case they tried to accuse him of something else. But he knew they weren't going to let her past the police station lobby. She wouldn't be with him when they fingerprinted him and took his picture. She'd be sitting on a bench, angry and frustrated, and there be nothing she'd be able to do for him.

He shook his head. "Find a lawyer," he told her, looking over his shoulder. "Get someone to get me out."

Now she was crying, and Hunt saw the young policeman smile. He wanted to kick in that bastard's teeth and wipe the smirk off his face. Beth drew on some inner reserve of strength and pulled herself together. "I'll find someone. I'll find out how to get bail." She glared at the young cop. "And Hank whatever-your-name-is? Badge number seven-seven-three? I'll be telling the lawyer all about you. And I'll see you in court."

The policemen pushed Hunt outside and held his head down as they forced him into the backseat of their cruiser. The rooftop lights were on and blinking—red blue, red blue, red blue—and they seemed to illuminate the entire street. Looking out the patrol car's window, he saw the faces of his neighbors peeking out at him from behind their living room curtains.

Great.

He was terrified that first night, so scared that he did not allow himself to fall asleep. He'd read enough books and seen enough movies to know how a "short eyes" was treated in prison. And while he wasn't technically in prison, was only in county jail, he was thrown in with the rest of the inmates in a general holding cell and left to fend for himself.

County jail.

He worked for the county, and he didn't think there was any

way possible to keep this secret from his coworkers, from his bosses. Even in an organization as large and diverse as county government, news and rumors spread quickly, and everyone was bound to find out. *Steve* was bound to find out. He'd probably lose his job, end up fired and unemployable.

No. He'd talk to the employees' association, find out what his rights were. He was only accused, not convicted, of a crime. And he was innocent to boot. Genuinely innocent. They couldn't fire him for that. And if they tried, he'd sue them from here to eternity.

This might be another nail in the division's coffin, though, the straw that would break the camel's back and give the higher-ups an excuse to contract out tree trimming. And there'd be no way to prove it. He might be able to contest a retaliatory firing based on false criminal charges, but he couldn't combat an impersonal budgetary layoff.

He'd half-expected a guard to come by, call out his name and announce that he was free to go, but obviously Beth was unable to find a lawyer at such a late hour and unable to convince the cops that this was all some hideous mistake. He had tried to talk some sense into the policemen at every turn, but the two who picked him up considered him a criminal and ignored him, the one who took his prints and his mug shots didn't care one way or the other, and the guard who led him to the holding cell probably heard exactly the same thing from every inmate he escorted.

It was the lack of communication with Beth that was the hardest. For all he knew, she had been murdered in a drive-by while talking to a bail bondsman, or killed in a car crash while racing home, or dragged off the sidewalk while walking to her car and raped in some alley. He knew his mind tended toward extreme scenarios, but the situation in which he found himself was extreme, and what he had learned from it was that absolutely anything was possible.

All the more frustrating was the fact that he was not even

sure of the specific crime he was supposed to have committed.
He knew he was being charged with child molestation, that he
had supposedly had sex with a little girl, but as for who and
where and when he had no clue. The police wouldn't elaborate. He would have to wait for his lawyer who, hopefully,
would show up in the morning.

Hunt made it through the night unharmed. Everyone ignored him and left him alone, and as he looked around at his
fellow inmates, he wondered if criminals were able to spot one
of their own, if they possessed some sort of sixth sense that allowed them to realize when an innocent man was in their
midst.

Who was he kidding? They hadn't beaten the shit out of
him only because they didn't know what he was in for. It was
as simple as that.

The lawyer did come in the morning. Midmorning, sometime after ten o'clock. His name was Raymond Jennings, and
he looked like a less pompous F. Lee Bailey. Hunt didn't know
how Beth had found him or chosen him, whether she'd asked
around and gotten recommendations or simply called the first
number in the Yellow Pages, but Jennings seemed like a good
guy, seemed competent and trustworthy, and he chose to believe that the lawyer was one of the best Tucson had to offer
and would have an easy time getting him out from under this
mess.

Hunt's exposure to the criminal justice system had been entirely through television and the movies, and he'd been expecting to meet with his lawyer either in a large cafeterialike
setting where numerous prisoners chatted with their loved
ones and legal representatives at long tables, or in a closed cubicle, talking on a phone while looking through safety glass.
The reality, though, was that they met in a room not unlike an
ordinary conference room, with a heavy table and four chairs
in the center, and a TV and VCR in front of a wall-long blackboard. Jennings was already seated at the head of the table

when a guard led Hunt into the room and unfastened his handcuffs, an array of papers laid out before him. He stood when Hunt entered, hand extended. "My name's Raymond Jennings. I'm your lawyer."

"Thank God." Hunt shook the offered hand, then sat heavily in a chair across from the attorney. "What in the hell am I being charged with?" he asked. "They wouldn't tell me any of the details. And since I'm completely innocent, I can't even figure out what I might have done that could possibly be misinterpreted as a crime. The only thing I can come up with is that they've got me mixed up with someone else and they arrested the wrong man by mistake."

Jennings picked up a police report from the pile of forms and documents spread over the table. "The alleged victim is a nine-year-old girl named Kate Gifford—"

Kate?

Lilly's friend?

Hunt felt as though he'd been sucker-punched in the stomach. "Jesus," he breathed. He slumped forward, let his arms fall to the table. He had not seen this one coming. It had not even been one of the increasingly remote possibilities he'd considered toward the end of last night's long, long stay in the holding cell.

"Her parents allege that there has been a pattern of inappropriate contact with the child over an extended but unspecified period of time, and that on yesterday morning, you orally copulated with the girl in Webster Park on a blanket behind a bush."

Her parents.

He had met Greg and Lana Gifford at Joel's New Year's Eve party. They both worked for Automated Interface, and not only were they nice people, but he and they had similar career backgrounds. He'd worked in computer operations and the two of them worked in programming, but there was a lot of common ground, and he found it invigorating after being away for so long to talk to people who were technologically literate. He liked the Giffords, and he'd hoped to see them again.

Her parents allege.

That meant Greg and Lana had filed the criminal complaint. He wanted to call Greg right now, talk man-to-man and sort out whatever misunderstanding had led to this totally wrong and outrageous conclusion. He would never do something so heinous, had never in his most perverse fantasies even considered such a horrendous thing, and he had the feeling that if he could talk to Greg, even talk to Lana, he'd be able to make them see that. They'd been lied to. This was a joke gone horribly wrong or a full-fledged plot by some unknown enemy to ruin his life. He'd been framed somehow, and he needed to prove that none of it had happened.

"It's a lie," he said angrily. "It's all a lie. I *was* at Webster Park yesterday morning—they got that part right—but I was working. I was trimming trees and I have two witnesses who can prove that this never happened. All three of us worked together, and we were never out of each other's sight. We left by noon. Whoever says otherwise is lying. Besides, that park's fifteen miles away from where Kate lives. How would she get there?"

"So you do know the girl?"

"She's the best friend of my best friend's daughter." He ran an exasperated hand through his hair. "I don't know what's going on here. None of this makes any sense."

"Well if you have two witnesses who can account for your whereabouts yesterday morning at all times—and I mean *all* times, without a single second unaccounted for—then that will help. But these are very serious charges, and I have to say that the case against you seems very strong and would play well to a jury."

"How's that possible? There's no evidence. There can't be. Whatever they have is completely fabricated."

"They have the girl's testimony. On tape. I just finished watching it, and it's pretty damning."

"Kate said this happened?" Hunt was stunned. "She says I . . . did that?"

Jennings nodded. "Yes. It's the basis for the complaint."

He blinked dumbly, trying to figure out why the girl would lie, what would make her say something so completely untrue. He'd naively assumed that the accusation had come from somewhere else and that Kate would be his main alibi, that as soon as the police talked to the girl she'd tell them that none of it had happened and they'd let him go and all would be right with the world. But obviously they'd talked to her before coming to arrest him, and he thought now that maybe she had come to them. Maybe she'd told her parents this lie and then they'd gone directly to the police.

But why?

"Can I see that tape?" Hunt asked.

"Of course." Jennings stood, withdrew a videocassette from its box. "But it doesn't look good." He walked to the front of the room, turned on the television and popped the tape into the machine.

It was almost in black-and-white, the color was so washed out, but the image was clear, the sound audible, and in the bottom right-hand corner was yesterday's date. Kate was seated at a small blue plastic table in a well-lit room. There was a large pad of paper in front of her and an assortment of pens, but she did not touch any of them. On the other side of the small table, crammed into an equally small chair, was an adult woman wearing a knee-length skirt. Only the bottom half of the woman was visible. The camera remained trained on Kate. She was not behaving like herself. She seemed solemn—traumatized, Beth would probably say—and Hunt suddenly had a very bad feeling about this.

There were no introductions, no explanations. The two were talking freely, referencing subjects they'd obviously vis-

ited before. This was apparently the middle of a much longer
conversation, and the tape had been wound to this point because this was where the important information was located,
this was the crux of the case.

Hunt realized that they were talking about a game of basketball he and Joel had played with Lilly and Kate. The
woman subtly changed the topic of conversation. "And what
was that other game you said Mr. Jackson liked to play with
you?"

"*Made* me play."

"Made you play."

Kate shrugged.

"You told me before."

"He made me play 'Lollipop,'" Kate said.

"What is 'Lollipop'?"

She squirmed uncomfortably. "I don't know."

"You can tell me, Kate."

She shook her head.

"The only way we'll be able to stop it is if you're honest
and tell us the truth."

She looked down at her hands, fidgeting in her lap. "He
pulls down his pants and tells me to pretend his peepee is a lollipop. He wants me to lick it."

"It's a lie!" Hunt shouted. "That never happened!"

He kicked over the chair, stomping blindly around the
room, hitting a wall with his fist. He knew now what was
meant when people said they wanted to tear out their hair. The
world had gone crazy, and his frustration level was so great
that he was unable to express it in any way that didn't involve
lashing out destructively.

". . . white stuff came out," Kate was saying on the tape.

"Turn that off!" Hunt ordered.

The lawyer pressed the power button on the television and
then ejected the videocassette. "Now you see what we're up
against."

"I've never even been alone with her! Not once!"

"I believe you," Jennings said.

Hunt took a deep breath. "She's a good kid, Kate. She really is. I don't know how they got her to say those lies or who put her up to it, but . . . it's not true!" He sat back down. "But she believes it," he said quietly. "Even I can see that. They brainwashed her somehow and she thinks it really happened."

"Yes." The lawyer patted his shoulder. "So long as you understand that, we can move forward. When I have clients who protest their innocence, half the battle is usually getting them to see how their case looks from the outside, how it will appear to a jury. You know already, which means that we can discuss strategy. What I'm going to do right now is get a statement from you, a point-by-point rebuttal to all accusations. I'll talk to your witnesses, then I'll come back, sort through what the DA has, what we have, and map out our legal strategy. My hope is that this will never have to go to trial. There's a bail hearing set for this afternoon, and I believe we'll be able to make bail. Once that first hurdle's cleared, I'll be meeting with the DA and we'll compare notes. I've worked with him before, he's a good guy. If what you've told me is true and all of your alibis pan out, we may be able to get the case dismissed."

"And if we can't?"

Jennings took out a portable tape recorder and a tablet of yellow legal-sized writing paper. "We'll cross that bridge when we come to it."

They spent the next forty-five minutes going over Hunt's side of the story, his recollection of names and dates, his refutation of all allegations. Finally, the attorney shut off the tape recorder, put away his pen and flipped back the pages of the legal tablet. "I think we have enough here to go on." He started clearing the table, putting away his papers. "It's nearly lunchtime, so if I'm going to get anything done before the bail hearing, I'd better go now. Keep going over everything in your mind and think about any discrepancies, any inconsistencies in the case against you, anything important that you might have forgotten to tell me. Sometimes details don't come when you want them to, sometimes pressure frightens them away."

Jennings closed his briefcase. He held out his hand. "Nice to meet you, Mr. Jackson. We'll be working very closely together for the next few days, maybe the next few weeks, so feel free to call me Ray. I'll be checking in with you at least twice a day, and I've arranged for a visitor's schedule. Your wife will be by to see you shortly after I leave, and she'll come again this evening. I will be there for your bail hearing, and possibly again later if something new comes up. If you *don't* hear from me, don't panic. I won't have forgotten you, I will still be working on your case. Jail and lack of communication do funny things to a man's mind, so just be aware that even though you're temporarily out of the loop and aren't aware of every little detail, wheels are still turning."

After he left, Hunt was led back to the holding cell by a guard. He felt better upon returning. Part of a lawyer's job, he knew, was to keep up the spirits of a client, to bolster the client's confidence, but Jennings's optimism seemed authentic, his analysis of the situation realistic, and from talking to the man, Hunt was convinced that he was an intelligent and highly capable attorney. Besides, if he had buoyed up Hunt's spirits so effectively, he was probably damn good at the rest of his job as well.

The bail hearing did not go his way. Because of the severity of the charges and Hunt's loose ties to the community, the judge refused to buy any of Jennings's arguments. She said that she considered Hunt a flight risk, and did not simply set bail high but denied it completely. Maybe this was his own prejudice showing, but Hunt had the feeling that if the judge had been a man instead of a woman, things might have gone differently. He was pretty sure that in the judge's eyes, he was guilty, a predatory pedophile, and he hoped to Christ that he got another judge if he went on trial.

If he went on trial.

For child molestation.

How could this be? He remembered a line from Albert Brooks's movie *Lost in America*: "We're in hell. When did we enter hell?"

Shortly after he was returned to the county facility, transferred out of the holding block and assigned his own jail cell, a guard unlocked the barred door, slapped some cuffs on him and, nightstick in hand, led him downstairs to a visiting room that really did look like one of those in a movie. There was a long expanse of bulletproof glass with little sections partitioned off for individual prisoners to meet with their lawyers or loved ones. He was led down the length of the room, past occupied and empty chairs to a small space at the end.

"You have a visitor," the guard intoned.

Hunt sat down.

It was the insurance agent.

He was waiting in the cubicle on the other side of the safety glass, and he picked up the intercom phone and gestured for Hunt to do the same. He looked different than he had before, not quite so nondescript. Maybe it was the harsh lighting, maybe it was just the setting, but he seemed a little harder than before, a little more assertive, less the ingratiating salesman and more the cutthroat businessman. There was a sharper cast to his features, and Hunt thought that the detective hat—

Fedora? Hamburg? Homburg?

—looked less silly, seemed to go more with his appearance. He was also wearing what looked like a trench coat, though it was a sunny day and quite warm. He was trying to cultivate an image, no doubt, something cinematic that he believed was impressive, but Hunt also thought that there was a less benign reason for the wardrobe, and he found himself thinking that the insurance agent really did have sort of an old-timey look about him, as though he belonged to another era.

Hunt stood up for a second, looked down the line of inmates and their visitors. He saw wives, sons, parents. Lawyers. But of course no insurance agents. Why the hell would an insurance agent visit someone in jail?

He sat down, looked at the man on the other side of the glass. Why indeed?

Against his better judgment, Hunt picked up the phone.

"How are you today, Mr. Jackson?"

"What do you mean, how am I? I'm in jail. I'm accused of a crime I didn't commit."

The agent shook his head in mock sympathy. "Mr. Jackson, Mr. Jackson. I'm not one for I-told-you-so's, but may I point out that if you had availed yourself of our offer of deluxe personal injury coverage with the legal insurance rider, I daresay this incident would not be happening to you right now."

"Is that why you're here?"

"Yes it is."

The man smiled in a way that was supposed to be sympathetic but was definitely not, and Hunt suddenly realized that this visit was not one of courtesy. He was being sent a message. The agent was behind these shocking charges. Or his company was. They'd done this to blackmail him into accepting their insurance, to flex their muscles and show him that he'd better play ball. What other reason could there be? If the agent was not involved somehow, he would not even know Hunt was here.

But how had it happened? What were the logistics? Could they have bribed the Giffords into lying? They definitely could not have bribed or intimidated Kate. From everything he could tell, the girl was bluntly honest and totally incorruptible. Besides, he'd seen that videotape. Kate thought he really had done those things.

So how had they convinced—no, *brainwashed*—the entire

family into believing that he had forced Kate into giving him oral sex?

There was no rational explanation, no reason he could come up with that made any logical sense.

The man was still smiling, and the sight chilled Hunt to the bone. Whatever was happening here, he was in way over his head. He thought of the guest room, the noises, the figure glimpsed in the mirror. There was an entire world of which, until recently, he'd been blissfully unaware. A world of shadows and substance, as Rod Serling used to say, and although he had never believed any of that mumbo-jumbo before, he did now, and it scared the hell out of him.

But he refused to show fear, refused to give the insurance agent the satisfaction. He sat there stone-faced, phone in hand, for several moments longer, and when the agent didn't say anything more, Hunt made as if to hang up.

"Wait!" the man cried, and Hunt was grateful to hear an edge of desperation in the tinny voice.

Once again, he put the phone to his ear.

"I'm here to offer you another chance," the agent said smoothly, and once again he was the ingratiating if overly earnest salesman.

"You want me to sign up again?"

"I'm afraid you're no longer eligible for legal insurance. No, the reason I'm here is to offer you protection against conviction. Again, you will be required to purchase a personal injury policy. Then, for a nominal fee that will be added on to your base premium you will be issued a supplemental policy that will insure you against any adverse judgment in a court of law."

"What exactly does that mean?"

"I think the coverage is pretty self-explanatory."

"You mean I won't get convicted?"

"Indeed, you won't. This is as far as it will go. You have been charged with this crime, but the charges will be dismissed or you will be found innocent, depending on the type of coverage you choose."

"That's impossible."

"No, it is not. As I told you before, we are a reputable firm with an outstanding reputation, and our policies, some of which are very targeted and precise, always insure our customers for exactly what the terms specify."

He stared at Hunt, and against his will, Hunt felt the stirrings of hope inside him. Hope was a dangerous emotion that more often than not led men into foolishness and peril, made them risk their lives and lose their wives and part with fortunes that they never recovered. He knew he was too close to this, was unable to look at his situation objectively, but he tried to analyze the offer and could not find any downside. Was this some sort of Faustian bargain? Was he being tricked into selling his soul when he purchased insurance? He didn't think so, but he would read the entire policy very carefully before he signed anything.

"How much extra would it be?" he asked.

The agent reached down below the level of the countertop and withdrew a calculator and an actuarial table from his briefcase on the floor. "Twenty dollars a month for personal injury, an extra ten for conviction. Combined, that's three hundred and sixty a year you'd be paying for peace of mind." He gestured around the visitors' room, but his motion took in the building beyond the walls. "You'd never see the inside of this place again."

"And it takes effect immediately?"

"Upon signing." The agent paused. "Of course, you do have to qualify."

There *was* a catch.

"What does that entail?" Hunt asked.

He shrugged. "You answer a few questions."

"That's it?"

"That's it."

Hunt thought hard, tried to see the offer from all angles. He had no idea how to estimate the efficacy of the unknowable, how to judge the merits of a promise that by any conventional yardstick was impossible to fulfill. But it *was* possible, he knew that now, and he needed a means by which to decide what was right and what was wrong.

What would his lawyer say? He wished Jennings were here right now. This was not exactly an ordinary legal question, in fact was so far out in left field that it was in another ballpark completely, but he trusted the attorney to look after his best interests, and he would like to have the impartial opinion of an experienced man.

As if reading his mind, the agent said softly, "I need your decision now. It's a onetime offer. Take it or leave it. I don't have time to wait."

He wished Beth were here.

"Mr. Jackson?"

"I'll take it."

The agent was all business. He took a ballpoint pen from his shirt pocket, clicked it. "All right. There are just a few questions I need to ask, some important information we need so we can determine whether or not you qualify for this coverage. You ready?"

Hunt nodded.

"Number one: how big is your wife's pussy?"

Hunt stared at him. This had to be a joke. But the agent gave no sign that this was anything other than a legitimate query.

Anger coursed through him. "What the hell does that have to do with anything?"

"We will ask the questions, Mr. Jackson. You will answer them."

"I'm not answering questions like that."

"Yes, you will."

"Next question."

"You still haven't answered the first one. How big is your wife's pussy?"

"Next question!"

"Come on. Is she tight down there, or do you have to strap a board to your ass to keep from falling in?" The agent snickered.

Hunt slammed down the phone. Looking through the window, he saw the insurance agent squint comically at a pinprick-sized hole he formed by the close convergence of his thumb and forefinger—then expand the hole until he needed two hands to make it and it encircled his head. He grinned.

Hunt spit at the glass, kicked over his chair, and walked away.

2

Joel stood on the back patio, looking over the roofs of his neighbors' houses at the rough pyramid shapes of the Rincon Mountains, their tan facades a hellish orange in the light of the setting sun. The temperature was dropping fast with the disappearance of daylight, but he made no move to go inside. Lilly was in there, and if he went back into the house he would be forced to have a conversation he did not want to have with his daughter. Better to stay out here until Stacy called him.

Cowardly, he knew, but he couldn't help it.

Joel looked up into the sky. Night had not yet overtaken day, but both the moon and Venus were out, shining brightly despite the dwindling presence of the sun. He remembered vividly when he'd first learned that that bright star was Venus. He'd been ten, and they'd gone on a family camping trip to Mt. Lemmon, bringing Hunt along. After dinner, after the sun went down, his parents had retired to their tent, but he and Hunt had remained outside, sitting on adjacent rocks. Hunt broke out a map of the night sky he'd brought along. He turned on his flashlight, trained it on the circular piece of thin plastic, then flipped off the switch. The map glowed in the dark, and Hunt rotated the map until he recognized the positions of the celestial bodies. He pointed to a bright star rising in the west. "That's Venus," he declared.

"That's the North Star," Joel said. It was what his father had told him.

"It's not north," Hunt pointed out. "And look at this map. See? Right here, it shows Venus."

Joel looked. "You're right," he admitted. He was shocked by the fact that his friend knew something his father didn't.

"Venus is usually the first star out," Hunt said matter-of-factly. "Although it's not really a star, it's a planet."

The location of Venus was still the extent of Joel's astronomical knowledge, and he still recalled perfectly the night he had learned it. Now he found himself wondering if Hunt had a window in his jail cell, if he could see the night sky.

Joel closed his eyes against a tension headache that had been pressuring his brain all day. There was no way in hell that Hunt was a child molester. He knew that as certainly as he knew his own phone number. Hell, since meeting Beth, even Hunt's ordinary casual interest in looking at other beautiful women seemed to have disappeared.

And he would testify in court that in all the times he'd been over to the house, Hunt had never once been alone together with either Kate or Lilly. Not even for a second.

Behind him, there was a click and a swish as the sliding glass door opened. He turned. "She's out of her room," Stacy said. "I think we should talk to her."

Joel nodded and followed his wife inside. Lilly had plopped down on the couch and was using the remote control to turn on the television. Stacy sat down next to her and gently took the remote from her hand. "We have to talk," she said.

Lilly shook her head. "I don't want to."

"I know you don't, sweetie, but this is important. We need to find out what really happened."

"I don't know!"

Joel sat down and faced his daughter. "You're her best friend. Did she say anything about this to you at all?"

Lilly looked uncomfortable.

"Honey?" Stacy prodded.

Lilly nodded unhappily. "Yeah."

"Yeah what?" Joel asked carefully. "She told you about it?"

"She said it was Mr. Jackson, but I knew it couldn't be because one time she called and told me right after it happened and Mr. Jackson was here with you." The words came out in a rush. Then she was silent, her face beet red with embarrassment.

Stacy touched her shoulder supportively. "Did she ever tell you anything else? Did you ever see anything when you two were at her house or at the park?"

"I saw a man once," she admitted. "At the park. We were riding bikes, and she saw him, too, and she stopped and turned around like real quick. I thought she might know him, it kind of seemed like she'd seen him before, but when I asked her she wouldn't talk about it."

Joel's pulse raced. "What did he look like?"

"I didn't see his face. He was standing by a tree and it was like, all dark, and all I could tell was that he was big and wearing, like, an old-time hat."

"Big?" Joel asked, worried by the word.

"Yeah. Like a football player or something. Well, maybe not *that* big, but kind of like that, you know? Not skinny. And he was kind of hunched over."

"Why didn't you tell us about this when it happened?" Stacy prodded.

Lilly shrugged uncomfortably.

"You thought we wouldn't let you go to the park anymore?"

She nodded.

Joel stood. "We have to tell the police."

Stacy put a hand on his arm, pulled him down. "This doesn't prove anything. It might help Hunt's case, but it doesn't prove that he didn't do anything."

Lilly looked her mother. "Did Uncle Hunt really do . . . that?"

"No, honey. We don't think he did."

"I don't either," Lilly said adamantly.

"But," she added softly, "Kate does."

3

The house seemed empty with Hunt—

in jail

—gone. Stacy had called to commiserate, and that had cheered her up a bit. Briefly. But she hadn't called any of her other friends because she hadn't known what to say. *Hello, I'm feeling depressed because my husband was arrested for child molestation?* She had never felt so alone in her life, and a call to her mother in Las Vegas, in desperate search for a shoulder to cry on, led only to the sharp-tongued "How well do you really know him anyway?"

"Well enough to know he didn't do it," she responded before hanging up, and it was true. Her one consolation throughout this hellish day was that she was absolutely positive of Hunt's innocence. There was not a doubt in her mind.

She was equally sure that the insurance agent had something to do with the trumped-up charges. Hunt thought so, too. As wacky as it might sound to an outsider, they both had no doubt that they were being taught a lesson, that they were being punished for refusing to partake of insurance they hadn't wanted and hadn't believed in.

That was their real crime. They hadn't believed. That's why

they were being subjected to this ordeal, that's why they were
being persecuted.

Why hadn't she listened to Hunt in the first place? Why had
she let the agent into their house? Why had she insisted on
buying a policy from him?

Beth snuggled next to Courtney on the couch. The cat
purred, pressed its moist nose against her hand.

Whether out of embarrassment or some twisted desire not
to burden his family with his problems, Hunt had forbidden
her to call his parents. And though she desperately wanted to
tell them, knew that they would have immediately flown out to
be there for their son and would probably be able to bring
some much needed experience to this battle, she abided by his
wishes and refrained from informing them, even though she
knew it was wrong.

So she was all alone in the house.

Just her and Courtney.

And the guest room.

The guest room had taken on an almost mythical status in
her mind the past two nights. She didn't exactly blame it for
what had happened, but it was an emblem of all that *could* happen, a symbol of that preternatural, paranormal realm that en-
compassed the insurance agent and all that he'd brought with
him.

Because it was haunted.

She never lost sight of that fact. Day or night she was always aware of it, and for the past two nights, alone in the
house with Hunt gone, that aspect of the room had been at the
forefront of her mind. She'd been spending most of her limited time at home camped out in the kitchen, as far away from
the guest room as possible, and when she went to bed at night
she left the light on in the master bathroom, the television on
in the bedroom, and closed and locked the door until morning.
She was only in the living room now because Courtney was
here, and she was so nervous that she kept sneaking glances

at the hallway, wishing that she'd turned a light on in there before the sun had gone down.

The phone rang, and she jumped. *Jumped a mile*, her father would have said. She picked up the phone and was about to say "Hello," but she heard a sound on the other end of the line, and it wasn't a voice. It wasn't even human. It was a low sort of whistle, like a nearly empty teakettle. She stood and dropped the telephone, backing away from it.

The room was calling her.

But there was no phone in the guest room.

From the fallen phone and from down the hall—in stereo— she heard the whistling sound spiral upward in tone. In her mind, she saw that figure from the mirror, that hulking stoop-shouldered man with the broad-brimmed hat. She had no doubt that if she braved the hallway and peeked into the guest room she would see that figure reflected in the glass, standing in the doorway, the same way it always was.

It lived in her house.

Whom could she call? What could she do?

There was a sudden rapping at the front door, and this time she not only jumped, she screamed.

"It's only me!" a voice announced from the other side of the door. "Your insurance agent! May I come in and speak with you?"

How big is your wife's pussy?

She thought of what Hunt had told her, and the fear did not abate but intensified. "No! Go away!"

"I thought this might be a good time to talk about some of your insurance needs."

A good time?

She ignored him, did not respond, hoping he would get the hint and leave. There were goose bumps on her arms. The insurance agent seemed as scary to her right now as the noises and specter in the guest room. If he had arranged for Hunt's framing and arrest, what else could he arrange? What more could he have planned?

"I thought you might want to purchase the employment insurance we talked about."

She remembered what he'd said when he'd try to sell them the insurance, that if they bought it they would not be outsourced or fired or end up resenting their jobs because of "extraneous factors at work." He'd smiled at her when he'd said that last part, and she remembered that smile now and it prickled the peach fuzz on the back of her neck.

"Can I come in?" he asked.

She refused to answer.

"You're busy," he called out. "I understand. I'll return later when your husband's here. He'll be back soon, and then we can go over all of your options."

He'll be back soon? Did the agent know something she didn't? Unreasonably, irrationally, hope bloomed within her.

"I'll be back next week!"

She peeked through the peephole, saw him back off the steps and tip his hat to her, as though he knew that she was watching him. He turned and strode jauntily up the walk, between the twin ocotillos that acted as an entryway to the yard, and then turned right on the sidewalk, heading around the corner of the block.

She didn't notice until he was gone from sight that the guest room was still whistling.

Beth awoke early, having set the alarm. The guest room had quieted down after an hour of that low strange whistling sound. She'd hung up the phone and it hadn't rung again, but the noise issued from the room itself until after ten, and only when it had finally stopped and not returned for forty-five minutes did she gather up her courage and go to bed. She did not dare check the guest room, but she was glad to see that the door to the room was closed, and she closed her own bedroom door, locked it and slept all night with the light on.

Beth walked into the kitchen, put on a pot of coffee, fed Courtney his morning Friskies, and popped a bagel in the toaster oven. She'd taken yesterday off to see Hunt and to get him a lawyer, and she wanted to take off today, too. But she had a limited number of vacation and sick days, and she had the feeling that she was going to need them later—when the trial started. There was nothing she could do today anyway, no way that she could help him, and since her visiting time was limited to a single half hour at five-thirty, it would be better for her to go back to work. If it turned out to be a busy day, so much the better. Work might take her mind off everything else. And it would certainly make the day go by faster than if she were alone, pacing around the house, endlessly going over everything in her mind, driving herself crazy.

She wondered if there was anything about this in the newspaper. The media loved to jump on molestation cases. She knew that Hunt was innocent, that all of the accusations were baseless, but she also knew how bad it would look for him in print, and she hoped to God that nothing got out that would taint the jury pool.

Beth let out a short sharp laugh, a spontaneous expression of frustration that shocked even herself. Gallows humor. She tried to imagine explaining to her friends and coworkers that the charges resulted from a manipulation of the truth by an evil insurance agent. How credible did that sound? An insurance salesman with supernatural powers had sold them a health and dental package, then offered them legal insurance, and when they declined had punished them by miraculously making Lilly's friend believe that Hunt had forced her to have oral sex with him? Just going over it in her mind, even knowing it to be true, it still sounded ridiculous.

She ate breakfast, got dressed, then put on her makeup and lipstick. Looking at herself in the bathroom mirror, Beth realized that, amazingly, improbably, she had already gotten used to her silver teeth. She didn't like them, would be overjoyed when once again she smiled and two rows of pearly whites shone back at her, but she was no longer as self-conscious about them as she had been, no longer dreaded going to work or going out in public because her mouth looked like a rap star's wet dream.

She had more important things to worry about now.

The rectangular glass skyscraper that housed Thompson Industries, the tallest in Tucson, looked forbidding as Beth drove up to it and under it, parking her car in the section of the underground lot reserved for employees. She sat in her car for several minutes, breathing deeply, trying to summon the nerve to get out and go to her office. Through the windshield, she saw Amy from Accounting and Gary Barnes chatting and laughing as they walked past the row of cars to the elevator.

Wiping her sweaty palms on her skirt, she waited for the elevator doors to close before getting out of the car. Bracing herself for confrontation, telling herself that any hostility was not directed at her personally but stemmed from that insurance agent's hideous machinations, she got into the elevator, pressed the button for the twelfth floor and waited, staring at the numbers as they lit up in sequential order. The elevator doors opened with a ding, and she stepped into the chaos that was the workaday environment of the Public Relations department.

Everyone knew.

She didn't know how they knew but they did, and she felt like a leper as crowds parted before her, as conversations stopped when she walked by. She continued forward, through the warren of cubicles, past the Xerox room and the photo lab, trying to look straight ahead and keep focusing in front of her, trying not to see the hostile glances directed her way or feel the heat of peripheral stares, trying not to hear the hurtful words whispered behind her back.

She reached her office.

Closed the door.

Locked it.

And burst into tears.

4

Morning dawned dull and gray through the high small windows of the county jail.

At breakfast, in the mess hall, a short fat man who looked like an accountant pushed his way past several inmates to sit next to Hunt on the bench. Hunt was forcing himself to gag down the runny eggs and cold toast, and he looked up when the man clanked his tray down next to his own. "Did you buy insurance?" the man asked.

Hunt's eyes widened in surprise.

"I was two windows down, talking to my wife. I saw you with the insurance agent."

In the warm stuffy room crammed with smelly human bodies, Hunt felt cold.

The fat man leaned forward. "Name's Del. I'm in for . . ." He shook his head. "Too many things to name."

Hunt cleared his throat. "How did you know he was an insurance agent?"

"How do you think I got here?"

It was the answer he'd expected to hear, but it still chilled him to the bone. "My name's Hunt," he said. "Hunt Jackson. I'm accused of—" He stopped himself, glanced around. He wasn't sure if any inmates knew why he was here, and he sure as hell didn't want to let them know. It was probably the only reason his teeth weren't littering the floor of the shower. "Let's just say he's why I'm in here, too."

Del nodded enthusiastically. "I knew it, I knew it! What happened? Didn't make your payments?"

"No," Hunt said. "I didn't buy legal insurance."

"Legal insurance. I wasn't offered that one. What was it supposed to do?"

"Keep me out of here."

Del snorted. "Typical." He took a quick swig of cold coffee. "So what'd he offer when he came to visit you? And did you take it?"

"Conviction insurance," Hunt said. "And, yeah, I'm going to take it." He hesitated. "*If* he offers it to me again."

"You turned him down?"

"He insulted my wife. Well, not really insulted her, but he said I had to qualify for the insurance and he started asking me these outrageous questions."

Del was nodding. "That's his way. But don't let it get to you. He's just testing you."

Hunt took a deep breath. "*Should* I have taken the insurance?"

"If it would get you out of here? Hell, yeah!"

"Why are you still here, then?"

"I didn't pay my premium. *Couldn't* pay it. It had just grown so big, and I'd lost my job, and . . . I was going to pay it, but I was late, and then . . . then it all fell apart. Things just escalated and then I was arrested, and I had no insurance to protect me. When I saw him here yesterday, talking to you, I thought that maybe he'd come by and see me, too. Maybe he'd offer me some new type of insurance that would get me out of here. But he didn't. He hasn't offered me shit." The fat man nibbled on his cold toast. "Maybe he will, though," he said hopefully. "Maybe he's just trying to teach me a lesson.

"That's why I say, take what you're offered. You've been given a chance, buddy. Jump on it."

Hunt nodded thoughtfully. "Say," he said, "did the agent ever give you his name?"

Del shook his head. "No. And I've wondered about that, too." He was silent for a moment. "You know, names have power. In certain cultures, just speaking a man's name gives you mastery over him. Like in that kid's story, what's it called? Goldilocks? Rumpelstiltskin? The one about the evil dwarf who gets the princess's firstborn child unless she can say his name?" He paused. "I'm only saying this because you know and I know that ain't any normal insurance salesman. There's a lot more going on here."

"I know."

"Well, I think he keeps his name secret purposely. Shit, before I got arrested, I even thought that if I found out his name I could . . . I don't know, blackmail him or something, use it to my advantage. But you're right. There's something there. He's not giving that name out to anyone."

A guard came by, a thin ferret-faced man with a wispy Prince mustache and an obvious chip on his shoulder. He poked Del with his nightstick. "Daley? Your lawyer's here to see you."

The fat man scrambled over the back of the bench. "Appeals," he explained. "I'm hoping I have grounds for a retrial." He waved at Hunt as the guard led him out of the mess hall. "See you at lunch."

But Del didn't make it to lunch. Sometime around midmorning, a harsh low-tech alarm buzzer echoed through the facility, and suddenly there were guards everywhere shouting "Lockdown! Lockdown!" Hunt didn't know what that meant, but after it was all over, after the commotion died down, he heard two inmates in another cell talking about a fight in front of one of the upper units, a brutal beating that resulted from an earlier racial incident. One of the combatants had been taken away to the hospital either comatose or dead.

When Del didn't show up in the mess hall, Hunt knew that it had been him.

He should not have been surprised, and he wasn't. Shocked, horrified but not surprised. He tried to tell himself that it had nothing to do with him, that Del had not been penalized for telling tales out of school, that whatever had happened was the result of unfinished business between Del and the insurance agent, but he could not quite make himself believe it.

Later, the thought occurred to him that Del had been *sent* by the insurance agent, that he had not really been an inmate but had been placed in county jail specifically to talk to Hunt and convince him to buy insurance. It was a crazy idea—but no less crazy than a lot of the other things that had been happening lately.

Just because you were paranoid didn't mean they weren't out to get you.

He was lying on his cot, staring up at the ceiling, when he heard footsteps and then the loud clang of nightstick on bars.

"You have a visitor."

Jennings was supposed to be stopping by that afternoon, but Hunt hoped that it was the insurance agent. He'd had a long night and an equally long morning to think about the coverage he'd been offered, and he'd come to the conclusion that he would purchase conviction insurance even before he'd met Del Daley.

Sure enough, the insurance agent was sitting behind the bulletproof safety glass at the far end of the visitors' room.

He picked up the phone, motioned for Hunt to do the same.

Hunt sat down, reached for the phone and put it to his ear.

"How are you today, Mr. Jackson?" The agent's voice was jovial and hearty. Not what he'd been expecting.

"Fine," Hunt said slowly.

"I understand that you are interested in taking us up on our offer of additional insurance coverage."

Hunt nodded, feeling vaguely guilty, as though he were acquiescing to an illegal or immoral act.

"I'm glad to see you finally came to your senses. Now you still have to qualify, and I still have to ask you a few questions. Will that be all right?"

"Yes," he said tightly.

"Fine, fine. I'll try to get through this as quickly and painlessly as possible. Now, question one—"

"Small enough to be tight but big enough to handle me. Does that answer your question?"

"Are you big down there? Got a lot of meat on your bone?" The agent chuckled. "Sorry. Let's stick to the questions. Now, in answer to our first query, 'Have you ever been convicted of a crime?' you answered that your wife's vagina is 'Small enough to be tight but big enough to handle me.' Do I have that right?"

"What is this? What the hell's going on here? Last time, you asked me—"

"I'm sorry. That was my fault. I was looking at the wrong form. Now can we just get through this?"

"Jesus Christ!"

"Mr. Jackson . . ."

"Fine."

"All right, then. Now, question two: does your wife enjoy anal intercourse?" The agent laughed, held up his hands. "Joking! Joking! I'm sorry, I couldn't resist."

"Fuck!"

"Why don't I give you the application form and let you fill it out. Do they allow you to have pens in there?"

Hunt took a deep breath, tried to calm down.

That's his way. He's just testing you.

"No," he said. "I'll answer the questions. Just read them off to me. I want to get this done as quickly as possible."

"That's a good attitude. Okay, have you ever been convicted of a crime?"

"No."

"Have you ever been arrested before?"

"No."

"Have you ever committed a crime for which you were neither caught nor punished?"

"Drunk driving, maybe, in college. Some vandalism when I was a kid, I guess."

The agent picked up the form, slipped it into his briefcase. "We're done."

He could not believe it. "That's all? Those are the only questions?"

"Yep."

"When will I know if I qualify?"

"Right now."

There was a long pause.

"So?" Hunt prodded.

"You qualify. Now would you like to purchase a personal injury policy with the supplemental conviction coverage?"

"Yes, both of them."

"Very well. I will fill out your application for you although I still require your signature. I'll have a guard bring in the form for you to sign when we're done." He withdrew new papers from his briefcase. Beneath the white top sheet, Hunt could see pink and yellow pages. The agent placed the tripartite form on top of a clipboard. "Name . . . address . . . occupation," he muttered. He began writing furiously. "Reason for arrest . . . type of charges . . .

"Okay!" He looked up. Holding the application next to the window, the agent went over the terms of the policy in detail. It was so specific, the provisions and stipulations so self-explanatory, that there was really no reason to go over every single line, but the man delighted in explaining the details of insurance coverage, and he savored the description of each and every condition covered by the policy.

He did this for both personal injury and the supplemental conviction insurance, either of which could have been accurately and succinctly described in single sentences, then stood, walked over to a guard, and spoke with him for a moment. The guard opened the security door and handed it to his counterpart on this side of the wall, who then brought it over to Hunt.

Hunt read over each form to affirm that no additional lines had been magically added since he'd seen them through the window—not an impossibility—then signed his name. He handed the application to the guard, who opened the door and handed it to the other guard, who brought it over to the insurance agent, who quickly and greedily snatched it from his hands.

The agent put it in his briefcase and stood, bowing slightly to Hunt. "You won't regret this," he said.

But watching the hard smile creep up the man's suddenly sharper face, Hunt already did.

Less than two hours later, he met Jennings in what he'd come to think of as the lawyer/client room. The attorney was somber and ashen-faced when Hunt walked in, sitting very still, and Hunt knew immediately that something was wrong.

There were no papers on the table this time, no tape recorder, no briefcase. Hunt sat down opposite Jennings and pushed in his chair. His heart was pounding in his chest. "Hello, Ray," he said. "What's happening?"

The lawyer didn't speak for a moment, and that in itself was unusual. Each time Hunt had met with him, he'd been ready with a response, prepared for anything at any time, filled with a self-confidence that was catching. Now he seemed doubtful, unsure, and Hunt found that troubling.

"I have to ask you a question," Jennings said.

"Go right ahead."

"I need a straight answer."

"Of course." His stomach was knotting up.

"Remember, we're covered under attorney-client privilege here, so there's no reason for you to lie. Do you . . .?" He paused. "How do I put this delicately? Do you have any ties to . . . organized crime?"

Hunt stared at him incredulously. "What?"

"I need to know. Are you in any way . . . connected?"

"Of course not!"

The lawyer sighed, pushed himself back from the table. "Then you have to be the luckiest man on the planet."

"Why? What are you talking about? What *is* all this?"

"Kate Gifford was killed this morning in an auto accident in front of her school."

Hunt felt dizzy, as though the floor had fallen out from under him. Two words kept echoing in his head: *conviction insurance, conviction insurance, conviction insurance . . .*

"How did it happen?" he whispered. "Was Lilly there? Was she hurt?"

"No, she wasn't involved. Kate was carpooling with another friend. She was in the backseat, and when the car parked in front of the school, she got out on the street side. A pickup truck was speeding by, way too fast for the school zone. The driver didn't see her until the last second, and couldn't stop or swerve over in time. He hit her and took off the car door."

"Oh my God."

Conviction insurance.

"Yes."

"She's dead?"

"Killed instantly. Not only that, but the videotape of her describing the alleged sex acts has disappeared. Or I should say *all* copies of the videotape have disappeared. The one in the police evidence room, the one in the psychiatrist's office, the one the DA has . . . and mine." He looked at Hunt over his glasses. "So you can see why I might start to wonder."

"I don't know how this happened," Hunt lied, "but I had nothing to do with it." He sounded insincere even to himself, and he was sure that the lawyer looked upon him with renewed suspicion. In his mind, he saw that creepy smile sliding slowly up the insurance agent's face. *You won't regret this.*

It was his fault. He had killed her. If he had not signed up for conviction coverage, if he had not agreed to pay the insurance company to save his own ass, she would be alive right now.

But if she had not lied about him—

No. He refused to go there. Kate was an innocent victim here. He didn't know how, but they had made her testify against him, had brainwashed her and even gotten her to believe the lies. All of this in order to convince him to buy insurance.

Which he had.

And now she was dead.

But what did he expect would happen? How else did he think a dismissal of his case could be guaranteed? Did he think the insurance company would buy off the district attorney and the police and get the charges dropped? For a measly thirty dollars a month? That would be too cost prohibitive with too high a possibility for failure. No, they'd gone with the simplest, cheapest, easiest answer.

They had killed the girl.

And stolen all the tapes.

Hunt thought about playing basketball with Kate and Lilly in Joel's backyard, remembered Kate's giggly infectious laugh. The emotions within him were all mixed up: horror and sadness, anger and relief. He felt everything and nothing.

"Needless to say," Jennings continued, "the charges against you are being dropped for lack of evidence."

He forced himself to speak. "What does that mean? I'll be able to leave?"

"As soon as the paperwork arrives and is processed, you'll be free to go."

"And that's it?"

"Theoretically, the DA would be able to charge you again if additional evidence came to light, but that is highly, highly unlikely. So, yes, I would say that's it."

Whatever rapport they had developed was gone. Jennings couldn't prove it, but in his heart he believed that Hunt was re-

sponsible for Kate's death. Hunt *knew* he was responsible—
but for entirely different reasons than the lawyer could ever
suspect. They completed their business together formally, im-
personally, and two hours later when Hunt was officially and
expeditiously released thanks to the attorney's diligent efforts,
the two of them met for one last time to tie up loose ends.

And then he was free.

Beth was seated on a bench in the waiting room next to
family members of other prisoners. She jumped up and ran to
him the moment he walked through the doorway, and he threw
his arms around her. She hugged him back, burying her face in
his neck. He did not know if she was crying from relief because he had been released and their hellish ordeal was over,
or because of the way it had happened, because a little girl was
dead. Probably a little of both.

Hunt didn't want to stay in that building a second longer
than he had to, so when her crying ebbed, he ushered her out
the door into the glorious fresh air of freedom.

They made love as soon as they got home—there was nothing like the potential of permanent separation to rev up the old
hormones—and it was rough and dirty the way he liked it, the
best sex they'd had in a long time. Afterward, they lay in bed
talking, and he told her about Del at breakfast and his last
meeting with the insurance agent in the visitors' room, when
he'd agreed to purchase personal injury insurance with its supplemental conviction coverage. He told her about Kate, although she'd already heard through Jennings.

"Maybe it *is* unconnected," she said hopefully. "I mean, we
haven't paid dime one of that premium yet."

"He said it took effect upon signing." Hunt shook his head.
"No, I killed her. I signed her death warrant when I signed that
application."

Beth started crying again.

And held him close.

*   *   *

The guest room started up after dinner.

They ate out to celebrate his release, going to Terra Cotta, ordering exotic and expensive entrees, watching the beautiful sunset through the floor-to-ceiling windows, and when they arrived home, it was dark.

They could hear the sounds of the guest room as they entered the house.

Knocking and tapping, as of wood on wood. The dry whoosh of a nonexistent wind.

Hunt was determined to be brave this time. After everything he'd been through, a little noise in an empty room didn't seem quite so frightening anymore. But when he was in the hallway and walking toward the guest room, when he saw the door slowly swing open and caught a hint of movement in the black shadows that hovered over the top half of the unmade twin bed, his fear returned full force.

Next to him, Beth's breath caught in her throat.

"We'll stay in a hotel tonight," he said, stopping where he was. "I don't want to put up with this. Not tonight."

She nodded, afraid to speak as, down the hallway, the door swung closed.

Fourteen

1

Monday morning.

Steve sat behind a stained and battered desk in his corp yard office, scowling. "If it was up to me, you wouldn't be coming back," he said. "I would've fired your ass the first day you spent in jail. And believe you me, if we were working for a private company, that's exactly what would be happening." His voice was filled with disgust. "But this is government work. Which means that every loser and layabout on the planet Earth can leech off the public trough. At least until the board contracts you guys out."

"If you hate it so much, why do you work here?" Hunt asked.

"That's enough smart-mouth from you! I may have to give you your job back, but I don't have to put up with insubordination!" The maintenance services manager glared at Hunt, who remained respectfully silent. "Now as I said, you'll be docked four days for the days you didn't work. You won't have a punch card for those days, so when your time sheet comes around, put down Z time before you sign it."

Hunt had been right. Word of his arrest had spread throughout the ranks of the county employees. One of their own was a child molester. Luckily, no one he knew had believed it, no one from tree trimming had given the accusations any credence. But belief in his innocence dropped off precipitously after that small circle of people, and no doubt everyone else in maintenance services and those in county government's other departments, believed him guilty under the "where there's smoke there's fire" rationale.

Steve was one of those.

"On a personal note," the manager said "you disgust me. I don't want to see your face in the morning, and I don't want you to talk to me. If I have anything to say to you, I'll say it in a memo."

Edward stuck his head in the open doorway. "Hey, Steve, how's the house coming?"

From the yard outside came derisive chuckles and several guffaws.

The manager stood and yelled angrily out the window. "You're *all* going to be outsourced if I have anything to say about it! And I'll be laughing every day as I sit here reading reports from the companies that took your jobs, you worthless bunch of goof-offs!"

"We go, you go, Steve!" Chris Hewett called out. "Ain't no need for a maintenance services manager if there's no maintenance services department!"

Steve turned back toward Hunt. "I'll settle for eliminating tree trimming. Now get out of here and get back to work."

The crews were already starting to leave. Edward and Jorge had hooked the mulcher up to their truck and were leaning against the cab, drinking coffee and waiting. "Ready to go, boys?" Hunt asked, jogging across the asphalt to meet them.

Edward grinned. "You're back?"

"I'm back, baby!"

Edward laughed. Jorge slapped him on the back. "Let's get out of here, bro."

Hunt was quiet on the drive out to Tanque Verde, where they'd be working for the next week. He was riding shotgun with Edward driving, but it was Jorge in the cramped backseat of the truck who kept up a steady stream of conversation and who kept pressing Hunt for details as they made their way through the stop-and-go morning traffic. He finally gave them an abridged account of events, a sanitized version of what had really happened, but Jorge was still not satisfied, and Hunt could tell that his friend sensed he was covering something up.

They reached the vacant stretch of county land where they were to work for the next week. Edward bumped over the curb onto the dirt, pulled up next to a burned palo verde, and the three of them got out. Hunt tossed the remains of his cold coffee onto the ground and threw the cup back on the floor of the truck. Unhooking the mulcher from the hitch, Edward looked over at him. "You can tell us if you want," he said. "Whatever you say goes no further than this."

Hunt was still not sure even his friends would believe his wild story, but he saw the expressions on Edward's and Jorge's faces, and he decided to take the plunge.

He told them everything. From the initial offer of a rider on a personal injury policy that would protect him from arrest, to Kate's death and the disappearance of all of her videotaped testimony.

"It's a little hard to believe," Edward admitted when he was through. "Your insurance agent as guardian angel?"

"More like guardian . . . maybe devil's not the right word, but he certainly isn't an angel."

"I believe it," Jorge declared, his voice a little too loud, a little too forceful.

Both Hunt and Edward turned to look at him.

"He's been after us to buy supplemental health insurance before the baby's born. He gave Ynez a pamphlet with pictures of deformed babies on it."

Goose bumps rushed down Hunt's arms.

"Wait a minute." Edward frowned. "Is this that same guy? That door-to-door salesman?"

"Yeah," they both said at once.

Edward shook his head. "Oh man. I knew you shouldn't've gotten involved with that guy."

"Then you believe us?" Hunt asked.

"I don't disbelieve." He turned toward Jorge. "Did you save that pamphlet? I mean, it seems like you could turn him in for something like that. Harassment or extortion or something. You could turn it over to the attorney general. The state investigates suspicious business practices."

"They investigate fraud," Hunt said. "This isn't fraud. This is real. This insurance works."

"Well, what do you know about the company he represents?"

"The Insurance Group? Not much. It's supposed to be a consortium of insurance carriers, all very old and well-respected. I gather they've won numerous awards for quality and customer service."

"You didn't even investigate them, find out who they are?"

"I was going to," Hunt said dryly. "But other things came up."

"I didn't know their name," Jorge admitted. "The card he gave me just said 'Quality Insurance.' "

"I'm going to see what I can find out tonight," Hunt promised.

"I just thought of something," Jorge said. "Do you think this could be related to your other insurance problems? Your rental house and your car and all that? You think there could be a connection?"

Hunt hadn't really considered it. He'd been thrust so fast into this new world that he hadn't had time to catch his breath, let alone analyze whether there was any connection between the insurance agent's bizarre policies and anything that had gone before. Now that he thought about it, though . . .

Half past a monkey's ass, a quarter to his ba-wuls.

Yes. They definitely could be connected.

"Probably," he said.

Edward nodded. "If Jorge's right, maybe all those other troubles primed you for this, made you more susceptible to say yes to some insurance salesman off the street."

He hadn't looked at it that way, but it made a lot of sense.

The truck's radio crackled as Steve attempted to contact them and get a status report.

No one made an effort to answer it, and they ignored the manager's barked order to respond as usual, but Edward picked up the mulcher's tow arm and started pushing the machine toward the weedy patch to the right of the burned tree. "We'd better get our asses in gear. We got a lot of work today. We can talk while we're cutting."

Jorge grabbed tools out of the back of the truck. Hunt slipped on a pair of gloves. "So what are you going to do?" he asked Jorge. "Are you going to get that extra health insurance?"

The other man sighed heavily. "What choice do I have?"

At home after work, Hunt signed on to the Internet to see what he could find out about The Insurance Group. The company had no web page—very suspicious in this day and age—but the search he conducted got over 27,000 hits for The Insurance Group. Unfortunately, as happened with Internet searches more often than not, the listings proved to be tangentially related or not related at all. He found ads for companies with the words "Insurance Group" in their title—such as The Hartford Insurance Group or The Insurance Group of Maine—and information and articles about every other insurance company under the sun—as well as a web page for The Group, which was some sort of swingers porno site.

Beth brought him dinner, which he ate at his desk, and by the time he quit after midnight, with well over 26,000 entries yet to go, he had not come across a single reference to the company that had issued their policies. How such a thing was possible, he did not know, but even though ninety-eight percent of the listings were still ahead, he had a sneaking suspicion that if The Insurance Group had avoided detection through entries that had the highest percentage of correlation with his typed parameters, they would most likely not be found in any of those ranked lower.

Still, he was a hardware guy, not a software guy, and he was tempted to call one of his old acquaintances from California, one of Boeing's programmers, and ask him about any way to narrow the search so that only articles and information that specifically mentioned "The Insurance Group," with no modifiers or qualifiers, would be listed. But it was too late to bother anyone. Besides, he knew that such an effort would be futile, so he didn't even try. The Insurance Group could not be found over the Internet. Or through the phone book.

They could only be reached through the insurance agent.

He didn't know how he knew that to be true. But he did.

And it scared him.

2

Steve arrived home from work tired and angry. The shell of his rumpus room greeted him as he pulled in to the driveway, and that made him even angrier. He'd long since cleared away the debris and had even started rebuilding again—as much as his dwindling funds would allow—but he was still a good six months behind where he'd been before the storm—

and the men in hats

—had destroyed his handiwork.

He was convinced now more than ever that that fanatic insurance agent was behind the destruction of his addition. The man had tried the old hard sell to pressure him into buying new homeowner's insurance, and when that hadn't worked, the psychotic fuck had hired goons to vandalize his property. Despite what he'd seen, or what he *thought* he'd seen, there was nothing mysterious about those trespassing thugs. They were simply agents of the agent, doing the job they were hired to do. He didn't even hate them.

He hated the insurance agent.

And if he ever saw that asshole again, he was going to thrash him within an inch of his life. Or more, if the opportunity arose.

But the insurance salesman seemed to have disappeared. After the addition went down, there were no more entreaties to buy a homeowner's policy, no phone calls or junk mail or surprise visits. He seemed to have dropped off the face of the planet.

Lucky for him.

Inside, Nina was in the bathroom, taking a dump. She'd left a message for him on the blackboard above the kitchen counter: "Call Insurance Agent." He stormed down the hallway and pounded on the bathroom door. "What does this mean, 'Call Insurance Agent'?"

"He called at lunchtime!" she shouted. "He wants you to call him back!"

"How? Did he leave a number or anything?"

"Go look at your mail! I put it on your desk!"

He strode back down the hallway to his den. On top of the desk was a pile of cards and envelopes at least three feet high.

Some of the bluster left him, replaced by an uneasiness that was unfamiliar to him and was uncomfortably close to fear.

The insurance salesman was back. Steve walked over to the desk and started opening envelopes. They were all filled with identical brochures for homeowner's insurance. The cards were postcards featuring the same photograph of a smiling family in front of a two-story colonial home, with a printed message on the back made to look like a personally inscribed note: *Call for details! Quality Insurance 520-555-7734.*

He suddenly did not want the opportunity to thrash the

salesman within an inch of his life. He wanted the man to disappear and never contact him again.

But he picked up the phone and dialed.

"Hello! Mr. Nash!" The agent answered even before the first ring, and the enthusiasm in his voice seemed downright creepy. "You got my message!"

"Yeah," Steve said.

"Then listen to me, bitch." The voice dropped about three octaves. "I'm coming over, and I'm going to put a bunch of insurance policies in front of you, and you're going to sign up for every one of them. Do you understand?"

Steve's mouth went suddenly dry.

"Do you understand, bitch?"

Steve gathered his courage. "You come over and I'll blow your fucking head off." His voice came out squeakier than intended.

The agent chuckled. "Then I guess you don't want insurance."

"Not from you." The phone in his hand was shaking.

"Good luck."

The line went dead.

Down the hall, the bathroom door opened, and in the silence of the house Steve could hear the last whoosh of the toilet's flush. He was still holding the phone in his hand when Nina poked her head in the doorway. "What did he want?" she asked, and the tone of her voice was so casually innocent, so unlike her usual annoying whimper, that he thought she must know already, that she was probably in on it.

He wanted to beat her head with the phone, but instead he slammed the handset down in its cradle. "Go make dinner," he ordered. "Leave me the fuck alone."

3

"But it worked!" Ynez paced back and forth in front of the kitchen table. "Hunt got out of jail and that whole nightmare just ended!"

"He's not a genie," Jorge said. "He can't grant your every wish."

"No, but maybe if we call him we can get some kind of insurance that, I don't know, guarantees that our baby will be born healthy and happy."

"I don't want to call him," Jorge repeated. "If he comes to us, fine. But let him take the initiative."

"He already came to us! And you turned him down!" She knelt on the floor before him. "I don't want anything to happen to our boy."

"Haven't you heard a single thing I said? This is a Faustian bargain. We'd be making a deal with the devil, and there's nothing in it for us. It's a lose-lose situation, as they say. If he came here and threatened us, okay, I might give in for the sake of the baby. But I'd be foolish to go *looking* for him."

"He already came. The threat's been made. We have to take it off."

There was a knock at the door. Jorge sighed and went to answer it. Behind him, Ynez got herself a glass of water.

The man standing on the porch was not immediately recognizable. He was tall and well-built with sharp distinctive features and a full head of black hair. Jorge had already started to say, "May I help you?" when he realized who the man was.

The insurance agent.

The man nodded, smiling. "Yes you may, Mr. Marquez. And I think I will be able to help you, too. May I come in?"

Jorge did not want him in the house, not where his wife and unborn child were. But he found himself nodding and stepping aside.

The agent breezed past him, and Jorge shivered. Cold fol-

lowed in the man's wake. If it had been for anything else, anything other than his wife and son, he would have told the man
to leave his home then and there.

Ynez was still drinking her water, and she emerged into the
family room. "Hello," she said.

"Nice to see you again, Mrs. Marquez. I probably said this
to you last time, but it bears repeating: you have a lovely
home."

"Thank you," Ynez said. She was smiling, but Jorge could
tell from her tone of voice that she was also wary. Thank God.
Seeing the agent in person seemed to have tempered some of
her uncritical desire for more health insurance.

The agent sat down on their couch, loosened his tie, and
opened up his briefcase.

Automatically, they sat on chairs opposite him, and Jorge
realized that they'd already lost. Before they'd even started.
Because no matter what sort of policy he put in front of them,
no matter how much it cost, they were going to buy it. They
couldn't afford not to.

He knew this already.

"I've taken the liberty of preparing a package that I think
will nicely meet *all* of the medical, dental, and life insurance
needs of your soon-to-be family." He passed them a thick
sheaf of papers held together with three brads. "If you'll look
on page one . . ."

The agent's attention to detail was exhausting. As far as
Jorge could tell, the policy was fairly straightforward, and he
paid particularly close attention to the portion of supplemental
health insurance that dealt with delivery problems and extra
hospitalization, grateful to learn that it seemed at once more
flexible and more comprehensive than his existing county insurance.

"Now I need both of your signatures for this coverage," the
agent said, pushing the application forms across the table and
handing them each a pen.

"So when does this take effect?" Jorge asked.

"Immediately upon signing."

Jorge looked at Ynez, filled with a wariness that seemed to be mirrored in her eyes. If he were a praying man, he would have sent up an entreaty right now. He signed his name on the blank line at the bottom of pages three and six. Ynez did the same.

The agent took the forms from them. "Now there's just one more little detail we have to take care of. The exam."

Jorge's heart rate shifted upward in gear.

"The exam?" Ynez said.

"Yes. It's customary for new signees to undergo a medical exam to make sure there are no preexisting conditions for which coverage of treatment would be exempt under the terms of the policy. Ordinarily, this consists of a blood test, but we have the records of both your doctors and copies of your charts, so in this case, the blood test will not be necessary."

"Then—" Jorge began.

"I just need to examine your wife's crotch."

What? Jorge blinked dumbly, unable to believe what he'd heard.

No, that wasn't true. He believed it completely.

He turned toward Ynez, who was shaking her head from side to side.

The agent was moving around the side of the table, crouching down on the carpet. "Now if you could just pull down your pants and spread your legs so I could see your pussy."

Jorge stood, practically knocking over his chair. "No!" he declared.

The insurance salesman straightened. His voice when he spoke was cold, hard. "Then your policy will be null and void."

"I'll do it," Ynez said quickly, her hands fumbling frantically, desperately at her button and zipper. Tears were rolling down her face.

"No!" Jorge told her.

"It's our son!" With difficulty, she lifted her buttocks off the chair and slid down her pants and panties, kicking them off. She spread her legs wide as the insurance agent crouched before her.

"That's a beautiful beaver you've got there, Mrs. Marquez." He grinned up at Jorge. "You're a lucky man."

Ynez held her face in her hands, sobbing.

"Let's hope childbirth doesn't ruin that miracle of nature, eh?"

Jorge wanted to kill him. He wanted to lash out and kick in those grinning teeth until the man's mouth was nothing more than a gaping bloody hole.

The agent stood, pulled tight his tie and closed his briefcase. "Looks good," he said. "Consider yourself insured."

Ynez was still sobbing, legs tightly together, doubled over in an attempt to hide her bare lap. Jorge stood between her and the agent, trying to hide her, although there was not anything he hadn't already seen.

The man smiled at Jorge. "Did I mention that additional coverage may be required at substantial extra cost?"

Jorge could barely contain his rage. "No you did not," he said in a strained strangled voice.

"Depending on the circumstances, we may require an added commitment from you in order to ensure that you are getting the coverage that best suits your individual needs. Information regarding this codicil will be included in your policy, when you receive it, but if you have any questions, don't hesitate to call."

Ynez wailed behind him, a cry of anguish and humiliation.

"Don't worry," the agent said, "I'll see myself out."

4

By Wednesday, Beth was almost ready to quit her job.

If not for Stacy, she probably would have. Stacy now seemed to be her sole friend at Thompson and the only one to whom she could speak freely. Unfortunately, Stacy wasn't here today, she was all alone, and even casual contact with anyone else in the office had become extremely uncomfortable. The hostility of her coworkers seemed to have increased tenfold since Hunt's release, as though they thought he had gotten away with his crime, and their attitudes toward her had been uniformly antagonistic.

The question was: did she wish she had signed up for employment insurance? So she wouldn't resent her job because of "extraneous factors at work"? Beth couldn't really say. Certainly it would have been easier coming to work knowing that she had more than one guaranteed ally in the building—a lot easier than it had been two days ago when she'd gone to the bathroom only to find "Beth Blows Fat Men for Free!" written in one of the stalls. But the idea of paying another penny to that insurance agent and his company galled her.

Especially after what Ynez had gone through.

The phone rang just as she was about to eat her lunch. Well, just as she was about to get her lunch out of the refrigerator and bring it back to her office so she could eat in peace without having to put up with the silent treatment or the outright animosity of her coworkers in the lunchroom. It was line three, her outside line, and she picked it up quickly, hoping that it was not Hunt, hoping that nothing bad had happened.

"Hello," the professional-sounding voice on the other end of the line greeted her. "May I speak to Beth Jackson?"

She breathed an inward sight of relief. Thank God it was just a business call. "This is she," Beth said.

"This is Rebecca from Dr. Moy's office. We have an opening this afternoon at two, and we can fit you in."

Dr. Moy? She frowned. Who was Dr. Moy? "I'm sorry," she said. "I'm not sure who you are."

"I'm Rebecca. From Dr. Moy's office."

"I don't know any Dr. Moy."

The woman sounded extremely apologetic. "Oh, I'm sorry. I just assumed that your insurance company had called you. Dr. Moy is your oral surgeon. He'll be replacing your teeth."

"Dr. Mirza's my oral surgeon," Beth said.

"You've been reassigned to Dr. Moy. I don't think Dr. Mirza is part of the plan anymore."

There was something ominous about that statement—*I don't think Dr. Mirza is part of the plan anymore*—and she hoped to God that she was reading too much into it, that it simply meant he was no longer participating in her specific insurance program.

She had a sudden flashback to Dr. Blackburn.

"Pussy for breakfast, pussy for lunch, pussy for dinner and a midnight snack."

She decided to press it. "Dr. Mirza's not part of *what* plan?" she asked.

"Oh, I'm sorry. I meant your new insurance plan. You recently switched insurance carriers, which is why you have been reassigned to Dr. Moy. Now, how does two o'clock sound?"

Someone passed by her office door, and Beth looked up to see who it was. Ruben from accounting held up an angry middle finger. Beth quickly swiveled her chair so that she faced the wall. She couldn't take much more of this. "This afternoon?" she said. "That'll be fine, that'll be great. Just give me directions on how to get there . . ."

Dr. Moy's office was not on a widened residential street or in a converted house. It was in a brand-new medical/dental complex just west of the university. The courtyard of the building was busy and crowded, and when she walked into the wait-

ing room of the oral surgeon, three other patients were waiting
as well, two of them holding their jaws as though they were in
considerable pain. It was as far from Dr. Blackburn's office as
it was possible to be, and yet . . .

And yet Beth could not relax. In her mind, this was all a facade, part of an elaborate ruse to trick her and lure her in. Like
the attitudes of her coworkers—both her friends and enemies.
Everything was suspect now, subject to manipulation, and she
had the feeling that this was part of the plan too, part of a con-
certed effort to keep her off balance.

Still, Dr. Moy's office seemed to run more like a regular
dentist's office, like the ones she remembered from childhood.
Looking back now, everything about her visit to Dr. Blackburn
seemed suspicious. Hindsight was always twenty-twenty, they
said, but she couldn't help feeling that if she had been more
alert, the whole nightmare of her teeth might have been
avoided.

She filled out a new-patient form and submitted her driver's
license to the receptionist, who made a copy of it. She didn't
have an insurance card, but the receptionist assured her that the
insurance company had specifically called to make the appointment for her and arrange payment. She'd probably be
getting her card in the mail soon.

Dr. Moy's office was not quite *ER*, but it was busy and
bustling, and as Beth was led back to an exam room, she saw
that all of the patient rooms in the office were occupied. Dr.
Moy himself was an older Asian man with a very calm and reassuring demeanor. He patiently examined her mouth, studied
the X rays that an assistant had taken only a few moments before, then explained exactly what he planned to do. It was a
long and involved procedure, and there would be much less
pain, he said, if he did only a quadrant at a time, but he could
do the whole mouth at once if she preferred.

She told him that she did want it all done at once, she'd
lived with these silver teeth for far too long, and he explained

that in that case she would have to be put under completely and would need to sign an extra consent form.

Ten minutes later, the form was signed. Hunt had been called and told to pick her up at the dentist's office in two hours because she would not be fit to drive, she was prepped and ready, and Dr. Moy gave her the gas. In the second before she went under, she thought she heard the oral surgeon softly say the word "pussy."

Then she was awake and groggy. She was aware neither of when she lost or regained consciousness, it was all part of a hazy continuum. All she knew was that she was lying in the same dentist's chair and that it was all over. The small room was empty save for her, and the door behind her was closed. She sat up, feeling around on the tool tray for a mirror, so she could see what she looked like. All she could find was a small magnifying mirror with a long handle like a toothbrush, one that the dentist used to peer into the back of her mouth. She picked it up, held it a foot or so away and smiled.

Her lips were swollen and bloody and her head hurt like hell.

But all of her teeth were once again white.

5

"Got a visit myself last night," Edward said. They were trimming trees along a county-maintained bridle trail that ran through unincorporated land. "Your insurance salesman. Bastard tried to sell me supplemental workman's comp. Like there is such a thing."

Hunt and Jorge exchanged glances. "You know what that means," Jorge said quietly.

He cut them off. "Don't give me that crap."

"The insurance works," Hunt said. "I'm living proof. You ignore it at your own risk."

Edward waved them away, but the truth was that he felt far less confident than he let on. The visit from the insurance agent had shaken him. His friends were right. There *was* something seriously skewed about the man, and it wasn't merely his Stepford salesman routine. Beneath that facade, so close it could almost be seen, was a different, darker, more elemental essence. Edward was not a religious man, didn't bandy about words like "evil" or "demonic," but those were the adjectives that came to him when he listened to the insurance agent, and it had taken every ounce of courage he possessed to throw that fucker out of his house.

Even now, he wasn't sure he had done the right thing.

Maybe Jorge and Hunt knew what they were talking about. There could be disastrous consequences for not buying insurance.

"Things *happen* when you don't buy insurance," Jorge reminded him.

"Coincidence," Edward said, though he was no longer sure that was true. He could see in his friends' faces that they wanted to believe him, that they longed for him to be right, and he could not quash their hopes by revealing his own doubts. "We're almost done here," he announced. "Why don't you two head over to the south quadrant. I'll meet you there in ten."

"That's okay," Hunt told him. "We'll all finish up here first."

"It's a waste. I'll do cleanup, and you take the equipment to the south quadrant and start. Maybe we'll get out of here before noon."

They nodded reluctantly, knowing he was right, and he exchanged his saw for a long-handled clipper and climbed up the ladder to whack the last few danglers off two adjacent trees while Jorge and Hunt piled the rest of the tools in the back of the cart and drove down the bridle trail to the south quadrant.

"Be careful," Hunt said before they left, and there was a

resonance to the generic warning that was echoed in the sober expression on Jorge's face.

"I'll be fine," he told them. "Hit the road."

But the minute they were gone, he was immediately sorry that he'd suggested they split up. An uncomfortable conversation was a small price to pay for the security that two additional bodies provided.

Security?

He didn't want to think about that, and he concentrated on the work at hand, lopping off three thin branches that had not been cut by the power tools before getting off the ladder, moving it to the opposite side of the path and chopping off two more branches from another tree.

He heard a rustling noise from off to the right. The sound of shoes on dead leaves.

He looked toward the sound, thought he saw movement behind a bush.

A chill, like an ice cube, traced along the vertebrae of his back, moved down his body. "Jorge!" he called out experimentally. "Hunt!" But the two of them were far out of range.

He glimpsed more movement out of the corner of his eye, a dark figure that ducked behind a sycamore off to his left.

Edward was not a man who was easily frightened. He'd been in more bar fights than he could count, often with the odds three-to-one against him, and he'd never hesitated. He'd been on the ground in Desert Storm, and while more than a few of his fellow infantrymen had browned their shorts, he'd forged ahead fearlessly. But something about these subtle noises and furtive movements in the bushes spoke to a more primal part of his being. They bypassed his rational mind and warned him of a danger that he could not combat.

Supplemental workman's comp.

Bogus or not, he realized that he would feel a lot more confident right now if he were protected by extra insurance for on-the-job injuries.

But insurance only paid for the medical bills and other expenses incurred by an accident. It didn't prevent that accident.

Maybe it did, though. Wasn't that what the insurance salesman had hinted?

Edward looked around, listened, but he saw no other figures, heard no other sounds. He was overreacting, he told himself. The visit last night and all of his friends' talk had spooked him and made him overly paranoid. Still, enough strange things had happened recently that he could not automatically deny them. Better safe than sorry, as his momma used to say. He started to step slowly down the ladder.

And then he saw them.

There was one next to each tree, for as far as he could see up the bridle trail. Heavyset men in long coats and broad-brimmed hats. It was a sunny day but they all seemed to be in shadow, and it was that more than anything else that caused him to scurry down the ladder and jump the last few feet to the ground. They remained unmoving, as though posed, and their faces were little more than darkened smudges, as though he was viewing them through dark sunglasses or one of those polarized sections of film that were used to look at eclipses of the sun.

He had too much self-respect to just turn pussy and run—there was still a remote possibility that they were ordinary people and that there was a perfectly rational explanation for this—but he gathered up his shears and clippers much faster than he would have ordinarily, and quickly loaded them onto the truck that was still parked in the adjacent clearing. He was very glad that Hunt and Jorge had taken the cart. The truck had a much bigger engine and much faster pickup.

He hurried back to get the ladder.

And they surrounded him.

He didn't know how it happened, how they had gotten there so fast, but suddenly ten bulky men were standing in a circle around him, closing in. He still could not see their faces. They were still in shadow though there was no shadow.

He was afraid.

The circle grew tighter.

Instinctively, he backed up to the ladder, and immediately, unthinkingly, he turned around and started to climb. Maybe he could scramble up a tree branch and wait there for someone to come along, for Jorge and Hunt to return. Maybe these men—

monsters

—couldn't climb, or maybe he could leap over them and run to safety. His plans were not well thought out. He had no plans, really, only a vague notion that he might be able to get away by climbing upward. He moved up to the top of the ladder, grabbed a branch. He had to keep moving. He'd figure out something along the way.

He looked down. They had circled the ladder.

And suddenly there were only five of them.

Where were the other—?

He heard a noise, looked up, and saw them standing on the branches, in the trees.

One of them laughed. A high wild giggle.

And in the brief second before the branches came down on his head, he thought he saw, in one of the dark faces, the bright white shine of teeth.

Fifteen

1

The mail came early on Saturday. Hunt was online again, trying to learn what he could about their various insurance policies, looking up not only the name of the company but the names of the specific policies themselves, comparing what they had to the texts of similar offerings published on the Internet by other carriers, when he heard the rattle of the mailbox lid.

He wasn't expecting anything important, so he waited until Beth called him for lunch before opening the front door to pick up the delivered mail.

There were so many cards and envelopes they could not fit in the box, so the postman had placed the overflow in three neatly stacked piles next to the front door.

What the hell was this? He picked up a postcard with a photo of a homeless man sitting on a curb next to a dead dog. On the other side was a computer-signed note advising him to call his insurance agent.

His insurance agent.

Hunt quickly scooped up all of the mail and brought it inside, dumping it on the coffee table. He picked up an envelope and opened it, noting before he did so that there was no return address. Sure enough, inside was a pamphlet advertising employment insurance and touting its supposed benefits. He started opening the other envelopes, expecting to see a whole array of offered policies, but to his surprise, the cards and pamphlets were all identical, a total of thirty advertisements for The Insurance Group's employment insurance. There was nothing for any of the other forms of coverage they had not yet purchased, nothing for supplemental health or workman's comp.

He thought of Edward, laid up in the hospital because he had not bought an extra workman's comp policy. Only his size and overall fitness had saved him from being more seriously injured or even killed. As it was, he would be in the hospital for several more days, in bed for at least three weeks and have to undergo a ton of physical therapy before he'd be on his feet again and back to work.

The insurance agent, Hunt had no doubt, originally intended something far worse.

Beth came out of the kitchen. "I said it's time to eat—" she began. And then she saw the mountain of mail on the table and the expression on Hunt's face.

"Oh my God," she said.

He nodded, handed her a pamphlet. He took another one for himself, and silently they both read through the text.

He put his down. "We have to buy it," he said, "or we'll lose our jobs. We'll end up unemployed."

"I don't care if I lose my job," Beth said stubbornly. "I'll find another one."

"Maybe you won't be able to."

"I'll react to that when it happens."

"One of us needs to stay employed," he told her, and the reason was the same as it was for every other couple in America. Insurance. Only in their case, they needed to be able to pay their monthly premiums because if they didn't they would be sick and homeless and incarcerated—everything their insurance protected them from.

She understood without him having to spell it out. "Better

it be you," she said. "At least you still like your job." She ran
a frustrated hand through her hair. "I was thinking of quitting
anyway. It's getting too stressful."

"You could quit," he said unenthusiastically.

She turned her face up toward his. "That's what's so insid-
ious about this whole thing. Did you read that pamphlet? Employment insurance guarantees that you won't resent your job,
that you won't be affected by office politics or personal issues,
and you'll be happy in a job you love. That's aimed directly at
me. And I'm still not sure if it's meant as an incentive or a
threat. You know why? Because it *does* sound good to me. *And*
it scares the hell out of me."

"I'll just buy the insurance for myself," Hunt told her.
"We'll see what happens. And I'll wait until he pressures me
into it. I won't volunteer. We're buying too much insurance,
we're becoming indebted to him."

But was there any way to avoid that? Del Daley had tried,
and he'd been imprisoned for it. Then he had been killed.

But was Del what he had appeared to be?

Was anyone?

Maybe the best idea would be to leave. To pack up and disappear under the cover of night. He had come to Tucson on a
whim, and he could leave the same way. He and Beth could
gather their belongings and just take off. Inform no one, give
no notice, simply relocate to another state under new names.
They could get jobs at a hotel in Colorado or on a farm in Ne-
braska or as sales clerks in Pennsylvania.

But they would still have the same fingerprints, the same
faces. They could be tracked. He remembered the first time the
insurance agent had come into the house and started figuring
estimates. He'd been mumbling to himself as he'd gone over
the forms, but Hunt had heard what he'd muttered, and he'd
known their birth dates and places, their former lovers, everything about them.

He had the feeling that they could have plastic surgery and

fake IDs and acid-washed fingerprints and move to the wilds of Canada, and the insurance agent would still show up on their doorstep offering termite insurance for their log cabin.

No, this was not a problem from which they could run.

They ate lunch in silence, listening to the raucus sounds of the Brett kids next door, each of them lost in their own thoughts.

"What kind of house do you think he lives in?" Beth wondered. "Do you think he has a wife and family? Does he sit home at night and watch *Everybody Loves Raymond*?"

It was impossible for him to imagine, Hunt realized. He tried to picture the insurance agent in ordinary circumstances, living an everyday existence like all of the other people in the workaday world, but he couldn't do it. When he imagined the man's house, he saw a dilapidated mansion, the kind kids would say was haunted. When he tried to imagine the home's interior, he saw Scrooge-like surroundings: a completely darkened building with only a single bare bulb over an old wooden table piled high with insurance policies.

"I should follow him the next time we see him," Hunt suggested. "See where he goes. Home or office, either way I'd learn something."

"But what if he saw you, what if he caught you?" Beth said, worried. "I don't like it."

The truth was, he didn't like the idea either. He could be caught. And he could easily see himself ending up a missing person, kidnapped and lost forever deep in the bowels of some labyrinthine insurance building, tied up and tortured, eventually left for dead. Or, more likely, the victim of some accident that would conveniently not be covered by any of his policies.

"Maybe if we don't respond, he'll go away," she suggested. "Maybe he'll move on to someone else and be done with us."

That wouldn't happen and they both knew it.

But they could hope.

After lunch, they went to Home Depot, and then to Barnes

& Noble, where Beth browsed leisurely through the cookbook section while Hunt checked out the CDs and used the headphones to listen to a bunch of music he'd read about but not yet heard.

When they returned, the agent was waiting for them, standing patiently on the porch, smiling as they drove up.

Beth looked as frightened as Hunt felt, but he fiddled with his seat belt, looking down at it. "Stay here a minute," he said softly. "Don't get out of the car. Make him wait. Let's see how long he keeps that smile on his face."

A long time, as it turned out. Beth pretended to look through her purse, Hunt turned around and did a bogus search of the backseat before opening the glove compartment and sorting through its contents. And still the man was smiling, showing no sign of strain. They ran out of things to do, couldn't come up with any new business to keep them from exiting the car, so slowly, reluctantly they got out. Hunt went back to open the trunk. Hiding behind the open trunk door, they both took their time about removing the items they'd purchased.

And still he was smiling.

"Have you thought about employment insurance?" he asked as they walked up the driveway. "Because losing a job can be very hard on a couple, very hard indeed. According to our research, it puts more stress on a marriage than even infidelity."

Neither of them responded.

"It puts an end to lovely weekends like this one, where you can go shopping and buy much needed items to beautify your home and garden. When you're unemployed, your weekends are spend scouring the classified ads, staying home so as not to spend money on gasoline and other luxuries." He chuckled. "No, I wouldn't want to be in that situation. Flush with money and gainfully employed. That's the only way to be, eh?"

Hunt dropped a bag of potting soil by the flower bed,

stepped onto the porch, stood next to the insurance agent and looked him in the eye. They were both the same height, he noticed for the first time, and it was almost like peering into a funhouse mirror, seeing a version of himself that was not quite right. The two of them looked nothing alike, had only their size in common, but there seemed to be some intangible underlying similarity that made Hunt uncomfortable.

"I know we've mentioned this before, but I thought it was time to make a decision." The agent grinned. "So can I put you both down for employment insurance?" He was practically bouncing on the balls of his feet.

"No—" Beth started to say.

"We'd like some more information about it before we make our final decision," Hunt cut in quickly. "Do you have a copy of the policy itself that we could look at?"

The agent was thrown for a moment. "I don't have a policy with me," he admitted. "Just an application."

Got him! Hunt tried to draw it out. "Well, maybe next time you could drop one by, give us a chance to look it over, and then we could talk."

Clearly this had never happened before. By this stage of the process, customers were supposed to be so beaten down that they docilely shelled out for any new coverage that was offered. "I can answer any of your questions about the specifics of the policy," the agent said. "I know everything there is to know about it."

"I think we'd just prefer to see it in writing," Beth said, catching on. "You know how it is."

The agent's expression darkened. "Yes, I know how it is when people are unable to meet the mortgage payments on their homes because they've been laid off. I know how it is when cars and furniture get repossessed because there's no money coming in and the bills can't be paid." He leaned forward. "Sometimes it happens like *that*." He snapped his fingers. "The whim of a CEO or even an immediate supervisor can put an abrupt end to a once-promising career. I've seen it happen many times, and I don't want to see it happen to you."

"Maybe the application," Hunt pressed. "Does it have a description of the insurance and what exactly it offers?"

"A detailed description," Beth added.

"I can tell you what it offers. Specifically. It offers guaranteed employment. Your current job at your current salary with your current conditions. You will not be demoted, fired, terminated, laid off, furloughed, downsized, rightsized, outsourced or contracted out."

"There's no room for advancement?" Beth asked. "I'd be stuck in the same position forever?"

"You can always move up, but you can never move down. Guaranteed." He was back on his game, and with smooth well-rehearsed patter, he delved into the precise terms and conditions of the coverage, growing more confident and more enthusiastic the longer he spoke, until his eyes were sparkling and he was smiling happily. "I'd jump at the chance if I were you," he told them. "Confidentially, this insurance will only be offered for a limited time. Like many boutique policies, we offer it to a select few customers only, and once the target number is reached in terms of signups, a cutoff is enforced and the coverage is no longer offered.

"Now"—he looked from Hunt to Beth and back again—"I need your decision."

Hunt had no choice, he'd run out of stalling tactics, and as much as he hated do so, he said "I'll take it."

"And Mrs. Jackson as well, I presume?"

Hunt was not sure how Beth would react, whether or not she'd be able to go through with her original plan, not after the effective and intimidating spiel to which they'd just been subjected. But she shook her head. "I don't think so," she said coolly.

He seemed not to have heard her. "Two job insurance policies at ten dollars apiece per month—"

"One policy," she stated loudly. "I will not be purchasing any for myself. My job is secure."

A slight tinge of desperation appeared in his smile. "As I attempted to explain, that could change at any time."

"I'll take my chances," she said, and Hunt was so proud of her he could burst. It was a little victory, but a victory nonetheless, and one made all the sweeter because it involved no compromise. He had to cave in, but Beth didn't, and as ridiculous and overblown as it might seem, he felt as though they'd thrown a wrench into an evil, complex, and intricately designed plan.

"You'll regret it," the agent said. His tone was almost nonchalant, but there was no mistaking the deadly seriousness of his message.

"I don't think so. By the way," Beth asked, "what's your name? It's not on your card."

"Hey! You! Jackson!"

They were distracted by a shout from the yard next door, their attention immediately drawn away from the insurance agent. Hunt looked past Beth at the source of the rough voice. Ed Brett was striding belligerently across his lawn toward them. His fists were clenched, and the expression on his face was one of hatred and hostility. He stopped at the edge of his property. "Sicko!" he bellowed, pointing at Hunt. "I want you out of this neighborhood!"

"Jesus Christ," Hunt muttered.

Brett heard him. "Don't you dare take the Lord's name in vain!" He continued forward, across their lawn, until he was at the driveway. His fist smacked the trunk of the Saab.

Angrily, Hunt marched off the porch. "Get off of our property!" he demanded.

"Hunt!" Beth cautioned.

"What are you gonna do about it? Huh? You're not man enough to handle a real woman, have to go around diddling little kids, and you think you can take me on? I'd like to see you try it, Jackson!"

Oh fuck. That's what this was about. The molestation charges. Somehow Ed Brett had found out. Hunt glanced quickly up and down the street. How many other people knew? How many of them believed it?

"What are you going to do next, huh? Try to cornhole my boy? I want you out of this neighborhood, Jackson. You and that slut wife. We don't need perverts like you living next door."

Hunt advanced on him. He had never been a physical guy, had not been in a fight since elementary school, but he was ready now to rip that asshole's head off. "I have not done anything wrong. I have never, never, *never* touched a child that way. And if you speak that way about my wife again, I'll beat the living shit out of you."

Behind Ed Brett, Hunt saw his wife rushing over across the lawn. The bratty Brett kids were cheering on their father from inside the living room. "Kill him!" one of them yelled out the window.

A sudden tug on his arm stopped Hunt. Beth was pulling his sleeve. "Let it go," she said. "They're assholes. Who cares what they think."

Brett's face was red. "Who are you calling an asshole?"

"Yeah!" his wife shouted, moving next to him. "We're not the ones raping children!"

"No one's—" Hunt began. And Ed Brett shoved him in the chest, nearly knocking him down. He was up in a flash, ready to take a swing at the Neanderthal, but Beth held him back. "No!" she screamed. "Knock it off! Don't take the bait!"

"Need your little woman to protect you, eh, pansy boy?"

Beth turned on him. "He's more of a man than you'll ever be, you fat disgusting tub of lard."

Sally Brett ran at her. "You take that back, bitch!"

And then the two women were going at it. Sally Brett

fought wildly, like an animal, all flailing arms and biting mouth and kicking feet. But Beth was smarter, quicker, stronger, and she bobbed and weaved, ducked and struck. "I'll rip your eyes out!" Sally Brett cried.

The husbands pulled them apart, Beth still tense and in a fighting stance, Sally Brett struggling against her husband like a rabid alleycat. "No one wants you in this neighborhood," Ed Brett said as he backed onto his yard. "Get out of here."

"Fuck you," Hunt told him. He and Beth made their way back up to the porch.

"Sign here," the agent said, shoving a pen and clipboard at him.

Angrily, Hunt affixed his signature without reading the application.

"By the way, there's an addendum to your homeowner's insurance that we like to call the Good Neighbor policy," the agent said helpfully. "I don't know if you've read it. But I'll make sure it's activated." He smiled at them. "Good day."

Whistling happily, he strode across the lawn to the sidewalk.

2

Steve sat atop the ridgepole of his addition, fastening the last rafter. The sun was almost down and it was really too dark for this kind of work, but he was at the end and he wanted to get this finished before he quit for the night. He repositioned himself, then put all of his strength into tightening the bolt.

Something moved below him.

He nearly dropped the wrench.

He'd been anticipating something ever since the last phone conversation with the insurance agent.

Do you understand, bitch?

But even though he thought he'd been prepared, he knew

now that he wasn't, and the fear within him was a thousand times greater than when he'd spoken to the agent over the phone. There was anger mixed in with the fear as well, though, and it was the anger that he tried to stoke, that he concentrated on boosting.

He sat up, glancing quickly around the yard. From this angle, he could look down into the addition as well as see everything on three sides on the house. A man in a hat was standing next to the remaining half of the tree, and another was lurking near the tarp-covered woodpile. Whatever had moved through the addition below him was gone, but in the dim diffuse light of the nearly extinguished sun, he saw a puddle of urine on the plywood floor, and that served to fuel his anger.

"Right now, motherfuckers!" he yelled, standing and holding up his wrench. "Come on!"

The ridgepiece beneath his feet cracked, fell, sending him flying, and only by sheer dumb luck was he able to grab hold of the edge of the house roof. The lower half of his body slammed into the stucco of the wall, and he cried out in pain but held on. His wrench clattered onto the plywood, and he looked down to see one of the men standing directly between his legs, holding a screwdriver.

From the shadows another one emerged, swinging a two-by-four.

They were going to try to kill him. He had no doubt about that. They were working for the insurance company, and they had been sent out to punish him for not buying a policy with their firm.

He laughed rudely, sharply. Who would believe such a thing?

Suddenly the door to the house opened, an expanding triangle of fluorescence growing across the plywood floor, glinting off the puddle of piss, illuminating the men in hats. Only they weren't illuminated. They remained in shadow, their faces unseen.

Nina stood in the doorway. She saw the dark men with their makeshift weapons but made no effort to do anything. She did not run, did not call out for help, did not run to the phone. She looked up at him, unreadable, and remained in place.

So that was the way it went. He shouldn't have been surprised. His grip was weakening, and there was suddenly another man off to the right, holding a hammer. His legs hurt like hell, but he used them to try and gain purchase on the wall, hoping to use his remaining strength to pull himself onto the roof. They couldn't kill him outright, he thought. They would have to make it look like an accident.

His fingers tightened on the roof edge and he tried to lift himself, using his feet as leverage, but he simply didn't have enough strength. "Nina!" he called, hating himself for being so weak.

The door slammed below him, there was sudden darkness in the addition, and from within the house he heard the sound of running feet. She was going to get help! She'd just been stunned, temporarily incapacitated by fear. Now she was calling 911. Reinvigorated, he tried to raise himself again. His muscles strained, and he tilted his head back, looking up at the roof.

A bulking figure in a dark hat peered over the edge at him.

And for the first and last time, he saw the man's face.

And his smile.

3

Hunt knew immediately upon driving into work the next morning that something was up. He was five minutes late, but not one of the crews had left the corp yard yet. The men, in fact, were not even separated into crews; there was only a single amorphous group of maintenance services workers milling about the open area between the warehouse, the garage and the gate.

"What is it?" he asked Jack Hardy, the first person he met.

"Steve," he said. "Fell through his roof last night and broke his neck. Chuck's trying to find out if he's alive or dead. No one knows."

Job insurance.

It couldn't be.

But he knew that it could, and he glanced around guiltily, filled with not only a feeling of culpability but a bone-deep sense of dread. He was in way over his head. Like the apocryphal child who played with a Ouija board and opened the doorway to a whole host of horrors, he had gotten involved with something he did not understand, and instead of extricating himself from his predicament, he found himself getting in deeper and deeper.

He was responsible for Kate Gifford's death, and now, maybe, Steve's.

Hunt searched the crowd for Jorge, saw him talking to Mike Flory on the far side of the corp yard near the gas pump. He wanted to talk to his friend, but not in front of Mike, so he simply nodded and said "Hey." The three of them stood around chatting while they waited for Chuck's status report, and the consensus seemed to be that Steve was an asshole but he did not deserve *this*.

"Maybe he'll live and eventually be all right, but he'll have to take an early retirement and we'll get a new manager in there who will actually fight for us," Mike said hopefully.

Jorge said nothing. He was behaving strangely, Hunt thought. He seemed fidgety and ill at ease, constantly glancing around the perimeter of the corp yard as though searching for someone, lapsing into an uncharacteristic silence each time Steve's name was mentioned.

Hunt took him aside on the pretext of getting coffee. He

stopped by one of the trucks, where they couldn't be over-heard. "You bought employment insurance, didn't you?"

Jorge nodded, relieved to be able to speak. "Yes!"

"I did too."

"And that's why—?"

Hunt cut him off. "Yeah. I think so."

Chuck Osterwald emerged from the maintenance services administrative office and held up his hands for silence. "The news isn't good. Steve is in a coma," he announced. "They don't know right now whether or not he's going to live. He has a ruptured spleen, a pierced lung, internal bleeding and severe head trauma. He's been through surgery, but even if he survives, they don't know how long it will be before he comes out of the coma. Or *if* he will. Len Rojas will be acting as temporary manager, and he called from downtown to say that everyone's to get their ass in gear and get to work. This week's schedules will remain as is. Len will decide what's doing next week. Let's roll."

The milling employees began splitting off into crews and teams, heading toward their particular equipment.

Jorge thought for a moment. "Steve wasn't the only one threatening our jobs," he said quietly.

"I know."

"Other people wanted to contract us out."

"I know."

"The board of supervisors—"

Hunt looked at him. "I know."

The orgy was the top story on the news that night.

No details were given, but even a general overview of the situation was titillating enough that reporters were stationed outside of the normally staid and visually uninteresting county administration building, breathlessly commenting on "the scandal that has rocked a government institution to its very foundation." The story ran at five, then again at six after the national news, and once more at ten o'clock.

Apparently, an intern from the U of A had been working late last night, trying to impress the office to which he'd been assigned with his diligence and commitment, when he opened the door to the board of supervisors' deliberation chambers, the room where they went to discuss matters in private session. There he had found all five of the supervisors as well as two unidentified department heads participating in what the NBC and CBS affiliates referred to as "an orgy," the ABC station identified as "an after-hours sex club" and Fox called "sizzling hot sexcapades."

The intern had gone straight to the chief administrator and then to his parents. All of the supervisors had tendered their immediate resignation, and a special election was going to be called before the end of the month to choose their replacements. The department heads involved had also resigned.

Hunt had a sneaking suspicion that the two unidentified department heads were proponents of contracting out tree trimming.

A vindictive part of him hoped that one of them was head of MIS.

Jorge called while he and Beth were eating dinner to fill them in on details he'd learned from a friend of his in administration. Helen Butler, the lone female supervisor, had been on top of the conference table when the kid walked in, all three inputs in use. Lee Spenser, a gruff, tough ex-marine, was on his hands and knees on the floor, taking it from behind, Reynold Lopez giving it to him joyously. The department heads had indeed been two of the most vocal supporters of outsourcing maintenance services in general and tree trimming in particular. One was stuffing Helen Butler's mouth, the other was alone in a corner, stuffing a rubber enema hose up himself.

Hunt could tell that Jorge took a certain pleasure in the comeuppance of these administrators who had planned to do away with his job, but beneath that was horror and fear, a recognition that what was happening went not only beyond the bounds of physics and rationality but also morality.

"What happens next?" Jorge asked. "Is that it?"

"Let's hope so," Hunt said. "Let's hope so."

Sixteen

1

"Jorge!"

He'd been half-asleep, propped up on the pillow that he'd leaned against the headboard, but Jorge was wide awake, out of bed and running for the bathroom the second he heard the panic in his wife's voice.

She was supposed to have been taking a shower, but instead she sat on the toilet, naked, skin dry, a stricken look on her face. Between her spread legs he could see blood in the water. "Ohmygod," he said, the phrase coming out as a single word. It suddenly seemed hard to breathe. "Ohmygod."

"Something's wrong." Ynez started to cry. "We're going to lose the baby."

"No, we're not! Stay right there!" He ran back to the bedroom and scrambled through the jumble of items atop the dresser until he found his wallet and insurance card. He grabbed the phone from the nightstand and, with trembling fingers, punched in the emergency number on the back of the card. Thankfully, he didn't have to navigate an automated answering system but was connected immediately to a real live person.

"My wife's bleeding!" he shouted into the phone. "She's pregnant and she's bleeding! What am I supposed to do?"

The voice on the other end of the line was composed and

unruffled, the voice of a no-nonsense older woman who had seen situations like this before—as well as things *much* worse—and in a way that seemed comforting. "Calm down, sir. Just explain to me what's happened. Start at the beginning."

He couldn't calm down, didn't even try, but blurted out that Ynez wasn't due for another five weeks and suddenly had vaginal bleeding.

"Is it accompanied by cramping?" the woman asked.

"I don't know!" He'd never felt so helpless in his life.

"Go immediately to the hospital," the woman said. "Bring your insurance card and go directly to the maternity ward."

"Are we going to lose the baby?"

"I can't tell you that, sir. But they will know what to do at the maternity ward. They deal with this all the time."

He wanted more than that, he wanted a definite *This is normal, it happens all the time, everything will be fine*, but he obviously wasn't going to get it and he didn't have time to sit around playing Twenty Questions, so he hung up the phone and ran back into the bathroom. Ynez was almost dressed, and he quickly pulled on a pair of jeans and a T-shirt, grabbing his wallet and keys. "They said go straight to the hospital," he told her.

"What about the baby? What did they say it is?"

He decided not to sugarcoat it. "The woman I talked to didn't know. She just said we need to get to the maternity ward right away."

"Oh God!" Ynez was sobbing again. "Why did this have to happen to us?"

Because we need more insurance, Jorge thought crazily, but he dared not speak it aloud.

The trip seemed interminable. They'd made a dozen practice runs, trying every possible route until they found the shortest one, but this time they hit almost every red light on the way to the hospital. Ynez was alternately moaning and crying on the seat next to him, and he kept asking her if she was in pain, if things were getting worse, but she just shouted, "No! Keep driving!"

It was late and he wasn't sure the main entrance of the hospital would be open, so he pulled around to the emergency entrance on the side of the building and parked in one of the empty twenty-minute spaces next to the door. Ynez had put on a maxipad before pulling on her underwear, but the blood had soaked through, and when she got out of the car, Jorge could see a dark wet stain at her crotch.

"Shit!" he said, trying not to panic. Holding her arm, he hustled her through the door. The small waiting room was nearly empty. In one corner, underneath a wall-mounted television showing an infomercial, sat a dirty man in a brown shabby coat who appeared to be drunk. In the opposite corner, as far away from the man as possible, a young couple sat anxiously to either side of their pale, lethargic son.

Jorge took Ynez straight to the admissions window. Behind thick glass, an overweight nurse sat before a computer, typing. She looked up at their approach. Her nametag read: *F. Hamlin.* "May I help you?"

"My wife's pregnant and she's bleeding!" Jorge blurted out.

Ynez gripped his arm tightly, as though she were about to fall. "The baby's not due for five weeks."

A metal drawer opened in the counter beneath the thick window, like a teller's drawer at the bank. "May I see your insurance card?"

"She's bleeding! She needs to see a doctor! Now!" But even as he complained, he was taking out his wallet, taking out the insurance card, dropping it in the drawer.

The drawer closed. On the other side of the glass, the nurse withdrew the card, looked at it, punched in a few numbers on the keyboard of her computer and looked up at them. "I'm sorry," she said. The drawer slid out again with the insurance card. "We can't admit you to Desert Regional."

"What?"

Ynez was sobbing again, holding her abdomen. "This can't be happening!" she screamed.

"We're preregistered at this hospital!" Jorge yelled at the nurse. "This is where we're supposed to go!"

"I'm sorry, but your provider has been changed."

"What the hell does that mean?"

"It means you have to go to Waltzer Community Hospital. We can't admit you here."

"We've been taking Lamaze classes here for the past two months! We just took a tour of the maternity ward last week!"

"Your HMO is no longer accepted by Desert Regional. If you had a PPO . . ."

"There's . . . this . . ." He was spluttering, unable to speak coherently. "This is the emergency room. This is an emergency. You . . . you have to let us in. We have emergency coverage. It's . . . it's on the card."

"We can't—"

He pulled Ynez back from the window, pointed at the growing stain on her jeans. "She's bleeding!"

"We can't admit her here."

Jorge thought of Mary and Joseph, forced to give birth to Jesus in a stable.

This was how the other half lived. The uninsured.

Ynez was crying, and he felt so angry and frustrated that he was damn near close to tears himself. He wanted to pick up one of the chairs in the waiting area, smash it through the fucking window and strangle that bitch. He was literally shaking with emotion, but when he spoke again only a single-word plea came out: "Please?"

The nurse softened, and for the first time he could see the person behind the job. "I'll call for an ambulance," she told him. Her voice was low, and he got the impression that she wasn't supposed to do this. "They'll take you over to Waltzer Community."

He was immediately sorry for what he'd been thinking. It wasn't her fault. She was just doing her job, just doing what she'd been told. She was simply a cog in the machine. It was the machine itself that was to blame. The system.

"Thanks," he told her.

Ynez whimpered beside him.

"Go out the door and to the right. The ambulance'll be here in a second."

Jorge nodded.

"You'll be all right," the nurse said to Ynez. "Your baby will be fine."

He didn't know if that was based on knowledge and experience or if she was just saying that to make them feel better, but it *did* make him feel better and he hustled Ynez out the door. A moment later, an ambulance pulled up from around the side of the building. Two attendants opened the back door. "Do you want a stretcher?" the older one asked.

Ynez shook her head.

"There are bench seats in the back, then. Just strap yourselves in and hold on. We'll get you to Waltzer."

"Are you paramedics?" Jorge asked. "She's bleeding. Could you just take a look and . . . make sure everything's okay?"

"Sorry, sir."

The back doors closed, and they were left alone as the two attendants raced to the ambulance's cab. The sirens and lights went on and the vehicle sped away from the hospital. Through the rear window, Jorge saw his car, still parked in the twenty-minute zone, and he wondered if he was going to get a ticket. Or how they'd get back.

Small stuff, he told himself. They'd figure it out later. What was important now was getting to the hospital and making sure the baby was going to be healthy and born without complications.

The ambulance zoomed through city streets, running at

least two red lights, and in a remarkably short period of time they arrived. Jorge had no idea where the hospital was located—the view out the back window of the speeding ambulance was confusing and disorienting—but when the attendants opened the rear doors, he was grateful to see that they were directly in front of the emergency room entrance and that an orderly with a wheelchair was rushing out to bring Ynez inside.

Both Jorge and the orderly helped her into the chair and all three of them hurried through the sighing doors of the hospital, directly into the emergency room. Either Desert Regional's admissions nurse or one of the two ambulance attendants must have called ahead and explained the situation because the orderly pushed the wheelchair through the ER and out another set of doors into another corridor, and when Jorge asked where they were going, the orderly said the maternity ward.

Ynez let out a sharp cry.

"What's wrong?" Jorge demanded, frightened more than he would have believed possible.

"I think it's a contraction!"

"That's good," the orderly said. "That means things are proceeding the way they're supposed to."

Ynez started doing her Lamaze breaths: "*Keekee heehee! Keekee heehee! Keekee . . .*"

They continued forward, moving fast. He didn't like this hospital, Jorge realized. The corridors seemed too dark, and even though it was late at night, the place seemed less populated that it should have. They passed several rooms that appeared to be completely empty, devoid of even a bed, and nearly all of the rooms that did contain hospital equipment seemed to be missing patients.

The maternity ward was arranged in a semicircle, with the nurse's station at the hub and the individual rooms fanned out around it. There were three nurses behind the curved counter, a skinny black woman writing down monitor readings from a series of electronic display screens, and two overweight white women discussing something between themselves in low hushed tones.

The orderly pushed the wheelchair in front of the nurse's station, rapped his knuckles twice on the countertop, then headed back down the corridor with a wave. "She's all yours, ladies."

Ynez let out another sharp cry.

"*Keekee!*" she breathed. "*Heehee!*"

One of the overweight women rushed over. "Don't worry, everything's going to be fine. We have a room all ready for you, sweetie." She expertly helped Ynez out of the wheelchair and led her into one of the empty rooms, turning on the lights as she did so.

"What kind of hospital is this?" Jorge said, looking around. The room was decorated like a child's bedroom, with bright primary colors and paintings of clowns on the walls . . . only the clowns appeared hateful, evil. Arched angled eyebrows lent malevolence to mysteriously deep-set eyes. Painted mouths grinned venomously at the birthing bed.

"All of our maternity rooms are designed to resemble nurseries. We want both mother and baby to be comfortable here, and we try to make it as much like home as we can."

Comfortable? Home? Those were the last things this place reminded him of.

Maybe his perception was skewed, maybe it was all in his head.

But no, he saw the look on his wife's face and knew that she felt exactly the same.

He glanced toward a fat clown next to the bathroom door, a white-faced demon with a forked tongue protruding from between rows of oversized teeth.

He felt cold. They were here because they didn't have enough supplemental insurance. What was it that the agent had said? Additional coverage may be required at substantial extra cost?

The nurse helped Ynez out of her clothes, wiped up the blood with a damp sponge, put a hospital gown on her, then assisted her into bed. She did a cursory examination, announced that Ynez was dilated three centimeters and that the baby would be born tonight.

Ynez clutched the nurse's arm. "But what about all that blood?"

"It's not as uncommon as you might think. The doctor will be here in a minute, though, to give you a thorough exam. We'll know more then."

The nurse left, and the two of them were alone. As in the rest of the hospital, the lights in here were dimmed, and though Jorge knew it was supposed to approximate night in the twenty-four-hour world of the hospital, though he knew it was done to make patients more comfortable, it made him feel unsettled and vaguely ill at ease.

"I don't like this," Ynez said weakly. "It doesn't feel right."

"Where? Let me call the nurse back. Does it hurt?"

"No," she explained. "I mean this hospital, the way they're acting, the whole thing. Everyone's too casual. No one seems concerned that I was bleeding. I should've been checked by a doctor in the ER, not just left here—" She broke off in mid-sentence, grimaced with pain, and quickly started breathing. "*Keekee Heehee! Keekee Heehee . . .*"

"Goddamn it," he said. "Where's the monitoring equipment? Why aren't they measuring these contractions? I'm going to get that nurse—"

The nurse's bulk filled the doorway. "The doctor is here to see you," she announced, moving aside.

And in walked a tall man in a black hospital gown, wearing the mask of a demented laughing cherub.

Ynez started screaming.

"What's going on here?" Jorge demanded. "What the fuck is this?"

"Shut up!" the doctor ordered from behind the mask, and his voice was high and sharp.

The voice of one of those clowns, Jorge thought, and the idea chilled him to the bone. He grabbed Ynez's arm, helped her sit up. "Come on, we're getting out of here. We're going to another hospital."

"You're not going anywhere," the doctor said.

Somehow, while his attention had been diverted, two burly orderlies had entered the room, but they were not dressed in hospital gowns or medical attire. They wore long coats and broad-brimmed hats. At a nod from the masked head, they grabbed Jorge's arms and held him tight.

"Let me go!" he demanded.

"Sedate him," the doctor said in his manic voice. "He's hysterical." And suddenly his sleeve was pushed up and Jorge felt the wetness of alcohol and then a pinprick of pain on his forearm.

The three nurses walked in, and the skinny one began laying out a series of wicked-looking medical tools on a metal tray attached to the foot of the bed. Ynez was not only screaming but trying to escape, instinctively attempting to protect her unborn baby. The two overweight nurses held her down and strapped her into the bed while the masked doctor spread apart her legs and fastened them in stirrups.

Jorge wanted to help her, wanted to rescue her, wanted to get them both out of this funhouse hospital, but his muscles had gone slack. If he had not been supported by the orderlies, he would have slumped to the floor. He could not even seem to make his mouth work.

But he could see.

Oh yes, he could see.

And hours later, long after he'd been deposited in a chair facing the bed, after Ynez had passed out from the pain and could no longer scream, while the nurses cleaned up the blood and took away the tools, the doctor came over with a bundle in his hands. Jorge stared dumbly for a moment at the blood-spattered black gown, then looked up at the mask with its laughing cherub mouth. The eyes peering through the holes in the mask appeared to be laughing, too. The doctor held out the bundle and showed Jorge the baby, which was screaming and kicking and flailing its arms. Blood flowed from a gaping wound between its legs where the penis had been crudely severed.

"It's a girl," the doctor said.

2

Jorge was not the same after the birth of his child. He didn't talk much about the baby, but when he did, his voice was filled with a haunted sadness. There was anger, too, but he didn't express it, and in place of the carefree easygoing jokester Jorge had always been was a dark troubled man who seldom spoke unless spoken to, and sometimes not even then.

It had been the lead story in the paper and on all of the local TV newscasts for several days. Police and special investigators talked to everyone at Desert Regional who could have conceivably come into contact with Jorge and Ynez, interviewing men and women from all shifts, but no trace of either F. Hamlin the admissions nurse or the two ambulance attendants who drove them to the other hospital was ever found. Waltzer Community did not even seem to exist—authorities could find no record of it and no one in the medical community who had even heard of the facility—and gradually the tone of the articles and news stories had changed from horrified outrage to cynical disbelief, and by the end of it, Jorge's credibility was completely shot. Rumors were circulating that

Jorge and Ynez would soon be charged with the mutilation of their infant and a whole host of other crimes.

Hunt and Edward, of course, believed their friend completely. As did Beth and Joel and Stacy. Most of the other tree trimmers were on his side also, although Len, perhaps inhabiting Steve's role a little too well, seemed to make a special effort not to show any sympathy for what had happened.

A week after returning to work, Jorge did not show up at the corp yard, and while drinking his morning coffee, Hunt was paged over the loudspeaker. Jorge was out on stress leave, Len told him in the office, and he was being reassigned. Until further notice, he'd be working with Mike Flory. With Edward out on disability and now Jorge on stress leave, they were shorthanded, so his and Mike's respective three-man crews would become two-man crews.

Stress leave.

Had Jorge bought extra insurance for that?

Hunt tried to call his friend, but the phone seemed to be permanently off the hook, and when he went by the Marquezes' house, no one answered the door.

"Leave them alone," Beth told him. "Give them some time."

"Yeah," he said. But he thought of Edward, laid up in bed, Jorge, out on stress leave.

Two down, Hunt thought. One to go.

3

"I keep waiting for the other shoe to drop," Hunt said. "I can't help thinking that, despite everything that's happened, we've been lucky. We've gotten off easy."

Joel knew exactly how he felt.

They were out back, on the patio. The women were in the kitchen, Lilly was playing a video game in her room, and all of the windows were closed, so they had some privacy and were able to speak more freely than they could inside the house. "We haven't even told Lilly about the baby," he said.

Hunt nodded. "She doesn't need to hear that."

"But are we doing the right thing, shielding her from what's going on around her?" Joel sighed. "You're lucky you don't have to worry about those kinds of things."

Hunt lowered his voice and looked behind them to make sure no one was coming outside. "Has he come to you lately? Have you seen him?"

"No thank God. In fact, he's never come to our house. Only to my office. Once."

"Maybe he's forgotten about you," Hunt said. "Maybe he passed you by, maybe you'll be okay."

Joel certainly hoped so. He'd been following exactly the train of thought, although it sounded odd to hear it spoken aloud. He turned to the side, looked over at Lilly's closed window. She was the one he was worried about. She was seeing a grief counselor to help her deal with Kate's death, and the counselor said she was doing extremely well, but at home around them she continued to pretend as though nothing had happened, continued to act as though everything was fine and they lived in a Very Brady world.

She even acted normal around Hunt—which was nice because he believed his friend to be completely innocent of all charges, and she obviously did too. But at the same time, Kate had told her some pretty awful things, in detail, and it seemed strange to him that there was no residual effect.

And all of this made him wonder whether there would be any signs or whether she would tell them if she encountered the insurance agent someplace. That's what he was really worried about.

No. That was not true. What he really worried about was that she would fall through the cracks, that she would not be covered by one of their insurance policies and her vulnerability would lead to . . .

He could not even think it.

The kitchen window slid up. "Time to eat!" Stacy called. "Come in and wash up!"

He waved. "Okay."

Hunt smiled wryly as they turned to go inside. "If I could buy an insurance policy to protect your family and keep you out of everything, I would."

"Don't say that," Joel told him, shivering. "Don't even joke about it."

Seventeen

1

Sirens woke them up in the middle of the night. Sirens and the smell of smoke. Hunt pulled aside the curtains, looked out the window and saw flames leaping from a hole in the Bretts' roof next door.

He'd been expecting something like this to happen. Waiting for it. Hoping it wouldn't but knowing it would. Ever since Steve had been put into a coma and the board of supervisors had been forced to resign, he'd know that the so-called "Good Neighbor policy" embedded in his homeowner's insurance would bring about ruin for the Bretts.

No, that was not true. It hadn't been since Steve and the board. He'd known even as the agent had promised to activate it.

So why hadn't he said something?

Part of him wanted Brett punished, no doubt, but that was a small raging piece of id buried way the hell down. He hadn't really wanted anything bad to happen to anyone. Not to that moron Steve, not to that asshole Ed Brett. But something had compelled him to be silent, to keep the insurance, a nagging itch at the back of his mind, a drive to be ever safer, ever more secure, to protect himself by guarding against any and every calamity. It was like people who got tattoos. They started out with just one but were soon getting every square inch of their body inked. They couldn't help themselves.

He'd even found himself lately inventing new forms of insurance, thinking up types of coverage that he would like to have: barbecue insurance, so that when he grilled steaks or chicken the meat would never be burned; sleep insurance, so that he would always get a decent night's sleep and be well-rested each morning; photo insurance, so that he would always take good snapshots.

Beth had been thinking along the same lines, only her ideas were nowhere near so benign.

"I've been wondering something," she'd said the other day, and Hunt could tell from her tone of voice that he did not want to hear what she had to say.

"What?" he asked

"Betty Grable had her legs insured for a million dollars. I think Mary Hart did, too. And didn't Jennifer Lopez or someone insure their butt?"

He could see where this was leading. Insurance coverage for body parts. "I don't think we have to worry," he said. "We don't have any famous body parts." But he *was* starting to worry.

She leaned closer, voice still low, almost a whisper. "What if he comes to us? What if he offers to insure my breasts?"

"Don't."

"You know what'll happen. I'll get breast cancer. Or I'll be in an accident—"

"Beth."

She grabbed his shoulders, and he saw the hysteria building in her eyes. "What if he wants to insure my vagina? Or your cock?"

"Jesus Christ!" He pulled away from her. "Get a grip. We can't start overreacting. We can't let him get to us. We have enough real problems to worry about without inventing fake ones."

"I'm not inventing fake problems," she said. "I'm brain-storming. Trying to plan ahead so we'll be prepared."

Now, staring out the window, he thought that maybe she was onto something. Maybe they should try to think outside the box in an effort to prepare themselves for whatever came next.

As he watched, a fire engine stopped in front of their house, two firemen running toward the Bretts' home carrying a hose hooked up to the truck, two others grabbing a second hose and connecting it to the nearby hydrant. Another fire engine immediately pulled up behind it. An ambulance came to a catty-corner stop in the middle of the road.

Were any of the Bretts hurt? He hoped not, although it would be hypocritical of him to pretend that he was concerned about any loss to their property. He didn't give a damn if Ed Brett lost his house, his car and everything he owned. Still, he did not want anyone injured.

Or killed.

How had the fire started, he wondered. Faulty wiring? A short in a small appliance? Ed Brett smoking in bed? Hunt was sure that there'd be a legitimate reason, an easily recognizable and understandable cause. At the same time, he knew the real reason for the blaze, a reason that no inspector would guess in a million years.

Good Neighbor policy.

He looked across his pillow at Beth, who was also watching the scene out the window. She met his eyes. Neither of them said a word.

2

I'll rip your cunt out you dried up bich.

Beth read the letter, then tore it up and threw it away, feeling both angry and frightened. They'd been getting threatening mail for the past several weeks, though she had yet to tell Hunt that she'd also started receiving letters at work. And the ones that came to her work were scarier, more vicious. One had vowed to kidnap her and take her anally with a cucumber and then make her eat the cucumber so she would know what it felt like to be molested. Another had promised to gut her and feed her innards to a javelina.

She thought about the message she'd just thrown away. It had been delivered by the post office—with no return address, of course—and had not come through the interoffice mail. The misspelling of "bitch" seemed suspicious to her, however, and while she was not a profiler, only watched them on TV, she thought that the error was a conscious attempt by the letter writer to make her think that someone less intelligent and less educated had sent it.

Which meant that it was probably one of her coworkers.

All of the letters took as their central premise the idea that she aided and abetted child molestation because she supported her husband. The missives they received at home were primarily aimed at Hunt, and they were basically death threats with some fairly graphic plans for torture and sexual mutilation thrown in. Neither she nor Hunt had any idea why these letters had suddenly started arriving, but they were pretty sure that radical children's rights advocates were making them the target of an e-mail and letter-writing campaign.

She wouldn't be surprised if the insurance agent or his company were behind it.

Maybe they were about to be offered mail insurance.

And e-mail insurance.

It was surprising how fast her perceptions had been altered, how quickly both she and Hunt had adapted their worldviews to encompass the concept of an all-powerful insurance company. These days there were very few events in their lives that they did not relate somehow to insurance.

Edward had suggested to Hunt that their current fast-track

acquisition of strange and unwanted coverage was connected to their previous insurance problems. Such a conclusion was unavoidable, but it also suggested an even wider conspiracy, not merely a treadmill onto which they had inadvertently stepped, but a pervasive insurance cabal that had been stalking them, targeting them, trying to recruit them. She and Hunt had discussed the implications ad nauseam, and they'd always ended up exactly where they'd started, in a state of gloom and hopelessness, unable to think of a way to break free.

Five letters with no return addresses and intentionally generic block printing were waiting in the mailbox when she arrived home. Hunt pulled into the driveway seconds after she did, and together they checked their e-mail. Fifty-five messages, all with lovely topic headings like "Die!" and "Child Molesters Rot in Hell."

Hunt deleted them unopened.

She was fired the next day.

Beth had been expecting to lose her job ever since she declined the employment insurance, but the timing of it was still a surprise. A Thursday? If asked, she would have guessed that it would happen on a Monday or a Friday.

And the way it was done was surprising as well. She walked into her office to find that all of her personal effects had been stripped from the walls and taken from their drawers and placed in boxes stacked neatly atop the desk. Next to the boxes, in a sealed envelope on which was printed her name, she found a letter of termination as well as her final paycheck.

The termination letter was signed by Earl Peters, Thompson's vice president in charge of personnel, and she decided to confront him in his office, make him fire her face-to-face instead of taking the coward's way out. She had nothing to lose. She hadn't bought employment insurance, so she doubted that another company or institution was going to hire her, especially with the bad recommendation she knew Thompson Industries would provide despite her years of outstanding service and excellent work. Whether she slunk quietly away or went out in a blaze of glory, she would not be employable again until they defeated the insurance company and all of this insanity was stopped.

Until they defeated the insurance company?

Yes. She didn't know how or when, but she realized that destroying the insurance company was their unspoken goal, was the end she envisioned. She had no idea how to go about such a thing—she wasn't some plucky heroine in a novel—but it was what she believed would eventually happen, and she knew that when the time came and an opportunity presented itself, she and Hunt would act without hesitation.

She looked down once again at her termination letter, at the hastily scrawled signature of Earl J. Peters, and she thought that this would be a good time to start honing her fighting skills. Letter in hand, she strode purposefully out the door of her office.

The news was already common knowledge. In the hall she was met with concealed smirks and amused whispers. She heard the word "witch" spoken under a man's breath, heard the word "whore." Just before the elevator, Stacy ran up almost in tears and threw her arms around her. "How can they do this? I don't know what I'm going to do without you."

Beth suddenly felt tears welling in her own eyes. She pulled away from her friend, not wanting to cry, needing to keep her edge. "I'll call you later," she said. "We'll talk about it tonight."

"But—"

"I can't right now," she said, carefully wiping her right eye with a fingernail. "I just . . . can't."

Stacy nodded. She understood. "Where are you going?"

"Up to see fat boy."

Her friend nodded, tried to smile through her tears. "Give him hell."

That she would, Beth vowed. That she would.

3

Edward did his exercises energetically, smiling, talking, trying his damnedest to impress the pretty little physical therapist the hospital had sent over. But the minute she helped him into the bed, gave him his shot and left, he slumped back on his pillow in misery and defeat.

"Just shoot me now," he said aloud.

He lay in bed, too tired even to turn on the television. Not only could he feel the agonizing pain accompanying every one of his multiple injuries, but his remaining muscles were unbelievably sore and strained. He closed his eyes for a few moments, hoping to fall asleep, but he was too miserable to doze, and he once more opened his eyes. Sighing heavily, he felt a sharp pang in his rib cage.

This was going to be a long fucking afternoon.

He glanced around his converted living room for about the millionth time. He was sick of this space, sick of this furniture, sick of these decorations, and once he was out and about again, he was going to renovate the whole damn place from top to bottom.

Things were not what they seemed.

He closed his eyes again. No, not that.

Things were not what they seemed.

That thought had occurred to him often over the past few weeks and it seemed to gain greater currency each time.

Things were not what they seemed.

He knew that was crazy thinking, knew he was being paranoid, but he couldn't shake the feeling that there was something different about his house, something wrong. He remembered reading a story where a family's possessions were substituted with identical objects in the middle of the night, and that's what this felt like.

Only . . .

Only that wasn't quite right. These were his belongings, he knew that, it was just that they seemed . . . corrupted.

Yes. That was it exactly. He didn't have any sixth sense, was not able to see or smell or feel the taint of those hat-wearing specters on his furniture, on his decorations. But the *On Any Sunday* poster on his wall now seemed genuinely malevolent, and he was convinced that the drawers of his bureau held more than clothes.

He thought of those men he had seen in the tree, around the ladder.

The teeth.

He remembered the teeth.

He was grateful when Hunt and Joel arrived to visit.

"How is it that people don't remember the word 'snatch-box'?" he asked as the two unlocked and opened the front door, walking in. "They know 'snatch,' they know 'box,' but somehow they've forgotten that the two used to go together. I tried to look it up in the dictionary the other day and it wasn't even there."

Hunt laughed as he replaced the key under the mat. "Using your time wisely, I see."

"Can't just watch soap operas all day."

Joel walked into the kitchen, got them all a beer. He tossed one to Edward. "How are the exercises going?"

He shrugged. Or tried to. "They're going."

"Any progress?"

"That exquisite little beauty they send over for my physical therapy says so, but truthfully I can't see it."

"How long before you think you can get around on your own?" Hunt asked.

"Too long," Edward sighed. "Too long."

They talked about things in general. Hunt filled him in on the gossip at work, and Edward said that Jorge had stopped by last night.

"I saw him, too," Hunt said. "He dropped by the house, said he'll be back at work next week. Thank God. I don't think it's good for him to just sit at home with Ynez and the baby all day. Brooding. I mean, let's face it, it must be hard to deal not only with that but with all of the gossip and the suspicion and the lawsuits hanging over his head."

Edward lowered his voice. "Have you . . . seen the baby?"

"No." Hunt shook his head. "I suppose they'll show him . . . *her* to us when they're ready." He shrugged. "Or maybe not. I just don't know."

"We didn't even know how to respond," Joel admitted. "I didn't know if I should send a congratulations card or a sympathy card. Stacy ended up just giving Hunt a package of Huggies to give them."

Hunt and Joel stayed another hour and promised to bring the wives next time. "You all set for everything?" Hunt asked. "Need me to make a grocery run or anything?"

"Not today. A few more days, maybe."

"All right, then. We'll see you later."

"Later," Joel said.

Hunt started to turn away . . . then stopped. There was a long pause. He looked back at Edward. "Has he come by?"

Edward knew exactly who his friend was talking about. "No," he said.

"Any phone solicitations? Pamphlets in the mail?"

"Not yet, knock on wood."

Hunt nodded, started to say something else, then thought better of it and gave Edward an almost genuine smile. "Later, then."

"See you. And thanks for coming by. Both of you."

He listened to them lock the door, heard their footsteps on the cement, the slamming of Hunt's car doors, the sound of the

Saab's engine, faint music from the radio. And then they were gone.

He was all alone.

Things were not what they seemed.

Not that again. He reached for the remote, turned on the television.

And tried not to look at his *On Any Sunday* poster.

Eighteen

1

It was Sunday morning. Hunt was mowing the lawn, and Beth was pruning her roses, weeding her flower garden. Across the open expanse of grass, the burned husk of the Bretts' house still stood, undemolished and surrounded by red ribbon warning trespassers to keep away because the structure was unsafe. Beth yanked out a long string of devil grass, tossing it in the pile of weeds next to her.

And the agent emerged from inside their house.

She just happened to be looking in that direction and she saw their front door open and the insurance agent step onto the porch, briefcase in hand. She gave a short sharp cry, quickly standing and instinctively running toward Hunt. It was impossible. They had been in the house all morning, had awakened late, eaten breakfast, read the Sunday paper, and then come outside to do yardwork only a scant ten minutes ago. There was no way the man could have gotten into their home.

She remembered with embarrassment that they had made love after waking up, an uncharacteristically strenuous bout during which she'd screamed out a kinky demand that she would not ever have wanted anyone else to hear.

Had the agent been there all that time? Had he sneaked in yesterday sometime and spent the night hidden away inside some closet or crouched down in a corner of the guest room, unseen? The only other possibility was that he had jumped the backyard fence sometime within the past few minutes and walked in through the kitchen door while they were busy in the front yard.

Or he had simply *appeared* inside their house and then stepped outside.

Hunt, no doubt alerted by her panicked reaction, looked up from the grass and saw the insurance agent on the porch. He shut off the mower's engine, and the two of them stood unmoving on the lawn as the man descended the three steps and started up the walkway toward them. "Good morning!" he shouted heartily. "I'm sorry if I startled you! Didn't mean to!"

"What were you doing in our house?" Hunt demanded.

The agent waved him away. "Oh, don't worry. Just a short routine inspection." He was wearing a strange, almost Victorian suit with pleated pants, a buttoned vest and a visible watch fob. The suit looked perfectly normal on him.

"What do you mean 'inspection'?" Beth had regained some of her self-possession. "That's called trespassing."

"I'm afraid not," the agent corrected her. "If you'll read your homeowner's insurance policy, article five, paragraph 2, subparagraph A, you authorize any representative of The Insurance Group to conduct random and surprise inspections at any time in order to verify that you are abiding by the agreement you signed and not in any way modifying your home so that your policy covers additional items not expressly stated at the time of signing." He grinned. "I'm happy to say, you passed with flying colors."

Hunt pretended to fool with the lawnmower's throttle. "What exactly do you want?" he asked. "We're a little busy this morning."

The agent chuckled lewdly. "So I heard."

He *had* been in the house!

Beth could feel herself redden. "Get out of here," she said angrily.

"I will. But not before offering you a chance to buy insurance that could very well save your life. I am speaking, of course, of physical protection insurance." He had not opened his briefcase, but all of a sudden two brochures appeared in his previously empty right hand. "Take one, please."

Reluctantly, they took the proffered pamphlets.

"I'm concerned about you," the agent told them. "I'm concerned for your safety. Particularly in regard to these lunatics who keep writing those threatening letters."

Neither of them bothered to ask how he knew about that.

"We have a physical protection policy for high-risk individuals that I think is tailor-made just for you. It protects your physical person from bodily harm."

"What does that mean?" Hunt asked.

It meant, she thought, that anyone who attempted to do them harm would themselves be harmed. Or killed.

It was as if the agent could read her mind. "You can't possibly have any moral objection to physical protection protection." He was dumbfounded. "It's entirely a matter of self-defense. And everyone has a right to protect themselves." He leaned forward. "Some of these people will kill you if given the chance. They're zealots, they're fanatics. The horrible punishments they threaten in their letters? They would gladly carry them out, in a heartbeat."

She saw the look in his eye and knew that not only did he *want* them to buy the insurance, he *needed* them to buy it.

Hunt cleared his throat. "I'm . . . I'm not sure that such a policy would be right for us."

"This policy is aimed specifically at people in your rather unique predicament. It is perfect for the two of you. And, may I add, it will undoubtedly prevent extreme unpleasantness from befalling your family."

Again, she heard the neediness in his voice. What if they did *not* buy the insurance? What would happen to the agent?

Would he be fired, demoted, reassigned? Any of those would
be good.

"You can't afford not to take advantage of this once-in-a-
lifetime offer. Your very lives are at stake."

"No!" Beth practically shouted. She grabbed Hunt's hand,
held it tight. "No more insurance. We have enough."

"You will be killed," the agent said, and it was not a warning but a promise. The expression on his face was dark. He'd
changed, she noticed for the first time. His appearance. Where
he had once been an average-looking man of average height
and build, now he was bulkier and seemed a little taller, with
features that were sharper, crueler, less bland. Although he
could still turn on the charm when needed and his smile remained ingratiating, the agent seemed more likely to intimidate than cajole these days. It was an odd and probably stupid
thing to think, but she wondered if all of the insurance they'd
been buying had served to strengthen him. Maybe that was his
commission. Maybe instead of receiving money from the
company for each policy sold, he gained strength and energy,
sucking it from the unfortunate men and women who were
beaten down by the increasing financial demands made upon
them.

And the financial demands *were* increasing. By her estimate—entirely unofficial since not all of the premiums had yet
been billed to them—they were shelling out nearly five hundred dollars a month just for *new* insurance. That was six thousand dollars a year.

And the amount kept going up.

"Perhaps you don't understand the terms of the policy." The
agent spoke slowly and deliberately. *Threateningly*, Beth
thought. "Let me explain them to you."

And there on the lawn, he went over the details of physical
protection insurance, fondly reciting entire paragraphs from
memory, growing ever more comfortable as he spoke, obvi-

ously relishing the opportunity to describe one of his precious policies.

"Best of all," he concluded, "the rate's locked in, guaranteed. They'll be no raised premiums."

There had to be a catch, but Beth could not think of what it was, her mind too distracted and unfocused to concentrate. She was still angry about the agent's invasion of their privacy and incursion into their home. That was one of the insurance agent's tricks, she thought. The man showed up at odd hours or caught them off guard, then gave them take-it-or-leave-it ultimatums so they weren't able to think through all of the consequences and potential pitfalls of any policy. Only afterward did the side effects of the insurance become clear, and by then it was too late to do anything about it.

"Let me guess," Hunt said acerbically. "This is a once-in-a-lifetime offer, and we have to decide right now whether to take it or leave it."

"No," the agent told them. "If you need time to think about it, go ahead."

Hunt, too, seemed to be trying to find a catch. "We don't have to make up our minds right away?"

"Well," the agent admitted, "I do need an answer by this evening. But I can leave and come back later. Tonight, if you'd like. We could set up an appointment."

In her mind, she saw the insurance agent stepping out of their shower at the appointed time. Or opening their locked front door and stepping inside. Or emerging from their bedroom closet.

She didn't want to see the agent tonight, Beth realized. She didn't want to see him again today at all. If they were going to do this, she'd rather get it over with right now.

"Can you give us a moment?" she asked.

"Sure," the agent said expansively. He started walking across the lawn. "I'll just take a short stroll over here and look at your neighbor's place." He shook his head. "Tsk, tsk," he said, and Beth wasn't sure she'd ever heard anyone actually say "tsk, tsk." "Too bad they didn't have insurance, huh? Could've saved them a whole heap o' trouble." He chuckled.

Hunt took her hand, and the two of them walked to the other side of the front yard. "What do you think?" he asked quietly.

"I don't know enough to have an opinion," she said in an equally subdued voice.

"Why don't we think about it and have him come back later?"

"He was in our *house*," she reminded him. "I don't want him coming back later." She looked over Hunt's shoulder and saw the agent staring at the ruins of the Bretts' home, bouncing slightly on the balls of his feet. "Besides, let's face it, do we ever turn down any of the insurance he offers us? Do we ever have a choice? You know damn well that whatever he says is going to happen *will* happen if we don't protect ourselves."

"Well, at least we should read a little bit about it."

They both opened their brochures, but beyond the colorfully printed cover with the gold-stamped words *Physical Protection Insurance,* there was precious little information. Three bulleted paragraphs inside the pamphlet stated exactly the same thing the agent had already told them, no more, no less.

Hunt sighed. "If we don't get it, we'll be hurt, injured or, like he said, killed."

Reluctantly, Beth nodded.

"Should we just take it?" She heard the defeat in Hunt's voice. "The rate's locked in and guaranteed. At least we won't have to worry about that anymore."

"We weren't worried about it to begin with," Beth said. "Not until he brought it up. That's his fucking pattern. He brings up things to make us worried, then offers to ease our minds about it." She stared at his back. "I hate him," she said fiercely. "I wish he would die."

Hunt smiled wryly. "Isn't there an insurance policy for that?"

"I wish there was. I'd buy it in an instant."

Together, they walked across the lawn to where he stood.

"I'd take it if I were you," the agent suggested, and she thought again of how he seemed so much bigger, stronger and more clearly defined since their first encounter with him.

What would he be like when they had purchased every type of insurance available?

She did not want to know.

But what if they refused to buy any more? Would he grow weaker? What if they canceled all of their policies? Would he wither away and disappear?

They would never find out. Because, as he said, they would die, killed by one of their unseen enemies. And he would find someone else, another couple, another family, to whom he could sell his ever more intrusive forms of insurance.

The agent was right. They had no choice. They had to sign up.

"We'll take it," Hunt affirmed.

The agent nodded, satisfied. "You've made the right choice," he told them. "The only choice, really. And in the long run, I guarantee you, you'll be glad you did."

But Beth seriously doubted that they would.

The three of them walked over to the porch, where the agent had left his briefcase. Beth let go of Hunt's arm. Unenthusiastically, he took the clipboard, accepted the offered pen and signed. She followed suit.

Joel drove up at that moment, parking on the street in front of their curb, and Beth looked up from the clipboard, trying to see through the tinted windows, frantically hoping that he was alone and had not brought Stacy and Lilly with him. He *was* alone, and for that she breathed an inward sigh of relief. The last thing she wanted was for Lilly to see this monster, for him to try and speak with her, and she thought that if Joel had brought his daughter, she would have run out to the street toward them, waving her arms desperately screaming for them to leave.

"Hey!" Joel was out of the car and walking up to the porch, and it took him a moment to realize what was going on, who was with them. When he did figure it out, his smile disappeared, and his gait slowed. Beth felt dirty, embarrassed, as though she'd been caught doing something shameful.

She handed the clipboard back to the insurance agent.

He took it from her and waved to Joel, greeting him heartily. "Hello!" he called. "Nice to see you again, Mr. Mc-Cain!"

Joel scowled as he reached the porch. "What do *you* want?" he said disdainfully.

"Why, I'm just selling your good friends here some of our valuable physical protection insurance, sort of a catch-all policy that covers a *wide* range of incidents and activities. You should really think of purchasing some for your family, Mr. McCain. It'll help you sleep better at night."

Joel's face turned visibly pale.

"Unfortunately, I'm on my way, and I don't have time to go over it with you right now." The agent put away the clipboard and papers, picked up his briefcase. "Got a busy day ahead of me," he told them. "Got a life insurance quota to meet. I'm expected to talk to fifty, sixty families before this day's done." He smiled. "Wish me luck."

They wished him no such thing, and the three of them watched in silence as he walked out to the sidewalk, hung a right, and continued jauntily down the block.

2

Hunt awoke with a feeling of dread.

Today was a holiday, so he should have been happy—no

work!—but outside, the heavens were gray, a solid ceiling of cloud cover that pressed down on the city and compressed the sky, imparting a leaden feeling to the world below and complementing the feeling of vague unease within him. The holdover from an unremembered dream, perhaps. Or some sixth sense that told him things were not right.

The space on the bed next to him was empty and cold. Beth was already up. It was unusual for her not to wake him, and he wondered why she had let him sleep. Even more odd was the fact that the house was silent: no radio, no TV, no stereo, not even the ordinary sounds of movement that would accompany her morning breakfast ritual in the kitchen.

His sense of dread increased.

Hunt quickly got out of bed, put on some pants, and walked out to the kitchen, where Beth was sitting at the table, staring at the front page of the newspaper. She had not made coffee, had not made breakfast, and she looked up at him when he entered, her face blanched. With trembling hands, she held up the paper.

FORTY-FIVE KILLED IN MOST VIOLENT NIGHT IN TUCSON HISTORY, the banner headline screamed.

He knew exactly why she hadn't awakened him, and he knew now that his oppressive feeling of dread was entirely justified. Feeling numb, he took the paper from her hands. Forty-five killed? On a Sunday night?

Got a life insurance quota to meet.

He had no doubt in his mind that these deaths were a direct result of the insurance agent's marathon visit to those fifty or sixty families. He was stunned, though, by the strength of the insurance company's power. Killing forty-five people in one night was not just an impressive feat or an amazing bit of logistics, it was an impossibility, and he understood for the first time how strong and almost omniscient was the entity they were up against.

Impressive feat? Amazing bit of logistics?

He was ashamed of himself for being so cold and clinical, but the scale of what had happened was so enormous that he was only able to think in such dispassionate terms. He could not focus on a single individual who would provide the intimacy necessary to generate real sympathy and real sadness. When tragedy was this large it was rendered impersonal, it became numbers and statistics rather than faces and names.

He sat down at the table next to Beth and read the article:

In what police are calling the most violent night in Tucson history, thirty-five men and ten women were killed last night in unrelated homicides.

"We've never seen anything like this," stated Tucson Police Chief Brad Neth, who added that the city's manpower was strained to capacity by the extraordinarily high number of violent deaths within the eight-hour period.

Murder-suicides and domestic violence were responsible for the bulk of the killings, with fifteen women and three men stabbed, shot or strangled by their domestic partners and another four the result of self-inflicted gunshot wounds.

Eighteen of the killings were the result of gang violence. Six drive-by shootings in the Old Pueblo district resulted in eleven deaths, and one direct confrontation between rival gangs on the west side, in which an estimated fifty to sixty gang members took part, left seven dead and three seriously injured.

Five deaths were attributed to random acts of violence.

Although figures were unavailable for comparison, the combined murders were greater than any single one-night tally in New York, Los Angeles, or Chicago, according to Sergeant Buck Wilson. Tucson hospital emergency rooms were overwhelmed by the—

The article continued inside, and Hunt turned to page twenty-eight to finish it, but his eye was caught by another small story on the same page: WOMAN DIES AFTER HIT-AND-RUN. He didn't know why he stopped to read such an innocuous and commonplace article, but his attention was grabbed by the generic headline, and he quickly scanned the two paragraphs to discover that shortly after dusk last evening a woman racing across Congress Avenue, half a block from a lighted cross-walk, was struck by an unidentified black van that immediately fled the scene. She was apparently killed on impact.

Hunt's mouth suddenly went dry.

It was Eileen.

He read the article again, carefully this time, then read it once more, not trusting himself to stop for feelings, wanting only an injection of the bare facts.

She was listed as "Eileen Marx," which meant that she'd gone back to using her maiden name. She'd died alone, he thought, and to his mind there was nothing more tragic. As bitchy as she'd been at the last, as terrible as their marriage had ended up being, he still remembered when it had been good, still saw in his mind and felt in his heart that innocent high school girl who had asked him to the Sadie Hawkins dance and who had shyly asked him if he thought they were going to be "just friends or more than friends."

Beth must have seen the look on his face. "What is it?"

"Eileen," he told her. "My ex-wife." And even the words had a sad ring to them, a forlorn description of a lonely woman he had last seen getting on a bus. He felt empty inside, much sadder than he would have thought. Part of it was for her, but part of it was for himself. Her death had closed the door on his youth, had nailed shut once and for all the door that led backward to younger, carefree, more optimistic days.

Beth didn't know how to respond. "I'm sorry," she said finally in a voice that betrayed her ambivalence, and he reached across the table for her hand, held it and squeezed reassuringly.

He read once again that stock headline: WOMAN DIES AFTER HIT-AND-RUN. Had it been a coincidence? he wondered. Or had Eileen been visited by the insurance agent, offered a policy that she should not have refused?

It made him sick even to think about it.

The phone rang, and Hunt stood up to get it, half-fearing that it was the agent, calling to offer them additional coverage. But it was Joel, who did not even bother with a greeting. "Did you see the paper?" he asked soberly.

"Yeah," Hunt said.

"Do you think—?"

"Yeah."

Neither of them spoke for a moment.

"He's going to offer me personal injury or physical protection insurance," Joel said softly.

"Take it," Hunt told him. "You have a child."

"How did this happen? How did we get involved in this?"

"I don't know."

"Oh my God!" Beth cried. Her eyes widened.

"Hold on," he told Joel. He put his hand over the mouthpiece. "What is it?"

She pointed to the front of the newspaper, to a photo of the location where the worst of the gang-related incidents had occurred. He had not bothered to look closely at the picture, but he looked now, turning the paper to face him, and felt his blood run cold. Bodies were lying on a section of street cordoned off by police tape. Patrol cars with lights on and an ambulance were at either side of the shot. In the foreground was a gathered crowd.

To the right of the crowd, standing by himself, was their ghost.

The one they'd seen in the guest room mirror.

The man with the hat.

Hunt's mind was racing. Maybe it wasn't a ghost. Maybe what they had seen in the guest room was something else entirely. Edward said several men in hats had accosted him by the bridle trail, had surrounded his ladder and knocked down the branches of the tree. "Thugs," he insisted on calling them, although they all knew they were much more than that. Until this, he had not put Edward's description together with the spectral figure they had seen in the guest room, but now it was all starting to make a weird kind of sense.

He looked again at the newspaper photo. These . . . *beings* seemed to show up wherever insurance problems escalated into destruction and death, whenever a point needed to be made about not buying insurance or the terms of a policy needed to be enforced. He had no doubt that when the Bretts' house had burned down, one of them had been lurking on the periphery of the property, that when Kate Gifford had been killed, the driver of the vehicle had been wearing a hat.

There'd been one in their guest room when he was arrested for child molestation.

They were agents of the insurance company. Not *insurance agents* but provocateurs. Men—or creatures—who were sent out to do the company's bidding.

"Are you still there?" Joel asked. "Hello?"

Hunt took his hand away from the phone. "Look at the picture on the front page," he said. "Bottom right."

"Holy shit," Joel breathed.

"When Edward had his so-called accident, he saw men who looked like that." He paused, inhaled deeply. "Beth and I saw one of them, too. In our guest room. We thought it was a ghost."

He expected questions. Not jokes and ridicule, as he would under normal circumstances, but an honest query.

Joel wasn't even fazed. "I saw one at school," he said. "Talking to that girl who hit my car. And that's what Lilly said the man who she saw with Kate looked like."

"She saw a man with Kate? You never told me that."

Beth pricked up her ears.

"You got released and Kate . . . Well, I guess I was just overtaken by events. But, yeah, Lilly might've seen the molester."

"Holy shit is right."

"What are we going to do?"

"I don't know," Hunt admitted.

"We've got to do something. Should we go to the police?"

"With what?" Hunt watched Beth as she examined the newspaper photo once more. "Talk to Stacy," he said. "I'll call you back later. We'll figure out a plan."

The phone rang again the instant he hung up.

Jorge.

"Get a copy of today's *Ledger*," he said without preamble. "There's a picture on the front page of one of the orderlies who drugged me."

Jorge sounded clear and lucid, anger having pushed aside the despair that had been his sole emotion since the birth. Hunt heard resolve in his friend's voice, a committed determination to see this thing through to the end.

He was back.

Hunt explained about Edward, Joel's school, Lilly, their ghost. "They work for the insurance company," he said.

"I'm going to get those bastards. I'll kill them for what they did. And if I see that insurance salesman . . ."

"Do you have any ideas?" Hunt asked.

"No. You?"

"No," he admitted. "But Joel's on it, too."

"Have you talked to Edward yet?"

"No."

"I'll do it right now. I'll call you back later." The line went dead, and Hunt hung up the phone.

"This can't go on," Beth said. "We have to do something about it. We have to stop them."

Hunt nodded his agreement. They had waited too long already, had stood on the sidelines and done nothing while lives were ruined, people were injured, people were killed.

But what *could* they do? How could they fight something that arranged for accidents and arrests at will, that had no compunction about killing, that was able to knock off forty-five—

forty-six

—people in one night?

"I'll go to the bathroom and then get dressed," Beth said. "You take a shower, and we'll head over to Joel and Stacy's and brainstorm."

"Okay." Hunt followed her out of the kitchen. She went into the small bathroom, and he was about to grab some clothes from the bedroom when he noticed that the guest room door was half open.

It had been shut.

A wave of cold passed through him.

There was a loud knock, and the guest room door swung inward, pulled all the way open by someone inside.

The insurance agent stepped into the hall, carrying his briefcase.

Hunt experienced the same visceral reaction he had the first time the insurance agent had arrived—an abhorrence, a loathing, disgust abetted by fear.

He was wearing a black suit, the type one would wear to a funeral, and he was now at least two inches taller than Hunt and much broader in the shoulders. His teeth looked too white, as though they'd been recently capped. And too big. As though the caps were two sizes too large.

He recalled how the insurance agent had made them invite him into their house initially, the way, according to legend, a vampire was able to gain entrance into a home.

They should not have done that. If they had not allowed him entrance, he might not have been able to gain a foothold, he might simply have moved on. Now the demon was able to show up at or in their house any time he pleased.

Vampires. Demons.

Exactly what the insurance agent was still eluded him, but it was somewhere in that ballpark. It was a mystery that might never be solved, though. In novels, in movies, when individuals became embroiled in horrific events beyond their ken, explanations were eventually in the offing. Through diligent sleuthing or the loquaciousness of evildoers, the protagonists eventually learned not only the how but the why, discovering what was going on, the reason for it and the way to defeat it.

Real life, however, offered no such ready answers. It was an ambiguous world, where actions sometimes had no meaning, where chaos reigned and no one was allowed to see the big picture, only their small portion of it.

"Good morning!" the agent announced with false cheer. He held out a hand to shake. The palms had no lines on them, Hunt noticed. And the knuckles bulged strangely. He had seen hands like that before somewhere—in a painting or a movie— but he could not remember when.

He kept his own hands stiffly at his sides, but the agent seemed to take no offense. "What a gorgeous day," he said, breathing deeply as if to savor the air. "What a glorious day to be alive."

From inside the small bathroom came Beth's short, shocked cry.

"Taking a piss, huh?" The agent grinned. "I bet she sprays up a storm."

"Get out," Hunt said flatly.

The bathroom door flew open, and Beth raged into the hallway. She'd put on pants and a T-shirt, and her face was filled with stone-cold fury. "Get out of our house!" she screamed. "We don't want you here!" She tried to push him, but he caught her hands and pumped them in some type of bizarre greeting. She recoiled instantly, as though her fingers had just squished their way through excrement.

"I'm only here as a courtesy to you," he explained calmly. "As I was telling your husband while you were so indelicately disposed, it's a glorious day to be alive. And that's why I'm here today, to make sure that you *do* stay alive, to protect you from the vicissitudes of this modern world and all of the horrible realities that we have to deal with on a daily basis." He motioned to the hallway before him. "Shall we retire to the kitchen, have a nice cup of coffee and discuss the very generous life insurance coverage we're offering?"

Life insurance.

Hunt looked at Beth. Neither of them were brave enough to kick him out of the house now, not with that hanging over their heads—

forty-six

—and, cowed but reluctant, they led the way back into the kitchen. They took up positions against the sink counter rather than sitting down at the breakfast table.

The agent placed his briefcase on the table and stood there, waiting. Hunt was determined not to ask about the insurance, determined to make the agent do all of the talking. A small achievement but one that he felt was important. He thought of lyrics from a Darden Smith song: *All these little victories.*

But the truth was that these little victories meant nothing. They were comfort food, feel-good panaceas in the midst of a losing battle.

Still, he remained silent. Beth did, too.

"Very well. I'll get the ball rolling." The agent's voice sounded clipped, annoyed. "I'm offering you life insurance. I won't go into the details since you don't seem to be particularly interested in what I have to say. Besides, I think the concept of life insurance is pretty self-explanatory." He opened his briefcase. There were no brochures or pamphlets this time, no concessions to the niceties of the ordinary world. He simply withdrew a long legal-sized form printed on card-stock paper and placed it on the kitchen table.

Hunt didn't want to look, but he did. He saw words and sentences so fine that he doubted they could be read without the assistance of a magnifying glass.

"This time," the agent said, "I'm afraid I must insist upon an immediate answer."

"We need to talk it over."

"An *immediate* answer!" He slammed his hand down on the breakfast table.

Hunt looked at Beth, who nodded unhappily.

Life insurance, he thought. It *was* pretty self-explanatory.

"Okay."

"Excellent, excellent." All trace of pique was gone from the insurance agent's voice. Once more, he spoke in the plastic tones of the professional salesman. "I congratulate you on making the right decision."

In a ritual that was becoming all too common but none the less heinous for that, he provided them with pens and they signed the insurance application.

The agent placed the application in his briefcase, shut it and then put it down on the floor. They expected him to bid them a cheery or ironic good-bye, but instead he stood there for a moment, looking out the window. "Come here, Mr. Jackson," he said finally. "Tell me what you see."

Reluctantly, Hunt stood next to him and looked through the window at the ruins of the Brett house.

"What do you see?"

He shrugged. "A burned house."

"That's what your home would look like if a terrorist decided to ram a plane into your roof or if . . ." He trailed off.

"It's a shame they didn't have insurance," he said softly, almost to himself.

It was the second time he'd said something like that about the Bretts' home, and Hunt thought that it must be some sort of obsession on his part. Had he offered Ed Brett insurance only to be turned down? Or was it the mere fact that they hadn't had insurance—*any* insurance from *any* company—that got under his skin, that preyed upon his mind?

He turned back toward Hunt, smiling brightly. "But you see, that's what you two will be able to avoid. You have ample coverage, and with this new addition to your insurance portfolio, you'll be protected against far more than the average policyholder." He patted Hunt's shoulder, and Hunt fought an instinctive urge to pull away in disgust. "I'm very proud of you."

Hunt glanced toward Beth, saw a strange unreadable expression on her face. She backed nervously up to the sink.

The agent walked over and picked up his briefcase before starting toward the kitchen door. "It's a business doing pleasure with you."

Hunt wanted to slug him, wanted to feel his fist smash into flesh and break the bone beneath. But he had the unsettling feeling that there wouldn't be bones underneath. And that the flesh wouldn't feel like flesh.

With a quick wave, the agent was out the door and gone. Hunt watched through the window as he walked up the path, past the ocotillos and down the sidewalk. Hunt was sorely tempted to run after him, follow him, see where he went. He had no idea if the insurance agent walked everywhere, rode in a limousine, drove his own car or took a bus. For some strange reason, the man's mode of transportation was never visible from the house. This was just one more tantalizing bit of secrecy, and it was one that Hunt had the means to uncover.

It was a place to start.

Beth was on the same wavelength.

"Let's follow him," she said.

"Are you sure?"

She nodded. "I have an idea."

She'd changed, but he was wearing only yesterday's pants,

and they quickly ran to the coat closet by the front door. He
grabbed a Levi's jacket, put boots on over bare feet, she
slipped on sandals, and they both hurried outside. The agent
was just turning the corner at the end of the block, and they
sped up, needing to follow at a discreet distance but still keep
him in sight.

There was no car around the corner, no black-windowed
deathmobile, nothing. The agent was simply strolling down
the sidewalk in a disconcertingly jaunty manner.

They watched him. Followed. Less than two blocks away,
he turned in the driveway of a low sprawling ranch-style house
and promptly sat down on the front stoop. They were nearly
caught off guard, but the second he stepped off the sidewalk,
they were ducking behind an oleander bush next door, and
they peered through the leafy branches, watching as the insurance agent put down his briefcase and sat.

He remained there, expressionless, completely unmoving,
staring at nothing. Like a statue. Hunt had never seen a person
so still, and the sight seemed creepily unnatural. He was afraid
that they would have to crouch behind the bushes for hours,
but less than five minutes later, a red Range Rover pulled into
the driveway, and the agent stood as though the vehicle had arrived just as expected, right on schedule.

Suddenly the Range Rover shifted into reverse and sped
back onto the street. Through the windshield, Hunt saw the
male driver's panicked face and the wildly gesticulating
woman in the passenger seat mouthing the scream "No!"

Grinning, the insurance agent jogged across the lawn and
into the street, standing directly in front of the SUV, blocking
its way.

"Get it!" Beth whispered fiercely.

"What?"

But she was already off, and before he could stop her, she
was pushing her way through the bushes and running across
the next door lawn.

To where the agent had left his briefcase on the stoop.

"*No!*" he wanted to yell. "*Get back here!*" But he dared not draw attention to her, and he kept looking back and forth from the street, where the insurance agent was calmly repositioning himself in order to block the SUV's escape, to the stoop of the house, where Beth was grabbing the briefcase and running like hell.

She broke through the bushes, and then they were both running, not needing to speak, not daring to do so, staying on the lawns of the adjoining homes, staying off the sidewalk. He expected any minute to hear a monstrous roar behind them, to feel the grip of cold fingers around his neck as the agent caught up to them and held them aloft. But they jumped over a small hedge, darted around a parked Cadillac, and then they were at the corner, turning right on Elm Street.

They did not slow down until they'd reached another residential intersection, turned left and were a good two blocks away from the insurance agent. They stopped in front of a too-cute home painted pink and gray, breathing heavily.

"We made it," Hunt said, desperately trying to catch his breath. "He didn't catch us."

"But where are we going to go now?" Beth said, speaking low, conspiratorily, as though afraid of being overheard. "We can't go home. It's the first place he'll look. When he sees the briefcase is gone, he might think he left it at our house and go back to check. He might stake the place out." She shivered. "Or have his buddies do it."

Hunt thought for a moment. "The library," he suggested. "We'll call everyone from there, have them meet us." The Dorothy Pickles branch of the library was only three blocks away.

"It's a holiday. They won't be open."

"Damn!" Hunt said.

"How about Kinko's? Over there in that strip mall across from Safeway."

He nodded. It was over a mile away, would take them a good half hour to get there, but it had plenty of chairs and tables they could use, was always open—and they could make copies of whatever they found.

But they had no money! He quickly dug through the pockets of his pants and found one wrinkled dollar bill, a quarter, a dime, a nickel, and three pennies. Change from groceries they'd bought yesterday. Beth was always after him to clean out his pockets, saying she was tired of washing money and business cards and other things he left in his clothes, but he was glad now that he had not yet broken that habit.

He took the briefcase from her. "Let's do it."

They walked quickly, turning at every intersection, afraid to remain on any one street for too long. They saw neither the insurance agent nor ghostly men in hats, however, and twenty minutes later they were approaching the copy store from a back alley. They walked around the side of the building, went in through the entrance.

Hunt found a study cubicle where people could pay for Internet access by the hour and placed the briefcase on the table.

He would not have been surprised to discover that it was not really a briefcase but only looked like one, that it could only be opened by the special touch of the insurance agent's inhuman fingers. But it felt normal, and when he pushed the latches on the left side and then the right, they opened immediately, revealing a compartment filled with papers and file folders.

They sorted carefully through the briefcase's contents. On top was the application for life insurance they had just signed, and below that was a folder marked with their names. He opened the folder and quickly looked at the papers inside, but found nothing unusual, only a computer printout containing personal information on each of them, followed by copies of all of their numerous insurance policies.

Beneath the file folder were glossy brochures and blank application forms and, most important, well-thumbed insurance manuals, books printed by The Insurance Group for use only by their representatives. Hunt's heart was racing, and for the first time in a long while there was hope within him. He pushed aside the papers and picked up a surprisingly thick book titled *Offered Insurance*. He opened it to the first page, saw the title again, then turned to the next page, where a short paragraph stated that the book listed the names and IT numbers (whatever that was) of each type of coverage offered by the company. The pages were thin, tissuelike, similar to Bible pages, and he had a hard time turning them one by one.

"Jesus," he said. "Look at this."

Beth moved next to him, held his arm protectively as he glanced through the book.

There was insurance for everything. Literally. In print so fine it was nearly impossible to read was an alphabetical listing of the situations and states, the people, places and things for which policies were offered. *Abandonment, Abdomen, Abduction* . . . He flipped randomly through the book. *Contamination . . . Overpass . . . Telescope* . . . He turned to the last page. *Zulu, Zuni, Zymotic.*

He closed the book, feeling overwhelmed. A company that could offer and enforce coverage of such a comprehensive catalogue was truly, awesomely powerful. At the same time, by poring through the nearly endless list, they might be able to discover something for which the company did not offer insurance, a loophole or Achilles' heel that they could take advantage of.

He placed the book on the table next to the briefcase and continued sorting through the other titles. Three books down was a digest-sized manual simply titled *The Insurance Group,* and Hunt eagerly grabbed the volume and opened it. There was no index or table of contents, but there did seem to be chapters and subchapters with headings offset in bold. He quickly turned the pages, scanning them until he found what he was looking for.

"Who Are We?" the heading asked.

Hunt read the following paragraph. The insurance agent had said that The Insurance Group was a consortium of different carriers, and here they were listed. Next to him, he heard Beth's sharp intake of breath as she read the names.

"They own UAI," she said. "And your rental insurance company and my old homeowner's company and . . . and everything."

Hunt nodded, feeling surprised but not shocked.

"So . . ." she said slowly, "we were right. All those problems we had, everything that happened to us, was done purposely, for a reason, to manipulate us and prime us for The Insurance Group's insane policies. All this time, they were guiding us toward what they wanted us to do."

"Why us, though?" he wondered. "Why did they target us? Was it something specific or just random? Did you or I do something? Did we fit a profile? Or were our names just picked out of a hat?"

She shook her head. "It doesn't make any sense. Why not hit on people with power? The governor or the president or Bill Gates or Ted Turner? People whose words and actions make a difference. If the insurance company controlled those people, it would have real influence, it could get everything it wanted."

"It can get everything it wants," Hunt pointed out. "It's obviously after something else."

What that could be, though, neither of them knew and neither of them cared to speculate about.

Hunt quickly looked through the rest of the book, trying to discover who had founded The Insurance Group and when, but if that information was to be found in the text, it was buried. He did learn that the company's motto was the nonsensical yet frighteningly focused "Insurance Above All Else," and that the company employed nearly three thousand people worldwide.

"What's this?" Beth asked as he was flipping through the pages. She withdrew a folded piece of yellowed paper from the bottom of the briefcase and proceeded to spread it out on the only section of the table not covered with pamphlets and manuals and forms. It was a map of the world, with X's marked over certain regions and lines drawn from the X's to notes scrawled in the margins. Hunt put down his book and scooted around the table next to Beth.

"Look," she said, pointing.

He had already noticed. The marks and notations were in the trouble spots of the world, the areas of unrest over the past fifty years: Cambodia, Bangladesh, Beirut, Angola, Kosovo, Afghanistan, Somalia, Iraq.

Beneath that map was another map, an older map. Iran was Persia, Istanbul was Constantinople, Thailand was Siam, Sri Lanka was Ceylon. This map was virtually buried under lines and X's and stars, scribbled notations leaking out of the yellowed margins into the blue expanse of ocean. He saw names he remembered from history, important figures in world events, the men behind wars and scourges and revolutions and assassinations. Suddenly everything became clear. He understood why these maps were in the insurance agent's briefcase.

He'd been *their* insurance agent.

Beth figured it out at the same time. "Oh my God," she breathed.

He nodded, not trusting himself to speak. Squinting, he tried to decipher what had been written at the end of one of the starred lines. The only word he could make out was "Hannibal."

"Do you think . . . ?" Beth swallowed hard. "Do you think all those wars and assassinations and everything happened because people didn't buy insurance? Or couldn't pay their premiums?"

That was exactly what he thought, although he'd superstitiously been afraid to speak the thought aloud. He nodded, licked his suddenly dry lips. "Yeah."

"This guy affected history. He *caused* history."

"If it was him." Hunt didn't want to think that he'd been around that long, that he was that old. "Maybe he just inherited the maps from his predecessor and so on down the line."

"No," Beth said firmly. "It was him."

Hunt traced a line from Rome—

The fall of Rome?

—to a side notation whose only legible word was "nonpayment."

"What *is* he?" Beth said. Her next words were whispered. "Maybe he's the devil."

"No," Hunt said. "He just works for the insurance company."

"What are *they*?"

For that he had no answer. He emptied his pockets. "See what you can get with that and start copying," He said. "I'm going to call Joel and Jorge and Edward."

All of his friends' lines were busy, and Hunt found that very suspicious. He imagined them dead or tortured, punished for his transgression. In his mind, he saw the insurance agent pacing in front of Jorge and Ynez, demanding to know the whereabouts of the briefcase while one of those dark burly men with wide-brimmed hats held up their mutilated son and threatened additional atrocities.

No. He was overreacting.

He hoped.

Still, he stopped calling, afraid that if one of the phones rang and someone answered, that someone would be the insurance agent.

With fifty cents taken out for the phone, they had enough money to copy fifteen pages. That wasn't much, so they used those pages to copy the maps, copying the two maps in eight-

and-a-half by eleven segments so they could reproduce the originals exactly. That took twelve pages. With three copies left over, they shrunk down each map on a single sheet of paper. In addition, Beth had found what appeared to be the address of The Insurance Group's Tucson office—Southwest Regional Headquarters, actually—and that went on the page.

Hunt wanted to go out to the insurance office and confront whoever he could find, or, at the very least, get the lay of the land. But they had no transportation, no money, and after talking it over, they decided to take a chance on going back home.

"We'll wait and watch first," Beth suggested. "Hide across the street or something. Or in the Bretts' yard. Then if it looks like the coast is clear, one of us'll go in and check."

"I'll go in."

She smiled. "I was hoping you'd say that."

The streets were safe on the walk back, the insurance agent was not striding through the neighborhoods in his funereal clothes or cruising in a company car, and when they hid behind the ruins of the Bretts' house, watching the exterior of their own home, they saw no sign of movement. Hunt went in the side door prepared for anything—the insurance agent, a trashed kitchen, a ghost in the guest room—but the house was clean, and after a quick tour, opening all closets and cupboards, checking the garage, he waved Beth in.

They worked fast. Hunt put on a real shirt and tennis shoes, grabbed his wallet and keys. Beth took her purse and put on sneakers. Not wanting to take their stolen goods into the lion's den, he hid the briefcase behind the extra freezer in the garage, while Beth hid the segmented copies of the maps in the house. They took the two small maps with them, as well as the photocopied address.

It was just after eleven.

"Ready?" Hunt asked.

"Ready."

And they were off.

3

Joel was in the car when his cell phone rang, having just tanked up on gas at Circle K because he had a sneaking suspicion that in the next day or so he might need it. It had been three hours, Hunt had not called back like he promised, and when Joel had tried to call *him*, no one had answered. After last night's massacre, his head was full of all sorts of wild possibilities, so he told Stacy and Lilly to stay home, to not answer the door or the phone, and he set out to fill up on gas and check Hunt and Beth's house to make sure they were all right.

He picked up the phone on the first ring, his heart slamming against his rib cage as though it was trying to escape. No one had this number except Stacy and Lilly, and they both knew never to use it unless there was an emergency. He fumbled with the phone, simultaneously trying to push the talk button and not scrape the side of the oversized truck in the lane next to him.

"He's here," Stacy said in a breathless whisper.

Joel thought he might crash into the truck after all. It was suddenly hard for him to control the wheel.

"How?" he asked, fully aware that she might not be able to answer.

Stacy was still whispering. "I let Lilly go out in the backyard to play basketball—"

"I told you not to go outside!" he yelled.

"I thought the backyard was safe." The fact that she continued to whisper, that his criticism did not goad her even to raise her voice, made him realize how serious the situation was. "And I was watching her. I just turned for a minute to get some orange juice out of the fridge, and when I looked back outside, he was talking to her."

"Oh, God." Joel felt as though he were about to throw up.

"I ran out back, and he was offering her insurance, personal injury insurance, telling her that if she was going to play basketball or soccer or any other sports, she might get hurt and need protection."

"Bastard!"

"Just listen to me!" Stacy said. She raised her voice, and he realized how urgent she sounded. Already he was moving into the left lane, preparing to make a U-turn and head back toward home. "He had the policy out by the time I reached them, and she was agreeing to take it. She was scared. He looked at me and told me that she was buying the policy."

"Oh my God, oh my God."

"The thing is, we have to sign it as her legal guardians. *Both* of us."

"I'm on my way!"

"But he's going to leave if you're not here in three minutes."

Even with perfect traffic, hitting every green light, he was still ten minutes away from home. "Stall him! Do what you can! Offer him food or drink, try to talk to him about insurance! Ask questions!

"No!" Stacy yelled and suddenly her voice was far away.

"Stace?" he called. "Stacy?"

He heard her voice in the distance: *"Don't go! He's on his way! Please!"*

Joel veered to the left, bumped over the median into the opposing lane and was nearly hit by a blue Mercedes-Benz that honked at him and swerved out of the way. He floored it, speeding back down the boulevard toward home, but then he heard the whine of a siren behind him, saw the flash of blinking lights as a patrol car pulled him over.

On the phone he heard nothing but the sound of Stacy sobbing.

Nineteen

1

"This can't be it."

"This is it."

"You must have the wrong address, then."

Beth shook her head. "No. This is the place."

Hunt got out of the car and stared over the Saab's roof at the ruined shell of a structure. It looked like a building that had been bombed. Only three partial walls were remaining, and the fourth wall, like the roof, had collapsed into rubble.

They were on the far outskirts of the county, near the Mexican border, parked before what appeared to have once been a warehouse. It was the only construction on an undeveloped cul de sac, and from the look of the weeds and vegetation that had begun to creep over the downed chunks of concrete and rebar, the building had been abandoned some time ago. Hunt could not quite tell what had brought the structure down. There was no indication of fire, and it was not demolished completely enough to be the result of a wrecking ball. If he'd been back in California, he would have assumed that an earthquake had caused the damage, but that obviously wasn't the case in Tucson.

Beth got out of the passenger side, and he locked the car's doors and walked around to where she stood on the sidewalk.

She was staring at chalk drawings on the concrete, a child's drawings of horned demons and fanged monsters.

Beth smiled weakly. "Yep. We're in the right place."

They could see from here that this was no insurance office, but Hunt still felt the need to go inside the collapsed building and see what, if anything, he could learn. This was the only lead, the only information they had about The Insurance Group, and he was not about to let the opportunity pass.

"Where did you put all the copies?" he asked.

"In my underwear drawer."

He looked at her askance.

"I couldn't think of anywhere else off the top of my head. I figured they'd be safe there."

"Yeah, unless some pervert breaks into our house."

They started up the long service driveway that led to the ruined building. For the first few yards the cracked concrete was littered with broken glass and rusted nails and the usual detritus that accompanied business abandonment. But after that, curiously, the driveway was clear save for windblown dust and the occasional dead leaf. As they drew closer, the bulk of the empty building blocked out the midafternoon sun, throwing the way ahead into shadow. It seemed cheaply symbolic, but it was effective nonetheless, and Hunt felt chilled as they walked up a sloping sidewalk past dead flowering bushes to the front entrance.

A rectangular shape slightly different in tint than the rest of the wall testified to the fact that a sign had once hung next to the double doors but gave no indication as to what the sign had said. The doors themselves were long gone, only one crumpled metal frame on the left indicating that they had ever been there. The place still looked like a warehouse, and he had a hard time imagining that it had ever been the headquarters of an insurance company. According to the information they'd gotten from the agent's briefcase, it was, though.

But where had the company gone? Had it relocated? Or,

more chillingly, had it gone out of business, leaving only the insurance agent, a deranged fanatic with supernatural powers, to carry on?

"I don't like this place," Beth whispered.

"I don't either," he said and found himself whispering, too. "But we have to see."

The wall before them was only partially extant, the entire right half collapsed, but it was faster to go through the doorless doorway than around the side of the wall, and they stepped through the entrance inside.

Before them was what looked like a mountain of debris, an insurmountable obstacle to anyone attempting to navigate the interior of the ruined building. Most of it was roof and rafters, gigantic metal beams and attached structural supports protruding at odd angles from piled concrete blocks. Whether by accident or intent, a vague path led through the wreckage, a narrow dirt trail that wound between the huge accumulations of steel and stone, and they started down it, Hunt in the lead.

They passed broken shelves crushed under chunks of cement, fragments of crates and boxes, even what looked like the remnants of a smashed forklift, but nothing that would suggest this had ever been home to an insurance company. Off to the side somewhere they heard the scurrying of rodents. Above, the caw of a crow.

In the center of the building was a concrete slab the size of a large bedroom, and in the center of the slab was a stairway leading into darkness. They stepped up, stood above the stairway and held hands, looking down into the gloom. The air from that space was cold and dank, smelling of mildew and rotten roots. Hunt knew he had to go down there, but he was afraid. He felt like a child confronted by a dark alley after just seeing a monster movie, scared of meeting up with the boogeyman, and that analogy was far more apt than he liked.

"There's a flashlight in the car," he said. "I'll go get it."

"You'll go get it? What am I supposed to do, stay here? No way, José. I'm coming with you."

"I think you should wait in the car," he told her. "Just in case."

"No. I'm coming back with you. We're both going down there."

"What if something happens? I think it'll be better if we pick a time, like an hour, and if I'm not back by then, you go and get help."

Beth frowned. "What the hell are you talking about? We're in this together and we're both going in."

"But—"

"No 'buts.' I'm of the 'two heads are better than one,' school, and there's no way I'm going to be the dainty maiden sitting out of harm's way to let the big strong man go walking into danger alone."

"But what if something *does* happen?"

"We'll deal with it. Besides, I have my cell phone. I can call for help just as well with you as I can by myself. Come on, let's go. We're wasting time."

Hunt had to admit that he was relieved. He hadn't really wanted to go in there alone. Together, they walked back to the car, got a flashlight and two screwdrivers—to be used as weapons if necessary—then returned to the ruined building and the stairway descending into the pit.

The pit.

That's how Hunt thought of it. The pit. Like a descent into hell.

He hoped to God he was simply the victim of an overactive imagination.

He went first, holding the flashlight. It was definitely colder down below, and that sickly smell grew stronger. He was reminded of overripe mushrooms and spoiled potatoes. The steps were cement but the sides of the passageway were dirt, hard-packed dirt so old it was almost like dried clay. The stairs did not go down nearly as far as he had expected—darkness had fooled him into thinking the tunnel went deeper than it did—and they descended maybe the length of a single story before the steps stopped and they found themselves in an empty room roughly the size of the concrete slab above.

Of course, he thought. A basement. It was stupid of him to have expected anything else. He *had* let his imagination get the best of him.

For a second time he shined the flashlight around the room. It was not really a typical basement, at least not the type one would expect to encounter underneath a warehouse or business. It was more like a root cellar. The ceiling above was cement but both walls and floor were of the same hard-packed dirt as the stairwell. The flashlight beam shone on flaking dirt, embedded rocks, a protruding root—

a wooden door.

Next to him, Hunt heard Beth's breath catch in her throat. The door had not been there a few minutes ago; there'd been only a flat expanse of that claylike dirt. Her hand reached for his arm, grabbed his sleeve. "You think we should go in?" she whispered.

He did think they should go in, but it was the last thing on earth he wanted to do. They stepped closer, and in the yellowish beam of the flashlight he could see peeling pale green paint and, in the center of the door, barely visible, the faint outline of three letters: TIG.

The Insurance Group.

They'd found it.

Hunt didn't know whether to be sorry or glad. He would certainly have felt more confident if they had come across this door in a building on the surface. Being underground left him feeling uneasy, and distinctly vulnerable. But they had no choice; they'd come here to discover what they could about the insurance agent and his company, and the only way to do that was to see what was behind the door.

"We have to," he said.

Next to him he felt more than saw Beth's nod of agreement.

A cold breeze was coming from the cracks around the door, a chill that permeated the basement in which they stood but was clearly much greater in the room or rooms beyond. Gathering his strength, clutching both the flashlight and screwdriver tightly, he walked forward. Beth's hand let go of his sleeve and grabbed his wrist, desperate for something more substantial to hold.

Hunt opened the door—and stepped back, gagging. This was where the smell was coming from, and this close to the source it was overpowering. Beth coughed deeply, and her hand left his wrist as it moved to cover her nose.

The two of them stood in the center of the basement, desperately trying not to vomit, holding their hands over their noses to filter out the stench. "Jesus," Hunt managed to get out.

"What do you think it is?" Beth asked, and her voice sounded strangled and thin. "Something dead?"

His imagination had been far less prosaic. He'd been thinking of slimy creatures that had never seen the light of day, hideous white mutants who lived underground on roots and rot and who occasionally made their way up to the surface and metamorphosed into . . . insurance agents. But now that Beth had made her suggestion, the idea seemed inescapable, and Hunt thought it highly likely that some sort of rotting corpse was in there.

Experimentally, he moved his hand away from his nose. The smell seemed less noxious than it had initially. Either he was getting used to it, or the heavily concentrated odor had mixed with the outside air and become dissipated. Whichever, he found himself able to move forward without retching, and he pointed his light ahead. Beyond the door, the flashlight beam died dully, its feeble illumination petering out after traveling less than two feet. The space in front of them could have been a closet or a cave. For all he knew, it stretched miles underground—or ended five feet away.

He felt Beth sidle next to him. In the thinly spread illumination from the flashlight, he could just make out the dark shape of her arm. "Are we going in?" she asked.

"Yeah."

"Take a deep breath. It's going to get worse before it gets better."

"On the count of three."

They both began inhaling deeply and exhaling shallowly.

"One . . . two . . . three!"

Flashlight and screwdriver extended, Beth clutching his arm, Hunt hurried forward into the gloom.

A light was switched on.

And they were in an insurance office.

Hunt blinked against the sudden brightness. The room surrounding them was so different from what he had expected, so at odds with the ruined building above and the dirt cellar behind them, that it took his stunned brain a moment to adjust.

They were standing on carpet: generic gray utilitarian office carpeting. In front of them was a wide wooden desk piled high with papers and atop which sat a computer monitor. Behind the desk was a wall of shelves holding books and bound volumes of what could only be insurance policies. To their left were several metal filing cabinets, and to their right a visitors' couch over which hung numerous diplomas and certificates.

At a sudden noise behind them, Hunt turned to look.

The insurance agent was standing in the doorway.

He was big and muscular, his frame almost filling the entire space, and both his stance and the expression on his face were menacing. He moved toward them, and both Hunt and Beth backed up a step. The agent laughed, a deep chuckle that was at once hearty and sinister.

"May I have my briefcase, please?"

"We, uh, don't have it," Hunt stammered.

"Come now, come now. You stole it."

"It's back at home," Beth said.

"I thought that's why you came by. To return it to me." The agent moved his hands in such a way that it looked like he was flipping his sleeves back, and suddenly the briefcase was in his hands. "That's okay. I took the liberty of getting it myself. I picked up the copies of my maps, too." He smiled at Beth. "Nice panties," he said. "They smell just like you." In his other hand was a pair of her underwear. He used them to blow his nose, then tossed them aside. "Down to business, shall we?" He walked past them around the side of the desk, where he sat down. He turned on his computer and immediately began typing. For several moments the only sounds in the room were their own ragged breathing and the rapid-fire click of keys as the agent typed.

"I don't have my glasses," the agent said finally, although Hunt had never seen him wear glasses. "Can you tell me what time it is?"

He motioned toward a clock that hung on the wall with the framed certificates. Hunt had not noticed the clock before, but as he looked at it now a chill passed through him. There were no numbers or icons, only a cartoonish drawing of a monkey's buttocks where the twelve should have been and a pair of hairy droopy testicles instead of a six. The clock's lone hand pointed at where the three should be, directly between them.

Half past a monkey's ass, a quarter to his ba-wuls.

The agent started laughing, and there was something manic in the sound.

He reached over, shut off his computer and swiveled his chair to face them. Now the expression on his face was one of anger and belligerence. "So why are you really here?" he asked. "What do you want?"

Hunt didn't have an answer.

"Insurance," Beth said quickly. "We suspected that you were keeping things from us, offering only the policies *you* wanted us to have rather than the policies *we* wanted to have. We came to see if we could find out what those policies were, and to go over your head if we had to and report your inadequacy to your superiors."

The agent's attitude changed instantly.

Hunt did not know what had made her say such a thing, by what stroke of genius she had come up with such an approach, but it succeeded brilliantly. The intimidating bully of a few moments before had been replaced by a groveling servile lackey.

"The job of an insurance salesman is to determine the needs of his clients and to secure policies that will meet those needs," he said placatingly. "I certainly never meant to give you the impression that I was keeping insurance options from you. Far be it for me to dictate the terms of your coverage. I'm here only to serve you." He spread his hands open. "Just tell me what sort of policy you're looking for. Whatever it is, I'm sure that The Insurance Group will be able to meet your needs and that I will be able to continue to provide the type of quality service you have come to expect."

He seemed to be speaking not to them but to some nonexistent observer, and Hunt found himself wondering if they were being watched, if this room was under surveillance. By whom, though? He had changed his mind when they came upon this office and determined that there was no company called The Insurance Group, that there was only the agent, acting alone. But the man seemed genuinely worried about the reaction of higher-ups to Beth's criticism, and once again Hunt decided that there must be an insurance company, a hierarchy to which the agent was answerable. Where was it, though? Who was behind it? And, whoever they were, could they really be watching the three of them here in this office behind the basement of a ruined building?

He had seen enough to know that, yes, the three of them could be under surveillance right at this very second, and that the means of observation was just as likely to be a crystal ball as a high-tech listening device. The agent had said more than once that the company he worked for was very old, and the maps and documents they'd found in his briefcase certainly seemed to verify that, but, not for the first time, Hunt found himself wondering how old. He was not sure when or where the concept of insurance had originated, but he had no doubt that the age of The Insurance Group predated the generally accepted date by . . . what? Decades? Centuries? Millennia? In his mind, he saw the agent in a Fred Flintstone sabertooth tiger–skin toga, selling insurance to other grunting cave men as he chiseled out the terms of their policies with a rock pen and a stone tablet.

How old was the agent?

Was he immortal?

Hunt suddenly felt demoralized, defeated and hopelessly overmatched. How could he and Beth ever have thought that they could go up against a force so ancient and powerful and obviously successful? Who were they? Nobodies. It would take the greatest minds of the age and all of the resources of the federal government to put a stop to the unholy practices of The Insurance Group. He had a brief ridiculous fantasy of filing a formal complaint with the FTC or some other government agency and letting them take on the insurance company, but he knew that was impossible—even assuming he could get someone to believe his outrageous story.

The agent was still talking. "Nowhere will you find a more full-service commitment to your needs and a more hands-on approach to satisfying your myriad insurance requirements."

Beth had obviously caught the same whiff of desperation from his near-manic defensiveness that Hunt had. "You don't seem to understand," she said slowly and clearly, as though talking to a small child. "We are not happy with the service you have provided us. We're accustomed to receiving much better, much more respectful treatment from our"—and here she sounded theatrically dismissive—"insurance agents."

"I'm here to serve you," he assured her and whoever else was watching/listening. "My goal is your complete satisfaction."

Here was their chance.

"Are you serious?" Hunt asked.

"Yes. Of course. Tell me what you'd like. Tell me what your needs are, and I'm sure I'll be able to find a corresponding policy to meet those needs."

Hunt faced the agent, took a stab in the dark. "I'd like life insurance. Your deluxe policy."

The sides of the agent's mouth spread upward in a predatory smile, and suddenly he was back to his normal self, brimming with confidence, all trace of servility gone. "Now you're talking, boy. Those are some hefty premiums, but that's our ultimate package." He stood, walked around the desk and threw a beefy arm familiarly around Hunt's shoulder. "I'm proud of you, boy, and I can guarantee you that for this you will be eternally grateful. And I mean eternally. There's absolutely nothing like this offered by anyone, anywhere."

The arm, Hunt thought, felt like a cushioned log, and this close to the agent he thought he caught a faint whiff of that foul rotting odor.

"How about you?" The man placed his other hand on Beth's shoulder, pulling her close to him. "Are you up for some added insurance? Want to spend the rest of your days— the rest of *eternity*—with your hubby here?"

Beth pulled away, slipped out from under his arm. "Count me out," she said coldly.

Again he gave out with that deep chuckle, half hearty, half hellish. His big hand squeezed Hunt's collarbone tightly. "I guess it's just you and me, hombre."

You and me.

He had life insurance.

Deluxe life.

Hunt was afraid to glance over at Beth, afraid of tipping his hand, but he hoped that she'd caught that as well. The agent had a life insurance policy that made him immortal. That's why he had been around for so long, that was how he had sold insurance to all of those people in all of those countries. And that's why he kept the pressure on Hunt and Beth and God knew who else. Because he needed to pay his own premiums—which were doubtlessly expensive beyond imagining. If they could only keep the agent from paying those premiums, if they could only . . .

Find the policy and tear it up.

That was it.

Hunt was suddenly filled with an irrational exuberance, a feeling he made every effort to hide behind a blank facade. They were in the game. They had a chance. He had a vulnerability and they knew it and they were going to bring that son of a bitch down.

Even as the agent led him over to the desk, even as he brought out a lengthy document and began describing the terms of the coverage, Hunt was mapping out a plan, trying to figure out how they could destroy the agent's policy. What they needed to do first was find the real headquarters of The Insurance Group, the corporate office. Then they had to break in, find the policy and torch it. Once the document was dust the agent would . . . what? Hunt's imagination could not go that far.

"You will live forever," the agent promised. "This policy can only be terminated by you and the company under joint agreement and may not be suspended or canceled by either of you alone. Only failure to pay your premiums will terminate the policy prematurely, and that event will bring about substantial penalties."

"What penalty could be worse than death?" Beth asked.

The expression on the agent's face sent goose bumps racing

down Hunt's arms. "There are *many* penalties worse than death, penalties that last *beyond* death, and believe me, you do not want to know what they are."

Then the agent winked, gave them a friendly smile. "But if you do want to know, simply consult the fine print on your policy. It's all there."

"So where do I sign?" Hunt asked.

The agent flipped over the document, pointed to an open line at the bottom. "Right there. Sign and date."

"It doesn't have to be in blood or something?"

The agent laughed, and for once there was real merriment in it. This he thought was funny. "No," he said. "Just grab a pen. Your signature's good enough. That's all we need."

Hunt reached over the document, took a pen from a pencil holder next to the monitor. With a glance at Beth, who shook her head slightly as if to say, *No, don't go through with it, stop this game now*, he put the pen to paper and signed his name, wrote the date. He didn't want to, but he had the feeling that it was the only thing that was allowing them to walk out of here alive. Besides, if all went well, this would all soon be over and both his and the agent's policies would be terminated.

"I guess our business here is done." The agent stood, shook his hand. "Thanks for stopping by. Although next time"—and once more he appeared to be speaking for the benefit of an unseen listener—"I will come to your residence rather than make you drive all the way out to my office. We offer full service to all of our customers and are at your beck and call. Our goal is to make buying insurance easy for you rather than convenient for us."

He started to walk around the desk in order to show them out, but they started for the door themselves. "We can find our own way," Beth said shortly.

"See you soon!" the agent called from behind them, and then they were through the door and back in the basement. They walked up the steps to the surface without speaking and did not say a word until they were safely inside the car. Hunt was not even sure they were safe here, but they could not live their lives thinking they were being watched twenty-four hours a day by some omniscient company.

"He has deluxe life," Hunt said after he'd slammed and locked the door. "It's what's keeping him alive."

"I caught that, too. What are we going to do about it? Try to find his original policy and destroy it?"

He smiled. "I like the way you think."

"I'm not as dumb as I look." She frowned. "But why did you sign that policy? Why didn't you—"

"Wait? You know his pattern. I might've been struck dead then and there just to prove a point. Neither of us may have gotten out of that office."

She nodded. "You're right."

"But now we are out. And free to find that policy and terminate it." He started the car, backed up, turned around, and started for the highway. "But where?"

She reached under the seat, smiling. "Let's look at the map, shall we?"

"He didn't get all the copies?"

"Only the ones at home. Not the two we brought with us. I guess he's not as omniscient as he thinks. We'll just scan these into the computer when we get home and print out about a thousand copies."

"I love you," he said.

"Me too."

And they sped north toward Tucson.

2

Both Stacy and Lilly were at home safe and sound, waiting for Joel when he arrived. He'd never been an emotional guy, but he practically wept with gratitude as he enfolded them in his arms and pulled them close. "I thought . . ." He closed his eyes. "I thought . . ." He couldn't even bring himself to say it.

"We're here," Stacy said. "Uninsured but here."

He laughed, let them go, wiping his eyes.

"That man was scary, Dad." Lilly sounded worried. "He reminded me of that man with Kate. The big one with the hat."

"I know, sweetie. But it's all right now."

It wasn't all right, though, and Stacy gave him an unreadable look. "What are we going to do?" she asked.

He shook his head "I don't know. I'm going to try and call Hunt again, and maybe . . . Did he give you his card?"

"No," she said.

"Well, then we're going to sit inside the house like the bubble family and make sure we don't put ourselves in harm's way. If we don't place ourselves in situations with potential danger, we can't be hurt, right?" He was saying "we," but he knew that Stacy knew exactly who he was talking about. Lilly. She had been offered the insurance, not them. She was the one at risk.

From upstairs came a thunderous crash. All three of them jumped at the sound, and Lilly burst into tears.

"What was that?" Stacy asked, eyes wide with fear.

Joel shook his head. "I don't know. Stay here."

He looked around, wishing he had a weapon handy, but there was nothing he could use, and he ran upstairs, taking the steps two at a time. He saw immediately where the noise had originated although in his mind there had never been any doubt.

Lilly's room.

He hurried down the short hall and through her doorway. A section of the ceiling had collapsed. Pieces of plaster lay everywhere: on the floor, on the desk, on the bookshelf, on the bed. A board, a two-by-four, obviously part of the house's frame construction, had also been dislodged and had fallen through the ceiling. It had landed on her bed, directly where her head would have been had she been sleeping, and it had hit with such force that it had knocked her pillow onto the rug and ripped a hole in her sheet and mattress.

Personal injury insurance.

Through the window to his left, he caught a glimpse of movement, and he moved closer to the glass and looked outside. In the backyard he saw a dark figure skulking between the house and the lemon tree.

A burly figure wearing a hat.

"Close the windows!" he yelled at the top of his lungs. "Pull the drapes!" He yanked down the shades in Lilly's room, sped down the hall and closed the curtains in their bedroom, then dashed downstairs, where Stacy, with Lilly right next to her clutching her belt, was drawing the drapes in the living room.

"What is it?" Stacy demanded. "What's happening?"

"The ceiling fell on Lilly's bed. And they're out there. I saw one of them." He ran into the kitchen, pulled the string that caused the venetian blinds to drop over the window above the sink. The backyard was empty now, but he knew that any sense of security he might have would be false. He suddenly realized what a death trap their home was. Light fixtures could fall on Lilly's head. The water heater could blow up. The old gas pump in the family room could topple over. Records from the jukebox could come spinning out like lethal Frisbees.

Lilly was sobbing. "I don't want to die!" she cried. "I don't want to die!"

"Mommy's right here," Stacy said comfortingly.

He ran into his office, pulling the shades, hyper-aware of the bookcases that could fall and crush a nine-year-old child.

Everything was done. The house was locked, closed, secure.

They reconvened in the entryway. "We stay here," Joel

said. "We don't go outside, we keep away from anything that could fall or explode or burn or be turned into a weapon."

The phone rang.

"Don't answer it!" Joel ordered.

Stacy glared at him. "He might be giving us another chance!"

She was right. He dashed into the family room and desperately grabbed the phone. "Hello!" he shouted into the mouthpiece.

It was Beth.

3

They met at Edward's house. Beth was in charge of logistics, and since Edward had not only survived a direct attempt on his life but had not seen any sign of the insurance salesman or his cohorts in the intervening weeks, she thought that he might have some immunity from the madness and horror that seemed to have engulfed the rest of them, and picked his house as their meeting place.

She contacted Jorge and Ynez, Joel and Stacy. Jorge answered the phone and when she told him of the plan said he would come over immediately. "Ynez won't leave Martina, though," he explained. "She'll stay home."

"I understand," Beth said.

Joel was freaked and angrier than she'd known he could get. But when he explained what had happened, she understood why. A sickening feeling rolled in the pit of her stomach as she thought of the insurance agent targeting Lilly. *Aunt Beth*, Lilly had been calling her since she was first able to speak, and she didn't know what she would do if something happened to the girl.

"I'll be there," Joel vowed. "I'm not going to sit around and just *wait*. If you guys are going after him, I'm coming, too."

"I'm not leaving my daughter!" Stacy screamed in the background.

"Let them stay," Beth said softly. "It's all right."

Joel sounded conflicted. "Maybe she'd be safer over there with the rest of you. They know we're home, they might try to get her here. But that's a long way to drive," he mused. "A lot could happen on the way."

"We're staying!" Stacy shouted.

"It's your call," Beth told him.

So Jorge and Joel both arrived alone, almost at the same time, and they gathered around Edward's dining room table, where Hunt had set up a mosaic made up of the scanned and enlarged sections of map that he'd printed on their computer before coming over. Edward himself had gotten out of bed and, using his walker, hobbled over to the dining room. Outside, the afternoon sun was sinking in the west.

They looked carefully at the two assembled maps, afraid that at any moment the insurance agent might walk through the front door or emerge from another room to confiscate the pages. Even now he might be watching them, and Beth forced herself not to think about it.

There was no address for The Insurance Group listed anywhere, but on the oldest map a series of mysterious lines with no corresponding arrows or notes pointed to the southern area of Mexico, nearly obscuring a small circle with a star in the center of it. Hunt found the circle and touched it with his pen. "If I had to guess," he said, "that's the point of origin. Everything seems to spread out from there. I'll bet that's where they're located."

"Or where they *were* located," Edward said. "This is one really old map. What if they've moved?"

"It's the only thing we have to go on. Does anybody know anything about Mexican geography?"

They all looked at Jorge.

"I think that's Chiapas, but I don't know for sure." He

turned to Edward. "You have any geography programs on your computer?"

He shrugged. "I don't know. I think there's something called Encarta on there, some kind of encyclopedia."

The encyclopedia wasn't much help, but an entry for Mexico and a general map of the country confirmed that the area in question was indeed the state of Chiapas, and they moved on to the Internet to find additional information.

It would have made more sense, Beth thought, if The Insurance Group's headquarters were in Africa or the Middle East. Syria, perhaps. The cradle of civilization. But if that had been the case, its existence would have been known, it would have been written about in other ancient texts, word of its existence passed down through various sources. No, if anonymity and secrecy were what the company desired—and that certainly seemed to be the case—establishing the business in the wild jungles of the so-called New World would have been the smartest move.

But how had its agents—

Their agent

—gotten around in those days? Papyrus reed boat? She could not see insurance salesmen sailing for months on end across dangerous waters, at the whims and mercy of nature, as they fanned out across the globe to sell their policies. There had to have been some other way of traveling.

Come to think of it, how did they get around now? Assuming they had to report back to the head office periodically, did they buy tickets and wait in airports and fly in planes? She had a hard time imagining that as well.

Hunt located a more detailed map of the region, which he immediately printed out. They all seemed to agree that the circled star was located close to Tuxtla Gutierrez, a commercial and manufacturing center that was Chiapas's largest city.

"Let's go," Jorge said immediately.

Joel nodded. "Let's kick some insurance company ass."

Edward grimaced, leaning forward on his walker. "I'm with you in spirit, guys. But there's no way in hell I'd make it."

Beth looked over at Hunt, nodding. It was their only hope. "All right then," he said. "Tuxtla Gutierrez it is."

Twenty

1

After a nearly three-hour wait in Mexico City, after transferring to a single-engine Cessna, after a bumpy turbulence-filled flight, the four of them finally landed at the Tuxtla Gutierrez airport shortly after midnight. They were the only Americans on board, the only ones brave or dumb enough to fly to Chiapas during this period of regional instability. But the night workers at the airport were very nice and very helpful, and after unloading their luggage from the cargo hold, they took a dirty taxi to a hotel they'd booked through an online travel agent. Surprisingly clean, the hotel was located next to a steel and glass office building and across the street from what looked like a windowless adobe structure transported from a pre-Colombian century.

Joel and Jorge were sharing a room, and since they both had to call their wives from the lobby telephone, Hunt and Beth tiredly took their leave, Hunt making sure that they would immediately be awakened if something weird had happened back in the States.

The room was nice, with a queen-sized bed, a table with three chairs next to a window, and a bathroom with a sink, a tub, a toilet and plenty of soap and towels. The only thing that differentiated the room from one in the United States was the conspicuous lack of a television.

They didn't need a television, however. It had been a hell-ishly long day, they were exhausted, and immediately after crawling under the covers, they fell asleep.

Hunt was awakened by Joel's knock on the door. "Get up!" he shouted. "Time to get going!"

"I'm up!" he lied, nudging Beth next to him. "We're both up! Be out in a few minutes!"

There hadn't been much to see at night, but in the mid-morning, the view from the window was breathtaking. They were on the third floor of a four-story building, and from this vantage point they could look out over most of the city and see the heavily forested mountains beyond. Hunt had never been to any part of Mexico other than Nogales and Baja California and could not remember ever having seen a panoramic shot of the Chiapas landscape. It was all television closeups of armed guerrillas and buildings riddled with bullet holes. And Tuxtla Gutierrez certainly hadn't been on his travel radar. But the country here was beautiful. A cloudless sky so blue it looked like paint presided over a countryside of dark rugged moun-tains and hills overgrown with native trees of the deepest, darkest green. In the foreground, Tuxtla Gutierrez looked as exotic as its name promised, with mustached men in brightly colored garb pushing carts through an outdoor marketplace. Everything was foreign and unfamiliar, and there was some-thing innately exciting about that. It occurred to him that he should travel more, that if they ever got out of this alive, he and Beth should make an effort to see the world, to visit the places they'd only read and heard about.

If they got out.

Beth emerged from the bathroom, and then it was his turn. Ten minutes later, they were dressed and ready to go. They knocked on the door of Joel and Jorge's room, and the four of them went downstairs. Hunt bought some sugar-coated bread from a vendor in the lobby, got four Cokes from a machine, and took everything over to a threadbare couch in the corner for breakfast.

They'd spent their time on the Cessna poring over the insurance agent's maps and trying to compare them with a contemporary tourist map of Chiapas that Jorge had bought at the Mexico City airport, but they were no closer to locating the headquarters of The Insurance Group than they had been in Tucson. What's more, now that they were here, finding the office seemed akin to looking for a needle in a haystack. They were not even sure where to begin. They could look in a phone book or wander the streets searching for a sign that read "The Insurance Group," but Hunt had the sneaking suspicion that the company was not so free with its self-promotion. Still, one of the locals might know something, Beth suggested. She nodded at Jorge. "We already have a translator."

Several moments of conversation with the desk clerk, the vendors in and outside of the hotel and two men who wandered into the lobby for no apparent reason made Jorge think better of that plan. "We need a guide," he said. "Someone who knows the area."

Hunt looked from Beth to Joel and shrugged. "Fine."

Jorge spoke rapidly to the desk clerk in Spanish, and the man picked up the phone behind him, talked for a few minutes, then nodded.

"He's on his way!" Jorge announced.

They opted to wait in the lobby rather than their rooms, Beth visiting the line of vendors that stood in lieu of a gift shop while the men alternately sat on the threadbare couch and paced anxiously. Twenty minutes later, a slightly built man with a thick Zapatista mustache walked into the lobby, directly over to them, and said in accented but easily understandable English that he would accompany them and act as their guide for as long as they wanted for twelve dollars a day, American money.

"Twelve dollars," Hunt asked incredulously.

"Okay, ten."

The guide's name was Manuel, and he said he had his own four-wheel-drive pickup truck and would take them anywhere they needed to go. Unfortunately, there were five of them including Manuel and only room for three in the cab—assuming one person sat almost on top of the stick shift.

"I'll sit in the back," Joel offered, slapping the wall of the truck bed.

"Me, too," Hunt said. "Beth? You and Jorge sit with Manuel."

"No," Jorge said. "You stay."

"We need you to translate."

Manuel was offended. "I speak three languages! I need no translator!"

"I'll sit in the back," Jorge said. He and Joel climbed in and settled down, backs against the cab wall.

Hunt felt like Indiana Jones, standing on the teeming street, and for a brief wonderful moment the horror of why they were here receded as he climbed into the dusty front seat of the rattletrap truck. Then reality came crashing back full force, he saw in his mind Lilly's mangled body, and he was filled with a new resolve to terminate the insurance agent's life policy—

and life

—and do what he could to bring down the entire damn company, although he was not at all sure how they could accomplish such an ambitious goal.

"Where to go?" Manuel asked before starting the vehicle.

Hunt showed him one of the printouts, the section of the map detailing Chiapas, blown up to cover the entire page. He pointed to the starred circle beneath the thick spiderweb of lines. "We are looking for an insurance company that is located somewhere in this area. It is called The Insurance Group in English, but I'm not sure if it has the same name over here. It's—" *A multinational corporation,* he'd been about to say, but he was not even sure that was true. He thought for a moment, looked up at the guide and decided to simply level with Manuel. They didn't have time to fool around, and they weren't going to get anywhere if they tiptoed around the subject "It's a company that doesn't sell normal insurance. Do you have insurance over here?"

"We have insurance, yes. Do I have insurance? No."

"Well, they sell car and home and health insurance, but they also sell good neighbor insurance and personal injury insurance. And if you buy these, your enemies are killed and you are not."

The guide's eyes widened. "You bought this?"

"We had no choice," Beth said. "We had to."

"Now I have life insurance, and they have promised I will live forever."

"This I not believe."

"It's true. I don't know if it works, and I don't want to find out, but I have it and I have to pay for it and I can't afford it. I want to find the company and . . . stop it."

"Does any of this sound familiar?" Beth asked. "Have you ever heard of anything like it or are you familiar with any rumors of something along those lines?"

He shook his head. "No, no."

"But can you help us find this company?"

"I don't know where to start," Manuel admitted. He grinned, revealing two missing teeth. "But this is why I agree to help you. I thought you did not wish to go shopping. That is why I am only charging you ten dollars a day."

"Twenty," Beth offered.

"*Gracias*. I accept."

"So where do we start?" Hunt asked. "The phone book?"

"Your American office is not listed, no?"

"No," Hunt agreed.

"Not here either, I think. I know a man, though, who maybe can help us. We start with him."

"Great," Hunt said.

Beth nodded. "We really appreciate this."

Manuel started the engine, which roared to life.

"Hang on," he said.

Away from the main thoroughfares, the streets of Tuxtla Gutierrez were rough and narrow, built in a time when there were carts instead of cars, when people drove herds instead of pickups. A lot of people still walked here, and Manuel's truck sped between the ancient buildings through these constricted roads, barely missing crowds of men, women and children. The vehicle had no seat belts or shoulder harnesses, and both Hunt and Beth held on for dear life, he bracing his hands against the dashboard, she clutching the armrest of the door.

Hunt could only imagine what it was like for Joel and Jorge in the back. Each time he turned around and peeked through the dusty rear window, he saw them sprawled in Twister positions, using arms and legs to keep themselves from flying around the open space, their mouths and eyes closed tight against the dirt.

They passed buildings of white-painted mud that looked like they had been shot at in more than one war and structures with ladders leading onto roofs that could have come from an Indian pueblo. Everywhere, clothes fluttered from windowsill clotheslines.

This land was old. Hunt had never had a sense before of just how young America was, but here he could feel the crush of the past, the weight of history. The very air held a sense of depth. These streets had been trod upon a century before the Pilgrims landed on Plymouth Rock, and many of them appeared to have changed very little in the intervening years.

He was thoroughly lost by the time they reached their destination: a two-story tan brick building at the end of an alley. A man with a machine gun slung over his shoulder emerged from the open doorway, and Manuel stepped out of the truck, shouting out what sounded like a greeting. The man disappeared back into the building and a moment later another man walked out, a jolly overweight fellow wearing billowy white clothes. He looked like an extra in a bad movie, the comic-relief father of the hero's love interest. But the man with the machine gun, obviously a guard, indicated that Manuel's friend was more than just a simple funny guy. Manuel as well seemed to show deference to the fat man, and though the two were obviously friendly, just as obviously one had far more power than the other.

Joel and Jorge hopped out of the truck bed and stood next to the passenger door.

"This is my good friend Rodrigo," the guide said. "If anything happens in the city, he knows about it. Give me your map, and I ask him about the insurance company."

"The Insurance Group," Hunt repeated, handing out the map. "That's what it's called in the United States."

"I will tell him of your life insurance. He may not believe it, but I know he will be interested. So if he does not yet know about the company, he will find out."

But the news did not have the desired effect. Hunt could tell that immediately from the expression on Rodrigo's face, yet Manuel kept on, talking faster, obviously trying to get in as much as he could before being shot down.

Suddenly, the fat man lashed out and slapped Manuel across the face. Stunned, the guide backed up a step. Rodrigo said something angrily, then shouted what sounded like an order.

"This is not good," Jorge murmured.

The man with the machine gun came running out, accompanied by two similarly armed guards. Rodrigo struck again, slapping Manuel's face, and Manuel made no effort to defend himself. There was nothing jolly about the fat man now, and he pointed toward Joel and Jorge, standing by the truck, speaking heatedly.

The man was a thug, but obviously one with clout, and

Hunt didn't know whether to step in and try to help Manuel or sit back silently and wait for it all to end. The fact that he didn't understand the language and had no idea what was really going on left him at a distinct disadvantage.

It was Beth who jumped in. "Leave him alone!" she ordered, opening her door.

Rodrigo stopped, out of shock if nothing else. Even if he didn't understand the words, he understood the tone of voice, and Hunt doubted that he was used to having *anyone* speak to him that way, let alone a woman.

Manuel was moving slowly away, back toward the truck, trying not to make any sudden movements. "Stay out of this," he told them. "You are not involved."

Joel and Jorge moved equally slowly away from the passenger door toward the rear of the pickup.

"I think we are involved," Beth said, and her voice was strong.

"He does not believe me. He thinks I am making fun—"

A gunshot rang out.

It was not the fire of an automatic weapon, and none of the three guards had moved at all, but they moved now, surrounding Rodrigo and quickly ushering him back into the building.

Beth reached for the handle, slamming the door shut. Another shot was fired from somewhere—a rooftop, the upper window of another building—and Manuel ran back to the truck. "Get down!" he ordered. "Duck!"

They already had. Hunt felt like screaming, but his mouth was completely dry and his voice wouldn't work. He could feel the beating of his heart in the back of his throat. He crouched on the floor of the pickup, an arm held protectively around Beth, and the only thought in his mind was that they would not be able to stop the agent and his insurance company because they were about to be killed right here.

But he could not be killed.

He had life insurance.

Deluxe life.

Maybe he couldn't be killed, but Beth could.

He sat up instantly, then moved back down, draping himself over her, trying to cover her body like a shield of armor. She didn't object, didn't say anything or try to push him away, and then suddenly Manuel was back in the driver's seat, the engine was revving, and they were speeding backward up the alley the way they'd come. When the pickup reached another cross street, Manuel swung the wheel around, the truck spun with the sound of screeching tires, and then they were shooting forward and away.

"It's safe!" he announced. "You can get up."

Hunt tried, but the velocity of the vehicle and the bumpiness of the road made it difficult.

"What the hell was that about?" he asked as his head slammed painfully against the underside of the dashboard. He pulled himself onto the seat and helped Beth up.

Manuel rubbed the raw red side of his face. "He thought I was lying to him. He thought . . . I do not know what he thought. Rodrigo has many enemies, and he cannot be too careful. As you have seen. But do not worry. I have another idea."

Hunt looked over at Beth. The expression on her face mirrored his own feelings: maybe they should find another guide, someone without any ties to the criminal underworld. They did not have time to waste, but neither did they want to end up shot in some back alley as part of some gangster's turf war.

But he could not be shot.

He was immortal.

Besides, someone with such a wide range of contacts was probably *exactly* the type of person who could find the whereabouts of the insurance company.

Hunt looked through the window behind him, saw Joel and Jorge still flattened on the bed of the pickup. "Are you okay?" he yelled, but they could not hear him. "Are you guys all right?" There was no response, but then they took a sharp corner and Jorge's arm reached out to grab the ridge just below the window. Joel moved his foot to compensate for the turn. He saw no blood on either of them.

They were all right.

"What's your idea?" he asked Manuel.

"The witch. Maybe the witch will know."

Hunt and Beth exchanged a look. "The witch?" Beth said.

Manuel smiled enigmatically. "You will see."

2

Beth got out of the truck when Manuel stopped, grateful for the relief. They had been driving down a series of dirt roads through an empty section of wilderness for well over an hour. Her thighs were numb, her buttocks hurt, and if she'd been sitting at a different angle, she probably would have had an orgasm. The ride had been vibratingly rough, and her ears were still buzzing from the noise of the engine. Her head felt thick, padded, as though she'd spent all day in a tiny club listening to ear-splitting music at the highest decibels.

She stretched her arms, arched her back, walked to get out some of the kinks in her legs.

The sun was low, the afternoon nearly gone. Whether or not this "witch" had any information for them, they would not be able to act on it until tomorrow. By the time they returned to the hotel, it would be dark. And she was still tired, even though they'd awakened close to noon. She could tell from the droopy expressions on the faces of Hunt, Jorge, and Joel that they all felt the same. Maybe tomorrow, after another full night of sleep, their bodies would be adjusted to the new country.

Hopefully.

If she had been hoping for some revisionist witch, one of those modern Wicca women found in movies living in con-

temporary surroundings, wearing street clothes, she could not
have been more off the mark. This was something out of a
folktale, a small shrewish hag who would have been at home
in the story of Hansel and Gretel.

She lived in a small hut at the base of a black volcanic cliff.
The dwelling was made of wood. Branches and twigs, to be
more precise, all carefully fitted together to form solid walls
and roof. She would have made some crack about the three little pigs had she not been so frightened, but as it was she
remained silent. The domicile was humble, but from it em-
anated an aura of great power—and great evil. That was an
old-fashioned word and not one she had often used since childhood, but it fit.

It fit a lot of things lately.

The witch was old and hunched over, her face weathered
and lined, flesh puckered over a missing right eye in what
looked like a permanent wink. She smelled of feces and spice,
but Beth forced herself not to gag, afraid of what the consequences might be. Next to her, she could tell that Hunt was
also trying to keep down his gorge.

The old woman did not seem to know Manuel, and she
greeted him with suspicion, despite his air of friendly obse-
quiousness. But he spoke clearly and sincerely, and the witch
listened to what he had to say. Unlike Rodrigo, she did not disbelieve him or dismiss his story out of hand, but seemed to
accept what he said at face value.

"What's he saying?" Hunt asked Jorge.

"He's just telling her what you told him. Now he's describing the insurance that makes you immortal."

Manuel pointed, and the witch looked at Hunt.

The guide took several coins out of his front pocket and
deferentially handed them to the old woman. She nodded her
acknowledgment of his offerings, then spoke a single word.

"*Sí.*"

"She knows where the company is located," he told them.

Beth was filled with an unexpected sense of relief. It was as if she had been holding her breath, waiting for the answer, and now that it had come she could breathe again. She reached for Hunt's hand, grabbed it, and was gratified by his returning squeeze.

The guide looked at Beth and smiled nervously, showing his missing teeth. "But she wants something in return. A lock of your hair."

Beth's heart skipped a beat. The old lady was smiling at her eagerly, and she looked away, turned toward the west wall of the hut, where she had the misfortune of seeing a child's skull with several pieces chipped off its cranium lying in a home-made wire cage. This couldn't be good. She didn't know much about magic or witchcraft, but in fiction and film, hair was usually used as a binding agent, to gain power over someone. She saw herself turned into some sort of zombie, working as a slave for this old hag, doing things against her will—ideas that she would have scoffed at six months ago but now seemed per-fectly logical and reasonable.

"How about *my* hair?" Hunt offered.

Manuel translated, but the witch shook her head angrily, said something, and spat.

Beth knew why he'd offered. Life insurance. He was pro-tected. She was vulnerable, had left herself wide open, and this might all be part of some elaborately planned scenario worked out by the insurance company to bring about her death.

Still, what choice did they have?

"Okay," she said.

"No," Hunt said at the same time.

They looked at each other.

"We'll find it some other way," he told her.

"Yeah," Joel said, and she heard the fear in his voice. "Don't do this."

"There may be no other way. It's been two days already. It's going to be three. I have to." She stepped forward, pointed to her head, and almost before she knew what was happening, the witch had scissors in her hand and was snipping off a lock of hair from over her right ear.

The old woman scurried to the back of the hut, placed the hair in a small crumpled paper sack, then returned to where they stood near the door. She talked rapidly, too rapidly for even Manuel or Jorge to simultaneously translate, and they could only wait until she had finished, then try to paraphrase what she'd said.

Jorge spoke first. "It's in the mountains," he said. "According to her, it's at the bottom of a canyon marked by a star carved in a cliff and a rock in the shape of a man."

"Yes," Manuel confirmed.

The witch said something else, something short, and the guide's face lit up. "*Sí,*" he said. "*Sí.*" He smiled, nodding. "I know where this is."

"How far away is it?" Hunt asked.

"A few hours. We will go tomorrow. The road is very rough."

Grateful to be able to escape the foul-smelling hut, Beth followed Manuel out the door into the bright light and clean air. Just before she closed the door behind them, the old woman said something else, something long and involved in a rapid-fire delivery. Manuel nodded, interjecting what seemed words of agreement, but he did not translate.

"What was that all about?" Beth asked.

He grimaced. "A warning."

"About the insurance company?"

"About babies," Jorge said, frowning.

"Babies?" Hunt said and then looked at his friend in awkward embarrassment, thinking of Jorge's own mutilated child.

Martina. They'd named him . . . *her* Martina instead of Martin.

Manuel walked across the dirt to the pickup. "There are more . . ." He searched for the word. "*Events* here than your insurance company. This is an old land. There are many religions here, many spirits."

"But what about the babies?"

"She said beware of them," Jorge told them.

She could hear the frustration in Hunt's voice. "What does *that* mean?"

Manuel shook his head. "I will explain to you on the trip back. We must leave now. She does not want us here at nightfall." Left unspoken was the fact that *they* did not want to be here at nightfall.

The guide did indeed explain about the babies on the trip back, shouting his story over the roar of the engine, and it was a strange and frightening tale indeed. She felt as though they'd followed one monster down the continent only to find that it came from the *land* of monsters.

According to Manuel, when babies in Chiapas died, they did not ascend to heaven or descend to hell or go on to any sort of afterlife. Instead, they remained bound to the earth, to the town or city in which they lost their lives. And they were angry. It became the goal of their fiendish existence to harass the living, particularly women of childbearing years, to keep them from sleeping and to frighten them at night. They were harmless as long as they were not allowed inside a bedroom. Whether in a home or hotel, they could roam the hallways and kitchens and other rooms, making noise, scaring people, but they could do no physical harm. Once allowed into a bedroom, however, through an open door or window, the babies grew strong and could hurt, attack. Kill.

"They want to punish their parents, the parents who let them die, but as far as they are concerned, any adult will do. They are tricky," the guide warned them. "You will think they have been left on your doorstep or are crying to get in like a cat, but do not believe them. They are trying to fool you into letting them in your room. Whatever you do, do not open any doors or windows. Stay in your bed. Go back to sleep." He paused. "The witch warned you to be careful. She says they come for you tonight."

Before their encounters with the insurance company, Beth would have dismissed such stories as so much nonsense. But now she promised Manuel that no matter what they heard, they would not open any doors or windows in their room until morning.

Sure enough, she awoke that night to the sound of a baby crying and the tapping of a tiny fist high up on the hotel room door.

It has to be floating in the air, she thought.

She sat up in bed, chilled, and saw that Hunt was awake as well. He quickly tried to close his eyes and pretend he was asleep, but she'd caught him, and when she elbowed his side, he sat up next to her.

"I hear it," he admitted without prodding, and she could hear the fear in his voice.

"I don't like this country," she said. "It scares me."

"The people are nice."

"Who? The thugs? Or the witches?"

"Maybe that's why the insurance company's here. They fit right in."

Beth sighed. "I don't like it. It's like . . . an omen. Like we're being told, 'Get out while you can.' "

"You don't really believe that, do you?"

She shrugged.

"I'm signed up for deluxe life now. We've got to get to the insurance company and find the agent's policy and put a stop to him. And quickly. Or else my premiums are going to come due and I'm not going to be able to pay them and . . ." He didn't finish the thought.

"Life insurance. Maybe that's why those criminals couldn't hurt you," she said. "Bullets bounce off you just like Superman now." She'd been teasing, sort of, but it came out more seriously than intended, and Hunt took it that way.

"Maybe so," he said.

Outside the door was a baby's cry. From behind the curtained window to the side of the bed came a gentle tapping against the glass. They huddled together beneath the blankets.

"Do you think Jorge hears them?" she asked, thinking of his child.

"I hope not," Hunt told her. "I hope not."

3

The witch, it turned out, did *not* know where The Insurance Group was headquartered, and her misinformation almost got them killed.

As arranged, Manuel arrived at the hotel just after sunup with a full tank of gas, and they drove into the jungle in the opposite direction from the witch's house—a harsher, more vertical landscape. He had brought his brother's truck this time, with room for all of them in the cab, two in the front with Manuel, two in the back on a narrow cramped bench seat.

Hunt held on to the dashboard as the pickup bounced over eroded ruts and jumped embedded boulders on its way into the mountains. The road they were on looked more like a hiking trail—he saw no other tire tracks in the dirt, only what looked like crowds of hoofprints—but the truck successfully navigated a narrow pass and climbed a switchback up a cliffside. After another hour of winding mountain travel, they reached a clearing, a small flat spot in which a spring-fed pond was ringed by the ruined foundation of a long-gone structure.

Manuel slammed on the brakes, came to a stop. Once the gravel settled, the only noise in the canyon was the ticking of the truck's cooling engine. "Here is where we get out."

"This is it?"

"No, this is as far as we can drive. From here on, we must walk."

"Have you been here before?" Beth asked.

"Not exactly. Here, yes. This was the site of a very famous battle. But beyond, where the witch told us to go, no. I have only her directions."

"You don't think we'll get lost?" she said worriedly.

"It is not far. We will be fine."

This did not feel right to Hunt. It was exotic and remote enough to be real—a secret canyon in remote mountains with directions provided by a witch—but he felt going in that this was wrong. The Insurance Group might be nearly as old as time itself, but it was an urban, not a rural invention. It should be where people were, not way the hell out in the boondocks.

Joel, at least, seemed to agree. "This doesn't seem like the kind of place an insurance company would have its headquarters. Not even *this* insurance company."

Still, they followed Manuel's lead, each of them taking out one of the canteens that the guide had packed in the back. Hunt drank until he was full, refilled his canteen from the spring, took a piss behind a rock, then waited until the others were ready.

The five of them set out on a foot trail up the canyon.

He'd been prepared to walk far, had expected to wander through a maze of hidden canyons for hours before searching around to find a star carved in a cliff and a rock in the shape of a man, assuming that if this battleground was so famous and the location of the insurance company so secret, the two would be located fairly far apart. But almost immediately after they started walking, Jorge pointed up ahead, and through the tops of the trees, high on a mountainside, was a clearly marked star in a circle, a gigantic pentagram impossibly etched into the face of the cliff. Hunt did not know how such a thing was possible. It appeared to be the size of a several-story building, and the only way he could imagine it being done was by someone on a scaffold. Yet there it was.

"Now we look for the man," Manuel said.

Shortly thereafter, the canyon split, trails forking off to follow each branch, and Manuel took them up the one to the left. The canyon on the right appeared to go around the mountain in front of them and away from the star, but the left canyon sloped upward toward the carving.

It was hot and they were sweating, and here in the jungle the humidity seemed to be hovering somewhere near a hundred percent. Joel took off his shirt, used it to wipe his face, then tied it around his waist. It was a good idea, and the rest of the men followed suit. Beth unbuttoned the top two buttons of her blouse.

The canyon before them seemed to peter out, and the trail climbed up the steep incline at such an angle that they were forced to stop every ten minutes or so to catch their breath and wet their parched throats. Finally, they were at the top, and here was a formation Hunt recognized. A mesa. Until now the mountains had been sharp and pointed, traditional triangles, but now they were on a flat arid plateau that stretched before them. The star was still visible off to their right—if it gave off light, it would have been shining down on them—and now they could see a tall boulder that, whether naturally eroded or man-made, resembled a standing soldier.

"Let us go," Manuel said.

It took longer to reach than Hunt thought it would, and he was not sure until the last moment that they would find anything when they got there. The space between the star on the mountain and the rock that looked like a man appeared to be merely a flat stretch of dry grassy plain.

But then they reached the rock, and he saw that the plateau ended here. The plain had been an—

intended?

—optical illusion. Before them was a deep gorge, and at the bottom of the gorge was a garden.

It was the most beautiful sight Hunt had ever seen, made even more so by its juxtaposition against the surrounding countryside. Below them, row after row of flowers, in all colors of the rainbow, moved to the strains of an unfelt wind, as though they were dancing. Gigantic tropical-looking plants with elephant-ear leaves and long-stemmed roses were growing happily next to smaller proud carnations.

He did not see any sort of building, but maybe there was a cave he couldn't view from this angle. He still was not convinced that this was where they would find The Insurance Group, but he was entranced by the gorgeous scene below, and when he looked over at the others, he could tell that they were as well.

A stairway was carved into the cliff, and at the bottom of the stairway was a gate attached to a white picket fence. The sight made him laugh—with happiness rather than amusement—and he grabbed Beth's hand, and the two of them started down.

It was midday, but at the bottom of the gorge the light was as dark as dusk. Hunt did not understand why. From above, the garden had been clearly visible, flowers basking in the sun, but down here all was in shadow, and the cliffs up top looked murky and gloomy, as though shrouded in storm clouds.

He was holding Beth's hand, and then he wasn't holding her hand, and then he wasn't sure where she was. Joel had been right behind them, but he could not remember seeing his friend since they started down the steps.

There was a rustle, a whisper, a soft sussurant sound that gave him goose bumps and spoke to him on some level he did not want to acknowledge. The whispering continued slipping slyly into his ear. It was not a language, not exactly, but there were words and there were thoughts and there were images accompanying those thoughts, and they seemed to bloom in his brain like flowers, opening up to full-blossom inside his skull. Suddenly, the sounds were everywhere, and he looked around for Beth and Manuel, but he could not see, could only hear, and the things he heard whispered of death.

He wanted to get out, *needed* to get out, *had* to get out, but he was trapped. Then he felt as though he were falling down a very deep well, and when he landed he was cushioned by a soft bed of flowers, and then the flowers were touching him, caressing him.

And then they were stinging him, biting him, eating him.

And then . . .

He was being pulled out through the gate and onto the bottom of the stairway by Joel and Manuel. Next to him, on the stone step, Jorge was helping Beth get groggily to her feet.

"I am sorry," Manuel said. "I should have been there faster."

"What happened?" Hunt asked. His lips felt dry, his eyes hurt.

"I wouldn't've believed it if I hadn't seen it," Jorge said incredulously. "It was like the *Wizard of Oz* poppies, man."

"The flowers tried to take you," Manuel told him. "We saw Beth beneath a bush, and after we pulled her out, we found you under flowers. They tried to take me, too, but I cannot hear them so well." He grinned. "I am deaf in left ear."

"She lied to us," Beth said angrily.

Manuel nodded. "She lied. She wanted to trap us here. Trap *you* here, probably. She has your hair."

"I never trusted that hag," Joel said.

"Do you think she's working for them?" Hunt asked. "For the insurance company?"

"The witch works for no one but herself She has no connection to your insurance company. I doubt she has ever heard of it."

Beth shook her head. "But why would she do this, then? Why would she try to throw us off the trail and get us killed?"

"That is her way. Do not think of her anymore. We are through with her. We will find your insurance company another way."

"But—"

"Do not think of her. It is not good."

Hunt looked back, past the gate, at the rows of beautiful flowers.

And started up the steps and the long walk back to the truck.

At night, the babies came back, looking to punish their parents. Hunt knew they were supposed to remain safely behind locked doors, but a part of him wanted to peek out of the hotel room and see what the babies looked like. He imagined them as evil-eyed infants with mouths filled with fangs, but they could just as easily have been invisible, fiends without faces. He would never know, though. While he would have liked to see for himself, he knew enough not to break the rules that had been laid down for them. They were visitors in this country, they knew nothing about these things, and if they were going to live to see the insurance agent brought down, they would have to remain focused.

He fell asleep to the sounds of tapping and crying and hissing.

In the morning, Manuel was all smiles. "Luck shines on us, amigos. I have been asking around, and one of my colleagues has a friend whose brother works for a man who killed himself last week because he could not pay for his insurance. I think this is what you are looking for."

"But we need to find out *where* this company is. We need to go to the actual building."

"And here we are in luck. My colleague's friend's brother *saw* the salesman who sold his boss the insurance walking down a street on the west side yesterday and the day before. It was at the same time both days." He held out two hands like scales. "If we're there and he's there . . ."

"We can follow him," Joel said.

"*Sí.* Yes."

Hunt shivered involuntarily. This sounded right, this sounded familiar. No secret canyons in remote mountains but a man walking the streets, making his rounds. Now they were getting close, and he was getting scared. The enormity of what they were attempting to do was starting to come home to him.

"What time does he walk by?" Hunt asked.

"Eleven-ten. We should be there a half hour early, just in case."

"An hour," Hunt told him.

"An hour, okay."

He hoped that this was another insurance agent, someone local to the region who was working for The Insurance Group, but he could not help picturing in his mind *their* agent wandering the streets of Tuxtla Gutierrez in his old-time hat and trench coat, selling insurance policies that caused upstanding pillars of the community to commit suicide.

They had an hour and a half to kill, and they spent it cruising the streets of the city's west side, trying to find The Insurance Group on their own. They had no luck, however, and shortly before ten, Manuel drove to a long low modern-looking building that he said was home to the construction company where his colleague's friend's brother worked. He bade them wait in the truck, and they did so while he walked inside. He emerged several minutes later with another man in tow, a tall well-built man with neatly parted hair wearing a western-style suit.

"This is Guillermo," Manuel said by way of introduction.

"*Hola,*" the man greeted them as he stepped up to the pickup's window. He said something in Spanish.

"He's asking if we have insurance problems, too," Jorge translated.

"*Sí,*" Hunt told him.

More Spanish.

"He wants to know if we want to get rid of the company and put it out of business."

"*Sí*," Hunt said again.

"*Bueno*," Guillermo said, and Hunt understood that. The man nodded emphatically, then spit on the ground and spoke rapidly to Manuel.

The guide nodded, replied, then got back in the truck. "It is two blocks away. He walks there and we follow. He shows us where to park and tells us when this insurance salesman walks by. Then he will walk back."

"Should I pay him something?" Hunt asked as Manuel started the engine. "For helping us out?"

"No. That is an insult. He is avenging the death of his boss, his friend."

They crept down the street and followed Guillermo to a relatively wide avenue, with vehicles parked on both sides of the road. He motioned for them to pull in behind a motorscooter, which allowed them to see the street in front of them clearly, and Manuel swerved into the spot, barely missing a scroungy dog who appeared to be munching on a piece of meat. He cut the engine, and Guillermo took out a cigarette and stood next to a fence near the passenger side of the car, smoking.

They waited a long time, and despite the open window, Hunt was starting to doze in the stifling heat of the pickup's cab when a dig from Beth's elbow jarred him awake. Guillermo was leaning in the passenger window next to them. "*Aquí*," he said quietly and then spoke rapidly to Manuel in Spanish.

"The man carrying a valise," Manuel translated as he looked in his rearview mirror and started the engine. "Here he comes."

Guillermo left the side of the truck, apparently bidding them good-bye, and Manuel quickly and quietly said, "*Gracias*."

The agent walked past the pickup.

He was dressed in the sort of old-fashioned gray suit favored by Mexican businessmen and politicians, he had dark skin, he carried a leather folder rather than a briefcase, but there was something instantly recognizable about him, and Hunt had to fight an urge to duck down behind the dashboard and hide until the man was gone. He did not seem as healthy or strong or powerful as their insurance agent—at least their agent as he looked now. Rather, he had the average build and ordinary features of their agent when they'd first met him, and Hunt thought that the man was on the prowl for suckers like themselves off whom he could feed, stable established individuals able to keep up with the graduated premiums.

The man rounded the corner at the end of the block, and Manuel put the pickup in gear and followed.

"Shouldn't we walk?" Jorge asked. "I mean, aren't we a little conspicuous? He's going to notice a truck following along behind him at two miles an hour."

"We will see what happens. We will see where he goes. I would rather be prepared to give chase should he get in a vehicle of his own than be caught off guard and miss the opportunity."

Many other cars and trucks were crowding the street and quite a few pedestrians. Manuel gave nearly all of them the right of way, impeding his own progress in a non-suspicious manner but never letting the agent out of his sight.

Hunt had expected to be taken somewhere on the edge of the city. Not an inaccessible location out in the middle of nowhere like the witch's house or the garden of evil to which she'd directed them, but someplace off the beaten path, in close proximity to the city but not right in the middle of it. Instead, the insurance salesman turned a corner, walked down another street, turned another corner—and they were there.

"I have never been to this place," Manuel said incredulously. He looked around. "I did not know this was here."

Amidst the maze of buildings and the teeming throngs of people in the center of Tuxtla Gutierrez was what looked like a dry reservoir the size of an American city block. It was in a hilly area of the city, and its placement seemed both natural and logical, but even before he saw the insurance agent stride briskly down the slope toward the bottom of the basin, Hunt had a bad feeling about the place. Manuel stopped the truck, and the three of them watched through the windshield as the agent reached the bottom and walked into a small stone structure in what appeared to be the exact center of the open space.

That structure looked familiar, Hunt thought.

It reminded him of The Jail.

He had not thought of that purposeless building since Edward and Jorge had taken him to see it, but now he recalled the dread he'd felt while inside, the claustrophobic sensation that both of his friends had experienced as well. He turned his head to look in the backseat.

"The Jail," Jorge said, nodding. "God*damn*, I wish my cell phone worked here. I'd call Edward right now and have him check that place out."

"But he wouldn't be able to get there," Hunt pointed out. "He still can't walk by himself."

Jorge shook his head. "Damn."

They waited five minutes, ten, making sure that the insurance agent was remaining inside and not coming out. Just when they decided to get out of the pickup and hoof it down the side of the empty basin, the man emerged carrying his folder. Without pausing, he walked up the opposite slope, traversing the steep bank as though it were flat ground before disappearing down a narrow street between two old buildings.

Again they waited, but not as long. They were anxious to get going. They were so close to entering The Insurance Group's lair, to breaching the mysterious company's inner sanctum, and they wanted to hurry up and get in there.

When it seemed clear to Hunt that the insurance agent was not going to return and that no one—

or no thing

—was going to come out, he reached across Beth's mid-section and opened the passenger door. "Let's go."

She got out, he got out, Manuel emerged from the driver's side, and Joel and Jorge clambered out of the backseat. The five of them walked across the gravel, stood on the edge of the empty basin and looked down. This was the place. Hunt was sure of it. Whether that little building led to a maze of underground catacombs or was some sort of time/space anomaly housing a gigantic office building between those tiny walls in direct defiance of the laws of physics, this was where The Insurance Group had its headquarters. This was where it had started, all those centuries ago, and this was where it still resided.

It.

He'd been thinking of the insurance company as an entity, a sentient being, and he decided now that that was probably correct. This was not like a corporation in the modern sense, a business construct that employed people and provided services. It was more like an octopus, a living creature with multiple tentacles, and if one of those tentacles was hacked off, another would grow in its place.

Another would grow in its place.

He had avoided thinking about what they really had to do here, had concentrated on destroying their insurance agent's immortal policy, but being here now and having seen that other salesman slip back into the city to cause more harm, he realized that he had to try and stop all of the agents, not just theirs—or else another would simply take his place and all their effort would have been for naught. He had no grand illusions, did not fool himself into thinking they could walk into that small building and put an end to centuries of terror—he had no idea how they would even go about destroying the company itself. Explosives? Water? Fire?—but he knew that they needed to destroy *all* of the immortal policies they could find, cut off as many tentacles as they could.

"Any ideas on how we'll get down there?" Beth asked.

"He just *walked* down."

"It looks a little steep to me."

It did look steep. But before they could talk about it any more, Manuel was squatting, crouching down, then pushing himself off and sliding down the dirt embankment on the soles of his feet. Hunt looked at Beth.

"Works for me," she said, and followed suit.

Hunt felt like a kid. Sliding down, he glanced over at Joel and, despite the circumstances, he could not help smiling a little. When they were kids, the two of them used to take pieces of cardboard they'd cut from refrigerator boxes or television boxes or washing machine boxes and use them to surf down a grassy amphitheater in a park by the zoo, and that's what this reminded him of. The embankment here was rockier though, the dirt not as smooth as grass and progress was slower. Which was fortunate. He almost fell over twice but was easily able to stop himself and then start down again. When traction slowed him to a crawl near the bottom, he stood and ran down the last few feet.

That was fun, he was about to say, but the sight that greeted his eyes at the bottom was that small outhouse-sized building, and he saw the somber expressions on the faces of the others and said nothing.

They walked cautiously forward, each looking up periodically at the rim of the empty reservoir to make sure that the insurance agent had not returned and was not striding quickly down the side toward them. They reached the small structure. Next to the building, not visible from above, was a hole in the ground, a square rimmed with concrete that looked like the entrance to a tomb. A foul odor wafted up from the hole, a stench of spoiled mushrooms and rotten potatoes that he recognized immediately.

Beth did, too. "This is it," she said.

"I am not going in," Manuel informed them. "I will wait here for you."

Hunt nodded. He understood. Hell, for only twenty bucks a day, he doubted he would have come this far. He reached into his back pocket, pulled out his wallet and handed Manuel fifty dollars in bills and a hundred dollars' worth of traveler's cheques. It had only been three days and he was technically owed just sixty bucks, but the man had been much more than just a guide to them, and deserved at least this much. Hunt would have given him more if he'd had the money on him.

Manuel tried to protest. "No, no."

Hunt forced the money into his hand. "Take it."

"We are not through yet. I still work for you."

Hunt looked at him meaningfully. "Just in case."

Manuel glanced over at the hole in the ground and the structure next to it, and nodded. "I understand," he said.

Hunt looked at the small stone building and took a deep breath. The entrance had to be on the other side, but he was not quite ready to walk around and peer into its doorway. He was afraid, and he suddenly realized that they'd brought no weapons with them. He'd been so obsessed with *finding* The Insurance Group's office that he'd made no preparations really for what he'd do once they got there. He obviously wasn't going to Jackie Chan his way through a host of sentries, but neither did he expect them to be able to waltz right in, tear up all of the agents' immortal policies and then stride on out without encountering any resistance.

Tear up?

He'd been planning to burn them. But he'd forgotten to bring matches or a lighter.

God, how unprepared could he be?

He cleared his throat. "Listen," he told Manuel. "Do you have a knife or something I could borrow? Some kind of weapon?"

"Like this?"

Hunt had expected, at best, a pocketknife, but the guide pulled from a hidden sheaf a scary-looking dagger with a six-inch blade.

"Yeah. That'll do."

Manuel was taking off the sheath. "Here. Tie this around your waist with your belt. It will leave your hands free."

"And do you have any matches—?"

"I brought a lighter," Jorge said. He smiled. "I thought you might forget."

"Thanks." He finished fastening the sheath, then slid in the knife. "I guess we're ready to go." Now that the time had come, he could sense in himself more than a little reluctance.

Fear.

"I wait for you here," Manuel promised. "If you're not back by nightfall, I will go for help."

"*Gracias,*" Beth told him.

"Yes, *gracias.* You've been our savior. We never would have made it here without you."

Jorge slapped the guide's back, gave him a hug. Joel shook his hand. "You've been a big help. Thanks."

"It has been my pleasure."

Hunt looked around at the faces of their small intrepid band. He saw anger, determination, fear pushed aside by bravery. They were unprepared, probably outnumbered, definitely at a distinct disadvantage, but they refused to let that stop them, and right now he was prouder of his wife and friends than he had ever been of anything before in his life.

They were doing the right thing. And whatever happened from here on in, they would always have that.

He nodded good-bye to Manuel and they walked around the corner of the building.

Twenty-one

1

Hunt had no idea what he'd expected to find, but it was not this.

The entrance to the small structure was open and doorless, and guarding it was a blind dwarf, a freakish little man with wide staring eyes and a nose that looked like a beak. The mouth, muscles pulled into a permanent smile, was toothless, gums blackened with disease.

The dwarf did not say anything, and neither did they. Hunt had no idea what to do. He looked over at Beth, back at his friends, but they were all equally blank. On impulse, he stepped forward and walked past the little man into the structure. The guard made no effort to stop him, did not move at all, in fact. He might as well have been a statue.

Like The Jail, there was water on the floor, as though the small building capped a spring, but unlike The Jail there was also another doorway. Well, not exactly a doorway, more like a trapdoor, a circular hatch awkwardly placed in the rightmost corner.

That was how they would gain entrance to The Insurance Group.

"Come on in!" he called, and though the room was small, his voice echoed. He waved his hand, beckoning the others.

Beth started to follow him inside, but when she drew close,

the dwarf leaped in front of the entryway. She screamed, jumped back, and Jorge appeared from the right to support her before she fell. The dwarf was making a sound like a rabid bat, an angry high-pitched squeaking noise that no human larynx should have been able to reproduce.

Instinctively, Hunt moved forward to help—

—and the dwarf stepped aside to let him pass.

There was no way the little man could have seen him from behind, and Hunt did not know by what mechanism the guard could have known the exact moment to move over and let him through, but he suddenly realized why he was able to enter the building while Beth could not.

Life insurance.

Deluxe life.

Only immortals were allowed inside.

Beth had figured out the same thing. "I didn't buy life insurance," she told him. "I can't get in."

"Let me try it," Joel said. He started toward the entrance, and the dwarf jumped in front of him, making that angry squeaking sound. "Jesus!" He backed up so fast he almost tripped over his own feet.

"I have an idea." Hunt moved in front of Joel, and the dwarf stepped aside. "Hold on to my shoulders and stay behind me. I'll shield you." Joel grabbed his shoulders, and Hunt walked forward, keeping himself between the dwarf and his friend.

They made it safely inside.

"It worked!" Hunt shouted jubilantly. Leaving Joel in the building, he walked back out and attempted to do the same thing with Beth.

The small sentry blocked his way, not squeaking this time but growling, a wild threatening sound that made him think of a cornered boar. Hunt stopped, waited for a few seconds, then took a tentative step toward the entrance. The dwarf crouched as if ready to spring, clawed hands opening and closing rhythmically. With his milky-eyed stare and grinning black-gummed mouth, he appeared dangerously crazy.

Hunt backed off.

The dwarf resumed his normal stance, and Hunt tried it again with Jorge. Like Joel, Jorge had no problem getting in as long as Hunt remained between him and the sentry.

Hunt walked out unimpeded, had Beth climb onto his shoulders for a piggyback ride, but before they had taken even a single step, the dwarf was in a crouch and growling.

Women could not get in.

It was the only conclusion possible. He was about to suggest another try, but Beth was already shaking her head. "Go," she prodded him. "Who knows what kind of alarm that set off. You need to get in and out fast, under the radar, before anyone finds out about you."

She was right, he knew.

He nodded, gave her a quick kiss, a quick squeeze, then walked past the dwarf and back inside.

"I watch her," Manuel announced from around the side of the building. "I guarantee her safety."

"What am I, a china doll?" Hunt recognized her humorous tone of voice, but Manuel began apologizing, afraid he had offended her.

Everything would be all right out there. It was in here that he had to worry about. He turned his attention toward the circular hatch on the floor, which Joel and Jorge were already examining. It had no visible knob or lock or handle, and he was not sure how to open it. He crouched down next to the closed trapdoor, thinking he might be able to just lift it, but it appeared to be flush with the floor. In fact, now that he looked carefully, it did not look like a real door at all but a painted one.

He stomped his foot on the floor, splashing water. The rock beneath felt solid. He moved over to the circle, ready to stomp on it and see if there was any sign of hollowness or weakness.

And the circle started down.

Joel and Jorge quickly moved next to him so as not to be left behind.

Hunt crouched, afraid of losing his balance, acutely aware that there was no railing or anything to grab on to. Joel did the same, but Jorge remained standing, and the three of them remained in those positions as the circle dropped below the level of the floor and the seeping water dripped onto their heads. Then they were traveling slowly through blackness, through what had to be a tunnel. Had Beth seen this? Had she been watching through the door? Did she know what had happened? He should have shouted out to her, gotten her attention. It was important to him that she not be worried, that she not think that he had just vanished into thin air.

He remained in a crouching position, afraid if he stood that he would fall. This was an elevator. An elevator used by people who worked for The Insurance Group. An elevator that *he* was allowed to use, that he was able to activate because he was immortal.

They thought he was one of them.

The circle stopped descending, and though they hadn't been able to see anything until now, they found themselves on the floor of what looked like an ancient temple or the main chamber of one of the great pyramids. Blocks of stone the size of Winnebagos were fitted together to form the walls of the gigantic room, and on the blocks were carvings. Words and pictographs and pictures. The words he could not read, ditto for the pictographs, but the pictures, while undoubtedly ancient, depicted scenes that were easily recognizable. Two parents and a young boy, arms around each other's waists, watching a building burn. A woman crying over a man who had been crushed beneath a fallen tree. Two men arguing over a pair of ox-driven carts whose wheels had gotten stuck together.

These were ads.

Insurance ads.

The massive chamber was illuminated, though there was no visible light source, but the far corners were dark, shadowed, and out of the corner of his eye he saw one of those shadows detach itself from the wall and move. He almost cried out, he was so startled, but an inadvertent stumble backward distracted his mind, and he hop-stepped to balance himself and managed to avoid making any noise.

The shadow was not a shadow, and when it moved into the light, he saw that it was a tan creature almost the same color as the stone or the sand. It shuffled slowly across the floor of the great room toward an open doorway on the opposite wall. There were legs, appendages that looked like arms, and the remnants of a face, although the features seemed blurred, muted, eroded, like they had been sandblasted or had simply disintegrated over the centuries. He could not tell whether this was some type of monster or whether it was a human who had been alive so long that he had been worn down into this shambling mummylike creature.

He waited until the thing had passed through the doorway and disappeared into the darkness beyond, then turned to his friends, whispering, "Should we follow him?"

Jorge nodded silently, and in answer Joel started walking toward the dark open doorway.

They should have brought flashlights, Hunt thought. How *could* they have come here so completely unready for even the most obvious situations?

He needn't have worried. The space beyond the doorway only looked dark. Once there, he saw that it was suffused with the same sourceless light as the previous chamber.

They entered a much smaller room, a place with a low ceiling and bare unadorned walls. Before them was a stone table, a huge slab supported by two equally thick columns. Behind it on some sort of bench sat the creature they had followed. This close, he could see that the being had indeed once been human, although its skin had taken on an aspect of petrification, and the features of the face had indeed been eroded away over the years. He had no lips, only a thin line that indicated the presence of a mouth, and the nose had been whittled down to a nostril-less nub. Rather than the large sockets of a skull, there were small crusted slits where the eyes should have been, as though the petrifying skin had grown over the eyes and hardened there.

Looking at the creature, Hunt remembered suddenly that despite its great age this was the home of an insurance *company*, and it occurred to him that the great chamber behind him was like the lobby of an office building. And this was where the secretary would sit.

He paused for a moment unsure of what to do. Should they attempt to communicate? Ask directions? *Pardon me, could I make appointment to see the CEO?* He decided they should simply follow the course they'd been following, and he nodded to his friends so they understood his intention, and walked past the seated creature and into the corridor beyond, waiting for a shouted order or a demand to stop that never came.

They found themselves in a maze, an endless catacomb of identical little rooms, the ancient equivalent of modern-day office cubicles. Nearly all of the small rooms were occupied, mummified beings of great age moving slowly at their stations, positioned behind sandstone tables and piles of parchment, shriveled heads turning on creaking necks to silently eye them as they walked by. These things looked different from the secretary at the front desk, vaguely humanoid but more mutated, less easily identifiable, and once again he had no idea if they had once been people or were of a different race of creatures entirely. Either way, they were far older than any living being should have been, atrocities that should have died naturally long, long ago.

As if by unspoken agreement, none of them said a word.

The beings they encountered were mute, and all three of them remained silent as well, not wanting to draw attention to themselves, afraid that any sound would alert the denizens of the insurance company.

They kept walking, down one hallway and then another, and no one tried to stop them, no one paid attention to them. He had no idea what he'd expected to find when they came down here, but this damn sure wasn't it. Although they'd talked about destroying the agent's life insurance policy, deep down he hadn't really thought they'd find a row of file cabinets they could look through or a series of desks they could rifle. Back in Tucson that had seemed plausible, but here in Mexico his expectations had changed, and he supposed that he'd expected to encounter a dark, dank underground world filled with slimy monsters they would either outwit or slide by until they reached the large and terrifying supreme fiend, with whom they would have the inevitable showdown— which, of course, they'd somehow win. After *that*, they would find the grail-like policy and torch it. The scenario might have been clichéd, but it was nonetheless frightening for that, and just the thought of it sent his heart racing now.

But this was even creepier. It was not quite as *scary*, but it was more unsettling, and its disturbing roots ran deeper. This was not some wild raging monster, and they were not dragon-slayers here to kill the beast. This was a well-oiled machine, a company that had been operating since before men were men, and its workers' utter indifference to them showed him just how puny and insignificant he and his friends were.

They continued walking, searching for something that would tell them where they could find the immortal policies, some indication that they were on the right track.

In one room, incongruously, was a computer and monitor identical to the one in the insurance agent's basement office back in Tucson. The screen was lit and filled with tiny detailed writing, but there didn't seem to be a power source in the room and Hunt saw neither plug nor outlet. The room was empty, at least temporarily, and he ducked in, hoping to type the word "Tucson" or "Arizona" or "United States" and at least find out *something*, but the keys on the keyboard were blank, and the characters on the screen were not English, not Arabic, not Cyrillic, not anything he had ever seen. He quickly left before the office's occupant returned.

In another, slightly larger chamber, skulls were piled in a bin—human, animal, and in between—and in the center of the room a flayed mule stared silently at him, eyes rolling in unimaginable agony. *This* was more like what he had expected, and he quickly passed by, continuing down the corridor, hoping that they were not drawing ever closer to some spectacular horror at the heart of the company.

There was still no noise down here, no talking or grunting or screaming, and the only sounds they heard were their own footsteps on the stone floor and the occasional sandpapery whisper of the office workers shuffling their ancient feet. The noiseless mule had made him even more aware that these corridors were silent, and he tried to walk more quietly.

The corridor down which they were walking stopped at a solid wall, and they backtracked and took another corridor that finished in an empty room. They were coming to the end of The Insurance Group's domain and had yet to find any sign of the original insurance policies. He wondered if they would ever be able to find them.

Then they went down another hallway, a hallway from which many others branched off, a labyrinth that reminded Hunt of something he had read about in Greek mythology. There were no rooms here, only endless corridors, and he walked slowly, carefully, making sure to remember the sequence of each turn so that he did not end up wandering these passageways forever.

Finally, they reached what appeared to be the nucleus of the labyrinth, the nerve center of the insurance company.

He smelled it before he saw it, and it was that familiar stench of moist fetid rot. The odor seeped from behind a red wooden door set into the stone wall, a door barely big enough for a child or the dwarf who guarded the entrance above. Hesitating only briefly, Hunt reached out, turned the flat metal handle, and the door swung open. Holding his breath, he crouched down and peeked in.

The room beyond was in sharp contrast to the monochromatic tan of the surrounding complex. The walls were festive and multicolored, painted with the most elaborately detailed murals Hunt had ever seen. As with everything down here, light from somewhere made everything visible, and what he saw was a pictorial history of mankind, artistic depictions of every important event to have occurred in western, eastern, and middle-eastern civilization since time began.

Events insured by the company.

The doorway was small, but the room beyond was large. Not spectacularly large like the lobby, but the size of a small-town banquet hall. In the center of the otherwise empty chamber was a shallow pit ringed by a miniature barrier less than a foot high, and within that enclosure was the power, the force, the brains behind the insurance company.

It was a creature of sand and earth, a hideous elemental abomination that twined and twisted in its lair and kept its loathsome mouth perpetually open in a silent scream. Despite the foul odor, the air here felt sticky and sweet—it was like breathing cotton candy—and a palpable aura of malevolence, a tremendous sense of negative energy radiated from the room. Everything about the creature was wrong and evil, and as it craned its vile neck upward, mouth opened impossibly wide, Hunt knew that this was a sight which would haunt his dreams to his dying day.

How something so profoundly alien could set up, organize and run an insurance company, could be behind the bewildering legalese that made up individual policies, could determine the rules and regulations that made covering a Volvo cost less than covering a Corvette, he did not understand. But he knew it to be true, and as he watched, the scenes on the mural shifted, changed. Now they were not artistic representations of the past but real-time views of individuals all over the world: agents and customers of the company. Hunt's eyes scanned the myriad scenes, and his heart leaped in his chest as in the bottom right corner he spotted Stacy and Lilly, huddled on the couch in their living room, afraid to venture outside.

If he had been braver or if this had been in a movie, he would have heroically taken out Manuel's knife, crawled through the doorway, and after a tense fight murdered the beast. But this was not a movie and he had never felt less brave in his entire life. This was an evil so far beyond his ken that he could not possibly fight it, and, without saying a word to his friends, he carefully closed the door and slunk away, trying not to draw attention to himself, hoping against hope that the awesome power of that horrible being was attuned to a much higher frequency and had not even noticed his intrusion.

"What is it?" Joel demanded, and Hunt heard the rage in his voice. They were the first words any of them had spoken down here, and they sounded unbelievably loud in the stillness.

He thought of the scene with Stacy and Lilly on the mural. "Nothing," he lied. He was convinced that destroying that monster behind the door would put an end to the insurance company, but there was no way that was going to happen.

He still remembered the series of turns that had gotten them to this point and he reversed the route on their way back until they were once again in a corridor where those worn eroded creatures shuffled slowly to their offices. After that thing behind the red door, they seemed familiar and almost reassuring.

He did not know where to go from here, was tempted to head back to the lobby and start from the beginning, but then he caught sight of *real* movement in his peripheral vision. Not the slow shambling undead walk of the office workers but the purposeful stride of—

an insurance agent.

It was the one they'd followed. He'd apparently left and come back, and Hunt ducked into the nearest empty office, Joel and Jorge right behind him. The three of them stood in the darkness, watching as the agent passed by.

They stepped out of the office, back into the corridor.

And followed.

They moved slowly, at the same pace as the other creatures so as not to draw attention to themselves, but they needn't have worried. The insurance salesman was oblivious, his mind set on one specific goal, and Hunt watched as he strode down the corridor and turned right.

He'd been prepared to walk endlessly through the labyrinth in order to find out where the agent went, but to Hunt's surprise the man stopped at the first doorway he reached and walked right in.

Hunt thought they'd already walked past here, but apparently not, because behind the open doorway was not another small office with an ancient drone working on some meaningless task at a stone table but a long room filled with wooden file cabinets. The agent was looking through the one closest to the entrance, and Hunt hazarded a quick glance and then walked by, not wanting to be spotted, Joel and Jorge right behind. He went into the first empty office beyond, then peeked around the edge of the doorway until he saw the insurance agent emerge a few moments later. The man did not even glance in their direction but headed back the way he'd come, and as soon as he turned the corner, Hunt was hurrying back to the file room.

This was what they'd been looking for.

"Holy shit," Hunt said softly. "Guard the door!" he ordered, and Joel quickly positioned himself at the room's entrance.

The ceiling was low, not like in the lobby, but the room stretched so far back that he could not see its end. Both sides were lined with file cabinets, and he opened the one closest to him, the one the agent had been searching through, and saw folders filled with papers and documents. He lifted one of the folders and found insurance applications identical to those he and Beth had filled out but written in Spanish. He put the folder back, moved to the next cabinet and saw applications in Arabic.

He closed the door of the file cabinet, looked around. Before him, the wooden cabinets stretched to infinity, but behind him, at the head of the room, to the left of the door—

—was their insurance agent's immortal policy.

It was on parchment and under glass, like an exhibit in a museum. There were only six such policies—*one for each continent?*—and Hunt assumed that meant that there were only six immortal agents canvassing the earth. Had there been more at one time and had those earlier agents been unable to pay their premiums and then killed off? Or were there only six positions available and once those were filled no one else need apply?

He didn't know, didn't care. The fact that there were only six made his work a lot easier. He stood next to the case and stared down through the glass at the parchment. Again, the Faust idea returned to him, but such a model was too conventional, too simplistic. What he had here before him was more complicated, more involved. And yet . . .

And yet it all boiled down to the fact that the document in the case granted him the power of life and death over the insurance agent. He was in charge now. He was the one who would determine the outcome of this battle. What was behind that glass was not the agent's immortal soul, it was his immortal policy. He didn't have a soul, a policy was all he had, and Hunt realized that the Bible was right. In the beginning was the word. And the word was more powerful, more important, more binding than the body could ever be.

"What is that?" Jorge asked.

"His life insurance policy," Hunt said. They were still speaking softly, as if afraid of announcing their presence.

He leaned forward until his face was practically pressing against the glass. The provisions of the policy were written in an alphabet Hunt did not understand—something far older even than Arabic—but the form and structure of the document were identical to his own immortal insurance, and he recognized the line at the beginning that contained the agent's name.

His name was Ralph Harrington.

Ralph.

It seemed impossible. The name of evil should not be so average, so ordinary, so laughably mundane. Ralph Harrington? It diminished the man in a way, brought him down to size, made him seem less intimidating, less like some supernatural bogeyman and more like a regular guy.

Hunt recalled what Del had told him in jail, that names had power, like Rumpelstiltskin.

Words. Names. These were the things that mattered.

Out of curiosity, he moved down the case and read the name on each policy. One was written in either Chinese or Japanese characters, another in either Greek or Russian. Two were in an Arabic alphabet. Only Ralph's name was written in English. (*Ralph!*) All of the names were in contemporary languages, however, and Hunt wondered if the names changed with the times, if they were automatically updated in some magical way each time the individual agents altered their names to conform with the current era.

No matter. Ralph Harrington was his name now. That was the name on the policy and it was to that moniker that he was

bound. Hunt searched for a clasp or lock, some way to open
the case containing the policies, but there was none, and finally he walked over to the nearest file cabinet, took out a big,
thick folder, placed it on the glass, and then brought his fist
down as hard as possible in the center of the papers.

The glass shattered.

Thank God it wasn't safety glass, or he might not have
been able to break through. He picked up the folder, tossed it
on the floor, then carefully picked up the largest pieces of
glass and dropped them until he was able to take out the policies.

Now had come the moment of reckoning.

If learning the insurance agent's name had brought him
down to Hunt's level, it had also made him seem more
human, and for a brief fraction of a second, Hunt hesitated before doing what he had set out to do. But then he thought of
Jorge's child, thought of Lilly, thought of Eileen, thought of
all the other people who had died or suffered as a result of the
insurance agent's actions, and he put down the other policies
and held up Ralph Harrington's.

He took out the lighter, flicked it on, and, holding the piece
of parchment from the top, lit the lower right corner. There
was no magic poof, no faint echo of a scream, but the ancient
paper caught fire quickly and burned steadily upward, and he
held it in his hand until the last moment and then let it fall. It
burned for a few more seconds on the floor, then went out,
leaving a small triangular corner containing no writing of any
kind. He was taking no chances, though, and he picked up that
little triangle, set it afire once more and then held it until the
small flame touched his fingers and the policy was completely gone.

Hunt looked toward the door. It had taken him several
minutes to break open the case, take out the policies and light
Ralph Harrington's on fire, but Joel was still on watch, and he

looked back and nodded, indicating that the coast was clear. Hunt saw relief in his eyes, relief and gratitude.

He went down the line, burned the other policies.

No one came to stop him. That was the weird part. No alarms went off as he sequentially set the policies aflame. No sprinklers in the ceiling, alerted by the smoke, turned on to douse the fires. He did not understand it. Back home, the insurance company had seemed attuned to their every movement, yet here he was allowed to just walk right in and start setting fire to the policies that kept each of the insurance agents alive. Was it that all of the attention was directed outward, that there had never been a security breach before or a traitor in their midst and there'd been no need for precautions? Was it that the individual agents kept tabs on their customers and were responsible for monitoring their movements? Or had life insurance granted him a free pass, given him a cloak of invisibility and the license to do whatever the hell he wanted?

"You bastard!" Joel suddenly screamed.

Both Hunt and Jorge were on it in a flash. They ran out of the file room after their friend, who was yelling at the top of his lungs and speeding down the corridor toward a figure walking across the intersection of another passage several yards away.

A very familiar figure.

Their insurance agent.

2

Joel was standing in the doorway of the file room, guarding it, while behind him Hunt and Jorge set fire to the life insurance policies of their insurance agent and his immortal brethren. In his mind, Joel imagined the agent crumpling into dust as his policy burned, like a vampire exposed to sunlight.

Which was why he was so shocked when he heard the sound of footsteps, looked up the corridor and saw the insurance agent emerging from a side passageway.

Joel was filled with a rage so immediate and all-consuming that he didn't know what he was doing until after he'd already done it. "You bastard!" he screamed, and took off after the agent, who ignored him completely and continued walking from a passageway on the right to one on the left. "I'll kill you, you son of a bitch!" he yelled.

If only he had taken the knife Manuel had given Hunt. He'd stab that fucker right through the heart.

But shouldn't he be dead already?

He should, but he wasn't. In fact the insurance agent looked none the worse for wear, indeed looked as strong and healthy as he ever had. But how was that possible? He was no longer immortal if he did not have a policy to protect him.

The man had been alive for hundreds of years, and once his immortality was revoked, he should have reverted to his natural state. Yet he hadn't.

Because he still had *his* copy of the policy.

That had to be it. The original policy was gone, but as long as written proof existed, as long as the agent himself possessed the words stating that he was guaranteed to live forever, the coverage stood.

Joel turned the corner—

—and was tackled by Jorge.

Ahead, the agent kept walking, not looking back, oblivious.

"What are you doing?" Joel spluttered, scrambling to his feet. "That's him."

"Yes," Hunt said, grabbing his arm. "And we don't want you getting yourself and all of us killed before we finish what we came to do."

"*That's* what we came to do." He heard the desperation in his own voice, the rage, the fear, and he took a deep breath, forced himself to stop, calm down, look at this rationally rather than emotionally.

Further down the hallway, the agent entered an office.

"Okay," he said, whispering once again. "What do we do?"

Jorge looked at Hunt, both obviously at a loss. Hunt sighed. "Well, now that you've found him . . ."

"You burned his policy," Joel said, keeping his voice down. "But he's still alive. Want to know why? Because *he* has a copy of it. As long as those words are written down, as long as a copy of that policy is extant, it's still in force, it still applies. We need to burn *that* copy, too."

"You're right." Hunt thought for a moment. "But where would it be? Where would he keep it? In his office back in Arizona? At his house? Here somewhere?"

The agent emerged from the office into which he'd walked, chuckling. He didn't have his briefcase, Joel noticed. He hadn't had it since he'd first been spotted. Something about that nagged at him. To his knowledge, the man was never without his briefcase.

The agent's clothes were different, too—more casual.

He was off duty.

If Joel had been a cartoon character, a lightbulb would have gone off above his head. He had no idea how their agent had gotten here, although supernatural transportation seemed far more likely than conventional air travel, but he was suddenly certain that this was where the insurance salesman spent his nights. This was his home. He lived in The Insurance Group's headquarters.

All of the agents did.

So if they could find out where his room was . . .

"Follow him," Joel whispered. "He lives here somewhere. *That's* where his policy will be."

Hunt nodded, understanding instantly—the advantage of playing to a smart crowd—and the three of them continued up the corridor, remaining a discreet distance behind the agent, hoping he would not turn around and spot them.

The office into which the agent had walked looked like some sort of locker room, Joel noticed in a quick glance as they passed by. He saw a long stone bench in the center of the narrow chamber, and the walls on both sides consisted of twin rows of open alcoves. The agent had been chuckling when he walked out, but there did not appear to be anyone else inside the room.

The corridor jogged to the right then curved to the left, and they lost the insurance salesman for a few moments, afraid to pick up the pace, not wanting to close the distance between them despite the twists and turns of the passageway. Then the corridor ended. At a closed door.

Painted on the solid wood, like the moniker stenciled on the dressing room door of an old-time movie star, were two letters: R.H.

"Ralph Harrington," Hunt said. "That's him."

"So what do we do?" Jorge asked nervously.

Both he and Joel turned to Hunt.

"Go inside," Hunt said.

3

They had no guarantee that the insurance agent was not directly behind the door ready to spring at them, but time was passing quickly and they could not afford to wait around and dilly-dally, as his mother always said. Hunt put his ear to the wood, listened for a moment, heard nothing, then tried the knob. It was not locked and turned easily.

They were in an apartment, a grottolike room lit by a single black candle atop a wrought-iron stand. There was a rusted metal sink in one corner and in the center a filthy mattress on the floor that they could smell from here. Hunt saw no stove, no microwave, no refrigerator.

Maybe he didn't eat.

At one end of the room was a black display case pushed against the rock wall, filled with what Hunt could only assume were trophies: the skulls of wild animals, the skeletons of cacti. Dead things from the Tucson neighborhood. He thought of that room with the bin of skulls and the flayed mule, and though it had made no sense to him at the time, he understood now what it signified.

Parchment.

It was The Insurance Group's tanning room, where they made the parchment for their most important policies.

He looked at the display case in front of them now and thought that it was not unlikely that the insurance agent was doing the same thing here on a smaller scale. For relaxation after hours.

He saw no sign of the agent himself, but to the right of the display case was a narrow wooden door that made him think of the door to a privy or outhouse. He was almost certain that the agent was in there, and as if to confirm his assumption, a strange creaking noise came from behind the door.

The three of them huddled quickly. "Look for a file cabinet," Hunt whispered. "Or a desk. Someplace where he might hide his papers."

The room was way too dark for them to split up, so Joel grabbed the candle from its stand and they walked the room, moving from right to left. They saw an old Victrola, pulleys from a schooner ship's riggings, a sword and bayonet leaning against a full-length mirror, but no place that looked likely to hide important documents.

Then a light was suddenly switched on and the room changed.

It was no longer a dirty grotto filled with relics of the past but a modern, well-ordered living space twice that size.

Where the Victrola had been was a giant plasma TV, in place of the black display case was a walk-in closet filled with clean, tailored suits from different American eras. The filthy mattress had been replaced by a white contemporary couch facing the television, and where the closed privy door had been was a wide arched opening leading into a bedroom with blond wood furniture. Another open doorway on the opposite wall led to a kitchen filled with stainless steel appliances.

And to their right beneath a framed Chagall print, was a computer desk and filing cabinet.

Hunt dashed over and quickly rifled through the desk drawers. Pens . . . paper . . . rubber bands and paper clips . . . diskettes . . .

From somewhere inside the bedroom came the sound of a flushing toilet. The agent had finished going to the bathroom, his lights had turned on, and he was coming out. Hunt felt like a child waiting for a monster to arrive, and he sped over to the file cabinet and opened it.

It was filled with manila folders, all carefully labeled with the name of the insurance policy they held.

He'd found it!

The flushing sounded closer, louder, as, within the bedroom, the door to the bathroom opened. The agent was on his way.

A . . . B . . . C . . . D . . .

Footsteps and the humming of a tuneless song.

G . . . H . . . I . . . J . . . K . . .

. . . L!

Life insurance!

Hunt grabbed the folder, yanking it out, and Joel and Jorge blocked him from view as he pulled out the lighter and tried to get the pages on fire. There was a brief scary second where it looked like it wouldn't catch, but this was a lighter not a match, the flame was constant, and the folder could not withstand the power of the heat.

It started to burn.

It was still burning when the agent walked through the bedroom and out, and it took him a moment to register what was going on. When he did realize who they were and what was happening, he let out an ear-splitting bellow and pushed Joel and Jorge aside as though they were rag dolls.

Hunt was still holding the burning folder, and he ran from the agent, using pieces of furniture as obstacles, going around the couch, over the coffee table, behind a chair. The policy was almost gone, the flames were starting to hurt his hands, but he dare not let it go, and he ran into the bedroom and then into the bathroom, where he shut and locked the door before climbing into the shower stall.

The agent threw the bathroom door open.

But he was too late.

Hunt dropped the last of the policy just as it was about to burn his finger, and it fell to the tile and sputtered on the shower stall floor, and then it was gone—a small charred scrap disintegrating into tiny ashes. Hunt withdrew Manuel's knife, keeping his eye on the insurance agent. If he'd expected him to crumble into dust, he was disappointed. Nothing like that happened. There was no seismic shift in air currents, no crackle of unknown energy, no indication at all that anything had changed.

But it had.

And they both knew it.

There was movement from the bedroom behind the agent. Joel and Jorge had made a quick trip to the kitchen, and both had long carving knives in their hands. Joel stabbed outward, face contorted with fury, but the blow glanced off, and Joel found himself flat-assed on the floor. With dawning realization, Hunt understood that while the agent might no longer have immortal insurance, he was no doubt protected by almost every other policy type imaginable. Finding a chink in the armor, a flaw or weakness for which the agent was not covered was going to be next to impossible.

But it had to be done. And fast. Within the next few seconds.

He thought quickly, looked behind the agent at Jorge, ready to spring. "No!" he shouted, but he was too late. Jorge jumped the insurance salesman who turned and swatted him away, sending him and his weapon flying. Jorge's head hit the footpost of the bed with an audible crack.

"Knock it off, Harrington!" Hunt screamed.

And the agent's head jerked toward him, eyes wide with anger and shock.

That was it!

His name.

Names had power. He remembered how the agent had laughed when he'd thought he'd have to sign the immortal policy in blood. *Your signature is good enough. That's all we need.*

That's all they needed. No blood, no souls. Just names.

It was what Del had tried to tell him.

"Ralph Harrington," Hunt stated clearly.

The insurance agent no longer looked so formidable. Joel was getting up, shaking himself off, and Jorge was struggling groggily to his feet, but Hunt said, "Stay there. Don't go near him."

"How do you know my name?" the insurance agent demanded.

"I saw it on your immortal policy. When I burned it."

Recognition dawned in the agent's eyes. "So you did it," he said and his voice was quiet and unnervingly calm. "Very resourceful."

"And I'm canceling all of my policies with The Insurance Group. You guys can go fuck yourselves."

"Canceling?" He slammed his fist down on the bathroom sink, cracking the porcelain.

Hunt backed against the rear wall of the shower stall, knife out.

"How do you think you're going to get by without insurance, huh? What's going to protect you from the horrors of life, from the hell that is existence? Did you ever think of that?" The agent's face was red and filled with rage. He stepped forward, reached into the shower stall and slapped Hunt across the side of the face. It was agonizing. His eyes watered and it felt as though he'd been smacked with a brick. But the agent made no effort to assault him further. "That's the problem with you people! You never think ahead!"

Hunt tried to ignore the pain and the swelling flesh that was already starting to impede vision in his left eye. "Listen, Harrington."

"DON'T CALL ME THAT!"

The expression on the man's face was unlike anything Hunt had ever seen, a primal visage that was at once horrifyingly enraged and achingly vulnerable. Hearing his name said aloud hurt him somehow, and though Hunt couldn't follow the logic of it, didn't know how it worked or why, he acted upon it quickly.

"Ralph Harrington!" he shouted, thinking of Rumpelstiltskin. He said it twice more, fast. "Ralph Harrington! Ralph Harrington!"

He was again disappointed. The agent did not disappear in a puff of smoke or fade away, did not stomp his foot furiously like the dwarf in the fairy tale and fall through the floor. But he did back up, did look stunned, and since he couldn't think of anything else to do, Hunt kept repeating the name. "Ralph Harrington! Ralph Harrington!"

Behind the agent, in the bedroom, Joel and Jorge took up the chant: "Ralph Harrington! Ralph Harrington!"

Hunt tried to think as he shouted, wracked his brain trying to figure out what else he could do. If there were a birth certificate he could burn, perhaps *that* would put an end to the insurance agent. But maybe there were other policies still extant, insurance coverage that protected him from—

"THAT'S NOT MY NAME!" the agent screamed crazily, and suddenly Hunt had an idea.

"What *is* your name?" he asked.

The language in which the single word was spoken was not like anything any of them had ever heard, a grating noise like speech from the bowels of hell—part metallic rasp, part shrill screech, part squishy slurp. The aural equivalent of the language in which the original policies had been written.

In the beginning was the word.

And suddenly the insurance agent looked tired. All of the anger drained out of him, all of the rage and hate, and he stood there, slumping, looking down at the floor. He lost his height, lost his bulk, was once again the ordinary average man who had initially come knocking at their door.

And he started to fade.

His home faded with him, the shower stall disappearing, the sink growing fainter, the doorway to the bedroom dissolving into air. They hadn't moved, but they were back in the original grotto, and the television became the Victrola and the Victrola became a skin drum and then the drum disappeared from view and became nothing. Even the dark volcanic rocks lightened in color, and then they were standing in an empty sandstone cave.

Only the insurance agent was still visible. But just slightly, and his form had changed as well. He no longer looked human but older and odder, of a kind with those beings shuffling through the hallways, working in the offices, but different somehow, young rather than old, the way they must have looked before time and work had worn them down.

He remained in the same position, though, slumped, unmoving, staring down at the floor, and then, in the blink of an eye, he too was gone.

In his place was a crumbling rock on which were chiseled several unidentifiable characters.

His original policy.

Hunt picked up the rock and threw it as hard as he could against the wall, where it shattered into pieces.

"Let's get back to work," he said.

4

Hunt expected the passageways of the insurance company to be teeming with angry agents, to be a swarming chaotic beehive filled with insurance salesmen after their hides, but not even the loss of one of their own seemed able to derail the glacial forward motion of the occasional creatures who shambled through the corridors and worked in the offices.

"We need to destroy all the files," he said. He took a deep breath, gathered his courage. "And the president or CEO or whatever it was I saw in that room behind the red door."

"Behind that red door?" Joel frowned. "I thought you said there was nothing there."

"I lied."

Jorge nodded. "Then let's do it."

Joel smiled slightly, feeling either more confident or more satisfied after their dispatch of the insurance agent. "All for one."

They returned to the file room and started opening up file cabinets, throwing the papers in the center of the floor. If they spent all day and night here, they would not be able to empty out every one of the filing cabinets, so the three of them worked quickly for the next ten or fifteen minutes, tossing out the contents of hundreds of the most recent files, as much as they thought necessary to start a big bonfire. They arranged the papers so that they made thick trails to the individual cabinets and then used the lighter to set fire to the edges of several documents. Quite a lot of papers had been dumped out, and they caught easily, the flames spreading.

A conflagration arose between the two lines of wooden cabinets at the thickest part of the paper pile, and before they left, Hunt tipped over the two closest ones, hoping they would catch and fuel the fire. He thought he smelled flesh as well as paper burning, but he left quickly, not wanting to be sure.

"Let's find that red door," he said.

It took them several minutes to retrace their steps and find the corridor that housed the heart of The Insurance Group, but rather than think of what they were going to do when they got there or how they were going to escape from the company, he found himself coming up with better rally lines, things he should have said instead of "Let's find that red door." *Let's find the CEO and cancel his policy.*

Then they were there.

Hunt knew he would balk if he waited, if he thought about it. If he gave himself too much time to dwell on the inde-scribable horror he had seen behind that door, he would back out, so he simply pulled open the door, got down on his knees and crawled in, Joel and Jorge hot on his heels.

The room was different.

Way different.

In place of the banquet hall-sized chamber with its low-walled pit was an enormous space whose dimensions were immeasurable. It sloped downward away from them, and for as far as the eye could see were row after row of burly stoop-shouldered men in dark coats and identical hats.

In the dim distance was an orangish reddish glow that seemed to be vaguely round in shape. *The gates of hell*, he thought, and though he wasn't even remotely religious, the idea remained with him and he believed it utterly. This was where the army of ghosts, demons, provocateurs—whatever they were—came from, and he wondered what else lived in the horrible heat of that diabolic glow.

Hell, he thought, was not a cave filled with fire and brimstone—it was an insurance office.

"What do we do now?" Jorge asked, and Hunt heard not only fear but awe in his friend's voice.

He had no idea. Taking on that elemental monster in the pit would have been bad enough, but the three of them with their kitchen cutlery taking on legions of ghostly thugs and fighting their way into that glowing maw behind them was clearly an impossibility. Their best bet was to go back the way they'd come, get out of here and be thankful they'd accomplished as much as they had. Even if they couldn't stop the power at the heart of The Insurance Group, they had put its agents out of commission and hopefully destroyed most of its filed policies. It would take a long time for the company to regroup, possibly longer than their life spans, and they could let someone else at a later time worry about finishing the job they'd started.

No.

"I have an idea," he said. "Back outside." He ushered Joel and Jorge through the small door into the corridor, then crept out himself. He slammed the door shut, then waited a moment and opened it again. As he'd hoped, that endless chamber with its hulking army and their hellish source was gone, and in its place was the empty room with the mural and the walled pit and the twisting writhing monster.

On impulse, he closed the door again, waited, then opened it and looked in. This time there was a much smaller room, one commensurate with the diminutive size of the door. Its walls were black, and in the center of its floor, on a stand made of metal that looked older than the earth, was a tablet of stone, what he had always imagined the Ten Commandments looked like. Hunt squirmed through the small opening and stood on his knees, looking at the tablet. He could not read the alien characters chiseled on the stone, but they were powerful indeed because he had a headache just from looking at them, and his skin felt hot and tingly, as though he'd been in the sun too long and gotten burned.

This, he felt certain, was The Insurance Group's charter.

In the beginning was the word.

There was room for only him in here. Joel and Jorge were still in the corridor, crouched down and staring at his back and Joel asked, "What is it?"

"I think it's their charter," he said. "I think it's what we have to destroy."

"How?" Jorge asked.

Good question. Manuel's knife would not do the trick, and neither would the knives they'd taken from the insurance agent's kitchen. They had seen no hammers or chisels or anything of that nature, nothing they could use to smash the stone.

Grunting with exertion—the damn thing was *heavy*—Hunt lifted the tablet off its stand and dropped it on the ground. It did not break as he'd hoped. He tried to push it along the ground, but it wouldn't budge, so using every bit of strength he had left, he picked up the tablet again and, waddling on his knees, ducking his head, shimmied sideways through the doorway.

The second he was out, the red door slammed shut behind him.

Only it was no longer red. It was black.

"Check it out," Jorge said, pointing. The fear was still in his voice.

Hunt stood, lifted the tablet as high as he could and dropped it. Although the stone landed with a hard thud on the floor of the corridor, it did not break.

But it cracked.

Joel, out of curiosity, was opening the small door, and once again there was that endless room, although this time that reddish orangish glow had grown, and the hordes of burly, hatted men were looking up and at them. Through the doorway, Hunt could see their faces.

And their teeth.

He knew now why Edward was so frightened of their teeth.

"Close the door!" he yelled, and Joel did so.

The corridor was beginning to smell of smoke. Far away, the files were still burning. It was too much to hope that the entire company would burn down—most of it was stone after all, not wood—but if they were lucky, a lot more damage would be done.

"Help me," Hunt said, struggling to lift the tablet yet again. His arms felt weak, his muscles hurt, but with all of them working together, they lifted the stone easily and were able to hold it above their heads. "On the count of three," he said. "One . . . two . . . three!"

They not only dropped the tablet but were able to apply some extra pressure and *push* it down, and it was that extra force, Hunt was convinced, which led to the tablet breaking into three irregular-sized pieces. The smell of smoke was stronger. It was getting hard to breathe, and if they waited much longer they would find themselves mired in thick haze, getting lost on their way out to the lobby or suffering from smoke inhalation. But they still picked up the individual pieces of the tablet, throwing them as hard as they could against the floor, against the wall, until those terrible characters were no longer readable. Hunt took the last chunk and heaved it down the corridor away from them.

The charter was gone.

The Insurance Group was no more

"Come on! Let's go!"

The smell of smoke was everywhere, and black tendrils were seeping into several passageways, obscuring visibility. Still the corridors were empty for the most part, with those shambling workers periodically passing by, entirely clueless.

They couldn't take a chance that would remain the case, however, and with Hunt in the lead, they ran, passing the maze of offices, dashing past the freakish secretary at the front desk, and making it out to the lobby.

Where Beth and Manuel were descending on the circle they had used to get down here.

"What are you doing?" he yelled at them. "Get out of here!"

The circle reached the bottom, and Beth ran for him. "We have to get *out!*" he shouted. "The whole place is coming down!"

"We come to help," Manuel said.

"That guard," Beth said, throwing her arms around him. "He just sort of . . . *melted.* Turned into a steaming hunk of goo. And we came in after you. We thought you might need help."

He hugged her back instinctively, more grateful than he could say to see her again, but his brain was in overdrive, trying to calculate their chances of survival.

Five other circles were descending from the lobby's ceiling. On all save one were insurance agents in various stages of decomposition. One, dressed in a gray Chinese business suit was still standing and still alive, but, as Beth had said about the dwarf, he was melting. The right half of his head was dripping onto his shoulder, and his left leg was twitching as though he were doing some sort of spastic dance.

Hunt pointed to the empty circle. "That's ours," he said. "Our ticket home."

Beth looked unsure. "Let's just go back the way we came."

Jorge nodded. "It's safer. We know where it goes, and—"

A chunk of the ceiling fell in, a gigantic hunk of stone as large as a small house that landed several yards behind them and caused the ground to lurch beneath their feet. Smoke belched out of the doorway through which they'd just run, expelled with such force that it ruffled their hair and left soot stains on their faces.

"Let's get back up quick," Joel said, coughing. "This place is going fast."

"*Sí!*" Manuel shouted, a look of terror on his features.

"Okay." Hunt led Beth back onto the circle. He looked at the elevating device.

It might hold four of them but not five. "You all get on," he said. "I'll take the second trip."

"No!" Beth cried.

"I'm the only one with life insurance."

"Not anymore," Joel said.

"Just go."

But the circle would not ascend, and Hunt realized that none of them knew how to make it go up.

Jorge stepped off. "You try it," he said.

There was a thunderous crack as a section of the far opposite wall collapsed inward.

Nodding, Hunt stepped into Jorge's place. Nothing happened. There was not even a wobble from the circle beneath his feet.

One of the other circles began to rise with its cargo of rotting bones and flesh.

"It's broken!" Manuel wailed.

"The other one," Hunt said, pulling Beth with him. "Even if it's not ours, it's got to go *somewhere*." He ran over to the empty circle, stepped onto it. Immediately, he felt a thrumming of power vibrate upward through his body. "Come on!" he yelled.

Beth shoved herself next to him, climbing onto his shoes, like a child playing games with her father, and Manuel pressed himself against Hunt's back. All five of them were just able to fit onto the circle.

And it started to rise.

From somewhere below them came a horrid wrenching

scream, a cry so loud that it blasted his eardrums. If he weren't afraid of losing his balance and falling, he would have plugged his ears, and he found himself thinking of that loathsome twisting monster in the pit, its mouth perpetually open in a silent scream that was no longer silent.

That cry loosed the fury and chaos of everything below, and all of those shambling ancient creatures came pouring into the lobby, hell-bent on destruction. Their circle was too high to be reached, however, and the only thing the employees—

ex-employees

—of the insurance company could do was jump and flail their arms wildly. They were still mute, and that made everything even weirder. Another chunk of ceiling fell, missing their circle by inches, causing him to clutch Beth even more tightly. It landed on a group of those slit-eyed beings with eroded features, who were crushed beneath its weight, their spindly arms jerking wildly before stopping.

The circle went up.

And out.

Water dripped on their heads. They were in The Jail. Hunt recognized it immediately, and he was almost overwhelmed with emotion at the knowledge that they were back home, that they'd fought the insurance company and won, that they'd finally and completely put an end to the horror that had been plaguing their lives for so long. He wanted to weep, but instead he stepped off the circle, which now looked like a manhole cover, and hugged Beth so tightly he could feel her bones. He had no idea how they had entered the insurance company in Chiapas, Mexico, and emerged thousands of miles away in Tucson, but they had and he accepted it—only for some stupid reason the only thing he could think about was the fact that their suitcases were still back at the hotel in Tuxtla Gutierrez.

They pushed past the partially open rusted door and hurried outside. It was midday, the sun high in the sky, and the temperature was warm and refreshingly dry. Desperate to get as far away from the destruction and pandemonium of the insurance company as possible, they ran across the sand toward the sloping, south side of the empty reservoir.

"*Dondé estamos?*" Manuel asked, and Jorge answered, "Tucson."

"Gives a whole new meaning to the term 'multinational corporation,'" Joel said.

It was a lame joke, but they laughed as they ran—laughed far out of proportion to the joke's value, Beth even wiping tears from her eyes. Humor, even attempted humor, always seemed funnier when you'd just escaped death.

They stopped at the edge of the reservoir before starting up the slope. "Look," Beth said.

Hunt turned around and saw smoke creeping upward from the small building, clearly visible in the midday sun.

"You did it," she told him. "You guys did it."

"Yeah. We burned his policy and all of the other agents' policies and a whole bunch of files that probably held the company's most recent paperwork—hopefully including ours."

"And we smashed their charter all to hell," Joel said, "which, if all the perverted laws of business under which they've been operating still apply, means that they're finished, done, over and out."

Beth looked nervously behind them. "We'd better get out of here. Maybe the whole thing's going to blow."

It was what they'd all been thinking, and though they were tired and sore, worn out and physically exhausted, adrenaline provided enough stimulation to carry them up the sandy sloping hill. They stopped at the top, but there was no explosion, no implosion, The ground beneath The Jail did not suddenly sink and cave in, and Hunt reminded himself that The Jail was merely a portal, that the insurance company was not really here.

Maybe it wasn't really in Mexico, either.

Wherever it *had* been, he thought, it wasn't anywhere now. Destroying the charter had put an end to the company. Words were what had bound them to their insurance policies, and the erasing of those words was what had brought the company down.

Jorge sat down beneath a palo verde tree. Dropping more than sitting down, actually. He squinted up at Hunt. "So what are we going to do about insurance now?" He grinned. "Go back on the county plan, I guess, huh?"

"I wish we didn't even need insurance," Beth said.

"But we do," Hunt told her. "And that's the problem. We'll never be able to escape it."

He thought of all those names in the insurance manual they'd stolen from the agent's briefcase. The Insurance Group had many tentacles.

Like an octopus.

Maybe *all* of the insurance companies on earth were part of the same corporate family, maybe they were all synergistically connected, subsidiaries of the same parent company. Maybe The Insurance Group owned *everything*, was the ultimate source for every type of insurance all over the world since the beginning of time forever and ever amen.

And maybe they'd put a stop to it.

Maybe so.

But he didn't want to think about it anymore. Sometime in the future, they might be approached again by another agent wanting to protect them from the vicissitudes of everyday life, but for now they had beaten it and he had the feeling that it would be a long, long time before they would be bothered again.

"*Qué* . . . What time is it?" Manuel asked. "Does anyone have a watch?"

"Does anybody really know what time it is?" Jorge said, pulling out his cell phone to try and call Ynez.

"Does anybody really care?" Joel took out his phone to call Stacy.

"I know what time it *isn't*." Hunt smiled tiredly. He glanced over at Beth. "Half past a monkey's ass, a quarter to his balls."

Manuel looked confused, but Beth laughed, hitting his shoulder, and Hunt looked up into the blue sky, breathing in the clean desert air, as she took out her own phone and used it to call for a ride home.

Born in Arizona shortly after his mother attended the world premiere of *Psycho*, Bentley Little is the Bram Stoker Award–winning author of thirteen previous novels and *The Collection*, a book of short stories. He has worked as a technical writer, reporter/photographer, library assistant, sales clerk, phonebook deliveryman, video arcade attendant, newspaper deliveryman, furniture mover, and rodeo gatekeeper. The son of a Russian artist and an American educator, he and his Chinese wife were married by the justice of the peace in Tombstone, Arizona.